In the pin
the pink v
men. An
turned sca

Later, she grew more careful. And later, too, she came to suffer with a relentless, endless guilt. So she hid herself in the isolated house where her mother had died, 'taking' only from the animals of the plains and woods, avoiding men.

Until Sand Vincent charmed his way into her life. Young, handsome and eager — he wouldn't leave her alone. And she had been starved so long . . .

The death of Sand set on her track a dark hunter, an avenging angel: Sand's brother — the powerful, brutal, magnetic Jace.

At last Sabella had met her match, the one man capable of destroying her.

SABELLA

Tanith Lee

UNWIN PAPERBACKS
London   Sydney

First published in Great Britain by Unwin Paperbacks 1987

UNWIN HYMAN LIMITED
Denmark House, 37—39 Queen Elizabeth Street,
London SE1 2QB
and
40 Museum Street, London WC1A 1LU

Allen & Unwin Australia Pty Ltd
8 Napier Street, North Sydney, NSW 2060, Australia

Unwin Paperbacks with the Port Nicholson Press
60 Cambridge Terrace, Wellington, New Zealand

© Tanith Lee 1980, 1987

This edition published by arrangement with DAW Books Inc. New York

British Library Cataloguing in Publication Data

Lee, Tanith
   Sabella, or, The blood stone. — (Orion)
I. Title
823'.914 [F]   PR6062. E4163

ISBN 0-04-823353-6

Printed and bound in Great Britain by
Cox & Wyman Ltd,
Reading.

PART ONE   *The Wolves*

           1   7

           2   36

PART TWO   *The Avenger*

           1   61

           2   84

PART THREE   *De Profundis*

           1   109

           2   128

Part
ONE

The Wolves

1

I was out hunting the night my aunt Cassi died. As she was taking her last breath of revitalized Arean air, I was high on the Hammerhead Plateau, under forty thousand stars burning like diamond bonfires. Maybe I even killed in the same minute she let that last breath go. I hadn't meant to kill, perhaps it was an omen. And did I feel her reach out to me in the black eye-star-burning darkness, reach out with her dead finger, pointing, beckoning, condemning me, me thinking it was only the chill night wind of Novo Mars?

Just after sunup (Novo Mars sunup like a bomb of light going off in the sky: sixty-second dawn) the mailman buzzed the porch. He was a real man, the mailman, I mean human, because mechanization doesn't stretch out too far into the Styx of Hammerhead. He stood against the fresh pink sky, his electric mail dolly sitting beside him. When I went to open up, he saw me just as he always did, in my black wrapper and my dark glasses, my hair like black coffee poured over me from the crown of my head to my shoulders. He thinks I'm a slut, a boozy drug addict. Thinks? Thought. Maybe still thinks, who knows.

"Miss Quey? Registered stellagram. Thumbprint right here."

He looked resentful, as he always did. He was wondering if I'd seduce him someday in my silky wrapper. But I wouldn't. He thought my name Quey, (pronounced Kay) was phony too. The name on the sender's docket was Koberman, Cassi's name.

"Thanks," I said, as I thumbprinted.

9

"Sorry to wake you," said the mailman. His stupid sad malevolent human eyes said to me: I guess all you whores have to sleep it off in the morning.

But I didn't argue, not then, with the tepid rosewater sun streaming in my door and my hands shaking a little and the lightweight stella like a pack of lead.

"That's O.K.," I said, and buttoned shut the smoked-glass door, and slunk back into the lovely shadows.

All the blue paper day-blinds were down, and the blinds of violet cotton. How beautiful it all looked, true virtue of necessity. But that one slap of light in the face had told. I remembered the striped deer and some weak tears oozed from my eyes.

Out in the hallway, over the stair, the stained-glass window cries too, staining the wooden floor with a big crimson patch.

When I finally opened the stella, I wasn't really interested in it, it was something else that had to be seen to. At first I thought it was from Cassi herself, and wondered why she'd suddenly recollected me and what she wanted that she had to send star-bounced telegrams for, and what it was going to mean. (Does anyone else ever read their mail like this? Trepidation always, occasionally fear. How I loved ads and circulars, things you could send for or forget.) But then I found it wasn't Cassi, but Cassi's brother-in-law, a lawyer's formal bit of paper with formal phrases on it. Cassi was dead, but she'd sent me an invite to the funeral. She'd fixed her heart on it. And to ensure I came, she'd left me several thousand tax-clear New Mars credits. I hadn't recalled she was wealthy. I hadn't known she recalled where I was or even if I was still on-planet. I didn't know either what her post mortem game was, but it seemed to me she had set out to nail me on a very special Revivalist Christian Cross. But then, would she, all these years, have known that *too*?

Why does everybody have to love money so much? I wasn't rich. They'd expect me to want to be, and if I didn't, they'd want to find out why not. And Cassi had remembered where I was and they'd traced me here. Even if I ran (I contemplated that) they'd follow me.

Sabella Quey, this cash belongs to you, they'd say, as we stood there in the bright delicate sunlight of rose-hued Novo Mars.

An hour later, I went to the music deck and keyed in the phones. I let the sinister marvel of a Prokofiev symphony wash up through the house and over me as the jets of the shower washed down.

But oh, Sabella Quey, the cross stands ready.

The funeral, the day after tomorrow, drawing me, as if by suction, back into the world.

Novo Mars is enough like old Mars to have been dubbed with the name, but a pink planet rather than red, pearl rather than ruby. I was born east of Ares. This little world is all I've ever known. It's sugar-mouse color skies with their pale blue clouds of oxygen revitalization that turn the air over the cities to a lavender soup, the tawny-rose sands, the knife-ridge plateaus like pasteboard cutouts, the rust-red crags dissolving in the five-second dusks.

The vegetation is all earth-import, the books tell you, and mostly so is the fauna that breeds and hunts and basks and leaves its bones on plains and heights and in the dry canals. But both flora and fauna have mutated here to fit new climates, zones and geography. The waters were also initially false, atmospheric stabilizers replenished by viaduct and sub-surface reservoir, yet they, too, like crystal tinted by indigenous skies and pointed mountains, have become one with Novo Mars. There are genuine ruins (beware tourist traps) here and there. Thin pillars soaring, leveled foundations crumbling, cracked urns whispering of spilled dusts— all the Martian dreams that old Mars denied to mankind. Though this prior race, whose wreck men inherited, left small self-evidence beyond their architecture. Maybe men find it, anyway, more romantic to guess.

But there are still real Martian wolves in the hills above Hammerhead Plateau. Fine nights, you can hear them howl in tin-whistle voices, like antique lost locomotives searching for a station. Periodically, men come out from the cities and shoot at them, and those nights, from Brade to Hammerlake, the uplands ring to lead-blast and electric flash-gun charge. But wolves that have survived so many things, a passing of peoples, drought of four-fifths of the water, death of half the air—they can survive guns. Their rough coats are like pink champagne, their genes programmed long ago to copy the dusts, but catch the glare of their eyes at night, disembodied blood drops seemingly framed in stars, and know them for what they are.

When they cry, when they cry, Sabella, the hair lifts on the scalp, and the eyes fill up with tears and the mouth with water.

I took the night flight to Aresport. It's a two-hour run by air-bug from the Brade lift-off point. To reach Brade, there'd been the nineteen o'clock flyer from Hammerlake Halt. I'd footed the five miles to the Halt, through the fading afternoon, the scarlet minute of pre-sunset, through the seconds of sunset, through the tidal wave of night. Five miles was nothing to me, and the road was good. Once the sun went out, I took off my black straw hat and the big black glasses and carried them with my sandals and my single piece of luggage.

The half-hour flyer ride was uneventful, the bus almost empty, though we picked up a pair of couples on route through Spur and Canyon.

When I'd checked into the cabin of the air-bug at Brade and fastened myself down in the plasti-plush seat, the first intimation of fate came over me. I'd been expecting it; not such force. After all, I'd undertaken a few unavoidable journeys before, and I'd survived, sometimes with fewer scars than others. Then I remembered my mother's death, the memory also expected and inevitable, and a dreary pang swept through

me. My mother, Cassi's sister, had understood me. Had
understood me so well that one morning I came home
and she was dead, lying there accusingly under the
crimson patch cast by the stained-glass window. I don't
know if she'd planned that, or not. (My paranoia, you
perceive, was that the dead were always in league
against me—worse than the living. The dead, plotting
to snare and to implicate, to trip and fell me and lay a
naked sword across my neck.) But my mother died of
natural causes, if heart attack is natural. The medical
man, who like the mailman caught me in my sunglasses, and who looked at me with the same unliking,
interested stare, cleared the death certificate for me dis-
appointedly. He would, of course, have heard stories of
the odd recluse duo, the mother and her daughter, living in the old colonial house under the hills. When I
was sixteen or seventeen and couldn't keep out of
Hammerlake town, nights, all kinds of tales were
spelled out about me. The boys would whistle after my
lean long flanks, nipped-in swaying waist and heavy
young-girl breasts. In those days (nights) I had no wisdom at all. None. When I think how lucky I was, I
tremble, even now. Caution came long after guilt, but
before then it got to my mother. It made a slim artery
in her heart engorge and burst. It killed her. I—killed
her.

Presently the plane began to clear its throat and the
fasten-up warning lights came on. I hadn't glanced
about. I'd learned not to where space is confined, for
this is a gregarious civilization; I too, if I could afford
to be, maybe. The bug lifted on its jets and stars
crowded the windows.

I don't often sleep at night, darkness has too much
to offer with its silences and mysteries. But the motion
and hum of the air-bug and the thick half lights gradually sent me under.

Then I started to dream. I dreamed about Easterly,
which was a logical progression from the rest, the
death of Cassi and my mother's death.

Easterly was the little township, sixty-two miles east

of Ares where my mother and Cassi were born, and
where I grew up. My father was an ore-blaster, and
when I was two years old the drill he was working on
caught fire. (Catalog of death.) My mother, his widow,
got the insurance payments the company awards to
survivors. Aunt Cassi, an adventuress, was way off on
Earth, then. My mother and I, alone without a man,
became briefly wealthy.

Consciously, I can perfectly recall the copper-brick
house at Easterly, on a street of copper-brick houses,
for Easterly was an ore town on the boom. Asleep, I
could see it in microscopic detail. Every brick shining
in the sun, the neat lawn of aniseed grass running into
the avenue of honeysuckle trees and the brindle oaks
across the way where black-haired boys kick a ball.
The mines were neatly hidden underground, but the
distant towers of the three refineries gleamed and gave
off tiny puffs of cotton wool. Beyond the refineries,
over the river and the crescent of the dam, the
meadows and the wildflowers faded into the rose-petal
sands. There are ruins at Easterly. At eleven, I didn't
know. One of the dry canals plunges in under the rock
of an old quarry. In there.

"Come out!" my mother calls. "Bel, come out of
that, it's nothing but a dirty hole. Bel, do you hear
me?"

But momma, I've come to place with a tall pillar like
a lily stem. Momma it's not so dark—

"Child, the sides may cave in—"

Why was I scared? I wasn't scared before. I was
eleven. It was the day I started to bleed for the very
first time. It was the day I found—

"Bel!"

Oh God, why am I so scared?

"Bel!"

I realized the tunnel was closing in on me after all,
was dragging me away, and I beheld my mother's terrified face snatched from me, receding—

And I woke up to discover myself crying softly,

"Momma, Momma!" Like one of those dolls of centuries before.

"It's all right," somebody said. "Really it is. You're awake. It's all right, now."

I could see the air-bug, quiet, and scattered with persons who slept on without the raw edges of dreams to slash them alert again. And next to me, on the twin seat at my side, but not fastened in, a shadow saying, "Honestly, it's O.K. now," very gently, as if to the child I had been two instants before.

"Is it O.K.?" I asked, to gain time.

"Sure it is. You're back."

"Am I?"

"Truly. I swear."

He laughed, this gentle still. I hadn't looked at him beyond the first uncalculated awakening gaze that hadn't assimilated anything. But he was young. My age?

I'll have to be extra careful now.

"That's better," he said. "Look, can I get you anything?"

"Anything?" No, I must not fool around.

"Well, a brandy?"

"No thanks."

"You must have something, to prove to yourself the dream's over. I've had dreams like that sometimes."

"How do you know what kind of dream it was?"

"A bad one. Come on. Oh, I know," he said. His voice was warm, melodic. Perhaps Prokofiev had written his voice. "Last year I was on Gall Vulcan, with my brother. I freaked out on mescadrine." (Some drug.) Now he was telling me how his big brother saved him, sat and held his hand, ran him into the ground to sweat the horrors out of him, rocked him like a baby. It was extraordinary. "I'm not ashamed to tell you," said the young man in the shadow. "We shouldn't be ashamed."

"I was ashamed. Afraid, ashamed. Excited.

This was the duck-catch syndrome. I'd ducked, but

the missile had still come straight at me. In avoiding it, I'd caught the ball in my ungloved, unready hands.

"If you don't want a brandy, what about an iced fruit juice?"

I'm going to a funeral. Don't make it two.

"All right. Thank you."

He went to the auto-dispenser, and I looked at him. And when he came back and we sat drinking cold juice, I looked at him then, too. He was sunlit, even in the night cabin. He had the light bronze suntan of Novo Mars I can't even take from a ray-lamp. His eyes and his hair, like mine, were dark, and his hair was worn rather long, the recurring fashion among the young poets, the dreamers. His clothes were casual, but of good quality, and he had one of those gold ropes around his neck that are jewelers' fantasies of snakes, and have narrow graven heads and gem eyes.

"I hope you're not angry that I spoke to you," he said.

"I'm not angry."

"I have another confession." He lowered his lashes and I felt sad. Old and sad, and tired, and alone. "I was watching you when you were asleep. I was planning something to say when you woke up, but then you had the nightmare."

How rare and chill the juice tastes on my tongue, the tip of which is burning now. I always imagine it's like champagne, which I've never tasted, but how could it be?

"I wanted to talk to you, you see."

Yes. I see. I know.

I mentioned those centuries-old dolls that used to say ('Momma!') Dolls nowadays are robotic and can do anything your child programs into them. Eat, sleep, sob, dance, urinate, tell stories. And like dolls, humans, given a certain programming, will do . . . anything.

I put down my fruit juice.

"A relation of mine just died," I said flatly.

"I'm sorry."

"We were very close. It's my turn to apologize. I'm not good company right now. I want to be alone."

That was difficult to say. Laughable, but difficult.

"O.K.," he said. "Of course."

He stood up. The snake about his throat had blue eyes that comprehended me, and that glittered. But his eyes were innocent.

"My name is Sand—that's really Sand Vincent. If you need anything."

Magic formula, the exchange of names, but I only smiled at him, as stiffly and coldly as I could, and he went away.

It was so easy to make them come to me, like filings flying to a magnet. I was a lodestone. The boys on the neon-striped black candy streets of Hammerlake when I was sixteen, seventeen, seven or eight years ago. Hey, sister! Hey, baby!

There are still wolves in those damned hills!

The sound of guns, and the lights over the ridges, and the scent of burnt electric air.

I watched the cabin clock. Less than an hour to Ares. I wouldn't fall asleep again.

The Brade air-bug landed at the Cliffton Terminus Strip. Aresport has twenty-seven landing strips. Ares is a big city, though not as big as Dawson and Flamingo in the north.

Cliffton was a ghost terminus at this hour, almost deserted. However, every port had its duty-check, for drugs, for guns, for stolen goods. Machines clear the luggage, and every now and then a bag was opened. Mine got opened. The electronic eye scanned inside and hit the metal cap of the container, and an alarm went off. Aresport is too sophisticated to let a mechanism handle such matters. Two human securi-guards walked over and asked me to remove the container. Apart from the cap, it's transparent, so they looked at the red juice inside.

"Christ, lady, what's that, blood?"

Sand, having got through the check right in front of me, returned.

"Is anything wrong?"

"This lady is carrying a bottle of blood in her bag."

The guards at the port were bored and power-conscious. But here was a malign brittle good humor I could match.

"Pomegranate and tomato juice," I said. "Half a liter, concentrated, with added vitamins. My physician makes it up for me. Like to try some?"

The guards grinned. Sabella the proud beauty was turning them on, and it had been, was going to be, a long slow night on Cliffton strip.

I uncapped the jar, and they fetched plastic cups and distilled water and we mixed some and drank together. I hope they enjoyed it.

"It smells of flowers. Or hash," said Sand, perplexed.

"You want to come round the back, son," said one of the guards. "We've got confiscated Vulcan-grown hash up to the roof, no duty paid."

"And good old frecking alcohol," added the other.

"Are you going to be O.K.?" Sand asked me as we went out of the terminus building. The wide port highway strode up toward Ares. You never see the stars above a city. The revitalized atmosphere is thick, but oh the colors of their lights chalked on the under-swag of the clouds, greengage and peppermint and opal and strawberry ribs of color, as if the cities were on fire, and this their smoke.

"Yes, I'll be all right."

"Only, things seem to be happening to you, don't they?"

"Yes, they do. But it will be fine now."

"I'm not trying," said Sand, outlined against the first hour of black cloud-blazing morning city, "to be a pain in the ear. But after this—the funeral—"

"Then, I'm going home."

Say: *To my husband and my twelve babies. Say* it. Nothing comes.

Sand turned to the city.

"Pillar of fire by night," he said. He must have had Revivalist biblical training.

My heart was racing. The sight of the city was hurting me with pleasure. I have none of civilization's taint. A landscape of steel towers against hills of concrete, sings to me as does a landscape of rock pinnacles and gullies. All landscapes are one, dissimilar, yet still landscape. All one to me.

I swallowed.

"I must go now," I said. I can't even be nice to him. Dare not. "Excuse me."

I brushed by him, and a cab crawled to the walkway.

I got in and gave it directions to drive me to any middle-price hotel. (Not cheap enough to attract random fellowship, not flashy enough to attract speculation.)

Sand stood by the window.

"You won't even tell me your name?"

"I'd rather not."

"That pendant," he said.

The cab drove away.

My tongue's tip was a scald of flame.

Sunrise was at six o'clock, sunset eighteen-thirty; Aunt Cassi's funeral was set for sixteen in the afternoon. That was fortunate. The sun would already be westering behind the tall gray pines and cumulous trees and the white marble groves of the Koberman cemetery that uncle-in-law Koberman had sent me a picture of.

Why do you wear so much black, Sabella, baby?

It keeps the sun out, my parasol black. The women in the east of Earth knew that long ago. They knew other things. Anyway, what else do you wear for a Christian Revivalist burial? Black frock, black stockings, black shoes that seem to grow into the legs, as if I were born with three-inch heels. Big black hat. I am a raven. No, the ravens in the Ares Zoo are white.

I slipped the pendant inside my dress. It must have wormed out when I fell asleep on the plane and I didn't properly notice. Only Sand noticed, and perhaps the securiguards.

The hotel had been sleazier than it should have been.

On the sidewalk, between the great golden towers and the glass shards of the city, the cab whooshed through the dust. But once I was inside, the cab disowned the city, throwing it over its shoulder, racing into suburbs of grass plantings and white colonial houses.

The shadows were long and red when I reached the cemetery. There were no drivers in these autocabs to argue. I put the necessary credits in the meter and left it parked among the pines.

Westering glow, yet the sun fell on my face, my hands, like embers. I walked quickly up the path and into the chapel. The Kobermans had a Gothic twist. The Christ was white and warped and screwed by pins to his length of wood and apparently screaming. To be mercilessly nailed forever in a window; who could blame him?

There were two or three people already there, dark figures kneeling between the white bench-pews in the white light of the window. The huge jeweled cross by the lectern took your breath away. If Cassi had paid for that, Cassi had been in clover. Now she was in a box. My eyes touched the coffin in its snow drape and the nausea began as it had to. The last coffin I saw had been my mother's.

"Miss Quey, I'm so glad you were able to come. When we received no stellagram, I'm afraid I'd almost given up on you—"

The big tusker in the black formal two-piece suit spoke to me in a hushed monotone. . . . This was how you spoke in front of the dead, because they mustn't overhear the huge secret of what had happened to them. He thought I'd come to listen to the will read, shed a crocodile tear (I've never seen a crocodile), and collect, like all of them, and so he was instantly at home with me. But he introduced himself as the sender of the stella, uncle-in-law.

"You'll be coming back to the house. For the er, to settle matters."

"Yes."

He was extra pleased. He'd got a word out of me.

"And stay over, naturally. Hammerhead is quite a way."

"That's all right. I have a cab waiting to take me back to town."

"But Miss Quey—Sabella. Come on, now. You must be worn out already."

No, I'm not worn out. The sun left a line of invisible blisters all over my skin, and through the blisters my nerves were thrusting like eager wires.

The chapel had filled up, and the priest appeared in his black cassock, the lilies of death embroidered on his shawl.

Uncle-in-law wedged me into a pew. Somewhere music started and my heart stopped.

Oh Christ, let me get through this. I shouldn't be here. I'm on fire.

"*Deus*," said the priest, authoritatively, as if he had a through line to God, "*cui proprium est misereri semper et parcere—*"

The Revivalists revived the Latin with the rest of the Revival. It's beautiful. It plays me like a harp. Everything's so bright and clear and full of pain and sorrow. Six years since I heard such words.

"*Dicit illi Jesus: Resurget frater tuus.*"

I was leaning on the pew, and weeping and I didn't really know her, and it was wrong. And it makes it worse if anyone thinks it's *right* I should be weeping.

If it goes on much longer I shall faint. They'll carry me out and the sun will smite me by day between the pine needles. It will kill me and they won't know why. They'll say I died of grief for Cassi and now I'm going to laugh.

I didn't laugh. Something made me turn, maybe the

acute instincts of the hills. And there, at the back of
the chapel, his dark head bowed over his gentle
mourning and the snake coiled round his throat, was
Sand Vincent.

Big hog uncle took me by the arm, and guided me,
guided all of us away, when it was over. At a C.R.
mass you often don't see the box go in the ground. I
don't know why not. Dissociation from the mortal to
the spiritual things, perhaps. The way to the house lay
across some open land, acres of the Koberman Ares
holdings. It was a distance of half a mile, but most of
them got into their cars to do it. Cars like black-sharks
nosed up the road. Uncle and I walked side by side—
between the tall hedges of stonework, over the lawns,
the ugly house like a big pillared air-raid shelter ahead
of us on the rise. Sand Vincent, head still bowed,
walked about twenty yards behind us.

What should I say? I didn't at that time believe in
coincidence.

"We've kept it as informal as possible. She wanted
it like that. Cassilda, I mean."

Who could I think he meant? Who else had died?

"I know you saw very little of your aunt since childhood, but toward the end, you were in her thoughts."

I didn't even know what she'd died of.

"One thing," I said.

"Yes, Sabella. May I call you Sabella?"

"The man behind us."

Hog Uncle Koberman shot a glance behind us.

"Yes?"

"Is he a relation?"

"I don't know who the hell he is, Sabella. He's not
with our party."

"He was in the church."

"The hell he was. Some funeral freak. Stay here,
Sabella, I'll deal with it."

I stood where I was while knightly Uncle Hog went
back and stopped Sand on the lawn. They exchanged
words I couldn't hear, didn't try to hear. Uncle's wide

back blocked out my view of Sand. I knew he'd followed me, all the way from the port. I didn't know how. I knew why.

Sand didn't try to look at me and now the exchange of words was over. Sand stood on the lawn, his thumbs in his belt, cat's paw velvet on the velvet grass. The Hog Uncle came to me with the blood dinning in his face. "That's that."

He didn't tell me what had been said. I didn't ask. Sand got smaller and smaller as we went up the slope.

Flowers wilt in too much sun. They were wilting in the hall of the air-raid shelter, petals like paper.

"You need something to eat," Hog Koberman said to me.

They were all at the buffet, like the sin-eaters of old, gobbling up the crimes of the deceased along with the paté, cakes and exotic fruit segments in silver dishes.

But I convinced him I'd eaten before I left my hotel, and I sat and watched the others. When the eaters glanced at me, they felt antagonism. Uninvolved in their activity, I was outside the pale, I had an advantage. Besides, I had refused to consume the sins of the dead. Hog Koberman introduced me to everyone, but their names slipped off the surface of my mind, and their breath smelled of sugars, proteins and digestion. They were only extras on the set.

After a while, we went into Cassi's library. One wall was book tapes, and the rest actual books, bound in leather. Long windows sliced between the stacks, and there was a globe of Novo Mars in polished rose quartz, pierced and mounted to demonstrate the axial tilt, and pierced by the sun rays, too. Even the dust was gilded by the last sun against the windows. In the middle of the oak table where we were seated was a jeroboam of wine, slightly cobwebbed from the cellar. Cassi had had human servants, who now served us with this ancient valuable drink. Cassi had really schemed things, for this was the one way you reached back from the grave, with instructions to be obeyed, rituals to be performed. I pretended to sip from my goblet.

The Hog read the will slowly and carefully. Everybody waited breathless, as if at a lottery. The prizes were big ones, and everybody got a prize.

I was last of all. Now they could observe me in turn. The sunlight lay over me in a broad shining spotlight.

"Of course, Cassilda wanted me to intimate to you, Sabella, something of the form of this bequest," said Uncle, displaying to the others, in parentheses, the reason for my mercenary attendance at the funeral. "But what it amounts to, and here I read, 'To my only niece, Sabella Quey, the entire stock investments of the Kobercor Trust, which come to her, tax paid, as the sum of eighty thousand credits.' "

The extras smiled archly. My prize was good, but not so good as the others.

The servants came around to refurbish the drinks and the Hog closed his portfolio. He drew me aside, against a blazing window.

"It may not seem a great deal, Bella, but with wise reinvestment, it could amount to a tidy sum in a year or so. How about you sign the investment procedure over to me? I'd be happy to assist any way I can."

The sun was pouring through me. I felt, maybe I looked, translucent. My skin often has that quality, but were my bones showing now? Uncle was blurred as if I stared at him through smoke. I thanked him. I'd had to keep thanking him. People like you to thank them. They do you kindnesses so you'll have to say thank you, thank you.

"And there's one other small item," said Uncle playfully.

I stood in the sun's X ray, waiting.

"Cassilda entrusted this to me, this extra small thing, to be dealt with privately. It's a little casket, and I think, well, I know, Bella, it has a very fine piece of jewelry in it, which your aunt meant you to have. Her mind was on you a lot, you know, Bel, the last days. But she wanted it secret. You know how families are,

Bel, squabbling, getting jealous. Not about the value of
the token, but its sentimental worth. Now, what I want
you to do. Our John Trim over there is going to go
out, and I want you to slip out after him. He'll take
you upstairs to Cassilda's bedroom and direct you to
the casket. O.K.?"

I nodded. The Hog turned away and John, one of
Cassi's servants, walked between the library doors.

As I stepped out from the sun, the room sizzled and
went dark, but I moved through the darkness, after
John, across the flower-garden hall. John was much
older than Cassi. Had John been mentioned in the will?

The stair was mobile with white carpet over the
steel. John operated the button and we rode up in
silence to the third floor.

His hands on the rail, and on the bedroom's enam-
eled handles were like parched old brown leaves. A life
of sun had done that to him. Were my hands shriveling
too?

"In here please, Miss Quey."

The bedroom was white silk, with bronze blinds
down over the windows, hot, with that smell of too-
much hygiene that supplants sickness. On the vanity
table, all was laid out as if in readiness for her return,
platinum-backed brushes, tetra-shell boxes; she should
have been buried in here, like a pharaoh's wife, among
her treasures, side by side with her long-dead spouse in
the big white bed.

The casket was on a separate table. It was made of
ivory, with gold on the clasps, and a gold key hanging
by a ribbon.

"Excuse me, Miss Quey."

Servant John shut me in with his brown leaves, closing the doors softly.

I was supposed to open the casket, so I took the key
and put in the lock, and as the lock clicked I thought,
Maybe it will explode.

But the box didn't explode. Inside it, lying on satin,
was a tiny replica of the gold jeweled crucifix I'd seen
in the chapel, a lectern cross from Lilliput. It was

worth about twice what she'd left me in credits.

The bedroom in the bronze blind-light was full of menace. Cassi had lain in here, propped up and guttering, and she'd plotted, and here was the result. And I didn't grasp what it was. Like death itself, the threat was invisible.

Then I saw the envelope tucked under the cross, and when I drew out the envelope my fingers were oddly desensitized, but I wondered if poison would spurt into my face when I tore the paper across.

Poison spurted. Poison pen.

I know what you are, Sabella. I didn't know until I came to God, but when I found God, He told me. His angels told me. I know what you've done. I know you killed my sister. I hope the cross cripples you, as it should. If it doesn't, I've made another arrangement. Don't try to guess what it is. You're just one of the wolves, Sabella, an animal, and animals can't guess things. Not till it's too late. But you don't have so long, Sabella. I hope it's soon, and then you'll rot, and your soul, if you have one, will writhe and shriek in Eternal Fires, Sabella, and God will let me hear you as I rest on His bosom.

I sat down on Cassi's bed and put my head between my knees, but it didn't help, and I'd known it wouldn't. So I lay back, with the letter balled in my hand, and presently I pushed it inside my frock, between my breasts where the pendant was. Next to my heart.

She'd found God, and she'd found out. Yes, that made sense. She'd had intimations, but they would seem so crazy, she'd have to go crazy before she could accept them.

When I felt a little better, I opened my purse and took out the miniature bottle of what I'd mixed up from the red juice in the container.

It's blood. We all knew it, didn't we? It's flavored with pomegranate and tomato and a synthetic grain of hashish, which acts as a preservative, and to disguise reality in the presence of securiguards. It's the blood of the deer on Hammerhead Plateau. Brought home and first stored cold with a concentrator, it thereafter keeps several days, even in my luggage.

It's going to help you, Sabella. Yes it is. Drink, it'll make you strong. In spite of the sunlight, in spite of Cassi, in spite of spite. Drink.

But the fruity odors, this time, made me gag.

I sat there shivering, feverishly turning my black straw hat between my hands. On this occasion, Sabella, it isn't going to work.

Get home, Sabella. Quick, Sabella.

Get home.

I put the cross in my purse and left the casket, and as I shut the bedroom doors, the crumpled letter stirred against my breast.

A black Pig lurked in the hall.

He'd seen me weeping in the chapel, and I must look awful now. I explained how affected I was by everything, how I wished I'd known her better. I put in a couple of lies about childhood meetings, when I was twelve or thirteen. (Cassi had visited Easterly, in the years before we moved house. I don't think she properly saw me. My mother bored her; it was duty.) But humanity loves confession and painful reminiscence. We're all bloodsuckers, one way or another. I sold my uncle on the idea that I had to go home and pull myself together and we would sign papers another day, and that was how I got free.

There were about ten minutes left of the sun as I hurried across the lawns to the pine trees. The gray shade came over me at the same instant the sun turned boiling red. I walked into the deep shadow, and threw up violently, wrenching every muscle in my body.

There was a silly little ornamental cistern nearby, for watering the lawns, recycled tap-water probably unrefined, but I rinsed my mouth and was thankful. (Do even cisterns require thanks of me?)

Then I went to the cab and leaned on it, sore and aching, too weak to get inside.

It was coming on dark. The sun had dropped while I was ill. The night was like a cool bath, even the top of the cab was cool to my hands, my forehead.

And then I heard him coming up, over the dry needles. I knew who it must be. You get to know one certain step from all others, the step of the deer, picking its path to you through the wolf-dappled night.

He put his hands on my shoulders. Gentle, gentle.

"Sabella?"

He knows my name. He must have heard the Hog using it outside the chapel.

"Sabella, are you all right? Oh, Sabella." Gently he moved me around to confront him. His handsome face was holy with its concern, eyes limpid, wanting to aid me any way he could. "You look ghastly. No. I don't mean that. You look wonderful, but you look sick." He was a saint. He was meant to be a saint. No, Sabella. He held me in his arms, tenderly, he smoothed my hair. I was trembling so much it must have been hard for him to soothe me so delicately. His skin was warm, aromatic of youth, cleanness, masculinity and desire. I could scent his life through his skin. I could scent his blood.

He eased me into the cab.

"Now, where to?"

"It has the directions," I said.

"But where? I'll pick up my transport tomorrow. I'm coming with you."

"I don't want you to come with me, Sand."

"You need someone with you."

"Not you."

"Why not me?"

My brain was going out. I was losing consciousness. He had gotten in beside me and pressed the starter, and the cab moved out between the trees onto the high road back to town.

Again he put his arm round me. I looked up against his shoulder, through his warm dark hair, into the knowing eyes of the snake at his throat.

We were at the hotel, and I didn't remember much of the journey. Sand Vincent had got my door-opener, and brought me into the room and pressed the master switch for the side lighting. Then he picked me up, (I weigh one hundred and seven, it was comparatively easy for him) and laid me down on the bed. Like a fool, I still had my sunglasses on. He took off those, and my shoes.

"You need to sleep," he said. "It's taken it out of you."

"Sand."

"Yes?"

"You've been very kind."

"I'm not leaving you," he said, "if that's what you're leading up to."

"I want—I need to be alone."

"I'll wait in the corridor, then. But that's as far as I go."

"Please, Sand. I'll call you tomorrow."

Tomorrow, I'll be in Hammerhead. Sand doesn't know my route beyond Brade. It's a big country.

Why did I leave, anyway? Would it have mattered? There are still investment papers to sign for Hog Koberman. The Hog will pursue me, grunting. Anxious to see me be a pig too, greedy for cash. No, I came here because Cassi reached out from the grave and summoned me.

"I'll wait in the corridor."

We'd been silently at work on each other all the way from the cemetery. Like two acids, smoldering each other away.

"Take the chair."

"I'll carry it into the corridor."

"No. Don't bother."

He sat down in the chair. I shut my eyes so I wouldn't see him studying me. Inside my lids, the room was empty. It wasn't Cassi that made me come here. It was I, myself.

Of course, I know now I'm going to do it. And now I know, I'm getting stronger. My pulse was beating against that scrap of Cassi's vitriol on my breast, but I could feel the second pulse, too. It was mild, lethargic at first. It was coming back from limbo, the limbo it goes to, between.

The excitement. What's it like? It's in every part of me. It's like—I don't know what it's like at this time, have nothing to compare it to, drink or drugs, or sex or religion. When I was thirteen, when I was—changing, my mother took me to Revivalist meetings. Christ had caught on in a big way in Easterly. It has been remarked, the manner in which colonies retreat to the old fashions of Earth, the clothes, the decor, the religions, as if in search of anchorage. But remarking it, it still comes fresh and sudden, new to the new planets as if they had invented it. In the new C.R. copper-brick church, momma held my hand tight, and I saw the faces of men and women burning as if the great light were about to shatter out of them, dynamite inside glass. You could almost take hold of the tension, the glorious poise on the brink of ecstasy, and then the fall.

"Sand," I said, and he started. I can lie so still I seem dead, let alone sleeping, "I'm going to take a shower."

His eyes were luminous.

"Yes," he said, and rested his head against the back of the chair.

It was altered between us. He'd ceased asking me if he could help. He sensed he could help me.

I went into the cubicle and ran the shower, and as it ran I took off my dress and undergarments and when I came to Cassi's letter, I flushed it away through the chem-flush lavatory.

I looked at myself in the jets of the shower, at my body. Sand was going to want my body very much. (Whores do it for payment, Sabella.) The pendant around my neck on the hair-thin white-metal chain was glinting, pulsing, though usually only I could see it pulse.

The sleazy hotel room was warm. I shut off the

shower and went out rain-wet, and I called his name
very quietly, and Sand moved out of the chair and
around and saw me. For a moment his reaction was
dual, arousal and nervousness, quite normal, human:
I'm beautiful, I've scared him.

I crossed to him, and slipped off his jacket. I was
unsealing his shirt, quietly, quietly, and he said, "Sabella, are you certain you—" And then no more, because it was a gesture of some kind the decent human
response was forcing him to make. The animal human
response was already making him tremble, as I
trembled when he held me before. He placed his hands
at either side of my face and leaned and kissed me long
and slow, and the unhuman response was beginning to
well through him, what the unhuman part of me was
causing to happen to him. He said my name several
times as he kissed me along my throat, my shoulders,
and put his mouth to my breasts. The stone lay against
his cheek. (Sometimes, stretched on the wolf hills, a
boy, misled by the white refracted gleam of the stone,
would say to me, Is this a frecking diamond, baby?)
But Sand brushed the pendant aside.

And then we were on the bed. His skin smooth and
marvelous, his loins blossomed into a single hard fierce
flame.

I always feel concern at this moment. Even with the
basest of them, I feel a concern to make them happy.
Of course, I know the reason. And I, I'd had no
exquisite delight in it, not before, and not with Sand.
The sensations of touch, of clasp, of physical excitement, are all for the other, the partner. Yet the prelude
is sweet, being a prelude. Inside me, his rhythm was
tidal. Numb to it, yet I could measure its perfection.

"Sabella—"

"Darling," I whispered, "there's something we're going to do now, something you'll like—"

"Whatever you want—whatever—"

I had the trick of this movement, being practiced.
We rolled a little, and he laughed breathlessly, and
then I was over him, and though we were still joined,

the wonderful rhythm had broken, to allow the second rhythm to begin.

The snake shifted under my fingers, upwards two inches along his neck. His neck was strong and vital, the color of amber. I ran my tongue along the vein there, the golden vein which throbbed and spoke to me. And then I put my lips to the golden tube of the vein and kissed with the drawing kiss which bruises, brings the thing within to the surface. This was how I found the way, through this kiss, this bruising kiss, tasting the blood beneath. Sand moaned and clung to me, closing his arms around my waist, my hips, to hold me to him forever. The eye-teeth don't require great length, they are nearly long enough in most of you. They only need to be razor sharp, with points like needles, to pierce without tearing, without hurt, as the sun pierced through the globe of quartz. I pressed the flesh, the vein, with my fingers, molding it for my mouth. As I made the wound, he shuddered, and when I began to draw again with my mouth, the shudder became convulsive. I was strong, stronger than he supposed, I could retain my position with total facility, and then I must, for as the pump began, he came. And continued to come. (How could we guess, in the beginning? How could we revoke when we understood?) This orgasm, which follows the rhythm from his vein into my mouth, this climax which goes on and on, long after the fluids of it are exhausted, while this other fluid lasts, on and on and will go on until I stop drinking, or until he faints. This is what the mystery is. This is what kills.

Why does it happen in this way? I don't know. I've thought of the story that hanged men climax on the rope, the trigger of the throat, the thrust of blood into the brain and loins. Or of a surge of life whose symbol is sex, is seed, life rearing against death, for blood flowing away is the symbol of death. I've thought of the sometimes sensual pleasure of the beast giving suck. I've thought of the female spider eating her mate during intercourse. I can think. But I don't know.

And for me?

My excitement had concentrated and changed. I was no longer excited, I was beyond excitement, beyond the world. A lion crouched over its prey, you see me like that. No. It was a quite spontaneous need, like needing air to breathe. And then I was breathing air when ten minutes before I was breathing mud. I could go on, like him, different but the same, on and on. But I mustn't. I forced myself, forced myself, as if fighting against gravity.

I could picture his face. You've seen the faces of those who die in agony; did you never note that lovers look like this at the peak of joy?

I *must*, I *must*.

I raised my head.

Who told you it was messy? Great gouts and slobberings—no. A slender trickle from the one (why more than one?) minuscule wound, a thread of scarlet.

Sand's head lolled aside. He was unconscious.

I loved him, just for a minute, I loved him and I grieved for him and my pity was part of the beauty, before the shame began.

It was four hours to sunrise when Sand came to. He felt slightly dizzy, yet flooded by well-being, and hungry, as generally they did. He lay on one elbow, sometimes smiling lazily, and I fed him the steak I'd dialed for, and told him I'd already eaten my share of. My feeding him seemed quite suitable, playful and friendly, to him. Subconsciously, I believed, he understood it was his right, as prey, to be cosseted. In the light wine I'd already mixed the vitamin concentrate I'd ordered from the hotel pharmacy, along with the food. By morning, Sand Vincent would feel no more than tired. In a day or so, not even that. Unless—but I wasn't going to consider an alternative. There was a five o'clock Brade lift-off from Aresport. Mine. Even though I'd have to travel some of the route by day. I could make it now.

"That was one hell of a high," Sand said to me as we lay on the bed. "But you're one hell of a lady."

He didn't remember it all, not consciously, just that I was a good lay. In the beginning, even after I learned to control myself, to stop in time, I'd kill them because I thought they'd remember. But they wouldn't have. The truth is too absurd, it gets covered over and forgotten.

Then he put his hand to his neck and ran his fingers under the snake, and winced.

"I'm sorry," I said. "I was enjoying it, too."

He grinned. Sometimes they said, "You're a vampire!" It was a joke. You both laugh about it. But any pharmacy sells coagulant creams and healfast jel in handy purse-size packs. There wouldn't be a mark much more than a pale bruise by sunup.

"You enjoyed it too, did you," he said. He skimmed his hand across my body. He slid himself toward me, stroking, me, eager again, the way they are always eager. Then, he saw the stone. "Christ," he said, "it can't be a ruby, this size, can it?"

The pendant stone is scarlet, pulsing, warm, alive.

"Just stained crystal."

"I thought it was colorless. Why did I think that? Sabella, you're lovely."

I let him kiss me, then I eased away.

"I'd like to, Sand, but I'm so damn tired. In the morning?"

"No, beautiful. Now." And he started all over me, dreamy and stupid, with this lust the lodestone brings.

"This is to be rape then, is it?" I said. He blinked, and his face emptied. He let me go. "In the morning," I said.

"Woman, I won't let you out of this room until we do."

He fell asleep almost immediately, and in his sleep, came back to me, lying against me trustfully as a child. But the sleep was too deep for him to wake when I left him, put on my clothes and took up my piece of luggage and went away.

I paid the hotel bill through until noon next day. Sand would be ready to leave by then. He'd start at once feverishly trying to find me, obsessed by me in a way he could barely figure. But the compulsion would shrivel gradually when he didn't locate me. As long as he never saw me again, he'd be safe.

It was four years since I'd had a man. I intend the word 'had' in all its meaning—sex, con-trick, sustenance.

Four years. I'd tried to stop when my mother died. And I'd stopped. Lapsed. Stopped. Two years of lapsing, regaining ground, four years of keeping ground. But the craving never goes away. The beasts of the field appease, but I am a huntress, and my natural prey strides through the steel prairies, rides the gold mountains of the cities, the neon caves of the towns.

There are wolves on all the hills, even the hills of glass.

In the plane, as the sun was slitting the sky below and I darkened my window, I thought for the first time, *If Cassi sent me her curse and a jeweled cross she wanted to scorch me, why did she also leave me eighty thousand tax-paid credits?*

2

We moved away from Easterly because one night
when I was fourteen, I went for a drive with a boy I
picked up on the highway near the bearshop. It was insane instinct on my part, callousness on his. He
deserved something but not what he got. The highway
auto-patrol found his body in the bushes. Everybody
thought he'd left his car for the usual reason, and a
wildcat had attacked him, which caused a stir since
Easterly isn't hunting country. He'd died of heart failure, as always. But I'd made a mess of his neck. If you
allow your teeth to meet in the vein there's a hemor-
rhage at once. My mother waited up for me that night,
and when I came home with strange hot colors on my
dress, she locked us in my bedroom, and she questioned me. Six hours of questioning, but the same question, which I answered truthfully, which she would
then ask me again, imploring me, mutely, to recant, to
say I'd lied. We were both sobbing and shouting, and
she hit me sometimes. She'd taken me to medics before, but she'd never really told them anything. The
medics would prescribe for anemia. As for psychiatry,
nobody reckoned it anymore, and religion, in my case,
had failed. Now she had this terrible thing to face, to
cope with. Her little daughter had done something
momma couldn't admit, couldn't even believe, and
momma still had to hide it from everyone. So she fastened on the believable aspect, that I'd been laid at
fourteen and had lizards in my pants. Then, I got really sick. I started passing out, getting heat stroke after
half an hour in the sun. There was a doctor who said it

was photophobia, and a doctor who said it was psycho-somatic. And then I killed a boy again, and the same story of wildcats went around and the men got up a shooting party, and momma and I moved west.

She'd had nobody she could confide in. Those years ate her away. The three years when it was starting in Easterly, and the four years on Hammerhead Plateau. Did I say she had no one to confide in? That wasn't strictly accurate. Sister Cassi was permanently on-planet by then, living with her husband in Ares, and him building up the Koberman Corporation. Momma must have written Cassi quite a lot. I don't think she spelled it out, the huge unbelieved terror that lowered over her days and her nights. But I suppose it was there, if you'd looked through the written lines at the howling fear behind. Cassi hadn't looked, then. Cassi had been tuned in to her man and his money, though she wrote so seldom we didn't really know about that. (She never even wrote us when he died.) Only at the end had Cassi presumably reread my mother's letters or re-dreamed them. And the angels had told her what I was, and she'd accepted their word.

The house at Easterly was isolated, twenty miles from Hammerlake, and five from the nearest flyer-halt. And it was only semi-mechanized. The ordinary mail came once a month, unless you went to town for it, but there wasn't much mail. Only registered parcels (few) and stellas (none) came to the door. The rest was left lying in the mail basket with the groceries half a mile off, where the road goes by. Hammerhead was a wild place, too. Wolves on the uplands, a dam project and dredging complex on the rim of the lake town, and bars like yellow musical boxes and those girls that somehow nobody ever properly legalized here, who still copy vamps of centuries ago, red nails, tinsel hair, winter eyes.

My mother chose the house from a catalog. Did she realize how cunning she was to choose just this house in this spot, or did she hide away the cunning, too?

There wasn't much cash left by then, enough to get

by and to add a handful of improvements, button-doors, air-conditioning, dust-eaters. (There was dust in Cassi's library. By now, dust also is fashionable again.) I got my tape deck. I'd lie on the parlor floor and listen. Prokofiev, Stravinsky, Vaeder, Nils. My music frightened my mother. It was the emanation, to her, or stimulus of my madness. She couldn't see it as balm, analgesic. She'd move to the other end of the house when I played music.

She'd try to get me to eat. I must have anorexia nervosa, now. She thought I made myself sick deliberately. I found ways to pretend, and she let herself be fooled. I'd take meals in my room, and tip them in a plastic box I kept for the purpose under the bed, and later I'd empty the box in the primitive incinerator resident behind the kitchen. School finishes on the pink planet at about thirteen or fourteen anyway, and after that you go on to mature studies at your own discretion. That could be done in the house with mailed library tapes and TV. That was safe. In the back yard, under the fifteen-foot orange tree, there was an old swing. Momma used to sit at her bedroom window and stare down at me, my nighttime insomniac swinging, swinging. When the swing was empty, she'd search the house. Often, the swing was empty.

I could run for miles on the ridges and over the star-blanched sands, among the rifts and through the fern-clotted, shade-thick canyons. I was never afraid. It was country I could comprehend, where no one knew me. Big cities are the same, you see. I learned how to hunt in the wilderness, the corridors of night, and on the things I hunted, I learned how not to kill, though it's harder with the animals, who sense the hunter from afar off, who, even when they lie down helpless in the pools of your eyes, are tensed to fly. And besides, there's no sexual communion to bind them, it has to be an act of sabotage.

One day when I was fifteen, they were repairing the road to Hammerlake Halt, and working half a mile down the slope from the house. My bedroom faced that way, and I'd looked through the blue blind, and the blued dust haze, and made out their shadows, the two men with their robot equipment. Then came this dulled-over day, sky a deep rose parasol against the sun, and I went down the road and sat on a stone, and watched. Perhaps they'd heard about a girl in the house and were keyed up to it. They turned their copper-skinned male bodies and they looked at me, and they smiled and offered me a beer.

It happens very naturally. If there are two, one is drawn more readily than the other, whichever I want the most. His name was Frank. He came back after it got dark, whistling softly, in a clean shirt. We went up into the hills, up head-on into the crushed powder of starshine. I liked him. He was thoughtful and curiously well-mannered. He told me I was Shakespeare's Juliet and I killed him and I was sorry. It was because he was the first, after so long. I couldn't stop myself. And—I liked the power over him, what happened to him, the way he clung to me.

I sat and cried, holding his hand, but his white up-turned eyeballs glared like parodies of the stars.

I'd frequently heard the wolves. You can always hear them from the house. At certain seasons they fill the hills like blown sand, at others they drift away toward Brade, or westward to Montiba. But that night they were suddenly all around me, just red star clusters under the white.

I wasn't afraid of them. I didn't put it in a sentence in my head, but I understood nevertheless. They and I. Cassi had it right. One of the wolves, Sabella.

Delicate as clouds, they began to shiver down to me, and like a cloud they settled on Frank, and hid him and what they did.

Earth-imported animals don't feed on the dead. But the wolves of Novo Mars will take a fresh kill, at least from me.

The local TV news had it: Young robot-ganger savaged by wolves.

The wolves will kill, anyway. People have died

through the wolves. Periodically men stray with a
weapon which doesn't fire, or in ignorance without, to
meet a girl. Later, other men hunt the wolves, and the
night sky leers with gun flashes.

When I was sixteen, Aunt Cassi sent me a check.

I bought some dresses and a box of face paint. I
bleached my hair. I could get to town in three hours,
running. I can run, a slow run, a lope, for hours. And I
could look like a free-lance bar-girl. I went with the
itinerants where I could, men who wouldn't be missed.
We rode back in solar jeeps, in runners, in old-fashioned gas-tanked mobiles, into the wide spaces of
Hammerhead. But soon I learned to take a little, only
that, and then I learned the other thing, that they'd
come after me for more, they'd beg me. They thought
they were begging to screw me, but they were begging
to die. Only three ever tracked me to the house. One
beat me. He slashed me across my back and stomach,
yelling. He pulled me under the orange tree and raped
me and somehow I didn't touch him, and he got up
roaring I was no frecking good any more, and he went
away. My mother was in the house, on her knees. I'd
had a toy, one of those loose-limbed things children cart
around. Somehow she'd found it, and there she knelt,
hugging it to her, and crying, and she said to me,
"What you're doing to yourself—oh, Bel, Bel, what
you're doing." But she was speaking to the toy. And
not so long after, she died and fell down in the crimson
blood pool of the old window. Momma. Momma.

I walked home from the Halt through the morning. I
felt strong. I could take the sun because I was ap-
peased. But around three-quarters of an hour on the
road in the shining pink dusts, filed my nerves. There
was a gas storm up over Smokey, the mountain that
holds up the sky beyond Montiba. The gas storms start
when the oxygen filler sufficiently irritates the Martian
stratos, generally at the level where high lands probe
the upper air. The sky veiled over a little, and claps

sounded, and a big pale wind blew across my left cheek.

When I approached the house, I was bone-weary. When I'd seen the shape of it, the tall blind-sealed windows, the orange tree in a marigold of bloom, it was as if I'd been away a year. The tension went out of my sinews and I could have dropped.

I tabbed the door, but before I went in, I sat a minute on the porch on the lacework bench. The storm was building, a storm by Vaeder or Stravinsky. Dust creamed by the house, the wind made a sound like a sea, or as a sea sounds to me who has only heard it on a tape: Audio-scapes of Earth. Vol. 2. There might be rain later, Rain, but nothing else.

The guilt wasn't so bad now, because there was no need for too much guilt, and presently the gnawing, the need, would go away, as Sand's need for me would go.

I went in, and closed up, and I was really secure at last.

My bed is a copy of an old four-poster. Carved doves and pineapples decorate these posts, and navy gauzes hang down. There is only space else in the room for the vanity table blocking the window with its litter and its mirror. I can see myself in mirrors. The idea that I might not comes from the same myth that says vampires cast no shadow. Shadow and mirror image are both primitive ciphers for the soul. The myth implies a vampire has no soul. Maybe I haven't, but I've met others who surely haven't too. We all cast shadows, we all show in glass.

On the other plaster wall, where I could see it through the gauze, was the picture.

It was the reproduction of a holy picture, painted by a medieval artist in the days when there was only one world, and they thought it was flat. It depicts Mara, the mother of Christ. Her name means bitterness. But God is telling her she is going to conceive immaculately, and the artist has used the then popular symbol of the pencil-thin ray of light piercing the crystal goblet in her hands—piercing but not breaking. The analogy

is flawless and beautiful. Her head's tilted back and
she's so happy, so exalted, but it won't last. Mara-bit-
ter. Her child will suffer. A mother always takes it
hard.

I woke in the initial blush of night. The storm was
over. The utter stillness of the wilderness hung like a
velvet canopy on the house, the land.

I had a vague cramp in my stomach, but that was
nothing, and would pass. But as I lay there in the deep
dark, I could see starlight through the blinds, licking
the oddments on the vanity table. And I recalled it was
Cassi's birthday check that bought me my disguise as a
bar-girl. Then I wondered about the credits again, but
pushed them mentally aside, because she'd gone crazy,
and that was why she'd threatened with one hand,
gifted with the other.

And then I wondered about the town, the neons,
and the boys who called after me, and the way my
tongue burned as if a drop of flame were on the tip of
it. I thought of how I had them. How I drank them.
Breathed them. I thought of Sand.

I got up and shivered, and went downstairs in antique Earth-model jeans and shirt. Perhaps I'll go out
tonight. Perhaps the deer are running, Montiba way,
where the corrals lie like supper tables on the rouge-
black rocky meadows.

I got some real orange juice from the freezer and
put it through the thaw box and drank it. I took a cigarette from the carton. They had each a couple of grains
of the synthetic hash you can buy at any druggist's. I
smoked, and the cramp dulled in my belly.

My coffee-black hair showed natural highlights like
pale brass reflecting in the windows. Remember when
it was acid-drop blonde, Sabella?

The stone glittered between my breasts. It was only
rosewater then, pallid, dying, the rich scarlet sunk
away. Faithful barometer. Once it was always red,
sometimes so red it was a coal, a wolf's eye.

I put a tone poem by Nils on the music deck.

I shut my eyes, and saw myself alone in this house for sixty years.

I waited till the Nils was done, then switched off the deck. I crossed the hall and buttoned open the door and stepped out on the porch.

And as I stood there, facing down the slope toward the road, I saw a pinprick of light ghosting along the road's surface, coming from the east, from Hammer-lake.

Traffic goes by on that road at night, not often, now and then. But this car came level with the dirt track that swivels up from the road, and the car swiveled with it. The car was coming for me.

The headlight threw a blank page of light across the house and went out. The car parked about forty yards away where the road flickers back into scrub grass.

It was my uncle, the Hog. He wanted me to sign his goddamn papers.

The car door lifted. Someone got out, the door closed.

Somewhere, there was a whisper of cicadas.

He was poised in the darkness with only starlight to see by.

It was Sand.

"Here I am," he said. He said it not boldly but with shyness. A bag hung from his hand. "I had to see you again, Bella. I didn't believe it when I woke up and you'd gone. Why did you? Sabella?"

"How did you find me?" I said, having to say something.

The cicadas, who rarely speak around the Plateau, intimidated by our larger voices, had crushed themselves again to silence.

"It's so simple to find anyone you really want to."

The Hog knew where I was, maybe others of Cassi's circle. Sand had followed me to Cassi's house before. Maybe Sand had paid the servants a visit and just been plausible enough to elicit information.

I want you, baby, said the night with a hundred voices (So many? Less? More?) the men who had re-

turned for me. Not twenty yards away, a man had torn
into me under the orange tree. Why hadn't I killed
him? He had earned it.

"Sand," I said. My voice was husky.

Sand, I don't want you. You make me sick. I hate
your body and the way you lay me and Sand—and
Sand—

"Bella," he said. His voice was one caress. He made
my name magic.

"I don't want you here."

"Yes you do. You do want me. Maybe we both
should be honest, for once. But then, it goes beyond
honesty, Sabella."

He dropped his bag and came to me and grasped me
against him, and he was breathing as if he'd swum for
shore from some treacherous river, and I was the
shore, and now he was home, he was safe.

"Don't cry, Sabella. Why are you crying?"

"I don't want you."

But I was pulling at his arm. We were actually
scrambling over the porch, into the house.

The door was still open. The night leans on the
door, staring.

Sand pinned me against the wall.

Flesh was grass.

He couldn't wait for me. He didn't know he would
react quite like that. He apologized even as he ripped
my shirt.

Centuries ago, men dying of tuberculosis, were discovered to have a high sexual drive.

Incubus and succubus imparted such exquisite
pleasure to their victims during intercourse that the victims could not resist them, shunning their human partners for the embrace of death.

Be patient. Don't kill him.

You will, but not yet.

He won't come back, of course. Another myth, vam-
piric resurrection. He won't rise from the grave. He'll
lie in it. And all his amber and bronze and sable will
combine to form decay.

He cried out, and then the whirlpool choked him and swept him under. He only thought he'd escaped the river.

And I breathe again.

We had three nights, two days between, some hours more. All the while I wanted to baby him, care for him. Don't turn away. *Quid est veritas?* This is mine. All the time I was killing him I wanted him to live. I wanted to help him. Perhaps others do this. Kill each other, but always wanting to restore. But he was a drug to me, I to him. Of the two, he was the more importunate. He didn't know for a long while, almost to the last, what I was doing to him. Sometimes they never knew.

We didn't go out of the house. We—he—made love. And I used his lovemaking. I fixed him meals, after I'd dialed groceries from town. My mother taught me to cook. I cook well. I gave him steaks and wholewheat bread, green vegetables, red fruits, clear wines like morning. I pumped vitamins into him. He wasn't truly weak until the ultimate night.

You're thinking of the farmer who fattens his pig for the kill.

Did you ever eat the pig?

It's love that made me preserve. Guilt, despair.

He talked a lot about his brother. That was the subconscious again. It became apparent from his dialogues concerning this man, his brother, that Sand had been rescued by him many times. Not only from the mescadrine trip on Gall Vulcan, but from petty crimes years before, a dangerous liaison or two, debts. Sand was born a victim. I say this not to excuse myself, for it does not excuse me. But he'd traveled twisting ways, and snares had molded to him. Sand was a prophetic name. Sand that blows and forms many configurations, that can never settle, that is a mere residue of rock. Then I began to wonder if his mind was clouding, if he were hallucinating, for Sand's brother became a massive figure on the skyline of everything Sand said, an angel with blazing wings. Was it that the subconscious, anxious to provide another rescue for Sand in this extreme cul-de-sac, kept supplying the illusion of a brother? Possibly, the brother was not real and had never been.

The second morning, the mailman came. I'd forgotten about mail. He brought the registered packet which contained my certificate of holdings and my uncle's drawn-up documents whereby I could sign the investment paraphernalia over to him. The Hog was taking a fee, naturally. His letter assured me he had to, to see things legal. But I looked at all this days later.

The mailman, who again required my thumbprint, stared at my wrapper, and in the lenses of my black glasses.

"Sorry to wake you, Miss Quey."

He pivoted against the fragile sky, gazing long and hard, at Sand's car parked on the scrub grass by the track.

"Long time since I seen one of them. Ares I.D. digit panel."

He went on gazing. I held the packet in my hand.

There's menace here. He means me to feel menaced. But what can he do, what is he insinuating he can do?

"Visitor?" he said to me.

I could keep quiet, which might goad him further, though to what?

"Yes."

"You don't get so many of those."

"Thank you," I said.

"Thank you," he repeated automatically. "That's a nice car. Old model. Self-drive or auto. Nice."

"Thank you."

"Some morning," he said, "I'm going to buzz this door and you're going to come out with your clothes on."

I buttoned the door shut, but he went on grinning at me through the smoked glass. I walked away before he did, and his grin was focused on my spine as I passed through the blood splash of the big window.

Sand was lying on one elbow, reading, among the cushions on the bed. The house was cool and sweet with the air-conditioning. The blinded room was blue, and Sand's body and hair filtered blue. Even his eyes, the pages of the paper book.

He glanced up and he smiled at me. "She walks in beauty like the night," he said, "and all that's best of dark and bright, meet in her aspect and her eyes."

I sat beside him, and he let go the book, and laid his head in my lap and looked up at me.

"I've never felt like this before. And I've known some trips."

"How do you feel, Sand?"

"Floating. And as if," he smiled once more, pondering, "as if I'm a pane of window glass. What are we on, Sabella?" I didn't answer and he didn't seem to need the answer, and next he said, "Last time we made it, did I black out? I think I did for a moment. But it was wonderful, Sabella. As good for you?"

"Yes."

"I keep thinking," he said, "I *haven't* been honest with you. Jace—did I tell you about him?" Jace was the big invented brother. "Yes, I did. Did I tell you about my father? My father was incredible. Daniel. He was like being alive. He was so full of life, he was like —some kind of sun. And he was crazy. I loved that man. And Jace, he's like that man all over. . . ." He fell asleep, and the fiery jewel, swinging above him, reflected on his cheek, which now was hollow.

A little after sunset, he wanted me. I tried not to take anything from him, but he dragged my mouth to his neck. *Dragged* me. It isn't the same without, you understand, not after it's begun. Finally, I am as incapable of resisting as he.

After midnight, he started to die.

He wasn't scared. He was floating, as he'd put it. The heart gets lethargic, its sluggishness compounded by the loss of blood. I'd seen it happen quickly, in a single night, or less. But with Sand, I'd had the chance to preserve him, keep him alive. I'd never had that chance before. To watch it happen, slow, then steady and sure, like light going from the sky.

He had opened his eyes as far as they would open, which was only now a third of the way, the pried lids like heavy shutters. But at his neck the snake was still alert. Those watching, knowing, unsensual eyes would never close.

I could kill him now, simple as turning out a lamp. We didn't need to couple. His body had learned the connected responses. If I took from him now, he'd spasm anyway, and die in bliss, not guessing.

He seemed to love to say my name, a thing I'd noticed with the others.

"Sabella," he murmured, holding my hand, "Sabella—Bella—Bella."

After Frank, I'd tried to cut my wrists. I say tried. I couldn't do it. When your whole process is geared to survival, as in the hunter it has to be, calculated suicide is as hard to accomplish as to kill in cold blood would be for someone else.

Sand was young, and he had been strong. It was so stupid to realize that transfusions, cardiac assist, rest and sedation, could save this life which was trickling steadily out of him. Seventeen miles away, this side of Hammerlake, there was a hospital. It sat on a rise among palm trees, a hideous white cube that saved lives. It would be straightforward. Sand's car with its auto-drive on the night-clear road, could cover the ground in less than ten minutes. Next, I'd leave the car and Sand in it, hit the emergency button on the hospital gate, and run. Who could run better than Sabella?

Oblivion might cure him of his obsession. If he came after me again. I could go up into the hills. The longer he was away from me, the easier it would be for him. For him.

But there wasn't much time.

I broke the plasti-cover on two of the vitamin shot dermics and pumped the goodness through his pores. At the same instant I was smoothing the heal-fast jel over his throat. At the touch, he roused.

"Sabella," he said drowsily, "have you been drinking my blood?"

O.K. To a medic bending over him: "I met a lady who sucked my blood." The medic wouldn't believe him.

"Darling," I said, "we're going for a drive."

"Sure," he said, smiling. I helped him to sit up, and I dressed him as best I could. He had no more stamina now than the floppy doll my mother had held to her, kneeling on the floor. "I don't mind" he said. "Eternal life. Beautiful Sabella."

I carried him down the stairs. I'm unusually strong, but it was awkward.

"Why, Sabella," he marveled dreamily, "You're carrying me. Jace used to carry me," he said, "but Jace is built like a gladiator."

I got him through the door, over the porch. I opened the car, and managed to angle him onto the rear seat. Not every car has a rear seat. It was lucky Sand's car was a throwback model.

"Sabella," he said, "there's something I have to tell you."

"Later, Sand. There'll be lots of time later."

I got in and shut the car. I switched on the auto and keyed in the directions. The car revved itself, exploding the framework of the night.

"I'm cold," he said.

Miserere mei, Domine . . . conturbata sunt omnia ossa mea. . . .

Forgive me, God. Let him live. Let me be quick enough.

Sabella, you're insane.

The car spun itself around, and flared down the track toward the road, going so swiftly you scarcely felt the bumps.

"Where are you, Sabella?"

"I'm here, honey."

"If I tell you something about myself, don't start hating me."

"There's nothing to hate."

"Please don't hate me. Your aunt Cassilda Koberman
—right? She had a guy who worked for her, an
old guy, a servant, John Trim."

"Sand, don't talk."

"You don't know what I'm going to say."

"That he told you how to find me, because Cassi
knew."

"Not—not quite. Christ, I'm cold, Sabella. I feel terrible, Sabella."

Horror fills me. If I'd let him die in the house he'd
have died without pain.

"It'll be better soon," I said. It will. It will.

I could hear him shivering then, his teeth chattering
as he pushed the phrases out. We were on the concrete
road, racing east to Hammerlake. The speedometer
showed one hundred and forty.

"I kept wanting to tell you, Bella. Once I understood
how wrong they were, and how I—felt about you."

"Hush."

"No, listen—Cassilda Koberman was your enemy.
She left you a handful of credits in her will, like bait,
to draw you out of hiding. Then she primed old Trim
with stories about you. She never told him what it was
you were supposed to have done, but she implied
plenty. The death of your mother was suspicious, you
were a whore—old John Trim got the notion he was
meant to hunt you down, bring you to justice. They
both had this godawful Revivalist thing. She left him a
stack of cash, privately, the way she left it to her
bloody church. I told that fat man at the cemetery that
I was a relation of Trim, but Trim had hired me to get
friendly with you, to suss you out. Can you hear me,
Bella? I've run a little private investigation agency in
Dawson for about a year. Business was poor till this
stunt came up. You see, Bella, that's how I was on the
plane to Ares. I was watching for you, and the check-
out tipped me when your name came through the
machine. That's how I always knew where you'd be:
the funeral, Cassilda's house. I even found you here on
Hammerhead. But that wasn't—I knew straight off on

the plane it wasn't my job any more, that they had it wrong." He stopped, gasping for breath. Then he said, "Am I dying? What have you done to me?"

The car streamed over the concrete, speedometer at one hundred and fifty-one, maximum.

I remembered the Hog marching to Sand across the lawns, returning to me with a congested face, boasting no triumph. I remembered John Trim's frail brown leaf hands shutting me in with Cassi's casket of bane.

I had to make a decision. This is the nearest to the abyss I've ever been. I ought to let him die.

But I can't.

And then the road bent into a tunnel of rock, and as the dark of the tunnel clambered over the car, I saw something beyond the tunnel about a hundred yards along the road. I slammed the brake button, and the car threw itself to a halt three feet from the tunnel's end. And in the dark I sat and stared out through the windscreen at a bar of light dividing the road, and the bright gems of neon that spelled the words RANDOM ROADBLOCK.

Sand asked me if I was angry, and if that was why I'd stopped the car. Then he asked where we were going. He seemed to have forgotten what he'd said previously, he seemed to assume he had a virus, influenza, something like that. Then he told me his father, Daniel, had never had influenza and then he asked me when Jace would arrive.

All during this, I was looking at the roadblock sign, and the barrier across the road. Such checks on traffic across the deserts are irregular but thorough, carried out on suspicion, or just precaution to see what's going where, and when, and why, and with what cargo. They'd search the car and ask questions about Sand, the state he was in. And who was I and what was my involvement. I'd taken chances in my adolescence, chances that made me shake when I recalled them, and I'd been fortunate. (Oh I don't mean the law would react to what I was. But pervert, murderess, to all of that.) And now trouble was on every side of me, on every side one slip and the precipice yawned.

I said, I'm geared toward survival. I was like someone with half vision, and what I could see was my own life, and just a blur by it that was the life of Sand.

I grasped quite suddenly what I had to do.

I opened the car door.

"Sand, it's just a little way. Will you help me? It won't be for long."

I carried him back down the rock tunnel out into the night on the other side, the way we'd come a minute ago. I laid him in the still-warm dust just out of sight of the road. The night-morning was black, cool, not cold. The stars were friendly above. He was out, all the time I carried him. But he was breathing, shallowly. I took off my jacket and spread it over him.

"I won't be long, baby."

I ran back to the car. I jammed the auto button with the self-drive, the thing they say idiots often do. It was dim in the tunnel, but I scooped up the dust and smeared the digit panel. Maybe they wouldn't bother to check it, anyway, if they checked the car and it wasn't packed with anything illegal.

I walked out of the tunnel and straight toward the roadblock and into the light.

There were three automatic electric flash-guns set half charge on the barrier. Two men in the uniform of the Hammerhead road patrol sprawled on the roadside bank with a bottle and a box playing out softly live news, weather, and slow-beat music from the Montiba Smokey Impulse Tower. Both men got to their feet.

"You know," I said as I came up, "God and his angels must have sent you to me."

The men grinned.

"What's the problem?"

"I've jammed my damn car button again. And there isn't a fixit place for thirty miles."

"Oh, we can fix it, lady," said one of the men. "But I'll have to check your car, too."

I saw the roadblock for the first time.

"You after me again? What did I do this time?"

"Not you, lady. At least, I hope not you."

They offered me a drink from their bottle and even a plasti-cup to go with it, but I explained I was desperate to get to Canyon where my man would experience apoplexy when I told him about the car buttons.

Still grinning, but with one of the auto guns unlinked from the barrier and trundling after to cover me, the bigger man strolled with me into the tunnel. He didn't check the digit panel, just the seats, the seat storage and the rear compartment. He did it all humorously, showing his powers of search but not supposing they were necessary. He untangled the jam on the dash with a device from his pocket. He told me where I could buy such a device in Hammerlake. Then he extracted a pack of cigarettes. He demonstrated no wish to leave me. I thought of Sand beyond the tunnel, his strained heart struggling through each pulse.

"You know," said the patrol man, "you're kind of nice looking."

"Am I?"

"I'd say you were. I'd say you might be nice all over."

"Hey," I said, "do you have something to write with?"

Once we got over the double entendre of this, I gave him an invented call number.

"Any time after ten. If a man answers, say you're the Hammerhead police. That'll knock the oxygen out of him."

He might never take me up on this anyway, the boredom of the roadblock being over. If he did, either he'd get the unlisted tone, or a surprise.

He said I could drive on now, they'd open the block up for me to go through, and he walked away out of the tunnel. As soon as he was twenty yards down the concrete, I turned and ran in the other direction. My plan was to bring Sand back to the car just as I'd unloaded him, in the tunnel's cover, lay him on the floor and drive straight through the block. They wouldn't flag me down again, and if they did, they wouldn't check the car.

I reached the tunnel and crossed to the dust-floor, and Sand wasn't there any longer.

My jacket was, but nothing else. Only the scuffed dust, and a slur that might have been a footprint, before the patchy shrubs took over.

I'd been with the patrolmen about ten minutes. Sand had been comatose. But presumably the air had brought him to. Either he'd panicked, or he had just started moving automatically, to find me, or someone. Maybe he was looking for Daniel or for Jace. Maybe he hurt too much to lie quiet. But he hadn't the strength to go far.

I called him, softly. I didn't want the men by the block to hear me. In any case, I only had a few minutes at most before one of them came back into the tunnel to see why I hadn't driven on out.

The wind blew like a lake's ripples across and across the wilderness. I picked up the jacket and put it on.

I went out over the plain, one way, now another. Even in the dark the stars were bright and there the land was almost flat, apart from the ridge that ran down to form the tunnel. Sand couldn't have climbed that ridge, but he could have wandered among the shrubs, the slender, dryly flowering clumps of trees. A parched watercourse, long abandoned, was cut like a scar in the soil. I stared into and along it, because he could have fallen there. But it wasn't there that he fell.

The road was two hundred, two hundred and thirty yards away. I could see the flush of the roadblock's light beyond the arched shapes of the ridge and the tunnel. They must have been going into the tunnel by then. It was too late. I couldn't get back to the car, even when I found Sand.

Then I found him. Of course, then.

He'd come quite a way, as if there were really something out there on that flat easel of earth and night that he had to get to. The wind stroked his hair as he lay there on his face. He was dead. I could have saved him, even with the roadblock, I could have, if he'd waited.

"Why didn't you wait for me," I said to him and I crouched by him, as if for an answer. One of his cheeks was pressed in the dust, the other half turned upward, and luminous, or so it seemed, and the lid of the eye was luminous as if the eye shone through, looking at me. Somehow the snake rope had twisted so that its eyes could look at me too. The dead are always in league against me.

Naturally, the men would have reentered the tunnel then, found the empty car. They'd search for me, then or the next day. They'd stumble on Sand. They'd think that strange, a magic trick, a girl into boy. The digit panel of the car is an Ares registration. A call to Ares could tell them who bought or hired the car. Then they would trace Sand to John Trim and discover who Trim wanted investigated and it was me. Then they'd remember the girl on the road was like Trim's description of Sabella Quey.

It didn't matter what they could tie on to me, or can't. One connection with one of these deaths, these men who die in the darkness, one connection could trigger others. Easterly. The wolves. A spark spinning along a fuse. But not without evidence.

I gathered Sand up in my arms. It was harder, much harder since I had to run with him.

Back there in the tunnel, I heard Sand's car cough as someone manually revved the engine.

Run, Sabella. And Sabella ran.

The incinerator came with the house. It was fashionably antiquated but functional, a five-foot square black drum with a chemical filter chimney that odorlessly smoldered day and night in my mother's time, that didn't often smoke in mine. But it had been at work the past day or so, because Sand had been with me. Leftovers, cartons, wrapping, the incinerator had been busy. The press-button chute was large enough to take an item a whole four feet around. Back before my mother and me, the chute had obviously had to serve larger objects than are common to domestica. And now. Now it had to serve a man.

It had been four hours, going home, carrying Sand. I'd had to lower him to the ground many times. Gradually he ceased to be handsome, pitiful and important. He became a sack of beans I had to haul, my penance, unhuman. I moved a mile or so off the road, because one of the patrolmen was sure to come looking for me or radio for others. As I staggered the last steps toward the house, the brink of the sky was rinsing itself colorless ready for sunrise.

I bore him to the chute. I pushed the igniter to feed the flame inside, and sat down while the furnace heated. I held him in my lap, and we were the Pietà.

Then, when the furnace was ready, I fed him in, let the outer door close, and heard the inner door open and the flames rush up as he dove through into them.

So callously she burned his body, the evidence which might condemn her.

There is no way I can prove it wasn't like that. If you held a knife, would you stick it in your heart, or would you throw it away? Sand had become a knife. But, no. The knife is also your child.

The smoke from the chimney was blue, and the sun came up in it.

The heat from the proofed incinerator was slight, but greater than I had ever known it, even in my adolescence, when my mother burned her old dresses from Easterly, and those albums she and my father had kept together, stills of their wedding and their two anniversaries and my birth. We all go up in flames.

I'm cold, Sabella.

Not anymore, my love.

The ash and melted residue was shunted away beneath into an underground pit. Here it slowly amalgamated with the soil, and if you dug down at the farther opening of the pit, ten feet from the kitchen door, there was an ashy compost. But we had never needed it.

I'm not leaving you, Sabella.

The jewel between my breasts, catching the sun, was the color of a dying rose.

Five days later, I walked down to the delivery box at the edge of the road.

I'd heard nothing. No one had come to the house. I'd been listening to all the news bulletins as I hadn't done for years. But even the local news from Smokey Tower hadn't carried word of a ghost-girl and a car, or a young man who'd been out this way and vanished. It had occurred to me that perhaps Sand had informed no one that he was following me to my very doorstep; that possibly the car dealer in Ares had mislaid Sand's name. Snatches of Sand's reveries came back to me. Possibly not everything was true, or legal. Possibly they'd never trace him through to me anyway. I'd remembered the mailman by then, who'd seen Sand's car parked at the end of the track. But if he'd been sure of a search or of his facts presumably by now he would have spoken out. His manner had registered as sly, a personal antagonism. When he came again, I'd know. As for the Hog, Sand had told him he was related to Trim. And in fact, the only definite potentially damning link between Sand and myself, was Cassi's servant, John. And again, his personal and suppressed form of malice might hold him silent and stultified.

There was a letter in the box, an unregistered letter.

When I opened it, I saw it was from the Hog. There was some grist about having sent me the papers I should sign if I wanted him to deal with my credits. There was a pompously sentimental footnote. He knew I'd be very sorry to hear that John Trim, Cassilda's manservant, had suffered a fatal stroke on the second night after the funeral.

I sat on the ground and read these sentences over. I think I laughed a little. Because, for once, the dead had aided me.

Perhaps it was the shock of seeing the whore-murderess in person that killed John. He had seemed remote, disinterested, in my vicinity, it must have cost him dear, boiling underneath for vengeance, justice. He was older than Cassi, he had looked ephemeral. Revenge had been too big a legacy to leave him.

Cassi, you failed. The prime agent is removed from the stage. And Sand—

My pendant is clear white, Sand. And all night the pain in my belly comes at me like the wolves. I'm living on diluted concentrates and the blood of fruits.

Your metal and your silk are cinders, trash.

And if you lay here dead, right now, I'd burn you again.

The tenth night I hunted, on the hills. The wolves were singing like broken silver saws.

The next night, I went to Angel Meadow, north of Hammerlake, the cemetery where my mother is buried.

Cassi didn't come to my mother's funeral. Nobody came but me, though curiously enough someone else was being buried at precisely the same hour in a neighboring plot, with a somber crowd, and an incredible importation of horses and carriages, emanations of that earlier world the colony planets cling to. It wasn't, in either case, a Revivalist burial. In theirs show took the place of religion. Soil rained on the coffin, and white flowers rained on it, and women desperately rained tears. Twenty paces off, the polished horses stamped. I'd never seen a horse before, certainly not with plumes. There were torches, too, though why these people also needed the night for their burying, I didn't know.

I hadn't cried over my mother's grave, though I cried in Cassi's chapel. Maybe my tears are the sweat of my calumny, and I had not yet learned I was utterly to blame for everything. I was eighteen. I was still blonde.

Obviously the gates were long shut that midnight when I revisited, but the wall was accessible. The cross leaned a fraction over her gray bed. I had never brought her flowers. I didn't pray or stupidly, humanly, attempt to speak to her; I just sat there on the turf, and I could smell aniseed grass, somewhere, like the lawn at Easterly.

When I came back over the wall, and started home, I had the urge to look behind me several times. There was never anyone there, and I think I imagined it. The pursuit had not yet begun.

Part
TWO

The Avenger

1

Two months after the smoke from the incinerator faded, a new mailman called at the house.

It was noon, the light hitting the walls like a frozen explosion, the tinted reflections of the blinds stamped in a patchwork on the floor. I'd been on the hills that night, and though I wasn't sleeping, I was lying on the parlor sofa with the music deck playing, when the buzzer from the porch drilled through. The Hammerhead mail might be delivered any time of day, for traditionally service to the Plateau wilderness is constant but erratic. But the buzz was like voltage going through me, for a moment, before my nerves dimmed down. For I was about to find out if this other enemy of mine remembered Sand's car parked on the track.

Yet, when I went to the door, even through the smoked glass, I could see it wasn't who I anticipated.

I opened the door, and he turned around slowly, like some big animal turning at a noise it doesn't fear.

"Mail," he said in a flat friendly drawl. He held a square package in one hand.

Behind him, pink noon heat shimmered, land and sky flowed over into each other. He stood out on the glare as if drawn on it and then blocked in with rich heavy color. He was six feet two. His skin was tanned like a brown-gold wood, and with the same sheened finish to it. His hair was black, and his pants and his shirt were black, and he wore black lenses over his eyes just as I did. It was as if we had both dressed in the same uniform in order to contend in some duel, in which, perhaps, sunglasses would actually become weapons.

Certainly, he wasn't wearing the uniform of the mail service.

"A very fancy order, lady," he said. "All the way from Flamingo." And he grinned. His teeth were beautiful, as if he had filled his mouth with winter snow.

"I didn't order anything from Flamingo."

He lifted the box. Black hair on hands and forearms and chest: each hair neatly done as if each were painted on with a fine brush and coal-black ink.

"Miss Ritter," he said.

"No. I'm afraid you have a wrong address," I said.

"It says here, Miss Ritter. You're Miss Ritter?"

"No."

"You have to be Miss Ritter."

The heavy colors of him, the heat that seemed to focus through him from the sun beyond, were becoming oppressive, almost frightening.

"Print here, please, Miss Ritter."

Like a scent, I could smell that strange odor which an intelligence gives off, a biting, honed intelligence, playing dumb.

"My name isn't Ritter."

Again he smiled. He invited me.

"What *is* your name then, lady?"

"My name is Quey."

"K-A-Y."

"Q-U-E-Y."

"Qwee?"

"Quey."

"O.K. Hannah Qway."

"Quey. Sabella Quey."

"That's sure a pretty name," he said. "Sabella. Still think this package is for you. Maybe you go in for made-up names."

I put my hand toward the door button. I can move quickly. He moved quicker. He was in the doorway, and the door wouldn't close on him. He didn't come into the hall, he stayed in the doorway. He looked immovable, in or out. He held out the package.

"Why don't you open it, Miss Qway?"

"It isn't for me."

"Look at the label and make sure."

"I don't need to look at the label."

"Ah, please."

So I glanced at the package. It had no label on at all.

"There's no label."

"Maybe there is, and you just can't see it."

I was afraid of him. Why? I'd met the pushy kind. I'd handled them. Handled some into the earth. My voice didn't show my fear.

"I can see there's no label."

"If you took off your sunglasses," he said, trying to help me, "maybe you'd see better."

"Get out," I said.

My heart hit my throat twice every second.

Then he took off his own dark glasses, and raised his head, smiling, and the glow of the stained-glass window revealed to me his eyes. They were like mahogany, but they shone. The black lashes were thick, almost coarse in their thickness. And because he was laughing at me, the outer corners of the eyes were scarred with hair-thin silver cracks in the gold.

"Ever play the imitation game, Miss Qwee?" he asked me. "I do it, and now you do it."

"You're not with the mail service."

"Then you'd better call the police."

The long silence filled the hall. The glare streaming around the edges of him was a crucifixion.

"What do I have to do," I said, "to make you get out. You want money?"

"It's true what the man said."

A pause. He continued to smile at me.

"He said you never answer the door with your clothes on."

I was not in my wrapper, but in a floor-length black smock, with an ornamental button-up, the top four buttons of which were undone.

"How about jewelry," he said, and I know he'd seen the glint of the pendant.

"What you're looking at is glass. You'd get twenty credits for it. There's nothing else."

"There's you."

When he said that, a constriction of terror came up through me. We know I'm not innocent. We know for me it's as if they comb my hair, rough or tender, no more than that. So why terror?

He'd been fraternizing with the mailman. He had a box he wanted me to open. I took it abruptly from his hands, ripped off the plasti-cover and the card reinforcer. One side of the interior gives, and something drops out onto the wooden floor with a clack.

It was the ivory casket, closed by its gold lock as when I had first seen it, and the key on the ribbon, the casket Cassi's heirloom had been in, and her poison-pen letter. I'd left it behind in the house at Ares. Now this man, who was eight inches taller than me and weighed around seventy pounds more, had brought the casket to my door. (Sabella, his height and weight don't matter. You aren't scared of those. What looms so great is the look on his face, in his eyes, that sense of a coiled spring. A thousand yards of coil ready to unwind like a whiplash.)

"You say this came from Flamingo." I sounded calm. I sounded indifferent. He knew I wasn't, but the control might throw him a little, not that he'd show that anymore than I was showing my own emotions.

"Flamingo? Did I say that? Ares."

"Who gave it to you to give to me?"

"Who gave it to me to give to you? The mail service, ma'am."

Now he was abruptly the simple dumbbell again; the dope, worried about his job, worried that I might misunderstand. I stood ossified, and he said, "My buddy is sick, ma'am. Something he ate. So I offered to bring this package out to your house. He couldn't make it, ma'am. He was puking. Real bad puking. Puking to left of him, ma'am. Puking to right of him. Volley and thunder . . . ma'am."

The mailman had gabbled about me. This one, this

new enemy, intrigued, had persuaded or coerced the
other into letting him bring me my package instead.
Could it be that straightforward? Did they really
gamble that I was so deep into shady dealings that I
wouldn't complain? And why no label on the package,
which seemed to have been opened and resealed. And
why the ploy with a false name and an erroneous city,
as if I must declare myself and my connections. There
was no letter in with the casket.

"Just need your thumbprint now," he softly reminded me. Soft, his voice was almost a mumble, lazy, a
beast purring.

But he *didn't* have the nail block for prints. Instead
he extended his hand to me, well-formed, hirsute, with
its sinews of fire under the skin. The gesture was another invitation. Then suddenly he grabbed my fingers
into his. His hand was hot and dry like the desert in
the sun.

He wrung my fist into a knot, as if he meant to
break the bones, and all the while he went on smiling.
But his eyes, were cold. I couldn't tell if he was merely
a sadist, if he was enjoying this. No, it wasn't that.
There was more. Only I couldn't read it.

Then he let me go. He saluted me and sauntered out
onto the porch. I walked slowly to the door button. I'd
learned, for he'd already taught me, that he could be
swift enough to negate that action if he wanted. At the
top step, he paused.

"While I'm on the premises," he said, "maybe you
can help me. I'm making inquires, you see, Miss Ker-
way. About my brother."

I didn't even blink. But then I hung by a thread.

"Could there possibly be two of you?"

He laughed. He made a meal of laughing. He rocked
around and clapped his hard palm against the porch
rail. He knew I wouldn't close the door.

"Nice, Miss Ker-woo. Nice, Well, Miss Ker-wuk,
I'm looking for my kid brother, Sand. Sand Vincent. I
guess you never heard of him."

Falling.

"I guess I never did."

"Your loss, Miss Ker-wak. Your loss." He swung down the steps. There was no car visible, not even on the road below, where the genuine mailman parks. When he turned once more, he had his sunglasses on again. "See you," he said, "Jezebella."

Why can't I take the sun, even the rays of a health-lamp? No, it's no part of a myth. The sun harms me. I think it's my blood. My blood is built of blood, purer, less opaque than human plasma, and more vulnerable. The sun affects all blood. In the daylight, the cells of mine begin to break down, shatter. The radiation of the sun, which would kill you if you were close enough to it, can kill me from a distance.

I moved around behind the blue and violet blinds all afternoon, all around the house, downstairs, upper floor, the attics, looking out through the blue and violet glare, checking to see that he had gone, that he hadn't come back.

He went toward Hammerlake, walking. Even through the blinds, he was definite, indissoluble. He must have known I'd be watching. He didn't glance over his shoulder.

Jace Vincent couldn't have known what was in the packet, not till he opened it. Someone had come on the casket in Cassi's bedroom, closed and locked it and mailed it to me, perhaps an unfriendly, painfully honest, self-effacing servant, hence the lack of a covering letter. Or Jace had taken the letter out and destroyed it, or lost it. . . . How had Jace found me? *It's so simple to find anyone you really want to.* I pictured Jace at Cassi's house, or with the Hog; with the patrolmen from the roadblock. Perhaps it was less complex than that. Perhaps Sand had kept in touch with his big brother (real brother) and there was a communication which mentioned me and Hammerhead. And what does everyone get? Mail. Jace and the mailman, a league of gentlemen against that dreaded witch, a woman alone. A woman who opened the door in her wrapper, who had visitors in cars with Ares digit panels.

And did any of that matter?

What mattered was that Jace Vincent had followed Sand to me. Probably from off-planet, for he had a glaze on him of recent other places, other globes. (Gall Vulcan, where he had nursed and sweated Sand out of the mescadrine D.T.'s?) Again, extraneous. He was here.

What now?

He couldn't be sure. He couldn't know Sand was in trouble, let alone dead. But Sand had often been in trouble. How did Jace know that anything at all was seriously wrong? Force of habit?

An itch in his brother-bone?

See you, he said.

And I couldn't call for help. I'd have to help myself. But there was only one way I knew of, and I couldn't return to that. I was being punished for that now.

The angel-gladiator, the winged avenger.

The house spontaneously self-locked, doors, windows. My mother's installation. No one could get in, at least not without a fight.

Perhaps he'd just wanted to rattle me. I thought I'd convinced him I was impervious; perhaps, therefore, guiltless. He'd just been testing me. He might not come back.

See you.

What had he said to the police, if he'd spoken to them? What had he said to the Hog, or Cassi's servants, or the mailman?

Was there some signal he and Sand had had between them, something missing, by which he knew Sand was dead?

The day crawled by. The sun flared and went out and the night closed its blind over the sky. I closed Cassi's casket in an empty drawer of my vanity table. Out of sight, out of mind? I sat in the parlor, so tense the muscles ached at the base of my skull, between my shoulder blades. I sat there and listened and waited. I couldn't go out. *He* was out there, somewhere.

I could move away from Hammerhead. There were other wildernesses.

It's so simple to find anyone you really want to. (Wherever they may be.)

See you.

When the morning sun came back, Jace Vincent hadn't. He was making me wait, a master musician, for the crash of chords, the brazen blare of trumpets.

I showered and changed into a frock. I put on stockings and shoes, which I hardly wore around the house or on the Plateau.

The door had a lectro-alarm, one of those force bars you can trigger to keep anyone from crossing through the open door, save the occupants. It hadn't been activated since my mother's time, but now I jammed a battery in the slot and switched it on.

As I was standing by the door, I heard the growl of a vehicle taking the spin-off track from the road and gunning for the house.

The center of my body, everything that held me straight, seemed to gush away, but I was still standing.

I'd have to open the door. To leave the door shut would be an admission of fear, and if you were afraid, you went to the police. I couldn't, and therefore I couldn't reveal that I had any reason to. I had to play it that he was just a crazy event in my life that I'd cope with.

The vehicle pulled up, and then there was a pause, then feet, over the ground, up the steps. Feet heavy on the porch. A shadow blossomed on the door glass.

It wasn't his shadow. I could tell immediately. In a way, I'd known they weren't his footfalls.

The buzzer went. I walked stiffly to the door and opened it. A boy about fifteen, in white overalls, was on the porch. He carried a crystal box, a transparent coffin full of green Savior roses.

"Miss Kerwow?"

"That's not my name."

"It isn't?" Concerned, the boy gazed at the docket on the box. His eyes had a puffy, almost tearful look of disorientation. He was at the age of confusion, when you can only get by through a series of perviously planned moves dependent on predicted responses. A reaction out of sequence could derail. I'd been meant to cry out Why, yes, and make a balcony of my arms and breast for the flowers. Then he could have smiled (what a charming boy!) and we would both have been satisfied. But now he fumbled at the docket, two wheels off the track. "It says, it says Kerwow here."

"Is there a sender's name?" He didn't guess his panic was one-ninetieth of mine.

"Sure is. J. Vincent."

"Take them away."

"But Miss Kerwow—"

"My name is not Kerwow."

"Lady, they're special delivery. They cost twenty-three credits, plus delivery charge—"

His eyes were bulging. He would never go. He would stand there forever, until the green blooms wilted into brown, and the natural-cloth overalls turned to skeletal rags on his body.

I made a balcony.

"All right. Give them to me—"

Something snapped. He didn't need pre-planning for a second, indignation was enough.

"Well don't do me any favors, lady."

I didn't tip him. I shut the door. He was fifteen and working on Mature Studies and he needed cash. But Jace had sent the flowers.

I put the transparent coffin on the floor. I had the same feeling I had with Cassi's casket.

But nothing exploded, there wasn't a message. Somehow, I didn't need a message. You lay flowers on a grave.

They were beautiful, the roses. That was my problem, I wanted to destroy them because they came from him, they're poison. But they were not poison, they

were loveliness. So I siphoned out water and set them
in one of my mother's pottery bowls. I'd thank him
graciously when he came.

I waited in the kitchen then. Through the blind of
the kitchen window I could see the broken swing, the
orange tree where the man beat and raped me and escaped alive. What was his name?

The flower vehicle had driven away, and now it
seemed to come back and the buzzer went.

My hands were shaking, heart booming.

But still it was not his shadow on the door.

"Miss Kervac, I have a crate of wine for you."

J. Vincent had sent me a crate of wine. It cost him
two hundred credits. I wouldn't let them in. I made
them leave it on the porch. Before they drove off, I
brought out the green roses in the pottery bowl and
placed them by the crate. I didn't deny that I was called
Kervak. There was no message.

I sat on the wooden floor in the hall, to one side, out
of the window splotch. I wasn't thinking. My heart
thudded slow and heavy. You drink wine at funerals.

The door buzzed.

"Miss Kweet?"

I broke. I laughed. It's funny, it's hilarious. And
he'd sent me a three-foot white-velvet bear. You unpop
the bear's guts and a white flagon of scent emerges on
a satin ledge. The bear's eyes are cold; cold blue eyes.
Like a snake's.

I closed the door and doubled over and retched. But
I was dried up inside, a burned-out ditch.

Presumably he wasn't sure of me. I might be on the
level, an honest nobody. I might yet call the police in
Hammerlake. So he threatened me with gifts I can't
complain of. Fragrance to perfume the dead. Frank-
incense and myrrh.

Then I waited again. I waited all afternoon. Sometimes the house creaks and my pulses stumble. I could
call the Hog: You're the lawyer, uncle. Well, there's a
man pestering me. The Hog wouldn't want to know, or
he'd want to know too much.

When he comes back, you'll have to, Sabella. Have to kill him. Which means you act friendly, you watch the lodestone have its effect on him, as on all the others. All you have to do is briefly want him. Is it so hard? His skin is flawless golden wood and his hair is jet. His blood's blood-color. Air to breathe, Sabella, *air*.

But there's something—something. He frightens me too much. I don't want to touch him, go near him. He frightens me.

Think of the man under the orange tree. You could have taken him any time. You held off, not because you were afraid, though you were terrified, but because you didn't want the guilt of his life. Remember?

You can kill this one. It's guiltless. It's self-defense.

When he comes back.

Out on the porch in the westering light, the wine bottles glinted, the roses withered, the white bear stared.

There was a wind blowing up, like the day I returned from Ares, the day before the night Sand found me.

Dust to dust, ashes to ashes, Sand to—sand.

But Jace wasn't dust, isn't sand, isn't jet and wood and metal. He was skin and muscle, bone, fiber, juices, enzymes, atoms. Nobody made him up. He wasn't like all the rest. He was real.

I won't answer the door again.

I left the bar switched on and I went up the stairs and lay down under the gauze curtains of my bed.

Paternoster. . . .

Sleeping—suddenly the room was black. It was night, inside and out. There was a noise. Someone was knocking on the glass door below.

Glass doesn't break any more, unless it's custom-built to do so. He'd know that. Why knock when the buzzer was there?

I lay quiet and waited for the knocking to cease. It

didn't, it went on and on. O.K., I can take the sound. Rap your bloody knuckles raw, you bastard.

Then, a girl's voice was shrieking.

I sat up, swung my legs off the bed. Certain reactions have to be learned, like those of the fifteen-year-old boy. A girl shrieking on my porch may mean different trouble, worse trouble. Once, in Hammerlake, a police patrol questioned me on the street because two girls had been fighting in the bar I had walked out of. This one shrieks again, and now I can make out the single word: "Hey! Hey! Hey!"

My night vision was developed long ago, and starlight comes in to help me through the stained window above the stairs, showing me the door, and a white shadow this time, thrown close on the glass. She can't see me, the shrieking girl. She knocks again, rat-tat.

He had sent her, this girl. She was out there with the wine and the flowers and the perfume-belly bear.

The fear was mounting up in me, the great orchestra.

The knocking, on and on and on, point counterpoint.

"Hey! Hey!"

I ran down the stairs; I didn't mean to. As I ran, I hit my fist against the old-fashioned light switch, a nipple in a lily bud, on the wall. Light burst through the hall, against the glass door, and my pupils squeezed to dots, but I still saw her. It was me. Sabella, when she was sixteen, seventeen, eighteen, low-cut dress, white powdered flesh, bleached hair, red nails. A vamp, (I perceived the ironic pun) a harlot from Hammerlake. How would he know what I looked like at seventeen?

I buttoned the door, and it swung wide, and I was face to face, eye to eye with Me. I don't mean she was my double. She was my past, is all. My past, that never ended.

"Hey," she said again, between perplexity and outrage, "Is this a *party?*"

Then she took in my face. Do I look like that? She

backed a step and demanded loudly of the darkness;
"Jay-yaice."

They must have walked from the road, for there was
no car on the track, shutting out the stairs. But as he
moved from the lacework bench, he shut them out. He
had on black again, but different clothes, no sunglasses,
just the black glass eyes themselves.

"Why," he said, "if it isn't my friend Jezebel."

I'm standing in the doorway. The lectro-chain's
switched on and he can see the faint glow of it, and
that this is as far as he gets.

"Is she welcoming?" Jace Vincent inquired.

"I should say not," said the bleached girl.

"What about my advance payment?" said Jace.
"Why, I anticipated finding you, Jezebella, sipping my
wine, carrying my roses, smelling like sixty credits a
bottle. And look," he showed me a wad of credits in
his hand, the bills you rarely see in a world of check
and auto-cards. "Down payment. More to come. For
services to be rendered. Or have the charges gone up
since my brother was here?"

I didn't say anything.

The girl sensed abruptly that this candy had a bitter
kernel.

"Jay-yaice? You said there'd be a pa-arty."

"Shut up," he told her companionably. "Unless you
want to remind this lady of the going rate of whores."

"Jay-yaice—"

"You scared she'll call someone? A patrol, maybe.
She won't. Not my old friend Jezebella. My kid brother
told me about this one. She's hot stuff. She does it like
nobody else."

With strange profundity, his harlot told him, "Nobody does it like nobody else."

Jace directed his hand, mildly, as if to reach in at
me, and the lectro-chain sizzled up, prepared to block
him. He smiled at me, as before, politely. Then he
leaned and hefted the wine crate, agile, as if it weighed
a quarter of what it did. He nodded to the girl. "The
rest of it's yours."

"Oh," said the girl, and her face was a child's face. "Can I have the bear, too?"

"Sure," he said.

She struggled and succeeded and had the bear and the roses, and she looked happy and very young. She'd forgotten me.

They walked away into the night as if nothing had happened, and he whistled a hymn tune, giving a lick to it it never had in church.

The car—Jace's?—revved about two-thirds down the track.

Green petals rushed along the porch.

The sun came up in a great mulberry ball and golden razors lanced the blinds. I lay on my bed and listened to the sun raining on the house, the tindery crackle it made, hitting the joists, the paint, the emanations. I felt enormously calm because there was no point in anything else. I had something in the freezer that would keep me going two or three days more. I had hash grains and tobacco and fruit juice and air-conditioning and music. I didn't need to go out. I didn't need to open the door. I could lie there, taking my time, making up my mind. And when I was ready, I could invite him in. I'd be glad to, then.

When something cracked on my window, I thought of Easterly. Boys used to do that in easterly, to wake you, little crumble stones flung at the glass.

"Oh, Miss Kwhore."

His voice was more familiar than my mother's, which had faded in my memory.

"Oh, Miss Kwhore, you have a very stylish residence."

Something smashed. Breakable glass—a bottle left over from the wine crate? If he'd been close all night, I never heard him.

"Yes, Miss Kweer, I'd say you had a fine appreciating property."

I half sat, then dropped back. I was going to look out at him. Silly.

The second time he spoke, he'd moved slightly, and then again, but I couldn't hear his steps. He walked soft, the way I can walk, a hunter's way.

And then he struck something with a stone, sounding it. It was away around the other side of the house, the tree side. I couldn't think what he struck, but suddenly he was at my side again, under my window.

"You have some charming antiquated features here."

And I knew what he'd struck, and slowly I sat up again, and I held my breath.

"Shit, Miss Kwack, you even have an incinerator."

And now I understood what it's like to be changed to stone. The limbs too heavy to move, the rib cage jammed so no oxygen will come, the eyes starting, the tongue grown into the roof of the mouth.

The silence outside told nothing. A stone can't ask, can't go to a window and see.

And then I heard his footsteps, he'd turned up the volume for my benefit. A deft crunching over the ground, and with it a low thin electronic humming, some machine that was trundling beside him up from the track. He walked with the machine, around to the back.

Suddenly the hum broke into a great chugging noise, a whoosh, and a vibration that ran through the frame of the house. And he too broke suddenly into a huge hoarse singing shout:

"Oh when we get there,
When we get there to that glor-yus town, o'gold
Jezus'll be waiting,
Oh yes Jezus'll be waiting—"

I picked up my stone body and moved.

Momma's bedroom looks out toward the orange tree. I can remember her pale face watching me as I swung the swing. I hadn't gone in her room for five years. I buttoned the door, and it was like cutting into a loaf of time, through a crust, through bread. And even though the dust-eaters and the air-conditioning did their work here as in the rest of the house, the atmosphere was thick as bread. I didn't look at anything. Only out the window, the one window that had no blind, merely the yellow gauze in front of it. The sunlight was like a knife, and the noise of the machine was roaring through the floor.

"Oh yeah, Jezus'll be waitin' as the Holy Book foretold."

A black rubber pipe went in the earth ten feet from the kitchen door. It quivered. It was attached to a cube of machinery with a blow-out chimney on the top, and an open rear end. I couldn't see Jace. I could see a haze of gray and black cinders showering out fine as pollen from the rear end of the machine. The machine was pumping out the belly of the pit under the incinerator.

. . . conturbata sunt omnia ossa mea . . .

I was running out of the room. No, not this way.

Brush your hair, Sabella. Straighten your dress. Put on your shoes. You look sick, Sabella, but for thirteen years I never saw you look less than beautiful. Pick up the half cigarette in the tray, light it. That's it. *Now*, run.

I switched off the lectro-chain and went out into the molten clamor of the morning and around the house. As if I had all the hours there are.

This side of the machine, Jace was. He stripped to black jeans, his body like a living carving, the round brazen muscles gliding in his arms as he manually shoveled through the piles of settled cinders. He'd left off singing. His face was concentrated, but though I'd made no sound, he knew I'd come out, and he turned and straightened up, and then he grinned.

"Hallo, Miss Kerwale."

"Hallo, Jace."

His face didn't alter, but he said, politely correcting me, "My name is Jason, Miss Kerwule. Only my friends call me Jace."

"And my name is Sabella, Jason."

Pleasantly he said, "Your name's just shit to me."

"Jason," I said. I looked in his eyes. They were hard, like the sun. "What are you doing?"

"Just sorting your dry compost, Miss Kerville. You see, a lady on her own can eat only so much, particularly a skinny jane like you. But a lady and a man. Some things don't burn. Metal tops, the check stamp on cartons, meat bones. I'd say you'd had a guest, Miss Kweele. Like my buddy the mailman told me."

I seemed to be looking at him down a funnel. He appeared small and made by an able craftsman. My nausea was a kind of feathering through my whole body. But he couldn't see it.

"I sometimes have guests, Jason."

"I thought you did, Miss Kwole."

The machine gave a sort of hiccup. Something a little too big for the pipe was being lugged up, sucked in. The dust would whirl off the top of the pit first, then the lighter noncumbustibles, the metal bits he spoke of. Down below, where the soil-returning mulch had begun, the machine wouldn't take hold. Between the two lay the heavier unburnt leftovers of the furnace. The pipe bucked a fraction, coughed, renewed its grip. Like a dog worrying a bone—

"Jason, leave that. Come in the house."

"Suddenly the lady is gregarious."

"Last night . . . just wasn't the right time, Jason."

Go to him, Sabella. Go closer.

I could scent him, and he was like Sand, a clean masculine odor, unmistakable, potent. In fact, he was very like Sand, but Sand crystallized, fused into essentials and into strength. Sand's weakness drew me to him. All their weaknesses. But this one wasn't weak.

The pipe gurgled.

He glanced at it. I was close enough to reach out and run my finger across his skin. Chest and belly were like sculptured rock. He turned back to me and I lifted my finger away from him.

"What did Sand tell you about me?" I said.

"A couple of things."

"Tell me."

I couldn't see any whites to his eyes, they were so dark and so still.

"Sand has a knack for permanent trouble. We keep in touch because that way I'm ready to bail him out. One stellagram a month, and if anything comes up, an extra stellagram. And he always tells me about the women he runs with. Women are mostly bad luck for Sand. So I know all about you, about Cassilda and Trim and how you turn Sand on and how he's following you to this old colonial house on the Plateau. And how there's two months' nothing from him after that. Which is what you're waiting to find out, Miss Kwek. Why I'm here."

"Do you know all about me, Jason? Why don't you come and see for yourself."

"First, you tell me where Sand is."

He's in that pipe, in that damn pipe, choking it, but it's going to spit him out, any moment, right where you're standing—

"He had something else to do. I don't know what, he didn't tell me. I guess he'll be back. You could wait around."

"He left his car in a tunnel on the Hammerlake Road. There was a girl. You have a sister, Miss Kwade?"

The pipe gave a big choke and dislodged the obstacle.

Black and brown, the sticks of bones hailed down into the dust and cinders.

We were both looking at the bones.

"What the hell is that?" His voice had changed. For a second there was no strength, no assurance in it after all.

"Oh God, how horrible," I said. "My dog. He got sick and he died. I had to burn his body."

The blazing day had turned to paper. Rose aluminum sky, reddish floor of congealed parchment. The

man, a paper cutout, with drawn-in shaded muscula-
ture, hair and features.

"A dog," he said.

Then the machine vomited out something else. It
ripped over the paper sky and landed, and skidded. It
skidded to our feet. It was unrecognizable, blackened,
jagged. But there was a dull glowing smear on it, like
melted debased metal. Jace Vincent bent forward a
little. Now he could make out the curious wedge-
shaped formation in the middle of the smear, and the
two calcified burned drops that glared up out of it.

It was Sand's snake, the gold jewelry around his
neck, what was left of it. And the two blue gem eyes of
the snake, no longer blue, were still unclosed.

There wasn't any time anymore. There was leisure
to let my gaze drift up to Jace's profile. His face had
gone yellow. He couldn't have known it all, then. Of
course, it was terrible to learn this way. I felt an in-
stinctive, momentary idiotic pity, and then I remembered that I was part of this.

I sprang and I spun and I ran. I'd run after the
wolves. I was quick. The open door was only around
the side of the house.

I could see the door, I was twenty feet away, when
he brought me down, his weight like thunder, like a
lion.

The ground hit me, the ground crammed into my
mouth and thrust into my breasts, and the man lay on
me like stone, and then he pulled off and I was flung
around, onto my back.

He knelt over me. His face wasn't vulnerable anymore; how could I ever have reckoned it was? It was
the face of God turned toward Gomorrah.

I brought up my hands and scratched at his face and
jackknifed my knees into his stomach and his groin—
but somehow his flesh eluded me, it wasn't there. He
caught my hands and impaled them on the earth and
he lay over my legs. I arched and strained my throat,
but even my mouth couldn't come near him now. He

said into my face, without expression, "So you killed him. How and why?"

When my voice came, I was surprised, it was hoarse and naked with terror. I screamed at him.

"You wouldn't believe me if I told you."

"Listen," he said, "I know that murder has become a sickness, and the Planetary Federation puts murderers in doll houses on a hill with pretty flowers and trees to make them happy. I know that. So this is our business, Jezebel. Yours and mine. Nobody is going to rescue you and institutionalize you and keep you safe. You have to deal with me."

I didn't fight anymore. The sun was washing me away like mud from a lake shore. I was blind, I was quiet, and blindly, quietly I said, "Sand was sick. I tried to take him to the hospital outside Hammerlake, but there was a roadblock and they checked the car and Sand wandered away and he died. I didn't want to get involved."

"Don't pass out," he says. "I'll only bring you around and we'll start again."

I was whispering, with my eyes shut tight.

"De profundis clamavi ad te, Domine . . ."

"Stop that," he said. He slapped my face lightly, wanting to keep me with him.

"Domine, exaudi vocem meam."

He held my hair, not really painfully, and repeated to me in English, *"Out of the depths I have cried to you, O Lord: hear my voice.* The only one who's going to hear you is me, Jezebel."

"Please take me in the house."

I didn't really think he would, but he did. He picked me up and carried me. He put me on the floor exactly where my mother lay when she was dead, under the crimson spillage of the window, and I wondered how he knew to do that, or if he knew.

I was listless. Was I afraid? Probably.

He didn't need a special weapon or ritual to kill me. Anything would do. A gun, a cord, a blow.

"What you're doing to yourself, Bel," my mother said, standing over me with her sad and fallen face.

"I know, momma."

I'm crying, momma.

"I know, momma."

I'm crying.

2

When I found the pendant, it was a few days after my eleventh birthday, and it was the day I started to bleed. My father had been dead for nine years, and our house was a woman's world. Women tend, as do men, to turn into clans when thrown in with too many of their own gender, and then those clans practice mysteries. From my tenth birthday on there'd have been these mystery hintings: *Once you start. Once you get to be a big girl, Bel.* I knew about menstruation, school took care of that. But somehow the science had never fully related to my body. A picture on a screen was just a picture on a screen. Then one day the picture happened inside me. Even when you know, it shocks. Even when you understand it's nothing bad, somehow it's still bad. Now you're different, not yourself anymore. In that moment, I turned for reassurance, applause perhaps, I turned to find myself in the eyes of another, because this is where generally human beings find themselves. But my mother gave me a tape book to play which told me what I had to do now, although I'd already heard it through at school. So I went out of town and along the road over the hidden mines and by the refineries and over the river into the meadows. Where a couple of the old dry canals opened under the rosy sands of Easterly's neck of the deserts, that still make up four-fifths of Novo Mars, I found a hole in the ground.

Anice (or is it Alicia?) fell into a hare's warren. Do bats eat cats she wondered, as she plunged into the dark. I suppose Sabella had climbed trees, dug into holes; I don't recall. I think I'd even seen this hole before, assumed it was but another pit in the quarry that overhung the canal bed. Why did I go in? I foresee an analogy, the womb of the earth, Sabella's womb. But I think it was just somewhere to hide, and maybe Alicia's was also a hiding place from her womanhood. Certainly, the tunnel had no exclusive feminine aura. In fact, an old catapult, the sometime gadget of most Easterly boys, lay near the entrance, but when I knelt on it it broke, brittle with age.

When I dreamed about the tunnel on the plane to Ares, my mother was there, but when it happened she hadn't been, I was alone. Nor were there tall thin pillars, as at Dawson, or up in the Calicoes. The tunnel roof was actually low, and I didn't go far before I came on a slab of rock set endways across the tunnel. All this I discerned by feel, because my body had shut out most of the light that came in at the entrance. Even then, I thought the slab was a grave.

The rock of the slab was worn or planed as smooth as satin, and, as with the other ruins of New Mars, there was no sand blown in, no dust, except their own, as if they had had dust-eaters at work. I was stroking the texture of the smooth rock when my fingers found a crevice. In the crevice was a pebble, also silken smooth.

When I took it out and held it toward the light, trying to see, it was opaque and dull, the shape and size of a small plum. But at the narrow end was a ring fixed through the stone. I was only eleven but I recognized the metal of that ring, the amalgam they christened areum, stuff of meteors that die here, unreproducible.

So I bore my prize out into the sunlight, holding it in my closed fist.

By planetary law, an item discovered on the site of a previous civilization is Federation property, which means property of Earth. I knew that, but I wasn't about to renounce what the day had given me when it had already taken away so much.

I sat in the rough meadows beyond the dam, and

picked the stone up, and held it, and put it down. It was ugly, but pleasing to touch and caress.

I watched the sun dive off the slope of the world, and then I got up to hurry home. I had my first cramps, and the tape book had recommended which analgesics were the best. When I was into town, I stopped at the drug store. I had been sentenced but I knew my rights.

On the street, as I started to smell the aniseed grass of our lawn, I looked at the stone, and it wasn't dull any more. It was clear and bright as crystal, as diamond, its facets all inside and winking, blinking back at the stars.

I made a deduction. The heat of my hands and my palm's pressure had burnished the stone free of sediment.

My mother hadn't told me I was wonderful to become a woman, so I didn't tell her about the stone.

I saved my expense money, and I bought a chain of white metal at a store on the far side of town. I never wore the stone then, except in my bedroom. Then I let it rest against my skin, between my breasts, which were growing fast now. I felt secretive when I wore the stone, and sensual and afraid and—as if I hungered, but I didn't know for what until that night when I was fourteen.

Six months before I was fourteen, I'd started to wear the stone all the time. Other girls wore crosses or medallions or good-luck pieces. The stone was mine. Nobody saw it. When I had to go into the school shower or the changing room, I'd have an adhesive tape wrapped round the stone. The girls laughed at that. They didn't like me. I was different, I didn't have a father, and their mothers didn't like mine because she was a widow with a bit of ephemeral money and maybe she'd seduce their men, so the daughters, catching the virus unconsciously, didn't care for me either. And now that I was beautiful they liked me less and less. And strangely, the boys didn't like me any more than the girls did. I didn't look soft or alluring or yielding or admiring at them. I was too beautiful to be pretty.

I didn't really know why I was on the highway near the beer shop that night. Restlessness, hunger. When the boy picked me up, I was flattered and amazed. He had very blue eyes and fair hair and he self-drove a car. He said we'd go to a cinemat, and to a roadhouse and dance. But he parked by the road under great dripping fern trees.

I knew about sex, too. We all did. We were taught about it and then told to leave it alone. The boy explained with his hands and his mouth that it wasn't to be left alone. I was excited, and then I felt the stone, pulsing against my breast. I became so fascinated by the pulsing of the stone, I lost track of what the boy did to me, all the burning sensations passing into each other, the stone their focus. And then he laid me on my back and he tried me, and when he couldn't ride easy, he forced me instead. It wasn't that I attempted to prevent him, but I felt roughly torn like a garment and the scald of blood. He'd taught me to kiss, the kiss that draws the blood against the skin. His neck was against my mouth. It was natural. I took his flesh into my mouth, and my teeth met through the vein. When he screamed out, I thought it was in pain. He was holding my arm, and he bruised it black; the other hand was clutched on the seat beneath us, and his nails went in the fabric. He was crying oh God, oh God, oh God, and then he didn't cry any more, and only the movements of his body went on, and then even they stopped.

I was satiated and drowsy and I lay there half an hour under him before I comprehended he was dead. I had continued too long, you see. I hadn't known.

I stopped menstruating when I was fourteen, about the time my body recognized I was no longer human.

"Is there some reason why you haven't killed me?" I said to Jace Vincent.

"There's a good reason why I might."

I couldn't see him. My eyes were still dazzled from the sun, though the dark glasses helped. He had let me put them on; at least he didn't stop me. There were no tears in my stockings, because nylon doesn't run any more, but there were runs in the long pale calves of my legs, and across my hands. I needed to replace what the sun had done to me out there. But it hardly mattered, if he was going to kill me. The fact was, he didn't want to kill me, not yet. He wanted to get the truth, or he thought he did. He wanted his vengeance drawn out, to break my back and watch me squirm, because he imagined I was a whore-lady who killed his brother for cash or kicks, and in a way he was right.

Presently I said, "Can I have some water?"

He didn't speak.

I didn't add anything, and then he got up and got my wrist and pulled me with him into the kitchen. I fell against the siphon unit. My fingers were cotton wool and I couldn't make the button work, so then he did it for me.

"What's the matter with you?"

"What does it look like?"

"It looks like let's pretend."

I drank the water, which nearly came back, but didn't. "Maybe I'm just afraid of you."

"It's more than that."

"I have photophobia. I can't take much sun."

"I know about photophobia. You don't have the right symptoms."

That's funny. I laugh, and he shakes me and lifts and holds me against the wall.

"Now, you tell me what you did to Sand, Photophobella."

My eyes are getting clear. I can focus on his golden throat. It would be easy. *Do* it.

I can't.

Why can't I?

"I told you, Sand was sick. I tried—"

"To take him to a hospital. Yeah. What did he have? Something he caught off you?"

I could see the orange tree through the blind.

"Let me down. I'll tell you everything."

I didn't know what I was doing, half-blind, dizzy. My instinct was, of course, still to run, but by day my escape route had to be limited. When he swung me down and let go of me, my instinct nevertheless mastered me stupidly.

I wasn't unexpected or fast anymore, I simply pushed by him and floundered out of the kitchen, toward the stairs, and up through the daggers of stained glass sun. He let me do this, although I had told him nothing, and I 'was aware that he let me. When I fell and pulled myself on hands and knees, he let me do that too. I had only one direction to go. I went into the bedroom, and thrust the door shut, and buttoned the lock. All that he allowed, but only in order to prove it was futile.

As I lay on the bed, stunned and mindless and panting with the effort, I heard that soft step of his that he permitted me to hear when he wanted me to. Then he put his shoulder to my door, a dazzling brazen machine, and the lock sizzled and shorted and the door crashed inward.

"Just so you know," he said.

I'm so tired. Suppose I told him the real truth. I killed your brother for his blood. He was beautiful. I couldn't get enough of him, I drank him nearly dry and his heart stopped because he loved what I did to him too much.

"I don't think we can go any further with this," I said.

"You don't."

"Because I told you the truth and you won't accept what I've told you."

"I can accept that Sand was working for the old guy, Trim, and that maybe Sand dug up some news you didn't want printed. Cyanide between bread and butter might be something you're good at."

"Would I tell you if I were?"

"You might," he said. "You see, Jezebel, you're

curling at the edges. I don't know what you're on, but there's some kind of stuff you have to have, and until you get it, you're shaking. When you start to shake enough, you'll tell me anything I want."

I could feel my mouth idiotically form into a grin.

Yes, I believe I am exhibiting the symptoms of drug addiction and deprivation, sufficient anyway to convince him, whose brother screamed and rolled on the floor from a lack of mescadrine.

"So I'll finally tell you I murdered Sand, and *then* you'll kill me."

"Don't worry," he said. "You have religion. I'll let you pray first."

"That's very kind." But he had already turned. "Suppose," I said, "suppose I have a secret stash of whatever drug it is you think I'm using, up here in this room?"

He turned back, and in his helpful voice he said, "If you do, then you'll use it, and that way I'll know. Then I'll rip the room apart and I'll find it. And then we'll wait till you start to need again." He went out, and from the place beyond the broken swinging door he said, "On the other hand, I reckon you have it ready-mixed in your freezer, like any store-minded junkie."

Don't flinch, don't move. Don't say a word.

Five minutes later, I hear cans explosing in the kitchen below, and the glub-glub of the waste-pipe, drinking the fruit juice he's pouring away. When the glass container falls, I hear that too. Unlike the glass of doors or windows or goblets, the container is disposable and smashes, and the red *eau de vie* will be gliding on the kitchen floor, amid the fragments of the glass. Presently the sun will dry the substance into a rich raw stain, just like blood.

"Say good-bye," he called up to me.

I said good-bye.

I need, I need. Every part of me is a hurt, my joints, my stomach, my tongue, my glands, my eyes. The sun took and I can't replace the sun's taking. I'm dying. No, not yet.

I lay on the bed. The sun was out. (Where did the day go to?) Sometime earlier he went down by the road where his car was parked, and brought back a pack of ready-food, which he heated in momma's old microwave-heater . Then he brought me a dish of this amalgam and urged me cheerfully to eat it. He only removed the plate when I informed him what would happen if he didn't. He offered me wine, too. Wine, he pointed out solicitously, would blunt the edge of the knife in my guts, for a while. His sadism was affectionate and intense, and under it he was a blank, not enjoying it at all, just using it, like the rack, the jump-chair, to get my confession.

Two hours after sunset, the first wolf let out his whistling howl, high on the razor-back hills in the star storm of night.

When I heard the howl my whole body began to jerk and tremble. I started to groan aloud and couldn't hold the sounds inside myself as agony and craving flung me about the bed. Then all the wolves in the world were howling out there, as if they called to me: Come, come, come to us, why do you wait?

Soon he reappeared in my door, dark on darkness, one glowing star caught between his lips.

"Charming cigarettes you have," he said. White smoke curled from his mouth as he spoke, and I smelled the incense smell of the loaded tobacco. He crossed to the window, passed by the mirror, raised the blind, and buttoned up the glass. The tide of wolf voices sang into the room, making it tingle, sparkle, like winter frost forming on everything.

Jace watched me.

"You like that sound?"

"Yes."

He moved around the bed and offered me the cigarette.

"No." I turned my head aside.

"You're hurting, honey," he said. "Very bad. Aren't you?"

"You know I am."

"Say a little prayer," he said, and he went away again.

Why can't I get over this unseen barrier and take him and have him?

The voices of the wolves were fading, blowing away. Out there, the hills are promises, there are four thousand neons in heaven.

Maybe he'd sleep. Sometime he had to. He was confident, he thought he'd beaten me.

The house was softly dislocating its tensions in the chill of the young night. Momma's ghost was sitting in her room, watching at the window. The broken swing and the broken door slowly swung to and fro in the wind.

The knife moved like a child in my belly, but then I began to drift, drift up out of the hurt. I began gently to hallucinate, or to dream. . . .

About how, over westward, Montiba way, the little deer may be feeding on the night-black plants, and how sometimes the heavy cattle, white as plaster in the dark, break their way from the corrals. . . .

Where do the wolves run to who hunt these hills, where do they run when they're invisible—back into time, before the civilization of this planet ended? Back to when the pillars upheld roofs like fluted water-ice and the urns were empty?

Dreaming, I struck west and ran ten miles. It was nearly midnight by the rings and spirals of the stars which seem immovable yet move. (No. The planet moves, not the stars. We must ignore the evidence of our eyes.)

There was a ravine, a memory ravine I remembered at once, its contours, its tiers ripe with leaves. A fragmentary wind rustled the papers of the leaves, and below, a rivulet of black water waded. I eased down through the shadows, and I could feel the dream deer as I always felt them, like a warmth in the night.

Near the bottom of the ravine side, where the eucalyptus trees grew sideways toward the water, I beheld the deer by the river, like young girls in a story, like Pharaoh's daughter at the river with her handmaids. No male in attendance, for the season is far off. Now a slender head, ears like curled leaves, lifts and listens. How lovely, the striped body, the fragile legs. Every one of them's a porcelain figurine.

I walked forward, and other heads lifted. The stone was burning softly on my breast, and I loved the deer as I moved among them. When I was fourteen, fifteen, and learned my hunting, I was surprised that I could go right into the herd like this, selecting from them the one I would drink from, like a precious wine stored in a vase of flesh. When I took from the deer, there was no human sexual act to encounter, to use as bait and placation. There was simply their instinct to fly from me, which only the chosen animal would exhibit. If they died, it was from shock, blood loss. I killed accidentally, through greed and carelessness, at first. And then I lessoned myself in how I need not kill. On the night of Cassi's death, I had chosen mistakenly a creature which had a weakness in it, and when it died between my hands, it was as though Cassi's cold breath, hissing from her corpse, had condemned us all. The deer, Sand, myself.

Here is the one I will have.

She comes after me instantly, her delicate steps pattering on the stones among the moss by the water. She came trustingly at first, irresistibly. In reality, I would feel now the excitement of hunger, and tenderness, compassion. In the dream, my limbs are leaden. I creep to the edge of the clearing, and in the cradle of the eucalyptus I drop down, and the deer follows me.

A yard away her struggle begins. She suddenly knows. She's come to the wolf. She tosses her head and stamps her miniature feet, as if she were tethered to a post, scenting death, unable to escape.

I go on gazing at her, at her soft antimony eyes, and finally she comes on again and kneels down. Her head lowers itself. Her eyes are glazed with terror, but her body is quiescent. Don't be afraid. I stroke her neck, whose nap is prickly velvet, (I can feel it, even dreaming.) Her smell is strong but healthy, (I can smell her, dreaming). My eyeteeth are slanted a fraction, outward, not enough to notice, enough to save my own mouth from their razors, (dreaming, I can analyze.) I make the single bite with enormous care. I must be very careful of her life. When I begin to draw out the wine, she quivers, tenses. Now she's ready for flight the moment I negate the hypnosis I've set on her. She feels, I think, nothing. She suffers it because she must. While I feel gratitude, comfort and boundless love.

Measure, Sabella. Don't drain her. Don't harm her. Love her and thank her. Let her go. (I don't remember any more that it's a dream).

No more, Sabella.

Let her go.

I wrench my head away, and at once the deer leaps to her feet. Memory of a hundred other deer.

They flash like bolts from a gun, through the nets of the shadows and the leaves, over the stream. The strong deer, who, when they had put distance between us, would rest and browse again, their cells refashioning what I had robbed them of. All the deer vaulted over the water and poured through unseen holes in the black.

The moss made a pillow for my body, and the pains were going out in me as if cancelled by a powerful analgesic, that yet left my brain quite lucid. I have evaded the avenger. How had I done that?

Perhaps, I had not.

I lay there in the dream and I thought, *he couldn't keep up with me, a wolf-bitch's running.*

But he was an athlete, his body gave evidence of that. He could keep up. Silently. But a night is full of sounds, of winds and grass and sands and waters. What you take for silence in the hills is only another kind of clamor. Yes. Jace could have tracked me, could have witnessed me. If I sat up and I saw him in the nightscape anywhere around me, then I'd know I'd told him every detail, after all.

There were none of the breaks, the edited sequences that come in dreams. All went forward logically, in progression. So I sat. And just across the trickle of the stream, the way the deer had fled, a black silhouette was inked on the night. It was not a freak form constructed of boulder, tree or shadow. It was a man. It was Jace.

I sat and looked at him, and eventually I could even see his eyes, their brightness, and then I could see the sheen of something slung behind his shoulder, a burnished tube that also was no part of any tree or branch; the long muzzle of an electric gun with which a man goes hunting wolves.

Dream Jace spoke to me.

"And that," he said, "the thing with the deer, is what you did to Sand."

"That and more." I wasn't afraid, not here, not in the dream-canyon, pain-freed, among the stars and the leaves.

I got to my feet. I was warm, and still, and easy with him.

"When I take blood from a man," I said softly, "it isn't the same as when I take it from an animal. When I find a man I want, when we make love; I take it then."

I was walking to him, I was stepping over the narrow stream. My tongue gently burning. My body burning. All the night was strung, like the strings of violins, resin-taut. As I walked to Jace, stepping over the water, I was like a bow, ten bows or twenty, drawn across those strings. And the note sounded deep in the womb of the darkness.

"Let me show you," I said to him. I knelt down before the man with the gun as the deer knelt to me. I was arching my back and the hoarse music of the night was soaring through me. He could kill me then. I didn't care. I wanted him to.

I turned my head, and offered him my neck.

"It's all right," Sand said. "You're awake. It's all right now."

But it wasn't Sand. There was nobody there. No one by me.

The wind was blowing the curtains around my bed, the wind which smelled of the hills and which had brought me my dream. But not all of my dream.

About me, the house was quiet as though empty.

His skin is sunburned, Sabella. He drinks alcohol and eats real food, Sabella, you saw him. No, that isn't the horrible joke. He isn't one of your own kind. You're still unique, and alone.

Why then. . . .

I was the victim. *Willing* victim.

It's sex, Sabella. What you missed. What you give but never receive. That's why you're afraid to touch him, Sabella.

I rested my head against my knees, doubled up to ease the clawing in my stomach. And I smiled coldly, remembering the Freudian dream symbol of the gun, and the Pascian symbols of the stream, the violins.

The house was so noiseless. Was he sleeping? Was he? The avenger, doubly my enemy, doubly to be dreaded.

I should like to see him asleep, just once. That face smoothed out, helpless and blind in sleep.

No, Sabella, let me explain this to you. All sadists are also masochists, one indulgence feeds the other. Sand kneeled to you. Now you kneel to the sword. But it's the night you need. Yes, I can, I must.

I crept out, and down those stairs which I've descended a thousand, thousand times. In the starlight from the window, pausing, reaching out to sense and avoid him. The darkness was deaf and dumb with waiting for me, the whole night a pool that I must cleave.

The glass door would open silently at my finger on its button. The night would open silently, and close over my head, hiding me.

The splotch of the starlight window was colorless yet

glowing on the wooden floor. I half turned, intuitively, feeling for the parlor, the sofa where I had slept, and where the man, secure in his assumptions, was sleeping now.

I ran forward soundlessly, and a huge blackness materialized from nothing, apparently from the bottom of the door, and reached out and seized me with iron hands.

I screamed in an ecstasy of terror, my whole body and my spirit dissolved in fear and loathing and despair. Pressed into the shadow, he had waited for me, like a great dog guarding a prison gate. Screaming, I couldn't stop. The whole night was screaming. The wolves, who waited on the hills for me, cheated as I am cheated, reciprocal of my terror, howled.

They were closer than I'd ever heard them, a ring of voices spiking the air, the stars.

"Shut up," he said to me.

I could only scream.

"All right," he said. He was forcing me, upright and wrapped against him, into the kitchen. Lights fired up. He was forcing me to look at something. I couldn't see. Then I opened my eyes.

My mother used to make homemade lemonade in that cut-glass jug. On the lawn at Easterly, lemons and sugar, and I was eleven years old, and I was almost happy and I don't remember—

There was blood in it now, blood flavored with hashish and pomegranates and tomatoes.

"Is that it?" he said to me. "Is that what you want?"

I was breathing and that was enough. He dropped me in a chair and poured a glass of the red juice for me with the detached accuracy of a bartender. It was deduction, he couldn't know. There was more of it than anything else and it had concentrator granules on the container rim. Maybe he understood, too, its scent is a cover for something else. He'd poured it in the jug, then smashed the container so I'd hear.

I drank carefully, almost primly.

My stomach griped, dulled, subsided.

It was over.

The avenger had saved me.

I could feel the imprint of his body against mine, even though he was no longer touching me.

The wolves had fallen quiet. I wondered if I'd imagined their cries rising with mine.

"Now, do I tell you about your brother again?" I said to him, not looking at him.

"Forget it," he said. "You're frecking crazy, Jezebel. Whatever you told me would be a pile of crap."

I felt drowsy, but it was a thin skin over my unease, my dread. Was this another snare? What's he playing for? Tell me the truth. No, any truth you tell will be a lie.

"If," I said, "you're not going to execute me, or hand me over to a madhouse somewhere, or even listen to what I say, or even credit what I say, why don't you get out and go to hell?"

"Maybe I will," he said. It's the mumble, lazy, indifferent.

I sat daintily drinking blood that tasted of fruit, and he sat, but I didn't look at him, didn't know what he did, his presence like red-hot metal a few feet away over my shoulder. I thought I'd become his experiment. In the morning, perhaps, he'd dissect me.

For sure, he wouldn't sleep. Watch and prey.

Like a picture of an invalid, I lay on my bed, propped up high, the glass of nourishment to hand, covered by a paper cloth. He didn't try to prevent me from coming back here, just watched me. I shut the window and pulled the blind and now the sixty-second dawn was beginning and the blind was a shining sapphire.

The juice wasn't enough, not really enough, to restore me after my dose of golden radiation. And besides, it wouldn't last long.

I'd tried to think of a way out of this. I'd tried to imagine some way I could appease him. But I didn't think he really knew anymore what he wanted from me. Maybe in the end he'd come up the stairs and beat me and rape me, and then he'd go away. Or maybe he'd just go.

Or maybe he wouldn't.

The day was overcast, the sky a gray-pink almond fondant. It was the kind of day I could go out on, the kind of day I used to wait for and use, for here, in the revitalized atmosphere of Novo Mars, that kind of overcast, once formed, remained till sundown.

Had the wind changed? I mean, the wind of ill-fortune.

I decided to display normalcy, what normalcy I could. I rose and showered. The shower was temperamental, being accustomed to my touch, because another had used it, and now it hesitated to respond to me, the hot too hot, and the cold too cold. I put on some of my black clothes, I brushed my hair, and fixed my face before the mirror. Then, on impulse, I brought my single traveling bag from under the bed, and packed it as if I were planning another trip, and when I'd stored the bag again, under the bed, I hung my black straw hat ready on the mirror. It was a premonition. Like the premonition I felt on the air-bug, going to Ares for Cassi's funeral, like the premonition I had the night I visited my mother's grave: foretastes of Death the hunter.

I walked downstairs, and I heard a sound thwack on the dry ground. The glass door stood open on the sugar almond day, and Jace was framed in the door and the day, twenty feet away along the slope. He was digging a grave for all the bits of his brother's bones. I glanced at the door, automatic and forewarned, since he wouldn't have gone outside without arranging the door. The lectro-chain was shorted, the self-lock quietly broken from inside, and bent.

A day like this, I didn't even need sunglasses. I could take in horizons, even the road, and a filmy high-speed dot of car. I stood on the porch, and looked at Jace working with the shovel. I felt a little twist of reassurance standing there in the safe morning. His face was all shut up and with its blinds down, unreadable, the way my face becomes when something is tearing at me. I wondered if he were torn. Of course he was. Why else his advent here and the cruel tricks of vengeance, undecided and malevolent as any of Hamlet's.

Around the other side of the house, by the pump which had excavated Sand, and which provided my mother's ghost with something fresh to stare at, Sand's bones had lain all yesterday and all yesterday night. Now they were in a neat indecipherable pile by the hole Jace was digging. It didn't have to be a large hole. It was already large enough.

Then Jace Vincent shocked me. Into the carefully dug, only ethically necessary grave he kicked, systematically and sparsely, the bones of his dead.

I went down the steps and crossed over to him and watched him cover them with dusts and soil.

"A ministering angel shall thy brother be," I said to Jace, "when I lie howling."

He tamped the soil flat, and let the spade go. He looked at me, and I beheld I had not reached him at any time, nor in any way. I had not even scratched the surface of what he was.

That second, the real fear caught up to me, the worse-than-fear. I had been trying to assess him by what I'd learned of men, and suddenly I saw none of these clues applied. He wasn't any kind, but neither was he of any kind I knew, and an overcast, a bag under a bed, a glass of red juice, were not sufficient talismans.

And then we both heard the high-speed car's rolling roar as it skimmed off the road onto the track.

"Who are you expecting?" Jace asked me.

I didn't say anything.

In a dust ball, the vehicle whirled toward us, already slowing on big silent brakes. As the fumes soaked down on the air, the size of the car became obvious. It was a four-seater auto-drive, the color of old copper, which rejected the dust that tried to settle on it as it overshot the track, and came to rest ten feet away. The polarized one-way windows were blanks. Then the side door lifted. Out climbed Cassi's executor, my uncle-in-law, Hog Koberman.

The Hog stared at once at Jace. Clearly, I'd guessed wrong before; they'd never met. The Hog didn't recognize Jace, but the Hog's features, his whole stance, implied disapproval, and uneasiness. This was to have been the Hog's party.

Then his eyes slid away from Jace, who presumably was impenetrably and intractably undiminished. The Hog's eyes lit instead on the spot of new-turned soil, and the fallen spade.

I can shriek: Uncle, save me from this madman who insists I killed his brother, the bones of said brother having just been buried where your eye is riveted. Jace can say: A woman who feeds dead men in her incinerator needs treatment. Neither of us is likely to say such things. I don't want trouble and incrimination, I don't want a planet-state institution any more than I want to die. And Jace, for whatever reason, doesn't want to surrender me to anyone else.

"Another burial, Bella?" the Hog asked me, with obscene accuracy and surprising lack of social taste.

Jace is silent, letting me make the first move, waiting for the cat to jump.

In a second or so, the Hog will also note the demolished lock fitments on the porch door.

"A thief broke in the house," I said, "while I was in town. He didn't take much, my dog scared him off." It's mostly the same story I attempted before. "But he killed the dog."

"Good God, Bel," said uncle, "this should be reported to the police." He risked a man-to-man antagonistic glare at Jace. "And who are you?"

Jace said, "Ask the lady, she'll tell you."

Confused, frustrated, the Hog swung to me.

"A neighbor. He helped me, with the dog."

"Jason," Jace said. "Name's Jason." He smiled at

the Hog suddenly, a snow-white smile of parochial gregariousness that threw the Hog off-balance instantly.

"Well then," the Hog said. He came to me and took my arm, angling us away from Jace. "Shall we go into the house?"

"All right."

We walked. Jace, naturally, came after us, sticking to us with a modest, eager-to-please doggedness. Uncle tried to ignore this dark and golden beast upon our trail.

At the door, uncle examined the two loose tongues of the lock.

"The police, Bella. You contacted them?

"Yes, of course."

"What are they doing?"

"Looking. . . ."

The Hog was satisfied but omnipotent.

"If you have any trouble—"

"Thank you."

"Strange I should drop by right now." he said. (Stranger than you think.) "I had some business out Brade way, and took a notion to drive over into this Styx of yours. I have the bimonthly figures of your investment program. There's also another matter—"

But really, it's just curiosity, uncle. You just wanted to see where I am, what I'm doing, the strange weeping girl in sunglasses, the social outcast of the tribe. Maybe you fancy me, too, your arm constantly around my shoulders, your hand on my arm, your breathing in my face. Whatever it is, you're here.

In the hall we paused.

"That's a fine window above the stairs, Bel."

Last night, this hall was an arena of the most basic savagery, of my screaming desperation. of Jace's blackness rising from the dark. My mother died out here. Now this stupid man stands and admires the damn window.

We went into the parlor. Uncle sat.

"I wonder if you have any iced tea?" wondered uncle.

Glibly, against my earlier statement, I said, "The thief took everything from my cupboards and my freezer."

"All she can offer you is water," added Jace obligingly from the doorway. He leaned there, shutting us in.

Unless you care for a drop of blood?

I laughed noiselessly and snapped the laugh off my face. Jason Vincent watched me. Uncle didn't see. Uncle was alone with two of the most dangerous creatures he was ever likely to mix with. Stop it, Sabella. Whatever you do, you mustn't feel part of a conspiracy with Jace; condemned and executioner aren't coupled in a primitive rite.

"Oh," said Hog Koberman, "Mr. Jason—pardon me, but there are some private matters I should like to discuss with Bella here."

Jace smiled accommodatingly. He would do uncle a favor and not mind. But he wouldn't move.

"Bel—" uncle said to me. I didn't offer a solution. The Hog made a wrong judgment he should wrongly have made some while before. His face engaged with his distaste, his disappointment. "Very well. If that's the way you want it, Bella."

"*Sa*bella," I said. I don't really know why.

Uncle's head jerked. "Excuse me?"

"*Sa*bella," I said. "That's my name." I looked at Jace. "*Sabella.*"

Uncle became very formal. Very proper.

"If you prefer. Sabella. Before we come to the investment figures, Sabella—"

"How about," Jace said, "Miss Quey."

Uncle jumped. He looked at Jace, and at me.

"Sabella—"

"Miss Quey," said Jace, "Spelled Q-U-E-Y. Pronounced Kay. Try it."

Hog Koberman was speechless. He looked at me, waiting for rescue, and then he stood up.

"I'd hoped to deal with this personally, Sabella." Nervously, involuntarily, he hesitated for Jace's interpolation, but none came. "Now I see a letter would be more in the order of things."

Jace stood aside from the door graciously, making way for Hog Koberman to pass through. Jace wanted to drive the visitor off, and he'd succeeded, the visitor was leaving.

Suddenly, a chasm split in front of us. The decision was so swift there was no space for doubt or conjecture.

I strolled quietly past Jace, and after the Hog, and I caught the Hog at the porch.

"I'll walk you to your car," I said.

"There's no need."

"I'd like to."

"Very well, Sabella."

We went out again. I took uncle's pudgy arm. Jace followed, slow, a guard hound pacing us, fifteen feet behind.

"Now," I said, "tell me what you wanted to say."

"What I *wanted* to say hardly comes into it, Bel—Sabella. I have a mystery on my hands, and I was in hopes you might throw some light on it."

I was barely listening.

"Yes, whatever you think."

"It's this business of old John Trim's death."

We were marching toward the big car, Uncle dragging me by my hand on his arm which he wouldn't acknowledge and I wouldn't release. When he said, "Old John Trim," it was like a record tape, snagged and repeating. I'd heard it before, yet it was meaningless.

"You understand, Bella—Sabella, I have responsibilities to the Koberman estate. After John's death I was sent certain documents of his. I learned from these that Cassilda had made Trim a private antemortem payment, which had at no time been declared for tax. A foolish illegality for Cassilda to have committed. On top of it, John was being harassed for money by some person who seems to have made a lucky guess about the payment. A term of detention at Trim's age would have finished him. In fact, the threat was enough. His stroke was doubtless due to worry at the harassment he was receiving. Among his effects was an unmailed letter, intended for the vulture who was threatening him, containing an enclosure of credit bonds. There was also evidence of the previous relationship of the two concerned. The reason I trouble you with the affair, Bella, is that apparently Trim had hired the man in the first instance at your aunt's instigation, in the capacity of a private investigator, the subject of the investigation being yourself."

We're all mad. The Hog's mad too.

Sand, a blackmailer, my gentle-voiced, sweet and sunlit lover?

Uncle was waiting for my reply, so I replied, but not verbally. I punched him in the stomach, a blow of such force he never could have reckoned my little white-knuckled fist would inflict it. And as he bent, choking, I threw myself past him into the car. Anyone can operate auto-drive.

The door sizzled down, and through the one-way window I had a final glimpse of uncle kneeling on the ground, his head in the dust. Behind him, Jace, running, but a fat hog in the way.

Then the car spun itself about, as Sand's car did just over two months ago. It raced for the road below. These big custom-built chariots, they do a maximum of two hundred, faster than most traffic there is. Jace's car, small enough to be parked out of sight, wouldn't have a speed like this.

The packed bag was only a symbol, and the hat for traveling.

I've left it all behind. And I've left another enemy, another witness for my prosecution.

"Say good-bye," Jace said, when he smashed the glass container. Now I've said good-bye to everything.

When I got near the Brade Highway, Route 09, I took the bills I found in Hog Koberman's wallet compartment. The credit cards I didn't dare to touch, not from honesty, but because card-users could be traced in minutes by the central computer of the banking system. That the Hog carried bills at all surprised me, as Jace's possession of bills had. I suppose they were a rich man's small-change, and for Jace, a good-faith token to the blonde whore he had brought that night to the house. I didn't feel compunction at robbery. In a world of enemies, compunction is a flaw no survivor could indulge. I'd stolen lives, after all. Cash was nothing.

After I'd pocketed the bills, I stopped the car. There was nothing on the road, either way. I got out, jammed on the accelerator, manually slammed down the door, and watched the vehicle plow on up the highway. A top-speeder has a built-in avoidance pattern to miss other traffic, halt at obstacles or roadblocks, or pedestrians. Meeting none of those, it will run until its solar cells dry out. With luck, the police uncle would undoubtedly alert wouldn't realize that the blank windows hid an empty space.

I walked into Brade Corner in ten minutes. The Corner is one of fifty outposts of Brade itself. People come and go constantly, and no one remembers faces. In a dim little underground parlor I let someone quickset my hair with a haphazard bleaching that would fade in streaks—I could refine it later. Somewhere else again, I bought a red dress and a large red bag, and somewhere suntan makeup for girls who come in from the cold planets. Then I took a cab to Brade lift-off point.

It was thirteen o'clock, unlucky thirteen, when I boarded the air-bug to Ares.

Who'd reckon I'd head for Ares, Koberman country? But Ares is like all big cities, like the Plateau, a wide tract of land where names don't matter, but the hunting is good by night.

I suppose I could have run to the hills, but years of human comforts had softened me. I couldn't live in a cave, not now. Besides I'd dreamed of those hills, and Jace Vincent had found me in that dream. Maybe I was just insane as well as full of hate and fear and an-

ger, and tired of making allowances, cheating myself.
Saying no, Sabella, no.

I sat in my bright bloody dress, and I looked around
the plane, and the dull sky shone in the windows. I
didn't care any more, you see. I'd tried, and my reward
was punishment. I wouldn't try anymore.

The name on my ticket was Sarah Holland. Sarah
was my mother's name, and Holland was the promo-
tion name on a long billboard advertising bottled water
as the Hog's car burned through Canyon.

Sarah Holland doesn't care about cold fanatical
Cassi, or shifty shifting Sand that Sabella had taken,
scorched in her own horror and guilt, while he had
been trying all along to take her too, and Trim, and
how many others, perhaps, back in his insecure, falter-
ing father-brother-haunted-past.

Even Jace has no part in Sarah's world.

When Sarah was fourteen, she went with a boy in a
car. And when she was sixteen, seventeen, eighteen,
she went with all the boys. Her mother never said to
her, "Sarah, what are doing to yourself?" Sarah's
mother hadn't cared.

Sarah has no pursuers, and no guilt. Sarah won't let
herself tremble with reaction.

Sarah can live with all she is.

Sarah will have to.

Part THREE

De Profundis

1

⸻

The nights I don't go out I sit and watch the skies above the city. I mentioned the clouds, and the lights of the city on the clouds, long ago. I explained about the hills of concrete and glass, and the valleys of neon and the trees of blue steel. The subways rumble wild as rivers. Great mountains of apartment blocks stand black on rays of white and indigo and violet. Sometimes jeweled birds fly over, planes coming into the landing strips of the port, or the golden tail of a phoenix, a space ship taking a fix on our glow, heading in to some point a thousand miles away.

In the end, maybe, I'll go off-planet. Maybe I should go to Earth. But the hills are green and the skies are blue, how strange, how oppressive. I think I could only go to Earth to die.

I move about a lot, anyway, a month here, a month there. Five days in Cliffton, ten in Iles, three in Dale.

My hair's pure blonde tinsel, but I have a wig which is black, woven of darkness. I wear white frocks and red, and stockings with silver seams. Guess what I do, nights?

I haven't killed yet. The whole Christawful city is riddled with men who are searching for me, the whore who gave them the lay of their life, but they can't recall why. I charge them cash, too, since I have to pay the rent somehow. Sometimes I even meet one of my customers again. I never say no. But then I move on again, and they're safe, till next time.

Did I say I never say "no"? Once I did. In a bar behind the spin-drive stadium. He was a racer and he came up to me. Jet black hair and golden skin. He reminded me of Jace.

"Come on, honey," he said. "Why not?"

Those fine black ink-and-brush-painted hairs were on his hands, lean and articulate with handling the blazing wheel of the spin-track. Had Jace done that, too? What had Jace done in any event, that I know of? Except hunt for me. Was he still hunting? Was the pig-man helping him now?"

"I don't do it with spin-racers."

"Yes you do."

"When I do it with a spin-racer, he crashes."

They have superstition on the track. As he got up and left me, I caught the glimmer of a gold cross on his gold skin.

I left Cassi's cross in the house, and the casket, and everything else.

I missed the house. The colored window, the deck of music, the wolves' music in the loudly silent nights.

An overcast day—the cities are richer in these, pale-blue oxygen overcast on lavender—I went out. I saw a tinstone C.R. mission, the House of the Shepherd. New and shiny, with a great white banner. The banner said: WHAT ARE YOU LIVING FOR? LIVE FOR JESUS.

It's been three months since I ran. Five months since Sand was burned to bones.

Sometimes it seems odd that they haven't traced me after all. Other times, I know they never will.

So what am I living for? For what happens when I take? I'll tell you something, when I take, now, nothing happens to me. It's a hunger and I feed it. Like sex to some of them, an itch to scratch. Not like breathing anymore. Each time I hunt on the slopes of concrete, through the ravines of metal brick, my excitement says to me, this time it will be special, like it was. Why isn't it? And if it isn't, why do I go on? Perhaps it is a drug, a habit, and I could break it. Perhaps I'm deranged, need help. Put me in a doll's house, lock me away. I'm preying on your city, sinking teeth in it, sucking its veins.

The pendant blazes. It's a ruby and never less than a ruby, and some nights it's a dragon's eye.

Before I became Sarah my life was just a series of roles. My mother's daughter, a hundred men's dream-lay, Sand's oyster, Jace's Hamlet-vengeance, Cassi's scapegoat. When was I ever my own?

Now I'm Sarah, I drink the air (which has become the mud). Now I'm truly me. But no, Sabella. Now I belong entirely to the blood-red stone around my neck.

Maybe, indirectly, Cassi's plan to destroy me is working after all.

Meantime, I watched the skies above the city.

There are about ten churches in Ares. Ten churches to around ten thousand bars, around ten thousand girl-houses, twenty-seven landing strips, fifteen spin-drive stadiums, twenty-five cinemats, ninety public swim pools, nine hundred hyper-markets, eight hundred automats, six hundred lavatories.

But once there were no churches at all. Till the Re-vivalists built them. Silver tinstone and white plasti-plaster, blue concrete, stained glass. Spires like metal pylons with crosses that light up by night.

I hadn't been in church for around eleven years, apart from Cassi's chapel, and the chapel at Angel Meadow when momma died. Sarah Holland had never been in church at all, nor did I suppose she'd have any hankering to be.

Of the ten or so, about half stay open at night, and the utensils on the altar have faintly glowing lectro devices around them.

I'd been hunting and I'd taken, and I was going home to where home was just then, which was an apartment block on Eighteenth Dale. The cross of the church, like an emerald badge pinned on the night, ap-peared between the tall stacks and crags of the build-ings, and then the pale wall, and then the wide-open doorway. I hadn't seen this place previously, though others like it many times. The warm-tinted soft light inside, the musty incense smell. Above the door was a treated painted panel. This Christ looked like Sand Vincent, the longish dark hair, dark eyes, amber flesh.

Before I knew it, Sarah Holland walked up the steps in at the door.

I sat on one of the polished benches, and looked at the altar. The cloth was dark red, embroidered with green and gold, the Cloth of the Blood of the Redeemer. A mutedly lit sign gave the times of the services, which were all done for tonight. No one was there but me; so I sat, my spine pressed against the hard supporting plank of the bench. I wondered why I was there, but the church was quiet. The peace was heavy on the air as any scent.

Then a priest came out of the back and began to walk along the aisle.

I meant to get up and go out at once, but my feet were heavy, had grown into the floor, I was weighted down on the bench. I stared straight ahead, but, of course, the priest would come to me. Presently he spoke.

"Can I help you in any way?"

His voice was young, younger than he'd looked coming toward me.

"No, thank you very much."

"Are you sure?"

I should never have come in here.

"Yes, I'm sure. I just wanted to sit for a while."

I know he's taking in my garb and my hair.

"Christ can help you," the priest said, "even if you won't let me."

I turned and stared hard at him, and I said, "If He knows the things I've called Him, He won't help."

The priest startled me by smiling. "Oh, I think He'd understand about that."

He was trying to draw me out, gently and kindly. And I felt the danger of a response. For three months I'd only really spoken to those I meant to have. And what was this? Childhood's theology hanging on my shoulder.

"Look," I said, "I won't discuss Jesus Christ with you."

"No," he said, "you don't have to discuss Him with anyone."

"You don't mind if I sit here."

"I'm glad for you to, if it helps."

Does it?

I wish I could tell him the truth and he'd pray with me and Christ would come down like a dove on the altar and make it all right.

The priest moved on and left me alone, but my own emotional prodigality had driven off the mood of peace from me, leaving me in the midst of the peace, in a little vacuum of dread and confusion.

You thought I was happy, did you, the wolf-bitch stalking the city?

I walked home to my unhome on Eighteenth Dale. I had a dream that night. I dreamed I was wandering through the house at Hammerhead. But the house was very old, ruinous and piled with pink rusting dusts of the desert. The blinds were torn and the doors broken and even the indestructible glass of the windows was cracked. In my bedroom, the bed was just a frame, and dust webs hung from the carved posts instead of gauze curtains. Then I came to the mirror and I saw myself. I wore the black night-hair wig I wore in the church, but it was thick with blood, and ends spiked stiff with it. There was blood over my mouth and down my dress (the way there'd been blood on my dress the first time, when I was fourteen, my own blood and the boy's). My nails were long and pointed and sheathed in blood. My eyeballs were scarlet. My lips were parted and I saw my teeth were very long, like white needles; and my tongue was a thin black whip. The terror that filled me was unspeakable, unutterable. And when I plunged awake, the terror was still with me, clamped inside me, a tumor on my invisible, shadow-casting, mirror-image-making, nonexistent soul.

The next sunset, I went back to the church. I went back without the black wig, in another dress, hoping the priest wouldn't recognize me. It was between services, and the church had emptied, all but for one woman kneeling, and the priest at the altar, who didn't seem to see me at all. Then there was another woman kneeling, and it was me.

You look like Sand, and I don't believe in you, or if I do, I resist the belief. I've cursed you and profaned you, and I'll do it again. I've never served you and I never will. Every minute that I'm not afraid I'll forget you. I can't make a bargain. But help me, help me. Help me, if you can, or you're there, or if anyone's there, or no one. Help me. Help me.

Then I went home to Eighteenth Dale. I brought a bottle of pills from the pharmacy across the way. But I only took five, and then I got sick, and it wasn't any use.

Next morning, the Ares sky was overcast, and my rent was up at Eighteenth Dale. I packed my red bag that I bought at Brade Corner with the things I bought at Cliffton when I arrived in the big city. It was time to move on.

I moved into a room at Iles, and I went with a blond spacer. His blood had been purified by the stars of space, but it was still mud, and I still had to have it. I also had to get out in the dark. He couldn't leave me alone, nor I resist his entreaties, and I was coming perilously close to killing him. At one in the morning I panicked, and when he was unconscious I smeared the jel on his neck and I ran.

I ran straight for the church in Dale.

The altar cloth was white and blue and I couldn't remember why. I huddled into the pew-bench and laid my head on the rail of the bench in front. I didn't know what I was doing there. If the priest had come out I would have bolted, but there was only a man near the door in the shadow, head on hands, praying.

And then I turned and looked, and he wasn't praying, and it was Jace.

I got up slowly, and slowly returned to the door, and he didn't react. Then I got outside, and he was there, and he caught my arm.

The touch of his hand on my arm, my skin, stopped me.

"How?" was the only word I could get out.

His voice was so familiar, I must have been hearing it in my sleep.

"You have religion," he said. "It was just a matter of when and where."

"Let me go," I said.

He said, ignoring that, "I've been to every goddamned church in Ares. I left a call code. I told them I was looking for my sister."

"Sister?"

The priest, the kind priest, wanting to be kind. Any woman can bleach her hair, wear a white dress. When I was praying to Jesus for help, the priest was looking at me, recognizing me despite blonde hair, black hair, from Jace's description. When I was vomiting up the pills, the priest was calling Jace.

I'm immobile in his grasp, except I'm shivering in the hot city night.

"Still want to kill me for Sand? Sand, the blackmailer, the cheat."

"I know what Sand was," Jace said.

"He looked like Christ over the door."

"Sure he did. That was his big number. Extortion, blackmail, those weren't new games for Sand. He raped a girl on Gall Vulcan. You find that hard to believe? So did she, till he did it to her. And I was the insurance, the demon brother who had to clean up whenever the stuff hit the fan, which it always did."

"So why come after me?"

"To see how far he'd implicated me this time, and in what. Whatever you and he had been into. He did write me. That was part of the fun, to show me what a great deal he was making for himself. Only the deals

stank, and they never came off. Then I'd get the stella
from the belly of the whale: Get me out, Jace. No
stella at all was special. After what he'd said about
you, it sounded as if the pot had boiled over. I'd say he
meant to take you for everything you had, but then
you did your magic act on him, and he shot for Trim
instead. Someone was bound to get Sand one day. It
just happened to be you."

I recalled Sand's confession, and his trying to run
away from me across the desert, when he was dying,
afraid I must be paying him out for discovered tricks. I
recalled Jace's profile, yellowing, when Sand's bones
landed in the dust.

"This is another trap," I said.

"Whatever it is, you're stuck with it."

"Does Koberman know?"

"The fat man? No. This is a private war, Sabella."

"Cozy-cozy," I said. My teeth chattered, as Sand's
teeth chattered when I tried to drive him to the hospital. "But Koberman will still be looking for me."

"I doubt it."

His tone was unequivocal. He'd obviously warned
the Hog away, perhaps merely by threats of violence.
Jace *is* violence, or at least, violent power. I should
know. I was held in the vise of it.

"Stop shaking," he said, "I'm not going to hurt
you."

"Because you hated your kiddy brother after all."

I'd tried to kill myself. If Jace killed me, it would
settle everything. Apparently, I was not a survivor anymore. Even Sarah wasn't.

"I didn't hate him. You don't hate the garbage."

"The great Daniel would be proud of you."

"Daniel," he said, so soft I nearly missed it.

"Your father. You forgot? Your golden marvel god
of a father that Sand worshiped, second only to you.
Your family has a truly biblical ambience, the Patri-
arch and his two sons. One with the mark of Cain on
his forehead."

"You're the lady with the incinerator," he said, "and the sick dog."

"And you still don't know how he died, or why." I paused. I watched the neons making flaming smoke of the clouds. "I'll show you."

"O.K.," he said.

He turned me unexpectedly toward him, and our eyes met, and I thought of the dream of the deer and the hills and the man with the gun, and I leered at him, and in my imagination my teeth were long as daggers."

"You've made a mess of yourself," he said to me. "Your hair, the way you've dyed your skin. You look as though you've slept hanging on a peg."

"Now I really want you to see," I said to him. "I want you to see what I did to Sand."

I knew I was insane, but I couldn't pull myself up. I'd raced to the brink, and leapt, and I was dropping through the air and I couldn't save myself if I tried. I was even exhilarated, horribly excited. I did want him to see. I did want him to know. An ultimate witness, to condemn me. As my mother was the first.

"Come on," I said. "We walk."

He shifted his grip to my elbow, and we did walk, down the steps of the church, under the reflected glory of the emerald cross.

There was a bar three blocks away; I'd been there before. Someone would be loitering, looking for a girl. There always was someone.

We walked without speaking, but at the street, where you could see the bar's bright sheen and three men leaning on the wall outside, smoking, I said to Jace, "Now for the demonstration. Let go my arm and watch."

His grip came off me immediately and for a moment I felt disoriented, adrift. How could he trust me? Could he read me so well he knew on this occasion I was on the level? Then I was walking on. I went toward the three men, and they looked, and I smiled.

"Hey, girlie," they said.

They reached for me. The one I wanted was in the

middle, the youngest, the most tender shoot. "Last dance tonight," I said. And I put out my hand, and the young one took my hand.

The other two laughed and congratulated us, and the boy and I came back up the street, past Jace, and Jace fell in behind us.

"Who's he? said the boy.

"My protector," I said. "Don't worry."

"Who's worried," said the boy, "but most of you girls are free lance. In case you have any ideas——" he revealed a switchblade, the old kind with the razor welded to the outer edge. This boy was younger than Sand. But then, Sand wasn't innocent either. I've taken so many and thought of them as victims, but maybe I'm the victim.

"You don't get it," I said to the boy with the razor switch. "If you let him watch, you needn't pay."

"Oh really?" The boy grinned. He grinned back at Jace. "Be my guest, mister." He's stupid. He's perfect.

A loading alley for robot carts ran between high steel walls. I led the boy, and we stepped over the rails, and Jace came behind.

"Here?" I asked.

"Freck it," said the boy. "I thought you had a bed."

"Come on," I said. "Who needs beds?"

He acquiesced and slid his hands up under my skirt and I released the sealer on his pants.

I didn't have any need, not really, and I was in complete control. Jace was standing a few yards off, black on black shadow, as in the dream.

I didn't feel pity anymore. Or a desire to give pleasure in return. I hated this boy working away in me, squeezing me, grinding me back against the metal wall. I called softly to Jace, "Now watch me, honey." The boy grunted his breathless contempt. I kissed his neck. He tasted of smoke and alcohol and darkness and sex. In the dimness, I wondered if Jace would see. Somehow, I knew he would. I was touching the vein, and the boy groaned. I was in control, but I bit hard and deep, almost carelessly. The boy yelped and then he reared against me, trying to thrust himself through me into the wall.

I took very little, then I let him go, and he fell away from me and on his face beside the rails.

I pulled my clothes straight automatically, practiced.

"Come and see, Jason," I said.

He came toward me, and I was going to tell him what to look for when he leaned over the boy, grasped his loose head by the hair, and examined the throat. There was more blood than usual, and the wound was glaring black in the dimness.

"That's what I did to Sand," I said. "And he loved it. He begged for it. I tried to save his life when it was too late. But there are plenty I didn't. I'm a lady with a past all littered with dead young gentleman callers."

Then I went by Jace and rubbed the heal-fast coagulant jel into the wound. When I'd finished, I straightened and Jace took my elbow and we walked away.

I looked up at his face. Unreadable.

"You do understand," I said. I looked unreadable too.

He didn't answer.

"I drink blood. I need to. The juice in the container was blood. Does it surprise you a vampire has religion?" I couldn't stop talking, and he apparently couldn't start. "It shouldn't surprise you. Jesus Christ, after all, was a vampire. Oh, yes, Jason, Jesus was a vampire. They drank blood at the last supper, and then the priests impaled him on a stake of wood. To be sure, they drove a wooden stake in his side. God made the sky go black by day out of pity for Jesus's agony in the sunlight. When he was dead, they buried him, but he resurrected, the way a vampire is supposed to. You can't keep a good man down."

See, Jesus? You wouldn't help me, so now I'm blaspheming you for all I'm worth. When I'm in hell, you can come and stoke the fires.

We'd crossed suddenly out onto one of the broad lit-up bridges of the Dale-Iles thoroughfare. A hundred feet below, an empty walkway, and traffic gushing on thirty-two lanes, like streaks of fire, a river of multi-colored lavas. And all around, the distant volcanoes and the mountains rose in impersonal waterfalls of neon.

"All you have to do," I said to Jace, "is lift me up over the rail and let me fall on the walkway. They threw Jezebel out of a window."

Jace had let go of me again. He rested his forearms on the rail of the bridge. The streaks of car-fire burned across his eyes. He was alone. I wasn't with him anymore.

"All right," I said. "I suppose you'll tell someone, sometime. Here's my address: four on twenty-sixth, Iles. The name on the tag is Sarah Holland. I'll wait for you, or who you send. Remember, every night you delay, I'll be out here, busy."

My head was up to look at him, and the wind, full of sparks and spirits of electricity and oxygen, blew back my cold-color hair. Then he turned his head and his eyes glared down at me, hard black surfaces, showing me what he saw. I'm dirt. I'm cheap and demented and filthy. He saw that. You don't hate the garbage.

I turned my back and walked on.

When they put me into the hospital they may cure me. Or if they don't I'll die.

But if my courage fails me, I'll just move out of four on twenty-sixth, Iles, and the circus will continue. I can keep away from churches now.

He found me. What was the point if it goes nowhere?

I hadn't wanted him to kill me. I'd wanted him to say to me it would be all right. Not a dove on an altar, but Jace. Not prayer, but Jace. Not Jesus.

Jace.

A mail chute slanted up into my room at four on twenty-sixth. A couple of random circulars came along the chute in the morning when I was drearily, restlessly sleeping. The package came later, and woke me from a nightmare like a grave. Awake, the grave persisted, since I knew what the package was. It was my haunting, Cassi's casket.

I opened the package, and I lifted out the casket. It was rather funny, had an element of burlesque, the way three times I'd been given this thing. There was the sinister quality, too. This version of the casting of runes. I knew who'd sent it now, delivered it by hand through the chute marked four, twenty-six *Holland*, ten stories down. But there was a miniature self-play tape in with the casket.

For half an hour, I couldn't make myself press the button to activate the tape. Maybe I never would have, but part of me, a very shamed foolish part, wanted to hear his voice, whatever it said to me. And this small part finally pressed in the button.

"Your friend, the Hammerhead mailman, hung onto the parcel with Cassi Koberman's box in it. Your recent life seems full of those of us trying to test which side of the law you walk. The mailman thought he could play games and you wouldn't report him. Then he sobered up some, and got scared you might. I know, because I had a couple of drinks with the bastard, the day before I took the box off him. I've talked with a few people about you Sabella. Don't backtrack on that. None of them can get near you, or has the guts to try. As for Cassi's box, I guess you couldn't have opened it the second time. When the fat man left, I went through your house on the Plateau, and I found the box, and opened it. Trim John sent it to you, just before he died. He put his own letter in the box. You haven't read the letter. Read it."

The voice ended there, and I paced about waiting for more, but the blank tail of the tape coiled on, with nothing, and then stopped.

I thought of Jace's eyes, on the bridge. The voice was unchanged, the lazy slurred drawl, even an edge of bevelled humor on the *"Trim* John." I thought of other things after that, but finally I set the key in the casket and lifted the lid, and took out the sheet of fine quality paper—finer than the paper Cassi's curse had been written on.

I expected to be cursed again. I spent a while looking at the thin, spidery, stilted writing, so I wouldn't have to read the words. "Miss Sabella Quey," it began. "Miss Sabella Quey, When Mrs. Koberman went to Easterly and came home with the warmth of God Almighty in her heart, I was glad for her. But then she had this notion that God's angels had warned her against you. And all her last days, she was planning how she would get to you through the law, because she said that they don't burn witches, and the law was the only recourse she had. To begin with, she provided you a sum in her will. She believed the chance of the money would ensure your presence at her funeral, while, if you had vacated the house at Hammerhead, a newscast announcement was to be made of your mention in the will, similarly intended to draw you from seclusion. Next, she selected a young man, a private investigator in Dawson, and instructed me to hire him. She had seen from the advertisement that the young man's name was Sand Vincent, and insisted that, because of his name, she understood God had selected him to carry on His work against you. Well then, Miss Quey, Mrs. Koberman died, and I did what she'd told me because you get accustomed to obeying a woman you've obeyed for ten-odd years. But Mr. Vincent isn't God's agent, Mr. Vincent is an evil man. The day after we put Mrs. Koberman to rest Mr. Vincent came back to the house for his rented car, which he had parked beside the cemetery. He told me he was driving out west to Hammerhead Plateau, to see you, Miss Quey. He said he had things arranged between you and everything was going as he wished. But then he threatened me over a certain payment that Mrs. Koberman had made to me. This evil boy is from the devil, and has not done with me, or with any of us. You see, Miss Quey, not being well, I can write these things, but I should be quick. I think that your aunt was led falsely in her supposings. I think that, rather than to chastise you, she was meant to bring you to salvation. It's a wonderful thing to approach God, and His Only True Son, Jesus Christ, whose love emcompasses all worlds and states and times. If you could know the comfort it brings me, even in my agitation, I believe you, too, would turn to Him. And for this reason, I advise you to go to Easterly, Miss Quey. It was there that Cassilda Koberman found her faith and there she learned what she upheld to be this bad thing which you had done, though she never confided in me as to what this thing might be. In Easterly there's a church, and here is where she said she was directed to discover this terrible thing. Or maybe we have all been mistaken. But I felt obliged to reveal all these matters to you, in hopes you also will seek redemption. And I ask you to forgive me if I have wronged you. I remain, most faithfully yours, John Michael Trim."

The extraordinary form of this letter. It's religious fever coupled to its curious formality; its blindness, its doubts, its pedantry, its childishness, linked to the stoicism with which John Trim recognized oncoming sudden death.

I visualized again his frail hands on the stair rail, his impartial, self-effacing solemnity. (Can I recall his face?)

But none of that took me nearer to any point of reference. So I reread the letter. John Trim advised me to go back to Easterly for the salvation of my soul. An old man's naïve fanatical deed of expiation. But why had Jace augmented it?

I pulled the blind of polarized glass over the window, for the day was burning bright. Easterly. Already I could smell the aniseed grass, see the cotton wool over the refinery chimneys. Already I could feel momma as she slapped my fourteen-year-old face in my locked bedroom, and hear the sound of men marshaling for a wildcat hunt, and the noise the wind makes, blowing over the river, the meadows, and the dry canals. And by the hole in the rock where I found my pendant.

Easterly's where it started. Maybe it had to end there.

I read Trim's letter yet again. 'Why did the name Sand Vincent make Cassi judge him suitable to her scheme?) Then I played the tape again, but all I heard was Jace's voice, not what he said.

He stood in the dark, and watched me with the boy from the bar. Jace watched me, and then he examined the boy, and then he walked with me, and he never spoke. "I drink blood," I said to him. Only the second time I ever vocalized it. The first time, momma hit me and yelled at me. He didn't answer. He didn't hit me, or yell, or laugh, or try to reason with or kill me. As if—

As if he'd been expecting it all. As if he knew.

I know what you are, Sabella. I didn't know until I came to God, but when I found God, He told me. I hope the cross cripples you, as it should. You're just one of the wolves.

His angels told me. I know what you've done.

Cassi had found God at Easterly, and her heart should have exploded with love, but instead she went crusading, and I was the Infidel and she knew it—

And Jace knew it.

How?

It was more than Cassi digesting my mother's old letters, those hints and evasions. It was more than Jace talking to a few people who mistrust me, and guessing. The kind of thing he'd never guess would be a thing like a girl who lives by drinking blood. I doubt if he actually believes it, even now. But he knew it.

It was at Easterly, whatever the truth was.

And then I realized that Jace has had the time, between when he opened the casket and when he waited for me on the off-chance in the church at Dale. He'd had three months since I ran from Hammerhead Plateau. Whatever was at Easterly, he'd been there, and *that was* how he knew.

But the dead are always in league against me. Momma, Cassi, Sand, John Michael Trim. And those others, Frank and Angelo and Benny and Lek and. . . .

Maybe all the dead were sending me to Easterly to die and Jace was the human spokesman for all those ghosts, so real and human and alive that I'd never figure it out until too late.

I sat in the room in Iles, and waited, but no one came to take me into any kind of custody.

So I packed my bag and I went out on the briefly sunset street, and dipped in the minute of fire, an auto-cab came to the walkway. And before the fire had died, I was riding east.

Besides, there was nowhere else to go but Hell.

2

At a car fixit place two miles outside Easterly, having had a moment's forethought, I went into the washroom and slipped on a black dress, took off my silver stockings, combed and pinned my bleached hair into a big knot on my head, and wiped most of the cosmetics off my face. When I was a child there, Easterly had a Puritanical flavor, and being sixty-two miles from Sodom (Ares) had only made it worse. I assume Cassi had gone to visit Easterly again out of nostalgia, and perhaps out of fear. It seems to me she understood death was creeping up on her, and she needed every anchor she could find. So she aimed for her roots, the town she was born in, and with true Koberman luck she caught God and holy war into the bargain. But what do I feel, with only the synthetic tan dye left on my skin, and my sober black dress, do I register anything beyond scents and alarms and old dusts?

It's true, I felt a kind of hankering for Easterly, the way you can look back at childhood, even when it's bitter, longing for all those firsts of life, and those endless wide horizons of unknowledge.

And remembered Easterly, of course, was bigger than I'll ever see it now, and younger, and more important. The brindle oaks, the honeysuckle trees, the children in the streets, the unmechanized bakery that baked real bread; the beer shops and dancing palaces and wicked 3-V cinemats outlawed out of town.

The first thing I saw as the auto-cab decelerated to eighty an hour and cruised in was the great chain of supermarkets built along the highway. And then I saw the surrealistic candy-parlor ballooning over the town, a large striped tent of magenta and white sugar fluorescents.

Everywhere new apartment blocks had been built up like toy bricks, and then spilled over and left lying in the meadows. Automated plants and factories overhung the dam. Where were the refineries? Their chimneys were hidden, like the mines, and only long plumes of smoke, pure bronze on the neonized darkness, flowed up into the night.

There were bars in Easterly, blazing on main street. The novel copper bricks of the ore boom town looked oxidized and pale. The houses crouched between the piles and pylons, a colony invaded by monsters. The old town was being squeezed out like paste from a tube.

Some of the streets were entirely gone to make way for improvements. My street was one of them.

I stopped the cab at the edge, where the half-remembered, half-familiar avenue ended, and where my street, momma's and mine, had begun, and now had ceased to be. It's very odd, the way it just isn't there. As if a chunk of my past had been rubbed out, as if it's only hearsay. Did we really live here? Did any of the events I associate with this spot actually occur? It suddenly seems memory itself could be a fake, come to that. What happened an hour ago, only the fabrication of a mind anxious to possess its background.

Even the trees had vanished.

The times I'd smelled aniseed grass, and thought of this place. And now the one place in my world that I wouldn't smell that grass was here.

I paid off the cab, and it sailed away into the lights and shadows. Then I moved slowly along the concrete sidewalk, through the arches and over the tiled plaza with its fountain of liquid glass. The house would have stood about here. Maybe I would find it. Maybe somewhere it was still here, meshed in the new brickworks and tiles, like those crazy drawings where you win a

prize if you can discover the shape of a flower in a
girl's eye, or a girl's eye in a flower.

But I didn't win the prize.

Only one thing was sure. The C.R. church had remained. Cassi came to it, and Jace had come to it.
John's letter told me that this was where the secret of
my sin was blazoned forth for all to see who could read
it.

Abruptly my legs were water. I wondered what I
was doing here at the whims of my enemies.

Over there, where the apartment blocks stride away
beyond the river, a tunnel ran into a quarry. Was that
the way I ought to go?

I walked through town, and over the river by a new
steel bridge. Then I walked on a new white fluorescent
road by the rims of which wild flowers still clustered.
My heart roused in my side as I got closer and closer,
closer and closer to that afternoon.

About a quarter of a mile from the border of the
two dry canals, a wall climbed up into the air. Through
an eyelet in the wall, I beheld scaffolding and other
walls and a pallid dome which ambiguously might be
intended as the future roof of a processing plant or of a
theatre. These buildings extended for two or three
miles into the night, beyond the point where the quarry
had gaped and the hole had gaped in the quarry.

Like vast dunes, they had swarmed over, and smothered it.

I went back to town, and then couldn't remember
where the C.R. church was anyway. Subconsciously, no
doubt, I had reasons. Consciously, I was simply confused and exhausted. There was a shabby hotel on the
corner of one of the older streets. The desk was mech-
anized, and the lift played tinny music. I went into a
room that was like the lift except it had furniture
squashed into it. I lay down on the bed and I listened
to the noise that Easterly made now, a noise like Ares,
but thinner and less sure.

I took ten showers in the closet of that room that
night. The room was hot and the windows wouldn't

open and the air-conditioning was faulty. I came to imagine there was nobody in the hotel but me, not one human. And I felt alone as I'd never felt alone, alone without even myself for company.

When the sun came and set Easterly on fire, I lay on the bed in the hotel, because it was too bright to go out, too bright and hot to go searching for any answers. But possibly the church would be shut after sundown. I considered waiting for an overcast, but to wait alone in this room and to walk the streets and the dry meadows by night filled me with an obscure fear. I didn't want to take, not in Easterly, where it started. The spacer had been generous, loading me with gifts, and then the boy from the bar had added the last dance of the night. I could hold out two or three nights on that, if I avoided the sun, but one day and night of the allowance were gone, and here was another day.

When the big sun began to wester, I put on my shade hat and my sunglasses, and walked down through the seemingly deserted hotel and out into the town. Long shadows I didn't recall were plastered on the ground from the new buildings. I asked someone on the street the way to the church. It was like seeing a movie I hadn't seen for years, recollecting the actions only as they happened—here the turn of concourse, there the angle of a store, now crushed between giants. The blackish shade trees were the same and the fence, discolored now like teeth. The church had been fitted with a door that opened as you approached.

I didn't really remember the church after all. Or else it was entirely changed. It had an austere whitewashed frame, through which had been stabbed great wounds of windows, like sliced pomegranates, green angelica and blue ink. The altar cloth was the blue and white I'd seen in Ares, and roses bled over their bowls in the hands of white marble angels with huge open-fan wings of tarnished gilt. A pool of incense hung in the air above the altar, like a mirage. The watch flame flickered in its little crystal canister, showing that God was present. But nobody else was home.

I stood on the tiled floor, staring around, my pulse a drum, searching for the vast scrawled words written in fire on the white wall; SABELLA QUEY IS DAMNED. But there weren't any words, and only the angels with their roses had any connection with Cassi's letter. Surely, there hadn't been marble angels here when momma and I sat among the congregation, tensed for the visitation of light out of or into our souls. Maybe marble angels would come alive, were granted the power of speech.

Their carved faces were frigid over the red flowers like blood. The blank eggs of the eyes stared back at me. Their lips must have parted slowly, and before Cassi's gaze they had stated the truth to her, as she kneeled astonished between the pews. Behold, the mouthpiece of the Lord.

And then one of the angels slowly opened its mouth.

I couldn't believe what I was seeing. I froze, with that feeling of the heart actually turning over which accompanies unpredicted horror. Wider and wider the lips of the angel stretched, as if snarling, as if preparing to bite at me. From out the lips came a huge high-pitched gale of sound, which seemed to split my head apart. Not till the shriek cut off did I scream, irresistibly, but helplessly delayed. The scream sounded far away, and so did the crack of my purse landing on the tiles.

There was a thud, and footsteps. I looked to see the angel running toward me, its mouth pulled wide to bite, but instead there was a man with a distraught face and two gray dog's ears of hair flopping at either side of it.

"Please," said the man, taking my arm, treading on my purse and jumping off it. "Please, don't be alarmed."

"The angel—" I think I said.

"It's just the calliope," said the man.

I looked past him. The angel's mouth remained wide.

"The calliope," said the man. "The organ pipes run up through our angels, there, and when I play they part their lips so they seem to be singing with the congregation. It's rather cute, I suppose. I always run over the hymns at this time. Usually the church is empty. But, oh my, I've really given you a shock, haven't I?"

I felt rather sick and very foolish. I sat down on the edge of a pew and the dog's ears man picked up my purse and put it by me.

He offered me a brandy from the medicine cabinet, but when I refused, he brought me a small tumbler of water instead, from the back room behind the angels.

"And you're a stranger, too," he said. "A newcomer, and now I've frightened you away."

"I'm just passing through," I said. "Some relatives of mine used to come here, years ago."

"That'd be before my time, then. Only been here a year and a half, part-time organist, and museum attendant on the side. If it's that you've come to see, I'm afraid it's not on show today." He seemed to expect a comment.

"Excuse me, what isn't?"

"The museum."

"I didn't know about a museum."

"The museum is generally what visitors to Easterly come in here to see. Or did. One time there was quite some traffic, but once the initial interest died down— Mother Earth gets the original and we get the bits, and everyone forgets. I say museum. I think I overstate."

The water, laying a cold gravitational center through my body, had steadied me.

"I'm sorry, I still don't understand."

"You mean to say, Miss—"

"Holland."

"Miss Holland, you mean to say you didn't know about the archaeological find at Easterly, two years back?"

There it was. It was like a gong booming through

the pit of the world, unheard, detected only by its massive vibration. I still didn't comprehend, yet I recognized the moment.

"What find?"

"Ah, Miss Holland. Are you interested in previous cultures? Are you concerned about the prior civilization of Novo Mars? Don't answer. Let's pretend you are. When they started to process the ground over the river for the New Easterly Complex, they blasted out an old quarry, and straight through it was this blessed confounded hole with a slab in it that dates back a thousand years before the first ships landed here. Just think of it. One thousand years before men started squeaking and picking about over the surface. That's older than the foundations at Dawson, older than the stuff up in the Callicoes. Not only older, but different. That's the real point. *Different.* The news had it, TV newsouts carried it for months. You never heard?"

"I suppose . . . I must have."

Recollect, I never listened to the news of my world, not since my mother died, except those days after I burned Sand Vincent.

"Well, it's a tomb. We've had them before, right? But they're urn burials. And this. This is a sarcophagus. Like the Egyptians on Earth, or the Plutonids—you get me, Miss Holland?"

"Yes."

"Oh, damn it," said the dog's ears man, then he glanced at the altar and said, "Pardon me, Sir. Miss Holland, we've put away the museum for today, but I've nearly scared you half to death. So if you'd *like* to see what we have down there—"

I wanted to say no.

"Yes," I said, "I really would."

He beamed at me.

"Better take off those glasses. The generator runs the lights below, and it's switched to half power now."

I took the sunglasses off, and the wounded window light shattered over me.

"Why, that's strange," said my guide, as he walked

me towards the angels and the room behind, "the very last visitor that came to see the museum—you wouldn't have a brother would you, Miss Holland?"

"No."

"That's strange," he repeated. We went by the angel with the open mouth, and I could see the hairline hinges in its jaw. "A tall man, what I'd call the piratical type. Of course much bigger built than you and black-haired, but you know—a distinct resemblance."

Is he talking about Jace? Do Jace and I look alike? I don't want to think about Jace, now now, nor Cassi, nor anything. They were leveling the ground out there, to create their complex with its ambiguous domes, when they found the hole I had crawled into, and disemboweled it. Whatever they'd found in there, one thing they hadn't found. That thing which seemed to be beating now, like a second crimson heart against my breast.

We were in the organ room, with a door to the robe room, and a static moving stair that led down through a trap in the floor. A notice in the wall said: REPLICATE REMAINS.

"Isn't that too nasty for words?" he asked me, indicating the notice. Then he invited me onto the stair, and pressed the down button. "This used to be the old robe room," he told me. "When they dug up the sarcophagi (or do you prefer 'guses?) it was reckoned the safest storage place in Easterly. Or rather, the safest place that would accept responsibility. Then, after they'd shipped the real relics off to the Federation archives on Earth, the replicas came in here, and here they stayed. Ares wants them, naturally, but we've held out. You know, I do think it would have been kind of nice to have held out all the way. We keep the real articles and have the Federation make the confounded replicas."

Cassi must have come this way, a year ago. Did she see the reality or the replicate? The replicates will be so perfect, I doubt it would have made much difference. Then again, suppose this stone around my neck were in a vault on Earth and a replicate were throbbing on my skin. What difference would *that* make?

As he warned me, the old robe room, now the museum, was dim, and after the rain of sun from the windows I was glad. Along the far wall were a series of blocks, the kind all genuine museums have, to contain and protect the objects inside yet leave them accessible to all around view.

"It's very dark," said my guide. "Of course, the blocks light up. Here we are." He led me, and we stood by the first block in the line, and it came alight like dawn.

The slab across my way in the tunnel, satin-smooth and almost featureless, save that there, there, Sabella, was the crevice you never saw before, only felt, in which your destiny lay like a pebble.

"See that little dinge, just there?" helpfully he pointed. "No one guesses as to what made that pock. You need laser power to cut into such a slab. And look, this next one shows the cut sections."

The second block lit. Inside, the tomb, split wide like a walnut.

My heart rattled. It couldn't beat so fast and let me live.

"And here we are, the insides—"

The third block lights. There it was. Whatever it was. It looked like handfuls of yellow string, and gray wire, and then I perceived a skull that looked to me human, ordinary and simply dead.

"That," he said, "is a Martian. A New Martian. Not dust, but bones. Now, just look at these wrappings from the body—" And he dashed to the fourth block and it lit.

Where the bones had staled, the covering hadn't. It was a sheet of a weave that looked like the best kind of synthetic silk, only a touch faded. The drawing, or maybe embroidery, on the cloth was photographically accurate. A man bent to drink from a cup a woman was handing him. Both were naked, hairless, beautiful. Beside them, stood another man and woman (or rather the first pair, repeated in the fashion of a cartoon), and the woman was kissing the neck of the man. The pictures were very calm, and quite innocent, except for the drop that hung from the woman's throat. These drops are two pieces of crystal, fixed into the design, and the first one colorless as white diamond, the second red.

"The theory is a little grisly, I'm afraid," said my guide. "Do you want to hear it? Originally, there was some outcry over such items being stored under the church if the theory was true, but of course, the safest place for every form of evil is directly under the eye of God. If it is evil."

"I'd like to know the theory."

"Well, first of all, the pictures were taken to mean nothing in particular—domestic duty, affection, between man and woman. Then the visual semantics people got on to it. The idea is that, since only two activities are shown, and quite specifically, they must interrelate. In the first picture, the woman gives the man a cup and he drinks. In the second, the man is giving the woman drink." There was a silence. He glanced at me rather apprehensively. After my outburst at the roaring angel, he wondered if I could take this. "I mean, she is drinking from his neck vein. Which leaves us, if the theorists are correct, with vampirism. Of course, there's nothing supernatural in it. It's probably a rite. We know so little about this people—" He starts to theorize himself, postulating many other acts which the cloth may really be depicting.

I stood, and I called to mind Cassi visiting in momma's house. Cassi not seeming to notice me. Not noticing me till she reread momma's letters, which must have mentioned several things, half hiding, half revealing. Momma, you must have seen the stone, and told her. You must have seen the stone, I know you did, when it was white and when it was red—and yet, even so, for Cassi to make the connection between this replicate under the church, the replicate she thought God led her to see, and myself—

"But superstition is a dreadfully clinging vine," my guide was saying. "The worst moment came for our collection here when the robot digger on the complex unearthed the bones."

I realized something about my guide. Despite his worry over me, which was quite genuine, he'd brought me down here because he felt assured, after my response to the angel, of a sensitive, perhaps hysterical further reaction from me. For months he'd had no custom for this pride of his, this find, and when I screamed in the church, he visualized, somewhere on the dark side of his brain, I might scream a little over these blocks. And so far, I hadn't. So now he was waiting. It was time to speak again.

"You mean there's another burial besides this one?"

"Well, in a way. What I actually meant was that human bones were found in the tunnel, outside the tomb itself."

It didn't register properly. It didn't fit.

"Human bones?"

"Well yes. Something of a mystery, and hence a lot of foolish nonsense, and opposition to us keeping the artifacts of the burial just here. I recall a lady who came all the way from Ares to shout at us. A big name. What was it now—Cooperman—"

"Koberman," I say, before I can hold myself.

"Ah, yes, I believe it was. How did you know?"

"The Kobermans are a big name in Ares."

"I can credit that. This lady now, she spoke a lot about God, and what she owed to Him. She scared me, I don't mind telling you. And as it turned out, her objections were virtually groundless, she didn't even know about the human bones. Then Pennington—he was guide down here then—he blurted it. She went as white as ash, this lady did. That was the first time we had a lady faint in our church, (you were nearly the second). And when she came to, you'd think she'd had some sort of vision. I love my God, Miss Holland, but that sudden turning on, like an electric current, it bothers me. . . ."

I didn't feel anything. No, not quite correct. I felt a sword poised across my neck, delicate as the wing of a butterfly. I couldn't prompt him, but I didn't have to.

"The thing was," he said, "this set of bones the digger unearthed belonged to a perfectly healthy little girl, about eleven years of age, just on the edge of puberty. There was no apparent cause of death, though I'd say she'd crawled in there and maybe the air was bad and she fell asleep and asphyxiated. But that's not good enough for the superstitions of our community. Something had to have lured her in the hole, and killed her. Now who in their senses would agree to that about a tomb full of dead remains?"

I was cold. Christ, I was so cold. Even the roots of my hair, my fingernails, even the moisture in my eyes, cold, cold. . . .

"But who was she?"

"The little girl bones? Well, it's a funny business, I'll admit that. The date of the decay was around eleven or so years before we got them out—they'd sunk back in the earth some, but we can date fairly accurately, even after Martian soil has done its work. But the trouble was, nobody had reported a child missing at that or any subsequent time, here in Easterly. The teeth are the usual way of identifying, and they were a dear little set, all flawless, but for a spot of work on one back molar. So they chased up the dental records in the town, and the only child whose record matched the teeth in the skeleton was a child called—"

Don't. Don't. Don't.

"—Sabella Quey."

He pronounced it Kee. Perhaps that made it all right. Perhaps that means it isn't—can't be—

"But this Sabella Kee (Sabella—that's pretty, don't you think?) Well, she certainly didn't go missing at any point. In fact she and her mother moved out of the area about three years later than the bone-decay date, and went to live over near Brade somewhere, I think the gossip had it, though we never traced them."

No. No.

This man is mad. And he told Cassi all this. And Cassi thought—no wonder Cassi thought—

I went in the tunnel. *I* went in, and *I* came out. I, me, Sabella. Sabella. Oh momma, why aren't you here with me to tell this man he's crazy, and that I'm your daughter, that you slapped and loved and died for.

He was saying something else about the bones, and missing children, and he was moving on and there was one more block, but I didn't want to stay there. I knew now what Cassi heard, what made her hate and fear me, and it was a lie.

But I must, as always, cover my tracks where I can. The tracks of the wolf.

"It's been very good of you—"

"But you must see the last one."

"I'm so sorry, I didn't realize how late—"

And the last block lit up, but I was on the moving stair.

"Come out!" my mother called. "Bel, come out of that, it's nothing but a dirty hole. Bel, do you hear me?"

But that was my dream on the plane to Ares, the dream when Sand woke me, and told me everything was all right. My mother wasn't with me.

But I remember. I do.

I was eleven, and nine years before, my father was killed, And I lived in Easterly, and I started to menstruate. And I was unhappy and I walked out of town and I found the tunnel in the quarry, which may have been a metaphor for the vagina, and—

And when I came back to Easterly last night, the house was gone that I'd lived in, and I thought it was as if a chunk of my past had been rubbed out, as if my past were only hearsay, and it suddenly seemed memory itself could be a fake, a fabrication of the mind.

And yet I can remember—

Everything since I came out of the tunnel, clear and absolute and washed with color and pain and shadings.

And everything before I went into the tunnel—yes, I can remember, but—

It's like a diluted painting, or a kind of tableau, where events and people are made of paper and pasted on. . . .

Yes, I know my father died. I know where I lived and where I went to school, and the shape of that room and this tree, and the color of a doll's dress and mother's hair and that it went gray after my father was killed and then she tinted it another color; and I know what my grades were, and when my second teeth came, or maybe a dentist fixing one, and perhaps I climbed trees and perhaps I loved lemon-acid ice cream, but then—

It was just as if I learned those things, the way I learned history dates in school. I could remember, but maybe only—

Second hand.

Outside the church, there was half an hour left of sun. A pink-copper light slicks off the walls beyond the churchyard fence.

Everything seemed to be whirling, the air full of specks, the trees coming undone, everything in shreds, returning to chaos. There was nowhere firm for me to stand, and even my flesh was whirling off, Sabella's flesh that wasn't Sabella's.

And then there was one dark solid, a static beacon in the flood.

The avenger, the dark angel. There was a bar across the street, and he was standing there. He'd been right behind me all the while, right behind this thing he knew wasn't human, not even the part-human thing it thought it was. In the whirling world, only he remained whole, but that was because he was death, just as I always thought.

He'd seen me, but he was waiting for me to cross the street and lie down for the stroke of the sword.

I turned and I ran. By the church and under the shade trees. The path was tiled, and there I could see a back gate and a street beyond.

He'd be running to catch me. He always caught me before. But now I knew what I was, now I was running not only from human vengeance but from my own self, that thing I dreamed in the mirror, its claws sticky with blood, its tongue a black whip, now surely I could run fast enough to get away.

I dropped my purse somewhere. The heel of my shoe twisted and I tore off my shoes and ran on.

I couldn't hear his steps behind me.

My hat was caught in the tree, a black raven. That was funny.

On the street, people got out of my way. Their surprised eager faces flashed past. Perhaps I wasn't running, but the world was dashing away from me, carrying Jace with it.

I ran over a road and a car dived by me, a hot breath of hell on my back. I never turned. I might see death behind me.

Here was a crowd. I ran, I pushed, I was trapped, I was free, I was through.

The sun was going. Try to catch the sun.

Sabella was running. No. Not Sabella. *Something.*

A pain in my side began to slow me, like a piece of lead shot in my vitals. And the red sky was being tipped out over the horizon and overhead the sky was already black.

What place was this? Did I need my fabricated memory, or the real one?

Real one. I was on the highway out of town. Beyond the hypermarkets and the giant stores, where the old beer shop used to be, and where the bars were now like yellow rips in the dark. This was where I was when I was fourteen and the boy with fair hair came by. That's right, that's fine. Full circle. And there was an open-top solar jeep slowing by the walkway.

"Hey, lady!"

Good. That's good. How it has to be.

I turned, and held out my hand, and three grinning human males lifted me into the jeep.

Even death can't outrun this jeep.

Then I looked back.

I couldn't see Jace. The pain was like tears now, like the tears I never did cry, the important ones I held inside me, keeping them, for they were all I had.

The boys in the jeep were laughing, touching my hair, my arms, insidiously my breasts, boldly my knees. They offered me a bottle of wine as the night burst on the front of the windscreen.

Where the plantations of trees ran out from Easterly, they spun the open-top off the road and down a track into darkness. Somewhere in the black they cut the engine and jumped out of the jeep, taking me with them. I didn't have to do a thing, they did it all for me, transported me, put me down, began to strip me.

They were all over me. If I'd have struggled it would have been pointless, but they missed the struggle or some sort of wriggling, panicky response, and so they began to slap me about.

I'd known it. I'm the masochist you suppose me to be. Because I want you to hurt me for what I do to you, I want to expiate my sins with your blows ringing on my flesh. None of this is happening to me. I died, thirteen years back, sitting by a tomb in a hole in a rock.

One of them was sprawled on me, fumbling for the door. His body was hot and wet through his thin clothes, and the other two were rolling on the ground, tugging my arms, yelling. Beyond their heads, I could see stars, as if it mattered. And then the stars went out.

The boy screamed, dragged up and backwards and flung, like a jointless bundle. I could just see his face, the big howling mouth like the mouth of the angel. And then branches crashing, and he was gone. The other two had started up like dogs. I was alone on the ground, but I couldn't really see what was happening. The stars kept going out then reappearing, as shapes went over them. And then one of the boys dropped down beside me, his face turned to mine, snoring wild-eyed through a beard of blood. His fists came scrabbling and were kicked aside, and I heard someone running away through the trees. My night vision had cleared, but I didn't need it any more. I knew the hands of death as they lifted me.

As soon as death touched me, I stopped being afraid. I relaxed totally, and let him carry me, with my clothes hanging off me in portions, and my hair white in my eyes.

There was a hire car parked up on the road. I didn't ask him how he'd got to it in time to come after the jeep. Perhaps he stole the car, perhaps he lost the jeep in any case and found it again merely by luck. It seemed to me that it was inevitable, that he couldn't lose me, he had never lost me.

The car started and he took the wheel. There was a crackle in the cab that must have been his anger, but I didn't look at him.

Then he gunned the engine so the car screamed up the road back to town, and he shouted at me in one long sustained shout. I couldn't hear half the words, and some I heard were off-planet obscenities. It was all distant from me, this shout. Then it stopped and there was silence. Then he said in the flat version of his voice, "Where are you staying?"

"You know everything, but not that?"

"Right."

I told him the location of the hotel, and for a moment I was almost amused. But then I remembered Sabella had died thirteen years ago. Whatever I was, I couldn't be amused.

We drove in silence again.

When we got to the hotel, he drove into the garage, told me to pull my dress together, and then ladled me out of the car and into the foyer and into the lift.

Sabella's head was hurting.

My—Sabella's—arms were bruised.

We went into my room and he shut the door.

He switched on the side lights. He said, "Go in the goddammed shower."

So I went into the shower, and took off the remains

of my clothes, and let the water wash the blood, their blood and mine, off me. And then I put my fingers to the chain around my neck. And I took off the pendant.

I held it in my hand, with the water splashing over my body and through my hair. The stone was paling again, a pale, pale rose.

I stood there, with the water falling on me, staring at the stone, and gradually the water beat me to my knees. I kneeled, and I could only see the stone in my hand, getting paler and paler, as if the life were rinsing out of it.

When Jace opened the cubicle door, I couldn't raise my head from looking at the stone.

"See," I said. "Just like the ghoul lady in the tomb." And then the proper words came, and I said to him, "I'm afraid. I'm afraid," and I couldn't stop saying it, it was the only thing I wanted to say.

He switched off the shower, and came and lifted me. He held me very quietly, and I thought of Sand holding me, rain wet from a shower, but the thought couldn't stay in my brain.

"I'm afraid, Jace."

"I know you are."

The stone was clamped tight in my hand, and my other hand held on to him more tightly. He took me through and put me on the bed, and rocked me. I'd supposed he was going to kill me. But of course he wouldn't. He was like the rest, the lodestone had magnetized him like all the others, and now he was mine. Yet, Jace wasn't like the others. Jace was like, was like—me. No, like Sabella, not like—*me*.

"Why did you want me to see the replicates?" I said.

"You don't know why?"

"Unless—to make me afraid, to—"

"No, Sabella."

"I'm not Sabella."

"You're as much Sabella as you need to be."

"I'm something that killed Sabella, took her form, her skin, her memories—"

"And that's all the memory you have. The human memory. No throwback Martian vignettes?"

I stared at him, at his real face, the only reality. He said, "You didn't see all those Martian blocks, did you?"

"One block I didn't see——"

"There's something I'm going to tell you, Sabella," he said to me. "But not just yet."

He'd stopped looking at my eyes. He looked now at all of me, and as he looked at me, I too began to become real again, alive. When he touched me now it was like fire sponging into me.

"No," I said. But he didn't take any notice of what I said, only of the answer my body was giving back to his hands. "Jace—don't."

"Such a beautiful mouth," he said. "Pity it's a liar."

"You saw me—with the boy in Ares."

"I've seen plenty."

"Jace, I can kill you."

"No."

"Yes I can. Like with the boy. Like Sand. I can, and I don't—I don't want——"

"Forget the others. When did you ever feel this before?"

Damn him, it's true, when did I? But I must fight him, for his own sake—or is it just——

As he raised me, I seemed to be lifted out of myself quite literally, as if my body slipped away and the new body inside rushed free. Then he brought his mouth down over mine very gently and undeniably, and began to kiss me. A wonderful feeling washed through me. It wasn't only sex, which I'd never truly felt before, it was a sensation of peace, of comfort almost. I couldn't fight him. Neither could I fool him. Suddenly I understood I couldn't do a single thing he couldn't handle; I couldn't take from him because he would leave me no space to take, no room for any response but one. Nor need I be ashamed, for I could commit no crime against him, only surrender, give in, let go.

That was what I'd confused with death. That was why I'd been afraid of him.

I was afraid now, but it was a different fear. It wasn't fear at all.

He was beautiful. He had the most beautiful male body I'd ever seen. He was terrible, too, that reality burning like the sun. But I couldn't resist and the sun flamed over me and inside me and I couldn't do a thing. I couldn't even be wise, or try to give him pleasure. I could only take. Take in a new, another way. So this is what they felt, this was what, prolonged, had killed them. Yes—it has the taste of death in it. The great blaze carried me up with it in long gasping leaps of solar energy. And then the world exploded, the sixty-second dawn.

He was lying over me, big golden animal, looking at me with his black, black-lashed eyes half-closed, lazy, amused, tolerant, in control. My fingers ached from grasping him so hard. I dropped the stone, sometime.

I said rather stupidly, with a very human attempt at wit, "Nobody ever gave me a present like that before."

"Relax," he said, "it's Christmas."

He made love to me twice more, before he told me what was in the last museum block. Partly because he wanted me, partly to have that symbol of sexual command clear and definite between us.

In the last block was the other string of bones from the tomb. It had been a double burial, a woman and a man.

The Easterly news archive, like the bars, stayed open all night. It was fully automated, and, because Easterly hadn't yet gained the city sophistry of Ares, there were no human attendants. Jace put me in a booth and dialed the year he wanted. The sheet came up on the screen and it read. TRAGEDY IN COPPER: *One man dead, twenty injured as ore-drill sparks on fire.* It's the year I was—Sabella was—two, the year and the day my father—Sabella's father—died a hundred feet underground in the New Mine, here, at Easterly.

Dressed in our black clothes, as if in mourning, Jace and I were framed by the large white screen. I shifted, disturbed, my body soothed, my mind staring, at odds with each other. "What—"

"Just read down the column."

I read. I read about Sabella's father's death, which left a widow and a two-year old daughter. I read about other injured men and company insurance. Then, at the column's end I read, *Luckier than some, Daniel Vincent, who should also have been at work on the ill-fated drill, had quit work that morning following an altercation with the drill ganger. Vincent, an off-planeter, who has lived in Easterly for five years, also found his luck holding good elsewhere. His twelve-year old son, missing for two days, came home yesterday, alive and well. The Vincents have another son, just one year old today.*

Jace touched the button and the screen went blank. My mind seemed to go blank with it, so when he began to talk to me, I saw what he said in pictures on the that blank brain-screen.

Daniel Vincent brought his family to Novo Mars in the hope of striking rich with the ore boom. But the ore boom, which benefited many, failed Daniel, and in the end, he had to work for the company in Easterly, in order to make up losses. Five years was a long time to Daniel, who was at heart a drifter. A rough, tough hell-raiser of a man, his first son, Jason, bore much of the brunt of Daniel's frustration. The head slaps, the off-hand beatings, were well outside the legal limits of assault, yet, they were brutal enough. They served to convey, more than physical hurt, the unlove that Daniel had for his first son. Then, the second son arrived, and on this second son, belatedly and bizarrely, Daniel fastened a savage possessive affection. If Jason's life was bad before, it got worse in the year which followed. The second son, named Sand for some romantic maybe drunken whim, was the blessing. Jason retained his position as the curse on the Vincent home. Jason ran with a pack of boys, caught in those bouts of hooliganism that plague all colonies once they become townships. Finally, trouble behind and the usual beating ahead, Jason, one sundown, didn't go home. Instead he went climbing in the dry canals outside of town. In an abandoned quarry, his foot kicked through a pile of loosened rocks, eroded by exposure, by time and the moistening of a revitalized atmosphere, and a black pit gaped at him. To Jason, it was a cave to spend the night, a place of shelter. He crawled inside, and when the rock slab blocked his way, he climbed over it to the far side. It was black in the hole, but it seemed like sanctuary.

He stayed in the tunnel, the far side of the tomb slab, one whole night, and the next day he tried to go to Ares, but someone spotted him eventually and brought him home, and Daniel Vincent beat the hell out of him.

A month after the drill fire, Vincent moved off planet. He took his family to Gall Vulcan, and here he periodically deserted his woman and his boys, returning at uneven intervals, like a chronic illness, to pet Sand, and to curse and to beat Jason. He went on spasmodically beating Jason until Jason was fifteen, and then Jason broke Daniel's nose and two of his own fingers. After that, Jace got free, becoming a drifter between the planets, enough of his father in him for that. Sand remained and let the father's petting warp and smear him out of shape in a way Jason had never been warped or smeared by those blunt crusted hands and the belt between them. It had been the father who had rescued Sand, in the beginning, from the blunders he made in his own world of twilight morality and confusion. Later, when Daniel vanished into death, Sand turned incredibly to Jason, and perhaps more incredibly, Jason answered.

Jace had stopped talking and the mind pictures flowed away.

"Sand—" I said.

"No," he said. "Ask me about the tunnel."

I paused, because even in my bewilderment I saw he was asking to be spared any more of Daniel and of Sand. At last I said, "You *made* the tunnel."

"I kicked it open again. It was already made."

"And you never noticed the stone? But all this was ten years before I—"

"We haven't finished with this, yet," he said, and he spun the dial again.

The blank screen lights, and it's last year's newsout, styled quite unlike the earlier crisper bulletin, with capitals that curl, the modern penchant for harking further and further back to the modish past of Earth.

Another skeleton retrieved from the relic tomb cavity. Last night, robot diggers clearing the further debris from the quarry tunnel where last year the unique New Martian tomb slab was discovered, unearthed another mystery find of human bones. These latest ossa, believed to be those of a male around thirteen years of age, are registering as having lain in the tunnel behind the area of the tomb for twenty-odd years or more. Readers will recall the rather uncanny previous disinterment of a prepubescent female skeleton some months ago, identified by dental records as a former Easterly child, still supposed living. There is a possibility no identification, accurate or false, can be made with the latest find, since all teeth are present and perfect and conceivably no dental record exists.

The screen goes out. I can't move. My brain, the blank screen, empty, frozen.

"The Calliope man could have told you about that other parcel of bones," Jace said, "if you'd given him a chance. He likes the buildup gradual." I didn't move. "Come on, Sabella," he said. His voice was slurred, playful, unafraid. "We're in this shit together."

"You're telling me that you're—That you and I— No. You eat and drink and walk in the sun—"

"Sabella, you're missing the sign."

He walked me out of the archive, and across the street into a bar. And then we sat at a table, he with a long glass of golden beer, the very color his soul must be, I thought, I with a glass of strawberry juice, the sort I used to drink in Easterly long ago, pale satin pink, the color the bloodstone goes just before all·color fades from it.

If you looked at us, we looked quite normal, and very splendid, very beautiful. You couldn't see my hands shake from where you're sitting, or my heart shake, or my mind.

I didn't believe him, or the newsout, because he was so calm, so uninterested: So, I'm dead. So.

"If you believe this," I said, "I just wish to God I could be like you."

"You don't have to be like me," he said. "I'll be like me for both of us." He took my hand lightly and looked at it, as if my mask of a face with the two distraught eyes in it, might distract him from his purpose. "You're scared," he said, "because you think you're dead. You're not dead any more than I am. We came out of the tunnel, but we didn't go in. Nor did we, you or I, kill those kids that we thought we were all of these years."

"What then? Something killed them."

"Maybe not. Maybe just bits of them got discarded. Or if not, just the shock of being copied. They walked up to a mirror and the mirror came alive. I'd say it was an impulse, a psychic trigger of some kind."

Somehow, words like "psychic" didn't fit in Jace's mouth. He had no gothic approach to any of this, no spiritual anguish. That was what was keeping him on the rails, and me too.

"You mean like a fly-trap plant," I said, "waiting for the first two flies."

He grinned at me. "We're alive. Even you're alive now, Sabella. You can't shoulder the guilt for a crime you don't even remember committing."

"We're *Martians*, then. Why don't we remember back when the place was all bloody lily pillars and damned urns—"

"I don't think it works that way. I think we got made on a blueprint, like two tin cans."

But I imagined the pink indigenous wolves on the hills, their voices, their running to me, and to my kill. They remember, if I don't, what fashioned me, and what I am.

A Martian. An old new reborn Martian. Do I laugh, now?

"Come on," he said, "you've got to live with it. Vampires resurrect, don't they?"

I clenched my hand in his, "But you're not—"

"Come on, baby. You know what I'm supposed to be."

"Before I considered it, I'd snatched my hand away, and half got out of my chair. But he took my hand back and I sat down again.

I said feverishly, "There are too many coincidences. It's absurd. Even to Cassi spotting Sand's name in an ad, and recalling it from Easterly small-town gossip, which I guess is what happened. Or am I to assume the coincidences are deliberate. This planet dragging its survivors together again."

Jace said, "If my goddam bastard of a father had stayed on in Easterly, you might not have had to make such a ballsup of your life till now."

"Stop patronizing me," I said. "All right, you know how to lay me. It doesn't give you the right to treat me like a child."

"That's the way I have to treat you," he said. "At least for now. And you sure as hell know why."

"No," I said.

But he stood up, drained the gold beer with swift gold undulations of the throat muscle that fascinated me, because I was reducing everything to detail, minutiae. Then he led me out of the bar.

On the street, he said to me, "For Christ's sake, Bella, I'm not afraid of you."

"I am. *I* am. You don't know—"

"I can turn you out like a light," he said. "Any time at all. And that's all you need tell yourself."

In the lift I started to shiver convulsively while the tinny music played. By the time we got to my room, I could hardly walk.

He sat on the bed and took me on his lap, and for all I'd cried I wasn't a child, I was glad enough to rest there in his arms. And I thought of Sand's descriptions—Jace the defender, the rock, Jace the comforter. And I wondered if these stories of Sand's were true, and still I didn't know just what love there had been between them, or hate, or if love could cancel all hatred, hatred all love.

Presently, Jace showed me the stone, which I'd left lying, and which he'd picked up.

"See," he said gently. "Meant for you, not for me. The infallible meter. You're almost out of gas."

"I can't."

But he moved my head until my mouth was against his throat, and easily he lay back and pulled me with him.

"Do it," he said.

So I did.

Instinct. And then, more than instinct. It isn't the same. Not the old thing, the sense of breathing, it's more than that, it's—but I can't say, I don't have the words to say. It isn't performed during love, that's a snare for enemies, the robber's way, the fool's way. But it's an act of love, nevertheless. And for the first time, I could kill a man only by excess of this, the drawing from the vein, the milking of life, and I would kill him out of love, not need. I could kill him then, but he said to me quietly, "That's it, Sabella," and I heard, and I wanted to leave him, but oh, I couldn't leave him, couldn't—and then he put his hands on my shoulders, and with his strength which was always greater than mine, just as he was generally a fraction swifter, he lifted me from him and held me away, and when the film of the great silence of the well I had been drinking at seeped off me, and my eyes unglazed, he put me down beside him, and for a while, we were quiet, as if after the other act of love.

"What," I said to him at last, "did you feel?"

"You kissing me," he said. "Very nice."

"But you can control it. You can stop me."

"Anytime."

"Even if I took when we were making love?"

"You won't."

"But if I did?"

"Try it," he said. "You won't sit on your ass for a month."

The stone was a drop of ruby in his hand, and he gave it back to me.

I was not afraid any more.

I believe in God. I think I believe in Jesus Christ. That night in Ares, I knelt, and I begged someone who was above bargaining to help me, And see, I was helped.

I've thought about it, and I have a conclusion to offer, though Jace doesn't care about it. It's a fact for him, insane but self-demonstrating. I am a woman he wants, and I want him, and he'll haul me with him to other worlds, or stay awhile here on this world which I perceive is ours, and which he takes as a stop-over point or a returning point, but which emotionally he views as just another hotel in space. Which makes me wonder if we are, in a way, still those two children who wandered into the grave-tunnel, not just exact copies of their bodies and their memories and their names. Certainly, we have no recollection of a past to set archeologists and spiritualists squalling and turn the Revivalist Church on its ear. The last impulse of two lovers in a last lost tomb, that's what formed us, and what pins us together, beyond sex and trauma and loneliness and need. We're utterly unlike, opposed, embattled. We can fight all we want, and we do fight. But this nail passes through both of us, a bolt of light as in a picture of Mars, piercing, but not breaking, the vessels of glass we are. Which to Jace is an idea to laugh at, the same as to liken him to earth, and fire.

And for the conclusion? It's all unround.

Before the Earth ships landed, started up their colonies, pumped oxygen into the air and water over the ground and planted things, acting like God in Eden, this planet was four-fifths dead. But before death came, what changes had occurred among a people who raised lily pillars and sealed death in an urn, a people whose technology was either so incredible or so obsolete that men can find no trace of it? I think when all but half the stores of the world were gone, they happened on, or evolved deliberately, a method of sharing. Of the little water and the little food there was, one would eat and drink, and when he was strong, the other would take from him the vital element which food and drink had made—his blood. So there were those who lived by feeding on the things of the earth, and those who lived by feeding upon *them*. It's a situation that admits no intolerance. A system that requires a careful pairing, a creation of partners, who could permit in love what could never be permitted in hate or greed. Except that some were greedy or reluctant, forcing, taking, pillage and robbery, and so the process of seduction followed, the murderous snare I had practiced, not knowing, (or could it be remembering?) another way. That destroyed them, or else, ultimately the planet had nothing left to give, even in half-shares. So the lovers had their tomb, and after them dust again filled all the urns.

It doesn't frighten me anymore about the tomb, the possession Cassi set out to destroy, the possession which is me. And Jace, if she had known. As for guilt, I still feel it, I'm still culpable, but it's become a familiar thing, a piece of me, no more. Because guilt is purposeless. I can undo nothing. Yet in the future, I can live without destruction. And more than that, simply, I can live.

We went to Hammerhead and tidied the house, heard the occasional cicadas and walked on the hills. Once three wolves came out in the dusk and briefly followed us, gilded by stars and blazoned with eyes. Jace

whistled them and they came to him. To him they're
dogs. He would have thrown them a stick, I think, but
they loped away before it occurred to him.

And yet, by that hole of a grave he dug for Sand,
I've seen him stand in the sunlight, while I linger in the
shade. I've seen his face, closed; I've seen him recall
his life as a human man, knowing he is no longer that.

We won't stay here forever, or even very long. I've
never seen another planet. This is all I know. I tell him
we're the last New Martians, and he says sure, baby,
forgetting graves, his light to my dark, his wide outward gaze to my introspection.

But we're not human. No humans are as we are.

The last Martians.

He has to dominate me, that's essential; for I take
his life's blood. The victim must be stronger than the
oppressor—or he dies. He has to tell me when and
how, and where to walk, and if I may, and I obey him,
but that's not for always. I've been anchorless for
years. I've wanted a discipline beyond myself, and
needed it to show me how to master myself, and I'm
learning this too, he's teaching me. In the end, maybe I
shall be the one to say that this planet is where we return to and where we remain.

And maybe the planet is a vampire too, taking from
the life that moves over it, waiting for its resurrection
from the deadness of a desert before it whispered to its
inner dead in their obscure burial places, Come, rise
up, taste of the oxygen in the skies, and the poured out
waters, and the spilled dreams of men.

Men don't own this world. And though the Federation of Earth leaves only replicates behind it, the
bloodstone between my breasts is real. I'm not a
woman in the human sense. A taker of blood, I don't
squander that gift at quarter season. But still it seems
to me that I may not be infertile. This traveling man
who has saved me, might not be of one mind with me
as he blows between the stars, but I can hear destiny
now in the whistling cry of the enduring wolves, the
cry of survival. There may come a time that whatever

brought us together will shout for its purpose to be ful-
filled through us, the last of our kind.

You will have noted I must still walk in shadows,
I'm still closer to the dark, the secret, the mystery.
Don't think me Jace's slave, for if you do, you miss all
truth in what I've told you, and you miss the promise
that one day I may choose to make this man the father
to our planet's children.

And on that day, or night, the last shall be first.

Also available

THE CENTAURI DEVICE
M. John Harrison

Born in the back-alleys of the universe, half-breed son of a spaceport whore, the last full-blooded Centauran, John Truck has been a loser all his life. He has scratched a living in the underworlds of the galaxy, surviving on his luck.

But suddenly he has become a valuable commodity, pursued throughout the universe in a deadly game of hide-and-seek. General Alice Gaw of the Israeli World Government is after him; so is Colonel Gadaffi ben Barka, and Dr Grishkin, mad priest of the Openers sect. Pusher-king Chalice Veronica wants him, and so does the Interstellar Anarchist.

For Truck is the last of the Centaurans, and only he holds the key to the Centauri Device, which may be the most terrible weapon the galaxy had ever seen; or it may be God . . .

A science fiction classic. Chosen as one of the 100 Best SF novels

THE SILVER METAL LOVER
Tanith Lee

Reared to be the perfect child, in permanent arrested development, Jane lives a sheltered life in a house in the clouds, until one day she falls in love with Silver.

Charming, witty, uncommonly handsome, an artist and a brilliant musician, it also turns out that he is a robot . . .

Who can Jane turn to? Perhaps her dazzling and untrustworthy friends — gorgeous, insane Egyptia, elegant Clovis, the lethal Jason and Medea . . .

But Jane is to discover that true love and loyalty is more to be expected from a robot than from humankind, as she flees the sterile luxury of her former life for the underworld of the city's slums to live with Silver.

But beyond her idyll, the force of government and big business are gathering against Silver and his kind. When machines are not only superior to, but more human than men, the only thing to do is dismantle them. . .

'Deftly written, moving, funny, totally convincing . . . this is quite simply the best sci-fi romance I've read in ages.'
                                        The New York Daily News

Also available

The Centauri Device *M. John Harrison*	£2.95 ☐
The Dream Years *Lisa Goldstein*	£3.50 ☐
Escape Plans *Gwyneth Jones*	£3.50 ☐
Second Nature *Cherry Wilder*	£3.50 ☐
The Silver Metal Lover *Tanith Lee*	£2.95 ☐
Time-Slip *Graham Dunstan Martin*	£2.95 ☐

All these books are available at your local bookshop or newsagent, or can be ordered direct by post. Just tick the titles you want and fill in the form below.

Name ....

Address ....

....

....

Write to Unwin Cash Sales, PO Box 11, Falmouth, Cornwall TR10 9EN.

Please enclose remittance to the value of the cover price plus:

UK: 60p for the first book plus 25p for the second book, thereafter 15p for each additional book ordered to a maximum charge of £1.90.

BFPO and EIRE: 60p for the first book plus 25p for the second book and 15p for the next 7 books and thereafter 9p per book.

OVERSEAS INCLUDING EIRE: £1.25 for the first book plus 75p for the second book and 28p for each additional book.

Unwin Paperbacks reserve the right to show new retail prices on covers, which may differ from those previously advertised in the text or elsewhere. Postage rates are also subject to revision.

He was still totally hooked on Gabrielle. Bad enough before when she and Kevin had been engaged. But now one glance at her made memories of his dying friend roil in his gut.

Hank needed to check on Gabrielle as he'd promised Kevin he would, pass along his friend's final words, then punch out of her life for good.

"Hank, what are you doing here?" Her emerald-green eyes went wide.

Again he felt an all-too-familiar snap of awareness. It happened every time she crossed his path, the same draw that had tugged him the first time he'd seen her at a squadron formal.

One look at her then, in the ice-blue dress, and every cell in his body had shouted *mine*. Seconds later Kevin had joined them, introducing her as the love of his life. Still, right now, those cells in Hank kept on staking their claim.

"I'm here for you," he said.

Dear Reader,

I'm thrilled to have a book included in the Billionaires and Babies series! As a mother of four children well past their infancy, I found it a sentimental treat to revisit the precious baby years through a story.

This book also offers a double joy in that I found the perfect venue to feature a character readers have been asking about for years. The Landis-Renshaw family offspring have all had their stories told except for Major Hank Renshaw, Junior—son of General Hank Renshaw and stepson of Ginger Landis-Renshaw.

Many thanks to all of you who asked for this book. I read and treasure the opportunity to hear from readers!

Happy reading,

Catherine

Catherine Mann
P.O. Box 6065, Navarre, FL 32566
www.CatherineMann.com
Facebook: Catherine Mann (author)
Twitter: CatherineMann1

CATHERINE MANN

HONORABLE INTENTIONS

Recycling programs
for this product may
not exist in your area.

ISBN-13: 978-0-373-73164-0

HONORABLE INTENTIONS

Books by Catherine Mann

Harlequin Desire

Acquired: The CEO's Small-Town Bride #2090
Billionaire's Jet Set Babies #2115
Honorable Intentions #2151

Silhouette Desire

Baby, I'm Yours #1721
Under the Millionaire's Influence #1787
The Executive's Surprise Baby #1837
Rich Man's Fake Fiancée #1878
His Expectant Ex #1895
Propositioned Into a Foreign Affair #1941
Millionaire in Command #1969
Bossman's Baby Scandal #1988
The Tycoon Takes a Wife #2013
Winning It All #2031
   "Pregnant with the Playboy's Baby"
†*The Maverick Prince* #2047
†*His Thirty-Day Fiancée* #2061
†*His Heir, Her Honor* #2071

*The Landis Brothers
†Rich, Rugged & Royal

Other titles by this author available in ebook format.

CATHERINE MANN

USA TODAY bestselling author Catherine Mann lives on a sunny Florida beach with her flyboy husband and their four children. With more than forty books in print in over twenty countries, she has also celebrated wins for both a RITA® Award and a Booksellers' Best Award. Catherine enjoys chatting with readers online—thanks to the wonders of the internet, which allows her to network with her laptop by the water! Contact Catherine through her website, www.catherinemann.com, on Facebook as Catherine Mann (author), on Twitter as CatherineMann1, or reach her by snail mail at P.O. Box 6065, Navarre, FL 32566.

To Noah—may you always feel your father's love
and know that his memory lives on through you.

One

"Laissez les bons temps rouler!" Let the good times roll!

The cheer bounced around inside Hank Renshaw, Jr.'s, head as he pushed through the crowd lining the road to watch the Mardi Gras parade. His mood was anything but party-worthy.

He needed to deliver a message on behalf of his friend who'd been killed in action ten months ago. Tracking down his best bud's girlfriend added twenty-ton weights to Hank's already heavy soul.

Determination powered him forward, one step at a time, through the throng of partiers decked out in jester hats, masks and beads. Lampposts blazed through the dark. The parade inched past, a jazz band blasting a Louis

Armstrong number while necklaces, doubloons and even lacy panties rained over the mini-mob.

Not surprising to see underwear fly. In years past, he'd driven down from Bossier City to New Orleans for Mardi Gras festivities. This town partied through the weekend leading all the way into Fat Tuesday. If former experiences were anything to judge by, the night would only get rowdier as the alcohol flowed. Before long, folks would start asking for beads the traditional way.

By hiking up their shirts.

A grandma waved her hands in the air, keeping her blouse in place for now as she shouted at a float with a krewe king riding a mechanical alligator, "Throw me something, mister!"

"Laissez les bons temps rouler!" the king shouted back in thickly accented Cajun French.

Hank sidestepped around a glowing lamppost. He spoke French and Spanish fluently, passable German and a hint of Chamorro from the time his dad had been stationed in Guam. He'd always sworn he wouldn't follow in the old man's aviator footsteps. While his dad was a pilot, Hank was a navigator. But in the end, he'd even chosen the same aircraft his dad had—the B-52. He couldn't dodge the family legacy any more than his two sisters had. Renshaws joined the air force. Period. They'd served for generations, even though their cumulative investment portfolio now popped into the billions.

And he would give away every damn cent if he could bring back his friend.

Chest tight with grief, Hank looked up at the wrought-iron street number on the restaurant in front of him. Less than a block to go until he reached Gabrielle Ballard's garret apartment, which was located above an antiques shop. He plunged back into the kaleidoscope of Mardi Gras purple, gold and green.

And then, in the smallest shift of the crowd, he saw her in the hazy glow of a store's porch lights. Or rather, he saw her back as she made her way to her apartment. She didn't appear to be here for the parade. Just on her way home, walking ahead of him with a floral sling full of groceries and a canvas sack.

Hurrying to catch her, he didn't question how he'd identified her. He knew Gabrielle without even seeing her face. What a freaking sappy reality, but hell, the truth hurt. He recognized the elegant curve of her neck, the swish of her blond hair along her shoulders.

Even with a loose sweater hiding her body, there was no mistaking the glide of her long legs. The woman made denim look high-end. She had a Euro-chic style that hinted at her dual citizenship. Her U.S. Army father had married a German woman, then finished out his career at American bases overseas. Gabrielle had come to New Orleans for her graduate studies.

Yeah, he knew everything about Gabrielle Ballard, from her history to the curve of her hips. He'd wanted her every day for a torturous year before he and Kevin had shipped out. The only relief? Since she lived in South Louisiana, while he and his friend were stationed in Northern Louisiana, Gabrielle had only crossed his path a couple of times a month.

Regardless, the brotherhood code put a wall between him and Gabrielle that Hank couldn't scale. She was his best friend's fiancée, Kevin's girl. At least, she had been. Until Kevin died ten months ago. Two gunshots from a sniper at a checkpoint, and his friend was gone. That didn't make Gabrielle available, but it did make her Hank's obligation.

Gabrielle angled sideways, adjusting the sling holding her groceries and the canvas sack, to wedge through a cluster of college-aged students in front of the iron gate closing off the outdoor stairs to her apartment. A plastic cup in one guy's hand sloshed foamy beer down her arm. She jumped back sharply, slamming into another drunken reveler. Gabrielle stepped forward, only to have the guy with the cup block her path again. She held her floral sack closer, fear stamped on her face.

Instincts still honed from battle shifted into high gear, telling Hank things were escalating in a damn dangerous way. He scowled, shoving forward faster without taking his eyes off her for even a second. The street lamp spotlighted her, her golden hair a shining beacon in the chaos. She pressed herself into a garden nook, but the sidewalk was packed; the noise of the floats so intense that calls for help wouldn't be heard.

Hank closed the last two steps between him and the mess unfolding in front of him. He clamped his hand down firmly on the beer-swilling bastard's shoulder.

"Let the lady pass."

"What the hell?" The drunken jerk stumbled backward, bloodshot eyes unfocused.

Gabrielle's gaze zipped to Hank. She gasped. Her emerald-green eyes went wide with recognition as she stared at him. And yeah, he felt an all too familiar snap of awareness inside him every time she crossed his path, the same draw that had tugged him the first time he saw her at a squadron formal.

One look at her then, in the ice-blue dress, and every cell in his body had shouted, "Mine!" Seconds later, Kevin had joined them, introducing her as the love of his life. Still, those cells in Hank kept on staking their claim on her.

The guy shrugged off Hank's hand, alcohol all but oozing from his pores into the night air. "Mind your own business, pal."

"Afraid I can't do that." Hank slid his arm around Gabrielle's waist, steeling himself for the soft feel of her against his side. "She's with me, and it's time for you to find another spot to watch the parade."

The guy's eyes focused long enough to skim over Hank's leather flight jacket and apparently decide taking on a trained military guy might not be a wise move. He raised his hands, a glowing neon necklace peeking from the collar of his long-sleeved college tee. "Didn't know you had prior claim, Major. Sorry."

Major? God, it seemed as if yesterday he was a lieutenant, just joining a crew. Okay. He sure felt ancient these days even though he was only thirty-three. "No harm, no foul, as long as you walk away now."

"Can do." The guy nodded, turning back to his pals. "Let's bounce, dudes."

Hank watched until the crowd swallowed the drunken trio, his guard still high as he scanned the hyped-up masses.

"Hank?" Gabrielle called to him. "How did you find me?"

The sound of her voice speaking his name wrapped around him like a silken bond. Nothing had changed. He was still totally hooked on her. Bad enough before when she and Kevin had been engaged. But now, one glance at her made memories of his dying friend roil in his gut again.

He needed to check on Gabrielle as he'd promised Kevin he would, pass along his friend's final words, then punch out of her life for good.

"You still live at the same address. Finding you wasn't

detective work," he said, guiding her toward the iron gateway blocking her outside stairway. His eyes roved over the familiar little garden and wrought-iron table he'd seen for the first time when he'd driven down with Kevin two years ago. Determined to gain control of his feelings, he'd accompanied his bud on a weekend trip to the Big Easy. Pure torture from start to finish. "Let's go to your place so we can talk."

"What are you doing here? I didn't know you'd returned to the States." Her light German accent gave her an exotic appeal.

As if she needed anything else to knock him off balance. Good God, he was a thirty-three-year-old combat veteran, and she had him feeling like a high schooler who'd just seen the new hot chick in class.

He took in her glinting green eyes, her high cheekbones and delicate chin that gave her face a heartlike appearance. A green canvas purse hung from one shoulder, her floral shopping sack slung over her head, resting on her other hip. The strap stretched across her chest, between her breasts.

Breasts that were fuller than he remembered.

Better haul his eyes back upward, pronto. "I'm here for you."

The rest could wait until they got inside. He pulled her closer, her grocery sling shifting between them heavily. What the hell did she have in there?

He slipped a finger under the strap. "Let me carry that for you."

"No, thank you." She covered the sack protectively with both hands, curving around the smooth bulge.

Smooth? Maybe not groceries, after all. But what?

Her sack wriggled.

He looked at the bag again, realization blasting through

him. Holy crap. Not a satchel at all. He'd seen his sister Darcy wear one almost exactly like it when her son and daughter were newborns. No question, Gabrielle wore an infant sling.

And given the little foot kicking free, she had a baby on board.

As far back as she could remember, Gabrielle had dreamed of being a mom. Her baby dolls had always been the best dressed, well fed and healthiest in her neighborhood.

Little had she known then how very different her first real stint at motherhood would play out.

No daddy for her child.

A sick baby.

And now an unsettling blast from the past had arrived in the form of Hank Renshaw. Standing in front of her, tall and broad-shouldered, he blocked out the rest of the world. He wore his leather flight jacket in the unseasonably cool night, looking as tall, dark and studly as any movie poster hero.

She still couldn't believe he was here.

Hank.

No kidding, Major Hank Renshaw, Jr., stood on her street in the middle of Mardi Gras. Only her baby's doctor's appointment could have drawn her out into this chaos with her child. If he'd been a few minutes later, would she have missed him?

She hadn't seen him since… Her heart stumbled as surely as her feet moments earlier. She hadn't seen Hank since she'd said goodbye to Kevin the day they'd both deployed from their Louisiana base to the Middle East.

For some reason, he'd come to visit her now. And no matter how painful it was to think of how she should have been celebrating Kevin's homecoming, it wasn't Hank's fault. She was just tired and emotional. God, she hated feeling needy.

But oh, my, how the shower-fresh scent of him chased away the nauseating air of beer, sweat and memories. How easy it would be to lean into that strength and protection. How easy—and how very wrong. She had to hold strong. She'd fought long and hard to break free of her family's smothering protectiveness two years ago, following her dream to study in the States.

She was a twenty-six-year-old single mom who could and would take care of herself and her son. She didn't need the distraction or heartbreak of a man, especially not now.

Although from the horror on his face as he stared at her baby's foot sticking out of her sling, she shouldn't have any trouble sending Hank on his way quickly.

She plastered a smile on her weary face. "Oh, my God, Hank, I can't believe it's really you. Let's step inside out of this craziness so we can hear each other better. When did you get back from overseas? How long have you been here?"

"I got back to base yesterday," he answered carefully, his eyes shouting a question of his own, directed right at her son.

She ignored the obvious, best to discuss it away from here—and after she gathered her shaky composure. "Just yesterday? And you're already here? You must be more tired than I am."

Bracing her elbow, his hand warm and strong, he guided her through the throng. "Seeing *you* topped my list of priorities. Why else would I be here?"

Her son kicked her in the stomach, right over a churning well of nerves. "Well, it's Mardi Gras." She tucked her hand into the canvas diaper bag, fishing for her keys. "I thought maybe you came for the celebration, some R & R after your deployment."

"No rest or relaxation. My being here? *All* about you."

"About Kevin, you mean." Saying his name, even ten months after his death, hurt.

She saw an answering pain in Hank's eyes. What a strange bond they shared, connected by a dead man.

Turning away to hide the sheen of tears, she fit the key into the wrought-iron gate closing off the outside steps up to her attic apartment. The hinges creaked open. Hank blocked anyone else from entering and stepped into the narrow walkway with her. He closed the gate and turned fast, clasping her by the arms.

His steely blue eyes weren't going to be denied.

He tugged her son's booty-covered foot. "And since I'm here about Kevin, that begs the question, who's this? Are you babysitting for a neighbor?"

So much for buying time to pull herself together. "This is Max. He's mine." And he was sick, so very sick. She shivered in fear, her head pounding in time with the beat of the jazz band. "Any other questions will have to wait until we're upstairs away from the noise. I've had a long day, and I'm really tired."

In a flash, Hank tugged her diaper bag from her over-burdened shoulder. He shrugged out of his leather jacket and draped it around her before she could form the words *no, thanks.* She'd worn Kevin's leather jacket dozens of times. One coat should feel much like the other. But it didn't. Hank's darn near swallowed her whole, wrapping her in warmth and the scent of him.

Kevin and Hank may have crewed together on a B-52, but their temperaments were total opposites. Kevin had been all about laughter and fun, enticing her to step away from her studies and experience life. Hank was more… intense.

His steady steps echoed behind her as she climbed the steps all the way to the third-floor apartment. After a long day at the hospital facing her fears and making mammoth decisions alone, the support felt good, too good. She fumbled with her keys again. Hank's jacket slid off and cool night air breezed over her. He snagged the leather coat before it hit the ground.

She pushed open the front door, toed off her shoes and tossed her keys on the refinished tea cart against the wall. The wide-open space stretched in front of her, with high ceilings and wood floors, her shabby-chic decor purchased off craigslist. She slept six steps up in a loft. The nursery, tucked in a nook, sported the only new furniture, a rich mahogany crib covered by blue bedding with clouds and airplanes.

Her studio apartment had been so perfect when she'd launched her dream of coming to the States to pursue her MBA. Since Max had been born, the place had become increasingly impractical. She'd considered caving to her parents' repeated requests to come home, but she'd held strong. She had money saved and a decent income from designing business websites.

Then the world had collapsed in on her. Her baby was born needing surgery for a digestive birth defect—to repair his pyloric valve.

"Gabrielle…" Hank's deep bass filled the cavernous room, mixing with the reverb from the parade vibrating the floor.

"Shh." She lifted her sleeping son from the sling and settled him in his crib, patting his back until he relaxed again.

One more swipe, and she smoothed Max's New Orleans Saints onesie. She cranked the airplane mobile to play a familiar sound over the noise from below. A familiar tune chimed from the mobile, "Catch a falling star and put it in your pocket."

A fierce protectiveness stung her veins, more powerful than anything she'd ever experienced before Max. She skimmed her fingers over his dusting of light brown hair and pressed a kiss to his forehead, breathing in the sweet perfume of baby shampoo and powder. She would do anything for her son.

Anything.

Weariness fell away, replaced by determination. She pulled the gauzy privacy curtain over the nook and faced Hank. "Now, we can talk. Max should sleep for another twenty minutes before he needs to eat."

Her son ate small amounts often because of the too-narrow opening from his stomach into his intestines. But hopefully the upcoming operation would fix that, enabling Max to thrive. If her frail baby survived the surgery.

Hank dropped the diaper bag on the scarred pine table near the efficiency kitchen and draped his jacket over a chair. "Is the kid Kevin's?"

His question caught her off guard, and she whipped around to face him. She'd expected anything but that. The doubt on his rugged face hurt her more than she wanted to admit.

Memories of happier times tormented her with how much she'd lost. The way they'd been coconspirators in reining in the more impulsive Kevin. How he'd helped Kevin rig a pool game so she would win—only to have her beat the socks off him all on her own the next round.

"Hank, you know me." Or she'd thought he did. "Do you really have to ask?"

"Between my sisters and my stepbrothers procreating like rabbits, I've burped a lot of babies. Your little guy looks like a newborn. It's twelve months since we shipped out." He shook his head, his knuckles turning white as he gripped the back of a chair. "The math doesn't work."

Her anger rose in spite of the fact he had a point about her son's small size. "Really? You think you know everything, don't you? Do you actually believe I would cheat on Kevin?"

Although hadn't she? If only in her thoughts.

"You wouldn't be the first woman to find somebody new once her guy shipped out."

"Well, I didn't." She crossed her arms tightly over her stomach. Her heart had been too confused to consider looking at another man. "Max is small because he has pyloric stenosis, a digestive disorder that has to be corrected by surgery."

Fear leached some of the starch from her spine. She sagged back against the corner hutch that held all her school supplies and books.

Anger faded from his face, his brow furrowing. Hank reached toward her, stopping just shy of cupping her face before his hand fell away. "Gabrielle, I'm so sorry. What can I do to help? Specialists? Money?"

She stopped him short, sympathy threatening to unravel her tenuous control. "I can handle Max's medical needs. I have insurance through the school. And you won't need your specialists to covertly check his age." Yes, she couldn't help but be suspicious of his offer. "His birth date is public record. He was born eight months after you and Kevin flew out. Max is four months old."

"So you were in your first trimester when he was killed. Did you not know about the baby when Kevin died?"

She swallowed hard. That, she couldn't deny. She'd lied through omission. "I knew."

"Why didn't you tell him before he died?"

How dare he stand there so handsome, self righteous and *alive?* She let her grief find an outlet in anger. "You two may have been friends, but my reasons are really none of your business."

His jaw flexed and he scrubbed a hand over his close-shorn hair. "You're right. They're not."

His nod of agreement deflated her anger. How could she explain when all of her reasons sounded silly to her own ears now? She'd been scared, and confused, delaying until it had been too late to tell Kevin. If he'd known, would he have been more careful? There was no way to answer that. She would have to live with that guilt for the rest of her life.

She tugged Hank's jacket from the chair and thrust it toward him. "You checked on me. Consider the friendship obligations complete. You should just go. It's late and you've got to be exhausted from your trip back. And honestly, I've had a long day with no time to eat."

A day full of stress on top of the exhaustion of feeding Max every two hours through the night.

She pushed the leather jacket against his chest. "It has been nice seeing you again. Good night."

He cupped a hand over hers. "I'm here to check on you, like I promised Kevin. And apparently my coming by was a good thing. Kevin would have provided for his child. He would want him to live in more than a one-room apartment."

Her head snapped back at the insult. "Back to the money again? I don't recall you being this rude before."

"And I don't remember you being this defensive."

Toe to toe, she stood him down. "I may not have the

Renshaw portfolio and political connections, but I work hard to provide for my son, and I happen to think I'm doing a damn fine job."

Her anger and frustration pumped adrenaline through her, her nerves tingling with a hyper-awareness of Hank until she realized... He still had his hand on top of hers. Skin to skin, his warmth seeped into the icy fear that had chilled her for so long she worried nothing would chase it away. Her exhausted body crackled with memories and heated with something she hadn't felt in a long, long time. Desire.

An answering flame heated in Hank's eyes a second before his expression went neutral. "Did you mean what you said about being hungry? Let me order us some dinner to make up for being rude."

"Dinner? With you?" She hadn't shared a meal with him since two days before he'd left for his deployment.

Since the night she'd kissed Hank Renshaw.

Two

Hank saw the memory of that one kiss reflected in Gabrielle's eyes. One moment of weakness that dogged him with guilt to this day.

She'd driven up to his base in Bossier City to say goodbye to Kevin before their deployment. The three of them had planned to go out to lunch together. But at the last minute, she had an argument with Kevin and he stood her up. Hank had bought her burgers and listened while she poured her heart out. He'd held strong until she started crying, then he'd hugged her and…

Damn it. He still didn't know who'd kissed whom first, but he blamed himself. Honor dictated he owed Kevin better this time.

Furrows trenched deeper into Gabrielle's forehead. "You plan to order dinner, in the middle of Mardi Gras?"

"Or we can leave and eat somewhere else. There's got to be a back entrance to this building." He kept talking to keep her from booting him out on his butt. "We can pack up the kid and go someplace quiet. It's not like he'll be able to sleep with all that Mardi Gras racket."

"This area's rarely quiet. He's used to it."

"Then, I'll order something in." He tossed his jacket back over the chair.

"Which brings us back to my original question. Who's going to deliver here? Now?"

He didn't bother answering the obvious.

She sighed. "Renshaw influence."

Influence? An understatement. But making use of it now was a rare perk in the weight of being a Renshaw.

"I guess even I would deliver a meal in this mayhem if someone paid me enough." She held up both hands fast. "But you're leaving."

He pulled out his iPhone as if she hadn't spoken. "What do you want to eat? Come on. I've been overseas eating crappy mess hall food and M.R.E.s for a year. Pick something fast and don't bother saying no. You're hungry. I'm hungry. Why argue?"

Hugging herself, she stared back at him, indecision shifting through her eyes. She was stubborn and determined, but then so was he. So he stood and waited her out.

Finally, she nodded, seeming to relax that steely spine at least a little. "Something simple, not spicy."

"No spices? In New Orleans."

She laughed and the sweet sound of it sliced right through him as it had before. He'd deluded himself into thinking his memory had exaggerated his reaction to her. And yet here he stood, totally hooked in by the sound of her laughter. Whatever she wanted, he would make it happen. He thumbed the number for a local French restaurant his stepmother frequented and rattled off his order from the five-star establishment. His dad's new wife brought hefty political weight to the family. And politicians needed privacy.

Order complete, he thumbed the phone off. "Done. They'll be downstairs in a half hour."

She placed her hands over his jacket on the chair, her fingers curling into the leather. "Thank you, this really is thoughtful."

"So I'm forgiven for my question about Max's father?" The answer was important. Too much so. Jazz music, cheers and air horns blared from below, filling the heavy silence.

"Forgiven." She nodded tightly, her fingers digging deeper into the coat. "You're a good man. I know that. You're just stubborn and a little pushy."

"I'm a lot pushy." The only way to forge his own path in a strong-willed family full of overachievers. "But you're hungry and tired, so let me take charge for a while."

"Look that good do I?" She rolled her eyes as she walked past him and dropped into an overstuffed chair.

Curled up with her long legs tucked under her, she looked...beautiful, vulnerable. He wanted to kiss her and wrap her in silk all at the same time, which she'd already made clear she didn't want from him.

So he would settle for getting her fed, and hopefully along the way, figure out why she had dark circles under her eyes that seemed deeper than from a lack of sleep. He crouched in front of her. "You look like a new mom who hasn't been getting much rest."

And she looked like a woman still in mourning.

Her eyes stayed on the nursery nook, the crib a shadowy outline behind the mosquito net privacy curtain. "He has to eat more often, smaller meals to keep down any food at all."

There was no missing the pain and fear in her voice. Right now it wasn't about him. Or even Kevin. It was about her kid. "When was the problem diagnosed?"

"At his six-week checkup we suspected something wasn't right." She adjusted a framed photo, the newborn kind of scrunch-faced kid with a blue stocking cap. "He wasn't gaining weight the way he should. By two months, the doctors knew for sure. Since then, it's been a balancing act, trying to get him stronger for surgery, but knowing he can only thrive so much without the operation."

With every word she said, he became more convinced driving here had been the right thing to do. She needed him.

"That has to be scary to face alone. Is your family flying out?"

"They came over when he was born. There's only so much time they can take off from work, especially since I live so far away." She set the photo down and crossed her arms again, closed up tight. "They offered to let me live at home, but I need to finish school. We're settled in a routine here with our doctors and my job."

"How do you hold down a job, go to school *and* take care of a baby?"

"I do web design for corporations—something I can do from home." She waved at the hutch in the corner. "Half my classes are online. Max spends very little time with a sitter, an older lady who works part-time at the antique store downstairs. She comes here to watch him when I'm away. I'm lucky."

Lucky? A single mom running herself into the ground to care for a sick child considered herself *lucky?* Or just so damn independent she refused to admit she was in over her head?

"What about *Kevin*'s family? Are they helping?"

Her chin thrust out. "They don't want anything to do with Max. They say he's too painful a reminder of their son."

Hank should have figured as much. The one time he'd met Kevin's family, they'd come across as self-absorbed, more into their vacation than their son. More likely they were ignoring Max because he interfered with their retirement plans. "At least Max has his father's life insurance money."

She stayed silent. Her fist unfurled to flick the gold fringe on a throw pillow.

Damn. He sat up straighter. "They did give him the money, right? Or at least some of it?"

"Kevin didn't know Max existed." She folded her hands carefully on her knees. "Kevin's parents were listed as his beneficiaries."

"I'll speak to them. And if they don't come through it shouldn't take much to contest—"

"My son and I are getting along fine," she interrupted. "We don't need their money."

Prideful? Needing to forge your own path? He understood that. Which made him the perfect person to help her. "You're doing an admirable job by yourself. I didn't mean to insinuate otherwise. I only meant that it can't be easy."

"That's an understatement." She smiled wryly.

"What about your parents?"

"Hello? I thought we already settled this. I'm fine."

"No one should have to carry a load like this by themselves. I recall from Kevin that your parents are good people." Although they lived an ocean away, in Germany.

"They are, and I did consider going home right after I found out I was pregnant. But I was already knee-deep in my graduate studies when I found out about Max. Sure, things are tight now, but I need to finish my degree, my best hope for providing a good future for my son."

"About those dark circles…?"

"I'll sleep after Max has his surgery because he won't be hungry all the time. He will feel happy, content…." Unshed tears glinted in her eyes. "I have to believe he'll be okay."

Her tears undid him now just as much as they had a year ago. He shifted from the sofa to crouch in front of her. He took her hands in his, her soft hands that had once tunneled into his hair, then down to score his back. Except now those nails were chewed with worry.

And he had to fix that. He couldn't let her go on this way alone with no one to help her. Staring at her bitten-off fingernails, he knew exactly what he had to do.

"That's the reason you're staying here rather than going to your parents, isn't it? Once you found out he was sick, moving to another country…"

"I couldn't start the medical process over again and waste precious weeks, days even. We're here, and we'll get through it."

He squeezed her hands. "But you don't have to go through it alone. I'm on leave for the next two weeks. I'll stay in New Orleans. I owe it to Kevin to be a stand-in father for Max."

A stand-in father?

Gabrielle froze inside. Outside. She couldn't move or speak. She'd barely gotten over the shock of Hank showing up here unannounced and now he'd said this? That he wanted to be some kind of replacement for Kevin with Max?

There had to be something else going on here. She'd heard of survivor's guilt. That wasn't healthy for him—or for her. "Hank, I don't know what you're trying to accomplish here. But Max already has a father, and he's dead."

His grip tightened around hers, almost painful. "Believe me, I know that better than anyone else." His throat moved in a slow swallow. "I was there."

Oh, my God. "When he died?"

"Yeah…." His grip loosened, his thumbs twitching along her palms.

His head dropped, and he looked down at their clasped hands, the strong column of his neck exposed. Her eyes held on the fade of his military cut. And strangely, she ached to touch him there, to stroke and comfort him. To hold on to him and let him hold on to her, too. They'd both suffered the loss of Kevin, and right now that pain linked them so tightly it brought the crippling ache rushing back full force.

Please, don't let her reach for him, which would have her crying all over his chest. The hint of tears a minute ago had brought him here in front of her…and when she'd cried before, they'd betrayed a man they both cared so much about.

So she gathered her emotions in tight and focused on him, and what he was saying.

"I tried to call you afterward from overseas, a couple of times, but calls out were few and far between."

"I got the messages," she whispered.

He looked up fast. "And you didn't write back? Email?"

His voice on those recordings had poured alcohol on her open grief. "It was too painful then." And his presence now? She didn't know what she was feeling. "I figured hearing my voice would hurt you as much as it hurt me to hear yours."

"Do you still feel that way?"

His deep blue eyes held hers, waiting, asking. She didn't have the answers and her life was scary enough just dealing with Max's surgery. She looked down at their joined hands and, holy crap, how long had they been holding each other like that?

She snatched her arms back, crossing them over her chest. "What are we doing here, Hank? Are you here to pick up where we left off after that kiss, now that Kevin's gone? Because you have to realize that was a mistake."

A dark eyebrow slashed upward. "If you have to ask that, you don't know me at all. I mean what I say. I just want to be here for Kevin's kid."

"But you didn't know about Max when you arrived." And why hadn't she thought of that until now? "What *are* you doing here?"

He shoved to his feet and paced in the space she'd decorated with such hope and plans, a blend of her dual roots. Then she'd met Kevin and thought, finally, she had found roots of her own, a sense of belonging.

Hank's powerful long legs ate up the one-room apartment quickly, back and forth in front of the nursery nook before pivoting hard to face her. "Kevin wanted me to deliver a message."

"A message?" A burn prickled along her skin until the roots of her hair tingled.

"I meant it when I said I was with him when he died." His body went taut, his shoulders bracing, broadening. "I was right beside him until the end."

She eased to her feet, steeling herself for whatever he had to share, for words that could haul her back into the agony she'd felt when Kevin died, when she'd given birth to their child alone. "What did he say?"

"He said he forgave us."

Three

Gabrielle looked every bit as stunned as he'd felt when Kevin said the words to him, that he forgave them. The memory blasted through him of that hellish night at the checkpoint when they'd been ambushed, the smell of gunfire and death. Then Kevin spoke and said the unthinkable.

That he knew Hank and Gabrielle had feelings for each other.

Her mouth opened and closed a couple of times, but no words came out. She pressed her palm to her lips, turning away.

He wanted to reach for her, to comfort her. Do something—since he couldn't seem to scrounge up the right words. He wasn't much of a warm and fuzzy guy. He was a man of action.

A squawk from behind him stopped him short.

"Max," Gabrielle gasped, rushing past him.

She swept aside the gauzy curtain and lifted her son out. Damn, the boy was so tiny. Scary small. The enormity of that little being going under the knife stole his breath and raised every protective instinct all at once.

Cradling Max to her shoulder, she patted his back. "I need to feed and change him."

"Yeah, okay. What do you need me to do to help? With all those nieces and nephews, I'm not totally inept."

"Unless you're lactating, I don't think you can help with this."

Lactating? Breast-feeding?

Ohhhh-kay. He grabbed his jacket off the back of the chair. "I'll wait downstairs for the delivery guy to bring supper."

She bounced the baby gently on her shoulder, his whimpers growing louder, more insistent. "The back entrance is just at the other end of the garden alleyway. Take the keys off the tea cart on your way out."

"Roger that. Wilco—" Will comply. "I'll be back in twenty minutes or so."

Pulling the door closed behind him, he stepped back into the waning Mardi Gras mayhem. The tail end of the parade blinked in the distance, the crowd following and dispersing. He scooped up a couple of strands of beads and a feathered mask that must have strayed over the gate. He wanted her out of here, somewhere safer. She had enough on her plate taking care of the little guy without worrying about someone scaling that fence one night.

He sidestepped the round iron table and chairs, decorated with a few potted plants and hanging ferns. Chick-pretty but not safe. He eyed the shadowy alleyway, not impressed with security. And he would damn well do something about it.

Reaching the back gate, he leaned against the brick wall to wait and fished out his phone. He thumbed through the directory until he landed on the name he needed. He hit Call. The youngest of his four stepbrothers worked renovations of historical landmark homes. Even a couple of foreign castles.

For right now, he would settle for something more local.

The ringing stopped.

"Hey there, stranger," his stepbrother Jonah Landis answered from on location at heaven only knew where. Jonah's projects spanned the globe. "Welcome home."

"Thanks, good to be back." Or rather it would be once he got some things straightened out. He needed to put to rest the feelings he had for Gabrielle and figure out a way out from under the guilt.

"How much longer until the base cuts you free for some vacation time?"

"Actually—" he crossed one loafer-clad foot over the other "—that's what I'm calling you about. I'm visiting a friend in New Orleans, and I'm hoping you can hook me up with a place to stay."

"What exactly are the parameters?"

Parameters? Privacy topped the list. His father was a retired general who'd been on the Joint Chiefs of Staff and now served as a freelance military correspondent for a major cable network. His stepmom—Ginger Landis Renshaw—was a former secretary of state, now an ambassador.

He hadn't grown up with that kind of influence. And even once his family stepped into the limelight, he'd lived a Spartan life, socking away most of his paychecks and investing well, very well. He could retire now, except that military calling to serve couldn't be denied. Even his family didn't know his full net worth. Only that his investments left him "comfortably" well off, enough to explain if he spent beyond a military paycheck.

Which he rarely did. But he needed something private. A place for Max to recover from his surgery, a place where Gabrielle would have help before she collapsed from trying to tackle everything on her own.

"Jonah, I seem to recall you were starting a renovation down here in New Orleans right before I deployed."

"Right, a historic mansion in the garden district that got whacked by a hurricane. It's an Italianate cast-iron galleried-style—"

"Right. I just need to know if it's finished and if it has a security system."

"Finished, security system installed last week, up for sale with bare bones furniture to help prospective buyers envision themselves living there."

Sounded perfect. "Think you can pull it off the market for a couple of weeks?"

"Any reason you're looking for a house rather than a hotel?"

"Hotels are noisy and nosey."

"Fair enough. What's mine is yours."

"I mean this as a business transaction. I insist on paying."

"Really, bro, we're good." Jonah paused for a second, the sound of sheets rustling and him speaking with his wife about going to the other room. "Seriously, though, why call me? Any of mom's or the general's people could have taken care of a low-profile place to stay."

Truth was easy this time. "Ginger would have heard about it, whether from her people or the general. She would have questions…."

"There's a woman involved." Jonah laughed softly.

No need denying that. And heaven forbid, he mention the baby and Grandma Ginger—his stepmom—would come running straight to New Orleans. "I want this to stay quiet for a while. The last thing I need is the press or our family breathing down my neck, not now."

"Understood." Of course he did. Jonah Landis's wife had royal ties as the illegitimate daughter of a deposed king. Privacy was a valuable commodity in short supply for them. "I can have the Realtor bring you the keys now."

"No need to disrupt anyone's Mardi Gras. I'll swing by tomorrow and get them myself."

"Party on, then."

"Thank you. I appreciate this."

"We're family, even if you hide out from the rest of us. Good to hear from you, bro."

And they were. Even if by marriage. His dad and his second wife, Ginger, had built something together after both of their spouses died. Hank looked up the iron stairs at the closed door leading to Gabrielle's apartment. She needed his help, just the way Ginger and Hank, Sr., had needed help with their kids. They'd turned to each other rather than go it alone. That's what friends did for each other.

Whether Gabrielle wanted his help or not, he was all in.

Gabrielle yanked her clothes off fast and tossed them all in the bathroom laundry hamper. Her knee bumped the sink. She bit back a curse, hopping around on one foot and trying not to fall into the tub in the closet-size bathroom. Any minute now, Hank could walk back up with supper and she needed to clean up after feeding Max. No bachelor was going to want to hear about—or smell— baby puke.

She didn't have time for a shower but at least she could splash some water on her face and change clothes. Not that she cared what she looked like around him. She was just excited over her first real meal with another adult since Max was born. Silly, selfish and she had to remember this wasn't a real dinner date.

Just supper with an old, uh, friend?

Oh, God, she was a mess. She sagged back against the sink. No amount of face washing or hair brushing was going to change the fact that she was a single mom, who wore nursing bras and eau de baby. Nothing was going to change that. She didn't want to *change* that, damn it.

Even if Kevin had somehow given her permission to fall for his best friend. The realization that he'd somehow known clawed at her already guilty conscience and made her feel like a huge fraud.

Frustrated and running out of time, she yanked on a pair of black stretch pants and tugged a long tank tee over her head. She grabbed a bottle of lavender spray she'd bought because it was supposed to be calming, soothing and she'd been searching for any help to relax her son.

Tonight, she needed some of that peace for herself. She spritzed her body fast, spraying an extra pump over her head and spinning to capture the drift. She scrubbed her hair back into a high ponytail just as she heard the front door open.

Time's up.

Her stomach knotted.

There was no more dodging Hank, that long-ago kiss and the fact that somehow Kevin had found out. She'd hurt the man she'd promised to love for the rest of her life. She rammed the lavender bottle into the medicine cabinet and padded back out into the living room barefoot.

And the breath left her body. Hank stood in the doorway, shadows across his face. In his flight jacket and khakis, he could have been any military guy coming home with supper for his family. Yet even with the anonymity of the shadowy light, she would never for a moment mistake him for anyone but himself.

The light clink of silverware across the room broke the spell, and she looked over to find a private waiter setting up things for them. Hank held out a chair for her at her little table that had been transformed with silver, china and a single rose. This was a world away from the sandwich and milk she'd planned for herself.

Their waiter popped a wine bottle—the label touting a Bordeaux from St. Emilion.

She covered her glass, even though her mouth watered. "No, thank you. I'm a nursing mom."

The waiter nodded and promptly switched to an exclusive bottled water as Hank took his seat across from her.

"Whatever that is smells amazing." She plastered on a smile as the waiter served their meal, then quietly left. "I concede you're the king of late-night takeout food. If that tastes even half as good as it smells, it'll be heavenly."

"So the little guy's down for the count?" His eyes heated over her, briefly but unmistakably lingering on her legs.

Was his head tipping to catch her scent? She had to be mistaken, sleep deprived and hallucinating. And if she wasn't, she needed to get her priorities in order. Max came first, and for him, she needed to eat and keep her strength up.

"Sorry about the wine but Max is nursing as well as bottle feeding." With his digestive problems, he fed more often than she could keep up with, even expressing. But that was far more detail than she wanted to share with him. "He will sleep for another hour and a half."

"You've got to be flat-out exhausted." He tipped back his water goblet.

"I'm not the only single mom on the planet." She set out silverware and napkins. "I'll survive."

And survive well with the meal in front of her. Aromas wafted upward to tempt her with hickory-roasted duck, cornbread pudding and on and on until her mouth watered. Reaching for the fork, she realized she was really hungry for the first time in months.

Sure, maybe she was avoiding talking for a few minutes longer, letting herself be *normal* for just a stolen pocket of time.

Until she couldn't avoid the burning question any longer....

Without looking up, she stabbed a fork into the corn bread pudding, mixing it with a roasted-corn salad. "What did you mean by saying Kevin had forgiven us?"

Hank set his fork down carefully on the gold ring edging the plate. "He didn't seem to know any details other than we had feelings for each other. He said he understood, and he wanted us both to go on with our lives."

Gasping in horror, she dropped her fork. Shame piled on top of the guilt. Kevin had known. Somehow he'd seen her confused feelings when she'd thought she'd hidden them so carefully. He'd been so argumentative just before leaving, picking fights with her about anything because she wouldn't agree to move closer. She'd held her temper in check because of his upcoming deployment—until nerves got the better of her.

He'd wanted her to skip out on work and party with him, but nerves were already chewing her over the last time he'd partied, gotten reckless and forgot birth control. She'd told him she was tired of always having to be the adult in their relationship. He'd snapped back, telling her to go hang out with Hank, then, since he was mature enough for ten people. The fight had been hurtful and a product of fears about him leaving.

How damn sad that a ridiculous fight led her to act on those feelings, to kiss Hank.

She flattened her shaking hands to the table. "Are you saying Kevin *gave* me to you in a dying declaration?"

"Not in so many words." He reached for his water glass. "He said he loved you, he forgave us both and then he mumbled something about being sorry for not taking you out for gumbo."

Tears welled fast and acidic. The enormity of what Hank had said, of his showing up here in the first place, exploded in her brain, then came back together like puzzle pieces fitting into an unsettling image. "You aren't actually expecting to pick up where we left off with that kiss, are you?" She pressed her fingers against her speeding heart. "Because that would be incredibly crass, if you came here looking for an easy pickup off your friend's death."

He choked on the water. "That *would* be crass."

"Glad we agree on that much. So why are you here again?"

"Gabrielle—" he set his glass down "—I'm here to tell you Kevin's last thought was of you, that he loved you and let you go. End of story. Or so I thought. But finding out Kevin had a kid? That changes everything."

Now he was sticking around because of Max? That should make her happy. Her son was everything, after all. Hank had said he wanted to be a stand-in dad. Yet something about the notion of him being here for her baby felt off. "Max doesn't have to change anything. You're free to go." She shoved her chair back sharply, just barely catching it before it tipped to the floor. "He is not your child, and he's not your responsibility."

Hank shot to his feet and grabbed her shoulders. "You know me better than that, Gabrielle. Do you honestly think I'm the kind of man who could walk away now?"

"You feel guilty." She gripped his polo shirt, the cotton warm from the heat of his body. "Even though he released you, you still feel bad about that kiss. Well, consider yourself absolved by me, too. I instigated it. My fault. Bye-bye."

She let go, pushed him away and raised her hands before she succumbed to the temptation to crawl right into his arms.

"Bull." He twined his fingers with hers. "What happened that night—it was me. I kissed you, and yeah, I still feel guilty as hell because if I had the chance, I would do it again."

Four

Hank stood so close to Gabrielle he could smell the lavender scent on her skin, on her hair. His body flamed to life, lust pounding through his veins leaving him hard and hungry. As much as he wanted to chalk it up to extended abstinence, he'd always felt this way around her. The day he'd met her, he'd been seeing someone else, a year-long relationship that he'd promptly ended. In fact, his abstinence stint had started that day, nearly two years ago.

Good God, much longer and he should get some kind of honorary monk status.

With Gabrielle this close, her hands linked with his, he remembered all the reasons he'd kissed her in the first place. Or rather *the* reason. He felt a crazy, inexplicable draw to this woman, a gut-deep need to claim her as his that wasn't dimming one damn bit with time.

Her lithe body was so close, motherhood having added some curves he ached to explore. She swayed, not much, but definitely toward him. Her sparkling green eyes went wide, her pupils dilating with unmistakable desire. Then she blinked fast, her shoulders rolling back. Slowly, she inched her hands from him.

"Hank," she whispered, her voice husky, accent thicker. "I think you should go now."

Disappointment whipped through him, quickly smothered by reason. Things were ten times more complicated than before and being with her had been damned convoluted then. He needed time to sort through the major bombshell the stork had dropped into his world tonight.

Hank stepped back, needing distance from her in more ways than one. He'd meant it when he said he would be here for her and her son during the surgery. He owed his friend—and he owed her.

The rest, he would figure out later, back at his place while soaking in his hot tub with a beer. "I'll be here at nine to take you to the baby's appointment."

She tugged at the collar of her loose tank top. "How did you know he has another appointment tomorrow?"

For a self-indulgent second, he let his eyes linger on the curve of her breasts under the silky cotton, her slim thighs hugged by black leggings. "You left the slip from the doctor's office under a magnet on the fridge. Some kind of early registration work at the hospital, right? He has surgery the day after tomorrow?"

"Yes to all, but Hank, this is my son, my life. I can handle it on my own."

"Yes, you can." And that was one of the things he admired about Gabrielle, her independence. God, he was so screwed. "But you don't have to."

The next morning, Gabrielle hitched the diaper bag over her shoulder, grabbing an extra receiving blanket at the last second. She was seriously scattered this morning. It was tough enough getting out the door with a baby, but leaving a half hour earlier than expected was darn near impossible.

Still, she was determined to go before Hank showed up. His sudden arrival last night, his words, his touch— just the sound of his voice—had tipped her world upside down. The twisted sheets and coverlet on her bed attested to how he'd plagued her dreams. First, he'd been wearing a mask, dark and mysterious with blues music and fog wrapping around him. Then she'd been the one in disguise, but her mask took on a more sensual tone, her clothes and inhibitions falling away....

Nerves tingling to the roots of her hair, she turned away from her brass bed. In her dreams, she'd spent the entire night there with him. She did *not* need more time with him today, especially not when she was so emotional over her son. She would just leave Hank a message on his voice mail once she got in her car.

She slipped the floral baby sling over her neck and settled her sleeping son inside. Today's blood work would bring them one step closer to having the surgery behind them. Two days from now, her son would have the procedure and life could return to normal.

Whatever *normal* was anymore.

She backed out the door, working her key down the locks. Hank's warning about the neighborhood, about providing for her child, tugged at her conscience. She turned around and pulled up short.

Hank sat on her top step. No *Top Gun* flight jacket today. He wore jeans and a button-down, loafers without socks. Old-school aviator glasses rested on top of his head without making a dent in his close-cropped brown hair. He had a casual air that worked for him without even trying.

How did he pull that off this early in the morning?

"Uh, Hank, what are—"

He held up a hand, and he gripped his iPhone in the other hand as he…played a game? The squawk, squeak and explosion noises coming from the handheld increased until a final blast and victory tune filled the morning. Hank didn't fist pump, but he smiled before tucking away his phone and reaching for his coffee beside him.

Shoving to his feet, he dusted off his jeans and slid his sunglasses down from his head and in place over his eyes. "Are you ready?"

She was so jangled from the explicit images of her dreams that she felt them simmer through her even now. She couldn't seem to draw a breath, as if just having him here stole all the air around her. Fighting for some distance, she shot him a level gaze and hoped her emotions didn't show.

"How long have you been there, and how did you get past the front gate?" She eyed the wrought-iron entry at the top of the alley. Still locked up tight. She looked back at Hank. "Well?"

"I've been waiting for twenty-five minutes to go with you to the doctor's appointment. As for how I got in, suffice it to say I've made my point about security." He drained his coffee cup with a final long swallow.

"Fine, you're right." She sighed and yanked off the diaper bag. She thrust it against his chest. "Make yourself useful and carry this."

Grabbing the handrail, she started down the stairs.

"Yes, ma'am." He laughed softly, his footsteps sounding behind her.

His laughter taunted and turned her inside out all

at once. God, he made her mad at the way he assumed he could thrust himself into her life, and she was even madder at herself for the leap of excitement over finding him waiting for her. "My car's parked in a lot a block away."

"I have my car right out front. I'll drive." He took her keys from her hand and opened the wrought-iron gate.

"You don't have an infant seat."

"Wrong. I do." He palmed her waist, guiding her past the shopkeeper sweeping beads and other Mardi Gras tokens littering the sidewalk.

"It's not even eight in the morning. Did the Renshaw-Landis influence make a baby seat appear in the night?"

He peered over the top of his aviator shades, blue eyes piercing and too darn appealing. "I went to Walmart Supercenter. Open twenty-four hours."

"Renshaws shop at Walmart?" She closed the gate behind her, stepping into her sleepy city and aware from the draw of just a look from Hank.

"For a car seat at midnight. Yeah." He pitched his coffee cup into a street trash can, then fished keys from his pocket and thumbed the automatic lock. Lights flashed on a dark blue Escalade. Not tricked out. Just understated wealth.

"Nice," she conceded. "Definitely more comfortable than my five-year-old little hatchback."

Forcing him to fold himself into her tiny econo car would be silly and pointless. In fact, fighting him every step of the way could be more telling than just going with the flow, pretending they were still simply friends.

He opened the back door and tossed in the diaper bag. "And does the infant seat meet with your approval?"

"Let me see…." She checked the belt, making sure he'd installed it properly.

"The air force trusts me with a B-52. I think you can trust me to follow instructions."

"It's my child's safety. I have to be sure." And she found nothing wrong.

Wow. It had taken her three hours to figure one of these out. She eased Max from the sling, her son so small in her hands, so perfect. Love and protectiveness welled up inside her—along with gratitude that Hank had gone to such trouble to make sure her baby had everything he needed.

Hank had to be exhausted, just back from overseas, then immediately on the road to see her. No wonder he needed the coffee. Her mouth watered at the thought of having a taste of something she'd been denied since getting pregnant with Max....

Uh, coffee. She missed coffee and chocolate and spicy foods, things she gave up while breastfeeding.

"Gabrielle?" Hank stood in the open door, her beautiful historic city behind him.

Her adventure. She'd started out here with such plans for taking the world by storm, launching a powerful career in international banking. Now she just wanted to help her child get healthy.

"Right, let's go before we're late."

She clicked Max in securely and thought about staying in back with him. But he was already asleep again and Hank was holding the passenger door open for her. Without another thought, she shuffled into the front, and Hank pulled out into the early morning traffic.

His GPS spoke softly. Of course he'd already plugged in the address for the hospital where Max would have his pre-admission blood work. Outside the car, people walked to work in business clothes. A mom pushed her kid in a stroller, passing by a homeless guy sleeping in a doorway. New Orleans was such a mix of history and wealth, poverty and decay. The city had looked different to her before her son was born. Her plans had looked different.

Hank's phone chimed from where he'd placed it on the dash. He glanced at the LED screen and let it go to voice mail. It was the same phone she'd seen him playing with earlier.

"I wouldn't have pegged you as the video game type."

He glanced over with barely a half smile, so serious for a guy who'd been blasting digital bugs on her steps. "I went to a military high school. One of my roommates was a computer geek."

"He got you hooked on games?"

"You could say so. His computer access was limited in school—conditions of not going to jail for breaking into the Department of Defense mainframe."

Her eyes zipped to his phone. "How did I never know you attended a military high school? Or that you're into video games?"

"You and I spent most of our time together keeping things light."

They had always avoided more serious subjects, like where they'd gone to school and their family histories. Until that day she'd poured her heart out over her fight with Kevin. How he'd wanted her to move in and she'd wanted the space to finish pursuing her dreams. Kevin had been living his. She just wanted the same chance.

She'd stopped short of telling Hank everything the fight had been about, unable to bring herself to share intimate details about a forgotten condom. How she'd been frustrated about Kevin's partying. The very playful attitude she'd originally been drawn to was beginning to pall. She was tired of always having to be the responsible one.

But God, she couldn't break up with Kevin right before a deployment, especially not when she wasn't even sure what she wanted. Talking to Hank, the harder she'd cried, the more she'd gasped, the more each breath hauled in the scent of him. Before she could think, she'd been kissing him, stunned as hell over the desire combusting inside her. She'd been attracted to him—sure—but she'd thought she had that under control. She was focused. She and Kevin were a good match. They balanced each other out, his humor lightening her driven nature. She didn't need more intensity in her life.

Except when Hank had focused all that intensity on her, she'd been damn near helpless to resist.

Her hands fisted until her gnawed-down nails bit into her palms. Their past time together was better left alone, especially today with everything he'd said last night still so fresh and raw. "Back to the DoD hacker high school roommate?"

"Once he turned twenty-one and got free of his cyber watchdog, he set up a small company that developed cutting-edge software. Computer games. Mostly save-the-world type of stuff."

"What game were you playing this morning?" she asked, intrigued by this side of Hank she hadn't guessed at before. Had he never seemed lighthearted around Kevin because Hank had been relegated to the role of mature grown-up? Had she lost some of *her* lightheartedness around her fiancé for the same reason, playing less rather than more around him? "Maybe I've heard of it."

"It isn't out yet."

"How nice of your friend to let you test run his material."

"I own part of the company."

That caught her up short.

"Really? Yet another thing I didn't know about you." Did his influence stretch to every niche of the stratosphere—political, financial, military and now even the geek-squad world, as well?

"I'm a silent partner, and I prefer to keep it that way. I've got enough notoriety hanging around my neck thanks to my family."

"Why this investment, though?" She wished she could see his eyes, read what he was thinking as her impression of him altered. "You're not a games kind of guy."

"But I'm a practical guy." He stopped smoothly at a red light. "The venture made good business sense."

The MBA part of her applauded him, although she suspected something else was at work here. "You're all about the military, not business. You don't care about money. You never have." Her more frugal upbringing applauded that, as well. "You risked the money to help a friend, and it just turned out well for you."

"When did you swap from a business major to psychology?" He slid his sunglasses down his nose, his eyes laser sharp as he looked over the top of the lenses at her.

What a time to remember a blue flame burned hottest.

"Hey, you inserted yourself into my life. Turnabout is fair play."

And damned if he wasn't doing it with complete ease.

This wasn't as easy as it seemed.

Midday sun piercing his aviator shades, Hank slid into a parking spot two blocks away from Gabrielle's apartment. He'd spent all morning helping through the pre-hospitalization blood work for her baby to have surgery tomorrow. There hadn't been a chance to speak over lunch, not between juggling the kid back and forth. So the day was slipping away and he still hadn't made any

headway in finding an opening to persuade her to stay
with him during the kid's recovery. Every time he got
close, something distracted him.

Like the way Max had cried when the lab technician
stuck his tiny toe.

Hank had wanted to tuck the kid under his arm like a
football and book it out of the hospital. Which was damn
silly. They were just doing their jobs around here. This
was all necessary to make the boy better.

Now, they were already back at her place again. It was
just past lunchtime, but felt as if it were even later. The
kid was getting cranky, so Hank just unsnapped the car
seat fast and hefted it out for expediency's sake. Gabrielle followed efficiently, the dark circles of worry under
her eyes even darker. Damn it, she needed more help than
just someone carrying the kid and supplying a meal.

Accordion zydeco music swelled from a street café,
although, strangely, the antiques shop below her apartment sported a closed sign. He was going to have to just
ask her to stay with him. And she would say no. Then he
would have to get pushy, which would piss her off. Hell,
it would piss him off. But he wasn't wrong.

Being right didn't comfort him much.

He pushed open the iron gate to let her through, prep-
ping his words and his will for the fight ahead once she
had her son fed and asleep again.

Gabrielle gasped and pulled up short. Instinctively, he
looked around for a threat—a mugger? Another drunk
like last night? How could he have forgotten they were
in downtown New Orleans—an undeniably cool place to
party but not the safest city on the planet?

Grabbing her around the waist with one arm, he tucked
her against him. "Gabrielle?"

Ah, hell. Her bottom nestled right against him, close,

intimate and too arousing. He took a breath and backed away. They had a cranky kid to take care of.

"Look," she said, pointing up toward her apartment.

He barely had time to process the sight of water pouring out from under her door before the front entrance to the shop burst open. A woman—probably in her fifties—rushed toward them wearing a 1920s flapper getup. Which would seem strange somewhere else. But New Orleans was an "anything goes" kind of place. A name tag pinned to her chest declared her *Leonie,* and the costume actually made sense for an antiques store employee.

Gabrielle brushed past him and clasped the woman's hands. "Leonie, what's going on?"

"A water pipe burst." She peered around Gabrielle with undisguised curiosity chasing away her harried look for a moment. "But a more important question, who's this?"

"Leonie, this is Hank, a friend of mine." Gabrielle chewed her lip before continuing. "Hank, this is Leonie Lanier. She works part-time in the shop and helps me with Max."

Interesting that she'd left off the Renshaw last name and hadn't referred to him as Kevin's friend. "Nice to meet you, ma'am."

"You, too, Hank." She finally peeled her gaze away and back onto Gabrielle. "The broken water pipe flooded all three floors. It's horrible downstairs. Yours is mostly damage along the floors. Still, even if your place isn't a mess, they had to turn off the water."

Gabrielle pointed up at the flowing stream trickling under her door. "And what's that if the water's off?"

"Everything that happened before we turned off the main valve." She pressed a hand to her forehead, right over the beaded band. "We're not sure what caused it, but I'm sorry, sweetie. All the renters in the building have to find somewhere else to stay. The second I heard that, my heart just sank for you and this precious little guy. As if you don't have enough to fret about now."

For the first time in ten godforsaken months, life was cutting him a break. He wouldn't have to fight or argue with Gabrielle. Persuading her to come to the house he'd rented would be a cakewalk now.

He clasped her shoulder, securing his grip on the car seat still in his other hand. "Gabrielle doesn't have to worry about a thing. She can stay with me."

"I'll check in to a hotel," she said tightly, stubborn to the end.

"Do you really want your son exposed to the germs of a generic hotel room?" He asked, swinging the car seat slowly to lull the restless baby.

"Since when did you become a germaphobe?" She perched her hands on her hips, cinching in her simple black cotton sheathe. "I distinctly recall you bragging about eating bugs in survival training."

"I'm not an infant facing surgery."

"Are you trying to make me cry?"

"I'm trying to take care of you, damn it!"

Leonie cleared her throat.

Damn. He'd forgotten she was there, forgotten they were standing in the middle of a busy street.

"Gabrielle, sweetie—" Leonie hooked an arm with her "—the hotels, motels, everything's full because of Mardi Gras."

Deflating, Gabrielle leaned back against the wrought-iron gate. "Of course they are. I should have thought of that myself. What are you going to do?"

"Don't worry about me. Just focus on Max," the older woman said, a helluva lot more subtle in exerting pressure than he'd been.

Resignation mingled with frustration on Gabrielle's weary but so damn gorgeous face. "But Hank, aren't you staying in one of those germy hotels?"

"Leonie can have my room." He stifled a wince since he'd actually already checked out of the place. But he could find somewhere in this overbooked town. There were always rooms set aside for someone with the right amount of money. He pulled out his phone. "Trust me. I can handle this. By the time you feed the kid and pack your suitcase, I'll have us in a house and your friend Leonie will be taken care of, as well."

Okay, so technically, he already had the house, but he didn't want to push his luck by letting her know he'd been working toward this victory since last night.

She eyed him suspiciously, hitching the diaper bag up higher on her shoulder. "Did you have someone sabotage the plumbing?"

"I would have if I'd needed to." Might as well give her the truth on that. "But fate has been kind to me today."

Still, her eyebrows stayed pinched together. She wasn't buying the ease of his plan for a second.

"Fine. You've got me." He whipped off his aviators and pinched the bridge of his nose. "Yes, I have a place to stay here. I arranged it last night, and yes, I was hoping even then that you would stay there for the duration of Max's recovery. The plumbing issue just makes the decision a no-brainer for you."

Gabrielle shoved away from the gate, fished out her keys and mumbled, "It's not my brain I'm worried about."

Five

Back in Hank's Escalade an hour later, Gabrielle wished everything in her life was as easy to decide as where to spend tonight. With her son's surgery scheduled for tomorrow, staying with Hank for the evening truly was a no-brainer.

After speaking to Leonie, she had gone upstairs to pack her things and nurse her son while Hank carried her bags and baby gear to the car. Thank goodness the damage to her place had been minimal. Clean up would be easy and her most treasured items were safe—her scrapbooks and photos.

Hank had made a couple of trips up and down the stairs lugging her stuff. Packing for tonight at Hank's place, plus the two-day hospital stay hadn't been easy. Where would she go afterward? What would she do? She would face that when the time came. For now, she could only think of getting through tomorrow's operation. Just thinking of her son going into the operating room had her stomach in turmoil, fears and tears bubbling to the surface.

That had to be the reason her feelings were so out of control around Hank. Once she had the procedure finished and her son healthy, her mind would clear. She would be rational again.

Hank drove through the Garden District and she settled deeper into her seat, letting the beauty soothe her ragged nerves. She hadn't bothered to ask Hank where they were going. Undoubtedly, they would have to drive for a while to reach anything available. She refused to think of her soaked apartment and the damage. She would sort that out with insurance later.

Passing historic home after home, they drove farther away from her apartment, slower and slower as if Hank sensed the peace she drew from soaking in their surroundings. Since Max was born, there hadn't been time to indulge in sightseeing tours. Even when she took her son for walks in his stroller, she was usually dead on her feet.

Like now, and it wasn't even suppertime yet.

Maybe she should ask Hank to swing into a drive-through on the way since she'd forgotten to eat breakfast. She looked over at him just as he turned the steering wheel, except he was pulling into a driveway not onto a road.

"Hank?" She sat up straighter.

A narrow, freshly paved driveway stretched beside a pink stucco house with metal balconies—Italianate style—all restored to former magnificence. The yard, while not huge, was a large plot in an area where land was at a premium. The lawn and garden did justice to its

Garden District address. She could only imagine what the place would be like in the summer.

When she'd dreamed of coming to New Orleans for graduate school, this was just the sort of place she'd envisioned visiting, maybe having lunch or treating herself to a night at a bed-and-breakfast. As a military brat with an American dad and German mom, she'd grown up all around the world, nowhere ever feeling like home.

New Orleans oozed with history, *roots.*

"Is this a bed-and-breakfast?" She rested a hand on Hank's arm, then pulled back quickly. "What a great idea, more comfortable, like a home. I don't know why I didn't think of that."

"It's not a bed-and-breakfast." He steered around back to an empty parking area with a three-car garage. "It's a vacation rental home."

"I don't remember seeing a Realtor's sign." She looked over her shoulder but the street had disappeared from sight as he stopped at the back door.

"The owners aren't the type to advertise." He shut off the SUV. "They work through a Realtor who sets up rentals for people who need space and privacy. Politicians. Actors."

"This is, uh—" She settled on "—thoughtful and a little overwhelming."

"Don't sweat this." He hooked an elbow on the steering wheel. "Really. This is nothing for me. It was easy, and I won't even notice the expense. So don't give me credit I don't deserve."

She looked at his casual wear and his old-school aviators. She'd allowed herself to be distracted from who he was. "I forget about your family sometimes."

"Thank you." Smiling, he swept off his shades. "I'll take that as a compliment."

"It is. But this—" she gestured to the yard, the no-kidding *mansion*— "is really too much."

"It's already done, Gabrielle. I have a week and a half left on my leave time, and I've already arranged to spend it in this house." He spread his arms, sunglasses dangling from his fingers. "So either you walk inside with me, or I'm stuck staying in there all alone for a week and a half, which sounds like an awful waste."

Shaking her head, she reached for the door. "Why do you keep making it sound like I'm doing you a favor when it's obviously the other way around?"

He leaned back and put his shades on again, pulling away in more ways than just physically. "Call it survivor's guilt. It's a real bitch."

What a sad situation they were both in here, trying to do right by Max and Kevin even when all these reminders of the past had to be flaying him raw inside, too. She blinked away tears and squeezed his hand.

"That it is," she whispered. "That it is."

An hour later, Gabrielle set Max's car seat on the floor and sagged back against the door to her temporary bedroom. Although the word *bedroom* seemed sorely inadequate to describe the luxurious quarters. Not a modern suite, per se, as the integrity of the old home had been maintained.

Grateful for some space to regroup before she faced Hank again, she carried Max's car seat deeper into the room and placed it at the foot of the sleigh bed. The large queen-size frame filled the space between two floor-to-ceiling windows. Slate-blue linens with splashes of yellow in the bolsters called to her to sneak a nap.

A fat yellow love seat was tucked in a nook. Persian rugs stretched over refinished hardwood floors that still bore the marks of past use. The beauty of the place was in how the imperfections were maintained so the home looked restored rather than gutted.

From what she'd seen, the rest of the house sported more of a skeleton set-up of basic furniture, the dining room with an antique table and sideboard with a gilded mirror on the wall. The living room was accented with a sofa and a couple of wingback chairs, along with sconces on the carved mantel. Mammoth windows, with airy curtains that pooled on the floor, added a whisper of color here and there to the otherwise whitewashed walls.

But beyond that, it was clear Hank had ordered additional items just for this visit.

A connecting door was open to the nursery, completely decked out in toile and stripes—black, white and gray— the contrasting colors perfect for a baby, yet in keeping with the historic home.

Beyond just the decor, the practical angles had been addressed, as well—diapers, sleepers, baby blankets and a monitor.

A mahogany end table—by the love seat—was actually a mini-fridge with a crystal bowl of fruit on top. She opened the small refrigerator to find—of course—bottled water, juice and milk.

When they'd hung out before, with Kevin, she'd known Hank came from a wealthy family, but he never flaunted his money. And he'd certainly never mentioned his savvy investment in a computer games venture. So this lavish display caught her off guard.

It also touched her.

Hank had given her time to unpack and then they planned to meet for supper. He'd ordered out and said they could dine on the side lanai. She had to admit, she welcomed the chance to soak up every wonderful detail of this dream home in her dream city.

With all Hank's help, she actually had time to take a more leisurely bath than the rushed shower she'd snagged in the morning.

She peeked into the bathroom and nearly groaned in ecstasy. Her gaze zipped right past the polished pewter-and-crystal fixtures to the deep claw-footed tub that lent an air of history, while spa jets inside the tub shouted pure modern decadence. She whipped her shirt over her head and ditched the rest of her clothes faster than she could think *Jacuzzi*—

Her cell phone chimed from her bedroom.

"Damn it," she whispered, then all but kicked herself. Before long, Max would be parroting everything she said.

She grabbed a thick, fluffy towel and wrapped it around herself on the run back into her bedroom. She couldn't afford to ignore ringing. What if it was a message from the hospital or Max's doctor?

Struggling to hold the towel in place, she fished through the diaper bag—like finding something in a deep black hole. Finally, her fingers closed around her cell and she yanked it free.

Her mother's number flashed on the caller ID. Relief warred with frustration. Already, she could imagine all the ways her mom would push her to come home.

She mentally switched to German and answered, "Hello, Mama."

"Why aren't you answering your phone at your apartment?" her mother asked, rapid fire and frantic. "I was worried sick some criminal had come in off the street and killed you both."

"I can assure you we're alive and not being held hostage by someone looking to hock my seventeen-inch television and costume jewelry."

Although she did have her diamond engagement ring, tucked away in a box and waiting for Max to give to his future wife one day.

"Well, if you're not being held at knifepoint and you're not dead in a ditch, then you were out all day. Too long for you to be out with a baby. Did your old car break down? You know your father could help you with things like that if you lived here."

She looked around the room and thought of how convoluted it would be to tell her mother everything going on with Hank right now. Especially when *she* wasn't even sure what was going on with Hank.

"Sorry, Mom, I just couldn't get to the other phone before you hung up."

"Tttt, ttt," her mother reprimanded. "You never were good at lying."

"Sheesh, I'm not ten anymore." She sank to the edge of the bed. "A water pipe broke in my apartment. My place is unlivable at the moment, so I had to find somewhere else to stay."

"My God, now of all times? Where are you?" Her mom still felt the need to keep tabs on all five of her kids, as if that would give her more control over a world where her husband got called away to secret locales at the drop of a hat.

In a way, Gabrielle got it. She wanted control over her own life now, too.

"I'm staying at a bed-and-breakfast."

Hopefully this time her lie played better to her mom's radar ears.

"A bed-and-breakfast? That sounds nice, almost as good as being home." Her mother's voice edged down a notch. "I just wanted to check on you. You promise you will call after Max's surgery."

"Of course I will." As a mother herself, she could well imagine how freaked out her mom must be right now. If only she could just be less...pushy about her own fears. It shouldn't take an entire ocean to create boundaries wide enough. "I know you're worried, too."

"I would be there, if you let me."

"Thank you, and I appreciate that. Honestly. But you already came out when Max was born." And when Kevin had died. Although she didn't want to talk about death, especially not tonight. "Thank you, Mama, but really, I'm managing okay."

Thanks to Hank.

Guilt pinched again over not being completely truthful with her mother. Her mom was an amazing woman, other than that "dead in a ditch" syndrome. She was a military wife, mom of five, two of which were still in junior high. She worked as a math teacher, swapping schools every time they moved. Her mother was so darn near close to perfect it was overwhelming sometimes.

Like now.

Gabrielle needed the space to be less than strong, less than perfect. She needed to just be upset for her child without worrying about making her mother even more smothering.

"Thank you for calling, Mama. But I should get some supper." And put on some clothes.

"Hold on just a few more minutes. Your father wants to say hello, too."

Gabrielle mentally switched to English to speak with her dad. She pictured her wiry, energetic mom zipping up all three flights of stairs in their fourplex searching. Gabrielle could hear her mom's repeated calls of "Gary!"

As a kid, she'd had nightmares about her burly, invincible dad dying in a war. Some of her mom's "dead in a ditch" syndrome had rubbed off. She'd grown up torn between a deep respect for those who wore a uniform and a desperate wish for her father to be someone different from who he was.

Even her perfect mother cried when she thought no one was looking.

Gabrielle gripped the phone tighter, questioning for the first time if she'd stayed in New Orleans for practical reasons—or because she hadn't wanted her family to see her grief.

"Gabby girl." Her dad's rumbly voice traveled through the connection, strong and familiar.

"Hello," she said to her father just as a tap sounded on the door. "Wait!"

She called out fast, but too late. The door was already opening after the hello.

"Ohmigod." She shot to her feet, towel gripped tight in her fist.

Hank stood in the open doorway, eyes wide. His feet were planted as if he was rooted to the floor in shock. He opened his mouth to speak, closed it and tried again. She held up a hand to silence him and damn near dropped her towel. She let the phone fall instead and grabbed fast to keep the towel in place.

Carefully, she knelt to pick up her cell without taking her gaze off Hank for a second. "Dad, love you tons, but I gotta go. Max needs me. I promise to call you and Mom tomorrow as soon as Max is out of surgery. Bye now."

She thumbed End Call, pitched the cell onto the bed and pressed both hands against the towel. Her body flamed to life at the stroke of Hank's eyes and yes, even more than that. Heat stirred because *she* saw *him*. More than just the breadth of his shoulders filling the doorway or his slim hips in khakis, she took in his face and, holy Gerard Butler, he was handsome in that rugged way made all the hotter by the keen intelligence in his blue eyes.

"Hank?" She cleared her throat and her thoughts. "Did you need something?"

Hank's slow, lazy blink spoke of hot sweaty sex. "Is there anything you need that hasn't been provided here?"

"Thank you, but we're fine. Everything's beyond perfect. I'll be down as soon as I get dressed." Although no way could she bathe now, not knowing that he would be thinking of her in the tub and she would be in that water thinking of how his eyes stroked her with unmistakable appreciation.

After months of pregnancy and postpartum body adjustment, she couldn't deny that his unhidden desire for her felt good. Who wouldn't be flattered, right? She was simply flattered.

Yet, the second he closed that door after him, her knees folded.

Hank sat on the lanai with a glass of sweet tea and listened to the distant sounds of a city that stayed awake late. Very late.

Draining his glass, he rocked the chair back and forth on two legs. He would have preferred a beer after the mind-blowing image of Gabrielle in nothing but a towel. Or maybe a few beers until he could pass out asleep rather than awake with the vision of her strolling through his mind every other second.

But he had to stay clearheaded and available in case she needed his help.

A dim light still shone from her room even well past— he checked his watch—one in the morning. She had to be dead on her feet after getting up with a kid all night, then the early start today. Not to mention the stress.

He'd already put into place a couple more plans for easing her life during Max's recovery. And damn it, there would be a recovery because Hank refused to accept any other outcome for tomorrow's surgery.

His chair legs slammed down on the porch.

He needed to check on her. Now. Find out why she couldn't sleep and see if there was something he could do. She'd been far too quiet at supper, eating in silence then excusing herself to go to bed. Except she still wasn't sleeping. Unless she left the lights on, in which case he would slip back out and grab some sleep himself.

These days he only managed about four hours of shut-eye anyway. That had started right about the time Kevin died. Hank was just wired. It would settle out as soon as he gained some closure by helping Kevin's kid.

A mocking voice in the back of his head reminded him he was here to see Gabrielle as much as the boy.

Hank strode quietly through the house. A good house. His stepbrother had done his standard stellar job on the place. A bit more furniture and it would be a worthy addition to the historic home tour circuit. He couldn't help but notice Gabrielle's appreciation. Felt good to get something right for her.

He took the stairs two at a time and stopped at the first door. Tapping once, twice, he waited...but no answer. He wasn't going to make the mistake of barging in on her again.

He started to turn away when the door opened. Gabrielle stood wide awake—and blessedly covered by a thick terrycloth robe. Max slept in her arms, his head on her shoulder.

Hank braced a hand on the frame, leaning toward her

without touching her. "Everything okay? Your light's still on. I thought you might need…a glass of water or something not here."

"There's water in the mini-fridge. The place has more amenities than I could have asked for." She rested her cheek on her son's head. "I just can't sleep. I need to hold him."

"Want some company?" The words fell out before he could rethink the wisdom of hanging out here in the late night with her.

Indecision flickered through her green eyes for a flash that had him thinking of emeralds. Nodding, she stepped back. "If we both can't sleep, might as well keep each other company."

Adjusting the baby on her shoulder, she curled up in a corner of the love seat. He dropped down beside her and waited. And waited. They used to talk for hours. Granted, they'd shot the breeze about lighthearted things or whatever was in the news. The one time they'd gone deep with the discussion he'd made the lame mistake of kissing her when he should have been comforting her.

He definitely needed to tread warily here.

Hank reached in the mini-fridge and pulled out a bottle of water, twisted off the top and set the drink beside her. "He's going to be okay."

"I know the odds are in his favor, but there's no way to be one-hundred-percent sure."

Grabbing a bottle of water for himself, as well, he nudged the door closed and leaned back, but the sofa brought them close, his leg pressed to her knees. He cleared his throat. "I looked into your doctors, and you're right, they're top notch."

She sat up straighter. "You investigated my son's doctors?"

"Shhh, you're gonna wake the kid." He waited until Max settled back to steady, sleepy breaths. "And yes, I wanted to check into them."

"You wanted to see if your money could bring something better." Her mouth pressed tight.

"Is that so wrong?" Although even if she thought it was, he would do it all over again. "Would you have turned me down on principle even if it meant settling for less for your kid?"

"Don't you think I already investigated them? As for the cost, I would have begged, borrowed or stole anything to make sure he gets the best possible care. I appreciate all you've done, but this is *my* child."

There was no mistaking the steel in her voice.

"I realize he's not my son, but he's my last link to Kevin. That means something."

You mean something.

The words hung out there, unspoken, but implied.

Understood.

She reached to touch his arm lightly, lingering. "It's hard for me to let people do things for me. My mom is a wonder woman in every sense of the word." She rolled her eyes. "I struggle to get both Max and myself showered by noon."

"You looked beautiful—and clean—this morning." He dipped to sniff her neck. "You smell good, like flowers, the purple kind. I think you're good on the hygiene."

She laughed. "Okay, technically clean since showers happen. Fast, of course…. The flowers are lavender. It's supposed to be relaxing."

He laughed along with her even though she was killing him with images of her soaked under the spray, and he found the sweet scent of her anything but calming.

Her fingers twitched on his arm. It was such a soft

touch, nothing overtly sexy with the kid around and her fears so thick he just wanted to haul her close until the next twelve hours could pass.

Her hand slid away. "You come from a family of amazing women, too. Your sisters juggle kids and military careers. Your stepmom was the Secretary of State, for goodness' sake. I've never even actually met them, and I'm already in awe. And then you've got all those stepsiblings...."

"Do you see now why I hide out here in Louisiana?"

"Hiding out? I can understand that." She winked at him with a splash of her old spunk shining through the exhaustion. "What about your mother? I've never heard you mention her."

"I don't remember a lot about my mom. She died when I was still in elementary school."

"And?" she prodded gently.

He didn't dwell on his childhood. Thinking about it wouldn't change a thing. But if that's what Gabrielle wanted to talk about, then fine. He would talk while walking on crushed glass if that would help her get through the night.

"One Christmas, my oldest sister made a photo album for me and for our other sister with all the family pictures taken before Mom died, some pictures from when she was a kid, too. There are days I'm not sure what memories are real and what's been created by those images."

"Does it matter if you remembered them or if she helped remind you of things you did together? I think it was a beautiful thing your sister did, gathering that together, helping you hold on to those moments you shared with your mom."

"Yeah, I guess. Better to have those memories than none at all. For some reason, both my sisters seem to remember more." And little Max would have no memories of the father he'd never even met. Hank rethought the concept of being "all in." This kid would need him for more than the next two weeks. Hank was a crucial link to memories of Kevin, especially if Kevin's parents were checking out. And who else would explain about Kevin's military service, how much he loved to fly?

"Hank." Her voice pulled him back to the moment. "What do you remember, beyond those photos?"

And just that fast, Gabrielle sent him into a fugue world between now and then, fusing the two. "I remember the sound of her voice when she read the *Gingerbread Man* at Christmas. To this day, the smell of gingerbread makes me think of her."

"That's a great memory of her to carry." She cupped his face, her eyes filled with compassion for him, even in the middle of her own crisis.

God, she was killing him here. He had to touch her back.

He grazed his knuckles along her cheek. "I guess what I'm trying to say is Max isn't going to care if you've got on makeup by lunch. When he thinks of his mom, he's going to think of the love in your voice."

Before he knew that he'd moved or she'd moved, she was leaning into his arms. Her back rested against his chest, his arms going around her and the baby.

She was right. He couldn't promise her everything would work out tomorrow. But he could damn well be there to hold her through the night.

Six

As the morning ticked away on the hospital clock, Gabrielle took comfort from Hank's arm around her shoulders. He'd been at her side on the waiting room sofa since the surgery started a half hour ago.

He'd been with her through the night each time she woke to feed Max, as well. His thoughtfulness—and the intimacy—wrapped around her as firmly as his arm. Why was it she could relax into Hank's comforting presence but not in her own family's?

She'd been so determined to face this on her own, and yet here Hank stayed, helping. And she couldn't deny his presence made things easier. She couldn't fathom what it would be like to sit here alone in this waiting room interspersed with others clinging to each other for support.

Although, if the surgery had occurred a few days earlier, she *would* have been here by herself to face the sterile air of fear and dying flowers. Somehow she'd lost sight of the fact he'd only just returned from a war zone.

Her head on his shoulder, she looked up at his deeply tanned face. "You must have had bigger plans for your homecoming than babysitting a distraught mom."

A smile fanned creases in the corners of his eyes. "My plans mostly consisted of food and sleep, so I'm good."

"What kind of food?" she pressed, needing the sound of his voice to fill the awful silence. It had been so hard walking away from Max this morning, leaving her precious boy in someone else's care to face the ordeal.

"Anything not cooked in a mess hall or prepackaged as an M.R.E." He lifted his foam cup. "And real coffee."

She inhaled the fresh roast scent steaming upward. "I hear you on that. I'm looking forward to knocking back an espresso someday. How ironic that when a mom needs the extra jolt from caffeine most, it's not good for the baby."

"Hadn't thought of it that way." He set aside his cup. "Anything else you're looking forward to getting back to once Max is healthy?"

"I haven't really thought about much but him. Looking into the future has been scary."

"You're going to be making plans before you know it." He squeezed her shoulder, drawing her closer to the warm press of his body against her side. "Why not get a head start? Today's for positive thinking. What are you going to do for yourself?"

The answer popped to mind fast, but it wasn't fancy and so very much *not* a guy thing that she held back. "You're going to laugh if I tell you."

"Me? Laugh at you? Not a chance in hell." The steady hold of his blue eyes reassured her.

"My wishes aren't lavish like your family's."

He tugged a lock of her hair. "Haven't you figured out yet that I'm the black sheep of the group? I prefer to fly under society's radar, so to speak."

From what she knew of him, that entirely fit. He was a man of grounded values. She'd always liked his lack of pretentions in light of such an illustrious pedigree. "Okay, when I'm playing, I like to do things that are totally different from my analytical MBA studies, totally hands-on rather than techno, like the computer work."

"What would that be?"

"Scrapbooking."

His forehead pinched in confusion. "Scrapbooking... Like...photo albums?"

"You are such a guy." She patted his chest—a flipping brick wall. Gulp.

"Your point?"

She laughed softly, so very grateful for the way he distracted her from her worries, from things she had no control over right now. "I've always held on to keepsakes. Moving around so much, I wanted something tangible from people in each city. With my father gone so much, I also wanted to be sure I didn't lose a single memory we made together. I collected ticket stubs, pictures, pressed flowers—filling up shoeboxes. Eventually it needed organizing and labeling."

"My mom would really like that." He nodded, his hand sliding along her shoulder to massage her neck. "My stepmom, too, for that matter. She has rows of shelves with photo albums. Now that I think about it, I've seen her with some of the wives and grandkids messing with photos and stamps."

"Scrapbooking has become an art form, with special papers and stickers and stamping." She resisted the urge to moan in pleasure at the magic of his fingers along the knotted tendons in her neck. "Some people make their own greeting cards—real works of art."

"And you get a creative outlet to balance your more analytical work." He pointed to a nurse walking past with a stack of charts. "Like how she has that funky fabric cover over part of her stethoscope.

"Exactly." How cool that he got it, rather than just dismissing her hobby as keeping junk—like Kevin had once said.

"I would guess you've started a scrapbook for Max... and have one about Kevin."

"Yes to both." She needed to capture those happy memories for herself and to share them with her son. "When my apartment flooded I was so scared something had happened to them."

"Are they okay?"

She nodded. "Completely undamaged. I boxed them up when I packed clothes for Max and me."

"What will go in the book for today?"

"Max's hospital bracelet. The appointment slip you saw on the refrigerator." She envisioned the page taking shape. "I'll stamp it with a stethoscope symbol maybe, and perhaps tack down the info with Band-Aids on the corners."

"And your book about Kevin?"

"You keep mentioning that." She pushed down feelings of disloyalty. It wasn't as if she was cheating on Kevin by sitting here with Hank. "I would rather not talk about him today."

"Why not?"

She leaned forward, grabbed his wrist and inched away. "Because it makes me uncomfortable to discuss him when you have your arm around my shoulders."

"Oh, really?" He gestured to the older couple across

from them. "He has his arm around her. Doesn't look like a big deal to me. Just comfort. Unless you're telling me you feel something more than that when we touch."

The air between them crackled with how easily comfort could lead to something far more physical. It was one thing to feel it without acknowledging it. But labeling the attraction for what it was—desire—that scared her. And right now, she didn't have the emotional reserves to play games or snap back with some witty answer that would deflect the issue.

She leaned in closer, lowering her voice so no one else would hear. "Is that what *you* feel when you put your arm around me? The need to comfort?"

"Yes, and more." He tucked a knuckle under her chin. "What about you?"

God, she couldn't lie to him or to herself anymore. "Yes, and more."

His hand slid behind her neck again, and he kissed her. Just lightly, a skim of his mouth over hers in a totally appropriate way for their surroundings. Anyone else would see them as a couple, connected and caring for each other. He rested his forehead against hers and she squeezed her eyes shut, her heart hammering in her ears, blood stinging her veins. She gripped his hard muscled arms and just held on, grateful to have him here. Confused about everything except the fact that she could not tell him to leave. Hank had a way of sliding into her life like a clean-fit piece to a puzzle.

So she simply sat, holding on to him while she said prayers for her child and drew in the steadying scent of this vital man who'd charged into her life again.

The sound of approaching footsteps drew her up sharply.

"Ms. Ballard?" the surgeon in scrubs called, walking toward her.

Her stomach clenched, and she instinctively reached for Hank's hand. He linked fingers with her without hesitation.

"Yes, Doctor Milward?"

"Your son came through the operation without any complications...."

The surgeon continued speaking, but the words blurred in the pool of relief flooding her. She sagged back and Hank's arm was right there to brace her, a solid wall of support, just like the man. But for how long?

Now that her child's surgery was successfully completed, so was Hank's role as stand-in dad.

For the past two days, he'd worked his tail off to be a stand-up guy for Gabrielle while Max recovered in the hospital. He'd brought her favorite local muffuletta sandwiches and changes of clothes. She'd slept in a chair by her son's bed—and he used the term *sleep* lightly. The circles under Gabrielle's eyes had deepened.

His plans to lighten her load needed to step up a notch before she collapsed.

At least now that Max had been discharged, she hadn't argued about coming back to the Garden District house with him. He stood in the doorway to the nursery, watching her swap out Max's diaper and put on a fresh onesie— Yeah, he knew the word *onesie* now, something he hadn't picked up from his nieces and nephews.

He took in the way her green cotton dress swirled around her legs as she moved, the glide of her silky blond hair as she leaned over the changing table to coo nonsensical phrases to her son. The joy on her face almost managed to chase away those lines of exhaustion. Regardless, right now, the glow of love and happiness radiating off her damn near blinded him. She was beyond beautiful. She was… He didn't even know the words or the label.

Not surprising. She'd turned his world upside down all over again.

The brief kiss they'd shared at the hospital had shifted something between them—actually, he would say the change started the night before Max's surgery when he'd held her until daylight. There was an acceptance of each other's presence, an ease to the way they spoke. More than one person at the hospital had mistaken them for a couple. And he knew before much longer he was going to have to think about that.

For now, though, he was focused on making sure *she* didn't end up in the hospital. Thinking of anything beyond that would place him firmly in jackass territory.

He rapped his knuckles lightly on the open nursery door. "Hello, gorgeous."

She looked up and smiled self-consciously, lifting her son to her shoulder and patting his back. "You mean, 'Hello, haggard.' But I'm cool with that. It's all worth it now that Max is home."

Home? He didn't even consider correcting her. "I've got supper downstairs. There's a porta-crib set up so you can keep him close. Unless you would rather just call it a day. I can bring something up to you."

"You've already done more than enough for me. I'm going to get spoiled."

"My sisters say all new moms deserve pampering."

Her smile faded. "Hank, I'm truly grateful, but you don't have to do all of this for me because of Kevin."

"What if this isn't about Kevin?"

She didn't move, barely blinked, her eyes locked with

his. His words hung there between them, linking them as surely as if he'd taken her hand. Or more.

"Uhm—" she chewed her bottom lip for a second "—you mentioned something about supper."

While she'd neatly avoided the topic, he took it as a victory of sorts that she didn't argue.

"Right, I did." He shoved away from the door frame. "Follow me."

He led her down the lengthy staircase, through the library and opened the double French doors out to the lanai. Live music from a party next door drifted along the evening breeze. A Cajun band played as the neighbor apparently sought to stretch Mardi Gras out even longer.

"I set up Max's porta-crib here in the corner. If we leave the doors open, you can see him from the table." He extended his hands. "Pass him to me, and I'll put him down."

She froze. What a time to realize he'd never held the kid. Surely he must have? At some point in the hospital, in passing? But the more he searched his memory, the more he realized, nope, he hadn't. Was it because she hadn't offered or because he'd never asked?

Slowly, she eased Max from her shoulder and placed him in Hank's outstretched hands. Holy crap, the kid was tiny and so damn fragile. He'd always thought his siblings were nuts when they pointed out how their newest offspring had somebody's nose or smile. But right now, he could see his friend in Max's eyes.

Hank put the boy into his crib, careful to position him just like Gabrielle did, but needing some distance from those familiar eyes.

Gabrielle tipped her head to the side. "Everything okay?"

"Sure," he said past the lump in his throat. "Let's step outside to eat."

The table for two had been set with flowers and a candle in a hurricane globe. A cart held their supper and dessert.

She lifted the silver lids on the chafing dishes one at a time, sniffing and sighing at the savory gumbo, crab cakes, all warmed by a flame underneath.

Pulling a chair out for her, he waited for her to sit. "I had the chef go light on the spices. These are things you've ordered in the past, so I figured it was a safe bet. There's a backup in the refrigerator, though."

"Another muffuletta?" Her eyes twinkled at just the mention of the super large, round sandwich with salami, mozzarella and olives.

"In a heartbeat, if you wish."

She paused by the chair, her head tipped into the wind. "Actually, you know what I would really like?"

"Name it." He would find it, buy it, build it, whatever necessary.

"Could we dance?" She swayed to the slower beat of a Cajun fiddle solo. "The music is amazing. It seems a crime not to make the most of it."

To hell with supper. He opened his arms. She stepped into his embrace, her hand fitting into his. His palm molded to the small of her back and with each step around the lanai, she relaxed closer and closer. Under his touch, the tension eased from her body. She hummed along softly with the tune, the vibration of her voice sweet against his fingertips.

She took such pleasure from such a simple thing— a dance and someone else's music. He wished he could shower her with more than just nice meals and a shoulder to lean on. The way she worked so hard, building a world for her son out of thrift store finds and scraps of memories pasted into books—well, it damn near broke his heart. He considered himself a practical man, but right now, he was feeling anything but sensible. She deserved spa days to recharge, a home like this.

A man in her life to help shoulder the load.

Next door, couples danced, friends partied at the catered event. A corner of the other lawn was open to view. Sprawling oak trees were lit up with twinkling lights. Sure the party was raucous, but not a huge gala. Rather, family and friends had gathered—much like the sort of thing his dad had said they wanted to throw for him, the sort of shindig he usually avoided.

And now?

He definitely didn't want his family around questioning what was going on here with Gabrielle. He wouldn't even know how to answer other than to say that he wanted her and couldn't walk away. But it wasn't as if they were actually dating. There was so much mixed up here to be sorted out. She'd loved Kevin. And yeah, he couldn't stop the sting of guilt from being here in place of his friend.

Her fingers circled along the back of his neck. "Thank you for this, for the past few days, as well. You truly made this so much easier for me than I could have imagined."

"That's what I'm here for." Being a stand-in for Kevin, even when it sliced him raw, because right now, he wanted to know that Gabrielle saw *him,* not a replacement for the man she mourned.

"I probably should have accepted my parents' offer of help. I really do love my mom, but she takes over rather than helping, and since everything's a battle, I end up even more exhausted."

"I get what you mean." His feet moved in perfect sync

with hers, his thoughts, too. "My dad casts a helluva large shadow."

She leaned back to look into his eyes, the wind lifting her hair. "So why did you choose to go into the same branch of the service, even the same aircraft he flew?"

"It's what I want to do. Call it genetics, if you will, but it's what I'm good at." He couldn't imagine doing anything else with his life. "Seems ridiculous to pick something that's not my first choice simply to go a different path."

"I can see that."

He rested his chin on the top of her head, breathing in the scent of lavender and pure Gabrielle. "Although, I gotta confess, it would have made life easier."

"Kevin told me you work twice as hard as everyone else trying to prove you didn't get anything because of nepotism—when it's clear to everyone you're a freakin' rock star at your job."

"A rock star, huh?" He could almost hear his friend's voice through her and, God, he missed Kevin.

"He said some folks knew the science of aviation and navigation, but you knew the art."

"His opinion means a lot to me. Thanks for sharing that."

Was Hank ever going to get past the way their lives linked up? Be able to look at Gabrielle without thinking of Kevin? Sure his buddy had been a lighthearted guy, but there'd been no missing how much he'd loved Gabrielle. He'd taken his commitment to her seriously.

Not that any relationship was perfect.

One night, Kevin had gotten drunk and rambled about how much he loved Gabrielle but worried about being the kind of man who could make her happy. He didn't want to lose her, but she wanted roots and a home.

What a kick in the butt to remember that right now since Hank didn't have anything different to offer her on that front. "Kevin really loved you."

She stiffened in Hank's arms, each breath warm against his neck as she continued to silently follow his dance lead.

"I was with him when he bought the ring." A day that had damn near ripped his soul out. He clasped her left hand and brought it between them, her ring finger bare. "He called your mom to get your size and some direction on what you wanted."

Her heart beat faster against their clasped hands. "I wore it on my right hand for a while after he died. I had to take it off at the hospital when Max was born, and I haven't put it on since. I've stored the ring for Max to give his wife one day."

"I'm sure Kevin would like that." He actually hadn't agreed with the ring Kevin and her mom had chosen. He would have picked something simpler, more in keeping with her streamlined style. But she'd seemed happy and that's what mattered.

"You really were a great friend to him. You still are."

"Other than making out with his fiancée."

She stopped dancing and took his face in her hands. "I'm the one that kissed you. I'm the one who deserves the blame."

"You really think you started that?" He gripped her wrists but couldn't bring himself to lower her arms, her cool touch enticing him even with his conscience chewing him up inside.

"I know I did, because I was eaten up with guilt over being attracted to you." Her fingers unfurled, and she swayed toward him. "Not just that one day, but weeks prior to that."

"Weeks?" He brought her closer.

"It wasn't some massive event that changed things. Just one evening we were on a riverboat dinner cruise and you were standing by the rail." She leaned into him, her eyes glimmering with tears and confusion. "Something just shifted inside me, something scary. But Kevin was so close to deploying. How could I tell him then? He and I wouldn't have had time to sort through anything before he left. I wasn't even sure what I felt for you. Then that day I fought with Kevin, cried in your arms…"

"You only acted on something I'd been feeling from the first day I met you. Once you kissed me, believe me, I was one-hundred-percent all in."

Her eyes went wide with surprise—and an answering hunger. Unable to resist her now any more than he'd been able to then, he dipped his head. He kissed her. He had to. Since he'd come back to New Orleans, they'd been shadow boxing with this moment. But here, tonight, under the stars, he wanted her, and he could feel that she wanted him too from the way she wriggled to get closer. He couldn't sense even the least bit of hesitation in her response.

She looped her arms around his neck and pulled him closer, a perfect fit just like a year ago. Her lips parted, and he didn't need any further invitation to take the kiss deeper. He cupped her bottom and lifted her more securely against him until her toes left the ground.

Pivoting, he backed her against an ancient oak. Her fingers roved restlessly into his hair. The press of her body against his had him hard and throbbing in a flash. Her soft breasts against his chest made him ache to peel away their clothes.

Now that he had her against him again, the taste of her fresh on his tongue, he had to savor the moment for an extra stroke longer. With each pounding of his heart against his ribs, he knew he couldn't let her walk away again without taking this to completion. Ignoring the attraction hadn't worked, in fact, it had only increased the urgent need to explore every inch of her body with his eyes, his hands, his mouth.

A cry mingled with the music, bringing him up short.

Max.

The infant's hungry wails grew louder.

Gabrielle froze in Hank's arms, then stepped away sharply. Her hands shook as she swept her hair back and rushed past him through the open French doors. He sagged back against a hundred-year-old oak and felt just about as ancient, the weight of what he'd almost done bearing down on his shoulders.

He couldn't—shouldn't—finish this, not tonight, not now when she was nearly dead on her feet with exhaustion. Her son had just gotten home from the hospital. She was feeling vulnerable. Only a selfish bastard would take what she offered and to hell with his conscience. She needed sleep—and they both needed to find a way to put Kevin's ghost to rest.

Because regardless of whether or not she wore that three-carat ring or not, Kevin's memory still stood firmly between them.

As the grandfather clock in the hall chimed midnight, Gabrielle stared at the blurry words on her computer screen, her foot lightly rocking her son's infant seat. The band still played next door, the neighbors' party going on into the night.

She wished she could blame her lack of focus on exhaustion, but she couldn't lie to herself, not tonight. While she should be catching up on work, her mind was too full of dancing with Hank.

Then he'd kissed her.

His mouth on hers, his hands on her body had felt every bit as earth-shattering as she'd remembered. So much so she'd almost forgotten about her son sleeping a few feet away. She'd grabbed her child and raced up the stairs, using Max's feeding as an excuse to gather her thoughts and composure.

Okay, hell, truth be told, she was hiding out in her room.

Once she'd fed and changed Max in the nursery, she'd come back to her room to find dinner had been brought to her. Dinner for one with a note from Hank.

See you in the morning.

He'd simply scrawled *H* for a signature, the stroke of the pen heavy and thick. Strong and bold like the man.

And smart. He'd been right to bring her food here and leave. They both needed space. So much was happening in such a short time.

Still, the meal had tasted bittersweet, each bite reminding her of how special the evening had started off. Dancing with him under the moonlight with live music lent a timeless air to the night. They could have been any couple, even centuries ago. Surely being any other couple would have made things less complicated.

Max's cry then reminded her of her responsibilities. She couldn't afford to forget them for a second. Rather than go to sleep after feeding her son, she'd parked her butt with her laptop computer to catch up on work she'd let slide while he was in the hospital.

The sooner she finished, the sooner she could sleep, and she would need a clear head to think through how she wanted to approach Hank in the morning.

Forcing her bleary eyes to focus, she clicked through the rest of her backlog of emails, then closed her computer. She glanced at her watch. One in the morning. With the time change, her mother should be waking up now.

Gabrielle shifted Max from his infant seat to his crib in the nursery so her conversation wouldn't wake him up. Still, she left the connecting door open so she could be sure to hear him.

Collapsing back into the pile of pillows and bolsters, she grabbed her cell phone off the bedside table and thumbed her parents' number. The billowy soft bed, the jazz music and the scent of Hank clinging to her dress stirred her already hyperaware senses.

The ringing on the other end stopped as her mother finally picked up.

Gabrielle clutched the phone tighter and rolled onto her side, staring out the window at the twinkling lights on the trees next door. "Hey, Mama, it's me."

"Is everything all right with Max? With you?" her mother asked in a panicked voice.

"Don't worry. Everything's fine." Empathy tugged at her heart. While she swore she wouldn't be as overpowering as her mom, she was starting to understand how easy it would be to let those parental fears take control. "I'm only calling to let you know Max is home from the hospital."

"Your apartment is fixed already?" The sounds of her cooking breakfast echoed in the background, clanking pots and water running, familiar sounds of home. "How perfect that could be taken care of while you were with Max."

"Uh, actually, I am staying with a friend."

"In New Orleans? Do I know this friend?"

"Him. Hank," she blurted out, even though telling her

mother was probably a totally stupid idea. And saying his name, admitting they were staying together, lent an importance to the relationship she wasn't sure if she could wrap her thoughts around just yet. "He's a friend of Kevin's. A friend of mine."

"Do I know this friend? This *man?*"

"Kevin's friend."

"Hank? As in Hank Renshaw, Jr.?" Most mothers would have been turning cartwheels over their daughter hanging out with one of America's most eligible bachelors, but there was no missing the censure in her mom's tone. "Gabrielle, are you sure now's the right time to get involved with anyone?"

Like she really had a choice? She couldn't ignore the truth now the way she had a year ago. Her attraction to Hank went way beyond friendship.

"Mama, I understand you're just worried, but I'm an adult, perfectly capable of handling my own life." She spoke quickly so her mother wouldn't be able to wedge a word in edgewise. "I love you, truly I do, but I need to hang up now and get some sleep. Give my love to Daddy and everyone else. Okay? Goodbye."

Gabrielle ended the call and tossed aside the phone, gnawing her lip. In less than two weeks Hank would report back to Barksdale Air Force Base. He would be hours away, and she would be back in her apartment. No. She needed to accept her life had changed. She couldn't live in this holding pattern. She would have to find a different, more kid-friendly place to live. And in order to do that on her limited budget, she would have to move outside the city limits. Time to shift out of the holding pattern she'd been living in.

Those changes included more than just her living situation. She needed to stop avoiding her attraction to Hank.

Starting first thing tomorrow, she would confront Hank.
No more pretending. No more avoiding.

She and Hank were meant to be lovers.

Seven

She ached to have him. Her flesh was on fire from months, years of wanting Hank.

And here in her dream world she could have him.

They could make love under a sprawling oak tree with twinkling lights that echoed the sparks of desire crackling through her. She could almost feel the silky inside of his leather jacket, spread on the ground beneath her. She could stroke and savor the hard planes of his chest as he loomed over her, thrusting into her, filling her, taking her so close to the edge of completion.

Her body burned for the fulfillment only he could offer. She moaned her need for him to take her the rest of the way there, not to leave her hungry, hurting, wanting....

Gabrielle bolted upright in bed, the scent of leather still lingering from her dream. Her dream that had been cut short before she'd reached satisfaction.

Blinking fast against the bright morning sun streaking through the window, she struggled to orient herself. She was alone in her bed, covers tangled around her legs. She kicked free of the sheets and her erotic images of Hank.

Or at least she tried to. The unfulfilled ache still lingered between her legs, echoing the near painful tingling in her breasts.

Her full and tender breasts.

Oh, God.

She pressed her hands to her chest and realized…it was morning, and she still wore her dress from yesterday. She'd fallen asleep just after hanging up with her mom. She hadn't fed Max since just before midnight.

Her son hadn't woken up.

Panicked, she shot from the bed and almost fell on her face tripping over the trailing comforter. Her heart lodged in her throat, fear threatening to strangle her. She raced across the room, past her damn computer that had kept her up so late. Had her son cried for her and she didn't hear him because of her exhaustion? Guilt tore at her. She ripped open the connecting door to the nursery, wondering how it could have drifted closed in the night without her hearing.

Her eyes homed in on the crib, the empty crib. A cry strangled in her throat. She looked around frantically until her gaze hitched on the corner rocking chair.

Her son was being held by…Leonie Lanier?

Max's babysitter—their neighbor from above the antiques shop—was here? And there were four empty bottles sitting beside the rocker, so she must have been feeding him the expressed milk Gabrielle had frozen and stored before the surgery. Gabrielle could hardly wrap her mind around what must have happened in the night.

She could only embrace the relief that her son was okay. She reached for Max. "Leonie, what are you doing here?"

Standing, her neighbor passed over the baby with a smile. "Helping you get a good night's sleep."

Gabrielle pressed five frantic kisses on her son's forehead. Her weak knees folded, and she sank into the rocking chair. Laying Max on her legs, she unsnapped his onesie and checked his three tiny incisions from the laparoscopic surgery. Her son squirmed in her arms, wide awake and cooing his "good morning" up at her as he pedaled his feet against her stomach.

Everything appeared to be fine, but he was her responsibility. Her son.

The trembling inside her wouldn't stop, months of stress and worry compounding. "That's very generous of you, but I wish someone would have told me. How long have you been here?"

Where was Hank? He had to know because only he could have let Leonie into the house. She hitched Max up to her shoulder.

"I arrived around ten last night. That cute Major Renshaw and I swapped off taking care of Max through the night. I've offered a million times, and you were always so stubborn about doing everything yourself." She crossed her legs, one tennis-shoe-clad foot swinging. She wore a track suit and looked surprisingly fresh for someone who'd cared for a baby all night. "Your friend and I decided to surprise you."

"Well, you certainly succeeded." Not in a good way. But she would save that frustration for later when she confronted Hank. That he would have gone behind her back... He'd even closed the door while she slept....

No wonder she'd been smelling his leather jacket. He'd been in her room.

Leonie sat on the daybed tucked against the window. "I really can't take credit for any generosity. Your friend knew the flooding put me out of my home, too—and I've lost my part-time job as long as the shop is closed. He offered me this position until I'm back to work, which is perfect since when I go back you'll be able to go back, too."

Position? "Hank's paying you?"

"Uh-huh. I already know Max's routine and I adore the little guy— Are you upset?"

"Surprised," she said tightly, patting Max on his back as he squirmed.

"Oh, my goodness, if I've overstepped, sweetie, let me know." Leonie's hazel eyes filled with concern. "It seemed like the perfect solution to all our problems and a great surprise for you."

"Of course it is. You haven't done anything wrong." Well, other than not speaking to her first, but chewing out Leonie wouldn't accomplish anything. Chewing out Hank, on the other hand, would make Gabrielle feel much better.... "Thank you for your help. You're one of the few people I feel comfortable with watching Max."

Max wriggled, his fingers getting tangled in her hair as he started to whimper with his "feed me" sounds.

"You do look better, more rested." She cupped Gabrielle's cheek. "That's a very good thing, even if you are still too tense. You're no help to Max if you wear yourself down until you're sick."

"You had the night shift, so how about I take him for a while? I need to nurse him." She worked free the front buttons on her dress and her son latched on, tiny fists flailing, then finally settling as he calmed. She stroked his impossibly soft cheek with one knuckle, love and protectiveness flooding fiercely through her. "Actually, I need to hold him. I'm sure it will take a while for the worry to fade."

"You're a mama now." Leonie winked on her way out the door. "You're never going to stop worrying."

Gabrielle sagged back in the chair, rocking faster, frustrated with herself as much as with Hank. Sometime last night she'd allowed herself to get complacent, to take all the help Hank had offered. She'd lowered her boundaries, and while his intentions may have been good, he'd steamrolled right over her. Hiring a sitter for her son without consulting her? Taking her son so she wouldn't hear him wake up?

She'd been delusional thinking she could just jump into an affair with Hank. Her life wasn't that simple. She had concerns and responsibilities beyond what she could have imagined a year ago.

Hank may not have changed, but she had.

Hank leaned back in the chair on the lanai, thumbs flying over the game on his phone. The late-morning sun beat down on his head. The clean-up crew next door clanked trash cans. Hopefully, they weren't waking Gabrielle. As hard as she'd been working the past months, he couldn't imagine how much sleep would be enough.

If she didn't catch up on her rest soon, she would snap. He'd heard the same advice in those end-of-deployment briefings they all got at the end of each tour. Decompress. Take time off. Play.

His thumbs flew faster over the video game, and he wondered why the kink in his neck didn't ease even when he hit the eighth level. If anything, the longer he spent away from base, the itchier he got. Which likely had more to do with the woman sleeping upstairs than any need to decompress.

The French doors swung open sharply. His chair slammed to the ground. He tossed his phone on the table just as Gabrielle charged through.

God, she was gorgeous and tousled.

And mad?

"A nanny?" She stopped short in front of him. "You hired a *nanny* for my son?"

Standing, he clasped her shoulders and resisted the urge to just kiss away her bad mood. "I thought you could use some sleep. I was being thoughtful, being a good... friend."

"Well, I'm being a mother, doing what a mother does. I'm taking care of my child." She swept a hand around her, gesturing to the historic home and gardens. "The house, the furniture, that's generous, thoughtful beyond belief, and I appreciate that you're trying to help. But you do *not* have the right to choose childcare for my son."

What the hell? He'd thought she would be turning back flips over a good night's sleep. "Is Max okay? Did something happen?"

"He's fine," she said tightly.

"Leonie Lanier is your regular babysitter. You've already chosen and approved her. I tossed some extra money at the situation." It's not like he would even miss the cash. "Consider it a baby gift since I wasn't here when he was born. So what's the problem?"

She ground her teeth, her fists clenched at her side. "You didn't ask me first."

"You're pissed at me?" He scrubbed a hand behind his neck.

"*Yes,* I'm angry."

His gift was definitely backfiring here. "Because I wanted to help you?"

"Because you made arrangements for my son—" she jabbed him in the chest with each phrase "—an infant, who just got out of the hospital, without discussing it with me first. You're overstepping. I'm perfectly capable—"

"—of taking care of yourself." He grabbed her wrist. "Yeah, I know. You've told me. Repeatedly."

She jerked her hand free and folded her arms under her breasts. "I meant I'm capable of asking for what I need."

"Doesn't appear that way to me," he snapped back, finding out he was pissed, too. He was working his ass off to help her, and she was giving him hell.

"Just because I didn't go running home to my family doesn't mean I can't accept help—the right kind of help." She shook her head. "And you're one to talk about reaching out to others, living your solitary life, dodging your family's calls. Why is it okay for you to be the only one who needs independence?"

"Whoa, whoa, whoa, let's dial this down a notch." When did this become about him? The last thing he wanted was anyone poking around inside his head or his life. "I'm trying to help. So I screwed up and didn't get it right. I'm trying."

She looked skyward, dragging in ragged breaths for thirty seconds before leveling a steely, strong gaze at him. "You may say it's not about Kevin, but I'm not so sure. Even you said on the first day back you're trying to be a stand-in dad. I get that. But it's not that simple." She held up a hand, backing away. "I've changed since last year. My life and my priorities have changed. Last night you were kissing the old Gabrielle. You don't even know the woman I am now."

Spinning away, she ran back into the house, leaving him floored.

And crazy turned on by the vibrant woman he was finding it tougher and tougher to remember had ever been engaged to his best friend.

How had she gone from totally turned on by Hank to totally furious with him in such a short time?

Gabrielle closed her computer for the workday and flopped back in the chair. Concentrating on business web designs—on anything—had been difficult with this morning's argument churning through her mind. She'd already been riding an emotional roller coaster since she lost Kevin, but now that Hank had come to town, it felt like she was stuck in a frightening loop without time for her stomach to settle.

Guilt pinched her over how she'd lost her temper with Hank. She still felt he'd gone too far in arranging care for her son without consulting her, but she wished she'd been calmer in relaying her point. He'd just hit such a sore spot with her, given the way her mom had micro-managed her life for so many years. She'd had to move an entire ocean away just to go to college without her mother checking in with her professors.

Although she had to confess, having the extra help from Leonie had been a real godsend today. She'd only asked Leonie to watch over Max while he slept, but just knowing she didn't need to keep her ears on alert, and having Leonie bring Max to her when he woke, had given Gabrielle longer stretches to catch up on business and school. She was actually—finally—back on schedule again.

Hank had steered clear of her all day, as well. Not that she could blame him. She'd seen his SUV leave shortly after their argument. Of course, he didn't have to check in with her. Still, she wondered where he'd gone. Had she actually scared him off for good? She couldn't fathom that he would just leave without saying goodbye, not matter how loudly she yelled. He wasn't that kind of man.

Which led her to the question, what kind of man was Hank Renshaw, Jr.? Besides her former fiancé's best friend. Beyond the pedigree. Beneath the uniform.

He was a good man who was trying hard to help her and her son when they weren't his responsibility. He was using his time off after a war deployment to hold her hand during her son's surgery. He was looking for ways to make her life easier, and sure, he'd bypassed her on the decision making, but she shouldn't expect him to understand parenting when he'd never been a parent.

Now that her temper had cooled, she had to admit she owed him an apology.

She shoved her chair away from the makeshift office she'd set up in her bedroom and crossed to the open nursery door. "Leonie?"

Her older neighbor—a treasured friend—looked up from her tabloid magazine as she sat curled in the daybed built into the window seat. "Yes, dear?" She set aside her gossip rag and a plate with a half-eaten sandwich. "What can I do for you and please don't say 'nothing.' I've barely done anything all day, and I'm going to feel guilty taking that generous paycheck your hot major is offering me."

"How generous?" she asked, wondering how in the world she would repay him.

"Sinfully generous, dear, and he was a total doll about the offer. Said he was doing his bit to help the economy."

Gabrielle rolled her eyes, turning away and checking on her son asleep in his bed. Seeing him sleep so peacefully, so much more content as he kept his food down better these days, warmed her soul. She had so much to be thankful for and instead she'd been stomping her foot and pitching a fit.

Leonie cleared her throat. "He drove back in about an hour ago."

Gabrielle didn't bother asking who Leonie meant. "I didn't see that."

"Ah, so you were watching out the window." She padded softly across the room and stopped by Gabrielle, covering her hand on the crib railing. "Go enjoy the rest of the evening. I have this. Really. I slept most of the day away and what little time I was awake, I was thoroughly enjoying this amazing home."

"Thank you, Leonie."

"For what?"

"For loving my son."

The older woman patted Gabrielle's cheek. "I love you, too. Now go play. Enjoy being young."

"Thanks again." Gabrielle pressed a quick kiss to her son's forehead and turned toward the hall door.

"Gabrielle, sweetie? Freshen up."

She looked down at her wrinkled T-shirt and torn jeans, coffee stains dotting them. It would be fun to dress up, to have time to do more than scrape back her hair in a hair tie. Smiling, she raced toward the connecting door back into her room and yanked open her small suitcase. Not much to pick from, but clean beat coffee-stained any day of the week.

Fifteen minutes later, she felt more like her old self in a black mini dress with red leggings, her hair loose around her shoulders. Each teasing brush along her neck reminded her of her dreams of Hank.

Was she apologizing so she could have those fantasies back and maybe bring them to life? Possibly. She wasn't sure. But she did know that for the first time in a year, she was truly…hopeful.

Her fingers trailed down the polished mahogany banister as she made her way downstairs, the sound of banging pots in the kitchen drawing her feet toward the back of the house. Standing at the six-burner gas cooktop built into the island, Hank lifted lids and stirred, three different pots going at once. A white apron splattered with red sauce looked delightfully incongruous on his hulking body. A lacy little hand towel was draped over his shoulder. An arm's reach away, he snuck bites from a serving tray with fat strawberries, soft white cheese and crostinis. Savory scents of something Italian filled the air until she salivated for everything in the room, the food and the man.

Tasting some kind of red sauce, Hank looked over the spoon at her. "Before you lose your cool, I'm cooking for me, not for you."

"Oh, really?"

"Yep, wouldn't want you to think I'm steamrolling you or anything." He dropped the spoon into the porcelain sink.

"You can call off the guards. I come in peace." She leaned against the door frame, and yeah, she relished every second of the way his eyes were drawn to her legs. The tingle of feminine power felt good, really good.

But first things first.

"Hank, I'm sorry for yelling at you earlier. I stand by what I said, but not the way I said it."

"Fair enough." He placed the lids back on the simmering pots of whatever aromatic magnificence they held. "And I apologize for not consulting you."

"You were right that I would have turned you down," she conceded with a grace he deserved.

He tugged the little towel from his shoulder and dried his hands, the island still looming between them. "And you were right. Perhaps springing the surprise on you during Max's first night home from the hospital wasn't the best timing."

"You're forgiven."

Something unsettling flickered in his cobalt-blue eyes, so fast there and gone it barely registered. "I take that to mean you're not packing."

"Staying here is best for Max." And was it best for her? It certainly shook her from her safe little routine.

Could she indulge in a no-strings affair with Hank? To hell with how different her life was now. What did it matter if this was just short-term? Even considering it made her tingle all over with the possibilities, what to-night might hold.

She shoved away from the door frame and crossed to the granite-topped island. "I'll admit, I'm frustrated that I can't give him everything he needs, but I recognize that a hotel and a worn-out mom may not be in his best inter-est."

He tossed the wadded towel from hand to hand. "Does that mean Leonie can stay, as well?"

"She needs the money." She circled around to him.

"And you need the help?"

"Don't push your luck." She snatched the hand towel from him in midair and snapped his hip.

He stepped closer, the air simmering between them as tangibly as the food in those pots. "I certainly don't want to blow my chances of getting lucky."

Her mouth fell open in shock. Before she could close it, Hank popped a plump strawberry between her lips. As she bit down, the explosion of flavor on her already heightened senses made her a strawberry fan for life. Life felt sharper, crisper—better—with Hank around.

She shifted her attention to the platter to give herself time to pull her thoughts together. "I'm guessing this is supper?"

"A late one, yes."

The way he said those last words felt layered somehow with a deeper meaning. But then, maybe she was searching for things she wanted to be true. "I'm here, and starving. I'm glad you waited."

Hank watched Gabrielle across the table from him, their lanai dinners becoming a habit. A very pleasurable habit. He'd spent the afternoon pulling this together for her, hoping to make up for their fight. Lights hung from the trees, like the party next door from last night. He'd cued up music, classical, like the concerts he remembered Kevin talk about attending with her and how he'd sworn his ears were bleeding by intermission.

Hank's smile faded as he looked across the table.

She was right about how it always seemed to come back to the three of them. Tonight, he needed to make this memory about just the two of them, damn it. If he couldn't do that, then he needed to walk away clean rather than tormenting them both.

He was still grateful as hell she'd forgiven him and agreed to eat supper. She'd even seemed to genuinely enjoy his homemade tomato basil sauce. His repertoire of meals wasn't that huge, but since spending a ton of money on help for her hadn't gone so well for him, he decided to opt for something more personal. She'd grown up in a family of more modest means, so he figured he might gain more traction in showing her how he'd come from a more down-to-earth family than their current media status would indicate.

She swirled her spoon through the dessert, a simple bowl of lemon sorbet. Baking a dessert stretched beyond his cooking talents.

"More?" he asked.

Groaning, she set her spoon aside. "I'm stuffed. Really. You went above and beyond, and you're making me feel guilty."

"You've been so focused on Max—and I can understand why—it seemed to me that you could use some extra TLC, as well."

"Well, you've certainly put together an amazing evening." She toyed with the hurricane globe in the middle of the table. "Who knew you're such a great cook and entertainer?"

"My sisters and I took turns setting the table. As for the minimal decorations—" he tapped the globe, with beads and a couple of Mardi Gras masks beside it "—blew over into the yard from the neighbor's party last night."

"Who would have thought a millionaire could be so thrifty."

It was billionaire, actually, but pointing that out was more likely to send her running rather than draw her in. Knowing that about her, actually drew *him* in. "My family didn't start out with all this. My dad was a regular guy, serving in the military. He earned his way through the ranks."

"You must be very proud of him."

Her comment startled him. People so often asked what his old man thought of him. Nobody turned that question around. "I am, actually. He's an amazing guy. When he was a squadron commander in Guam—"

"Guam? You lived in Guam?"

"Awesome place, like Hawaii but without a crazy crush of tourists." He preferred to remember it that way, not to think about darker times for his family after his mother died. "I'd like to take you there sometime."

"Sounds like you miss the old days, when things were simpler for your family."

Another insightful comment from the hot chick across the table, the one who totally ignored his comment about taking a trip together. He was flying into dangerous territory here, talking about his past. Lots of painful memories just waiting to shoot him down. But if he wanted to get further with Gabrielle—and he did—then he needed to suit up and soar right in.

"Life was easier before, without question."

"When did it all change?" She toyed with a feathered mask tangled up in purple beads.

He cocked his head to the side. "Are you sure you're not related to Sigmund Freud? You are half German, after all."

She swept up the mask and placed it over her eyes. "I am a woman of mystery."

Her smile sent a bolt of desire straight through him. Even if being with her could only lead to a crash and burn, he wanted her. Bad.

The mask fell away and her smile turned sheepish. "But no, I'm not Freudian, just curious about who you are. You keep so many walls up. I'm only just realizing how much you let Kevin do the talking."

"What do you want to know?"

"When did things change for you, growing up? What made you go from admiring your dad to keeping your distance?"

Pinpointing one specific event was tougher than he

would have thought. "In stages. My mom's death certainly shifted the whole family dynamic. She was a real rock for our family during all those moves. While I say she was a rock, she was actually the most flexible, light-hearted person in the family."

She touched his hand lightly. "What was her name?"

"Jessica. The world thinks of my dad and Ginger as a couple, and honest to God, I don't begrudge them what they've found together." He stared into the flame until the world blurred. "My mom gets lost in the mix. No one remembers her."

"Your parents had a good marriage, then?"

"I don't remember a lot, actually. I remember my mom was the only person I ever saw stand up to my huge father. My oldest sister said they would argue loud enough to rattle the windows, then make up just as fast."

Next thing they knew, his mom was clearing the house of the kids, passing his sister Alicia money to take him and Darcy to the corner mart for soda and a candy bar. *And take your time, kiddos,* his mother had said, winking back at their dad.

God, that seemed like a world ago. Alicia grew up to fly fighter jets. She had earned a Silver Star and Distinguished Flying Cross. Little Darcy flew cargo planes around the world.

"When I was in elementary school, Mom died a couple of weeks after Christmas, a fluky aneurysm. No one could have seen it coming. Some said it was a blessing she didn't know."

"It must have been tough for you, though, not having the chance to say goodbye."

"Sure." Except he'd been there to say goodbye to Kevin and it hadn't made things a damn bit easier.

Hank raked up beads from the table and twisted them

around his fingers like he did when his sister Darcy made him play cat's cradle. He would have done anything for his sister after what she'd been through when they lived in Guam....

"My dad's notoriety wasn't tied into money or being married to Ginger. He gained attention for who he was. We all did." He worked the beads, passing them over his fingers by rote. "When we lived in Guam, my sister Darcy was kidnapped."

Gabrielle set the mask on the table and went completely still, her whole attention focused on him. It seemed even the night bugs went quieter, the traffic on the street fading away.

"An extremist group that wanted the military base gone from the island took her, grabbed her during a squadron family luau." From him. "They kept her for a week. She wasn't assaulted—thank God—but something like that marks a person."

"It marks a family, I imagine."

He let the beads slither from his hands. "I'm not sure why I'm telling you all of this."

"Because I asked." She slid from her chair to kneel in front of him, the feathery mask still clasped in her hand. "I'm wondering why I never asked in the year we knew each other."

He tapped her forehead. "Turn off the analysis, Dr. Freud. There's no hidden meaning here." He slipped the mask from her hand and tucked it in his shirt pocket. "Just facts."

Clasping his wrist, she pulled his hand down, kissed his palm, then pressed it to her cheek. "Facts that explain to me how it could be scary as hell for you to let a woman get too close to y—"

He hauled her up by her elbows and kissed her silent.

It was one thing to fly into the painful midst of his past. It was a whole other matter to have Gabrielle peel away any defenses he had left.

Her lips parted without hesitation, the lingering taste of lemon sorbet on her tongue. He pulled her onto his lap, his hands finally, finally touching her, roving over her back, grazing the side of her lush breasts. He skimmed down her waist and over her hips. He'd waited so long to touch her, he soaked up every detail. The hem of her mini dress bunched in his hands and next thing he knew he was touching bare flesh above the waistline of her leggings.

She thrust her fingers in his hair, pulling him closer, not protesting one damn bit. Heat seared him inside and out. This attraction was no figment of anyone's imagination, no faulty memory. This was real and intense.

And about to become more so.

Eight

Moving from the lanai to Hank's bedroom passed in a blur of kissing, touching and frantic hands exploring as they climbed the steps and sealed themselves away from the world.

The door clicked shut, nestling them in the privacy of his bedroom.

Gabrielle pressed closer to Hank, couldn't get near enough after so long of wanting to touch him, to explore the hard muscled planes of his body. She'd been trying to hold back from this ache for so long, and now she could finally have him. If only for tonight or whatever time he had left in New Orleans, she could finally surrender to the tenacious passion that tugged at them.

Her leg hooked around his, her foot stroking his calf. The scent of oregano and thoughtfulness clung to him. The home-cooked food, the lighted trees and table decorations all put together by him touched her more than any catered meal.

He nuzzled her ear, his breath almost as hot as her tingling flesh. "Are you sure this isn't moving too fast for you?"

She gasped for breath, her pulse throbbing in her chest...and lower. "The way I kissed you last night didn't clue you in?"

"I was hopeful, but there's no timetable here, no rush," he vowed against her hair, stroking her neck, her shoulders, cupping her breasts in hands both bold and gentle at once.

"We've both been waiting a long time for this." Even hinting at the past, at the conflicting feelings of a year ago chilled her, threatening to steal away this beautiful moment. "Let's focus on here and now."

His arms slid around her, steely bands of strength. "I always knew you were a brilliant woman."

She kissed along the bristly texture of his jaw up to his ear. "This whole night has been amazing."

"I hope it's about to get even better." He tunneled up her mini dress, thumbs hooking in the band of her leggings.

A delicious shiver slid over her at the feel of his touch on her bare skin.

"I would say that's a safe guess." Her head fell back, giving him free access to her neck.

His hands cupped new curves, lingering with infinite tenderness and appreciation. He made her feel beautiful and sexy, all the more special in the wake of having been pregnant. She reveled in the feel of his hard thighs pressed to her, his hips tight against hers.

He nudged aside the collar of her dress with his chin and nibbled along her shoulder, sending wisps of pleasure over her skin. "We need to move to the bed or this is going to happen against the door."

"Is the door so wrong?" She tugged his chambray shirt from his khaki waistband and tucked her fingers in to urge him closer.

"Not at all—" he kissed upward until he looked in her eyes again "—except I've waited for you too long to rush."

His voice rumbled with promise. He clasped hands with her and walked backward toward the looming mahogany four-poster bed. The rest of the room came into focus for the first time.

Seeing his sparse room made her realize just how much trouble he'd gone to for her and for Max. The spacious master suite contained only the bed, a massive armoire, since there were no closets in the historic home, and two wingback chairs by the fireplace. The space was as stark as the man, a wealthy frame but Spartan in presentation.

Her legs bumped the back of the mattress. She was really going to do this, steal a night with Hank. Nerves and anticipation mixed into an intoxicating swirl flooding her veins. Her fingers sped down the buttons of his shirt. She whipped the fabric from his shoulders and flung it aside, the feathery mask sailing out of the pocket.

She'd seen him in swim trunks before, but this was so very different, so intimate. She allowed herself the pleasure of just looking at him, taking in the thick column of his neck, his sculpted chest honed from the sun and exercise.

A scar grazed his collarbone.

Frowning, she traced the inch-long pucker of scar tissue. "What happened here?"

"Shrapnel." He dismissed her question, clasping her

hand and kissing her wrist, taking his time along her racing pulse. "Nothing big."

Nothing big? The scar looked deep and close to his jugular vein. An inch over and she would have lost him, too. One heartbeat tripped over another before settling back into a regular rhythm.

Could this have happened when Kevin was killed? The thought threatened to ice her from the inside out.

Hank bracketed her face with his hands. "Stop thinking about it. That's the past. Come back to living in the moment."

His thumbs stroked her cheeks until she hooked her arms around his waist. "Make me forget, Hank, please."

"I can't think of anything I want more." He slanted his mouth over hers again, his mouth warm and familiar now.

His bold, confident hands bunched her dress up— breaking the kiss for only a second—and swept the clothing over her head. His eyes turned blue-flame hot as he nipped his way down her body, between her breasts, further down to peel off her leggings, his mouth following his hands. Kneeling in front of her, he tossed her pants into the growing pile of their clothes.

She hadn't been with anyone since Kevin—since having a baby—and her body was different now. She didn't consider herself shallow or overly vain. But this was her first time with stretch marks and an extra few pounds. Her mouth went dry.

Hank's eyes filled with admiration, grasping her hips with a low growl of approval. "You are even more beautiful than I imagined. And believe me, I have imagined you this way more times that I can count."

His hand stroked up again, holding...

She looked down. He'd picked up the feathered Mardi Gras mask, trailing in a silky teasing path, along her leg, over her hip and higher until he stood in front of her again.

Already gasping in anticipation, she made fast work of his belt, his zipper, until he kicked away his khakis and boxers. She grazed her fingers down the ridged six-pack of his stomach, to his narrow hips, sliding over to encircle his erection, which strained upward against his belly. Slowly, she caressed him, stroked him, working her thumb over the pearly bead on top, slicking her hand. Watching his face, the way he bit his bottom lip, sent a rush straight through her.

His jaw flexed with tension, his eyes sliding closed for two heartbeats before he clasped her wrist and drew her hand away. In a flash, he bracketed her waist and tossed her gently on the bed.

Climbing up the bed, he stretched over her, large and restrained all at once. And in his hand, he still held the Mardi Gras mask. He stroked the feathers along her neck with just the right amount of pressure to tantalize without tickling. Hmm…that felt so unexpected and good.

Her head lolled to the side and thank goodness he got the message to continue along her collar bone, back and forth until goose bumps rose along her skin. He trailed the silky softness between her breasts, circling one then the other, again and again, until she bit her bottom lip to keep from crying out at the tingling pleasure, to keep from begging him for more.

He flicked one taut nipple, then the other. Back and forth, he drew patterns of pleasure along her skin while she murmured a mix of pleas and demands. She gripped his arm, her head pressing back into the pillow.

The feather skimmed along her stomach, then around to the inside of her thighs, so close to teasing where she needed him most. She gasped for air—for release—her pulse thundering in her ears.

His fingers replaced the feathers. Then his mouth. Her hands went to his shoulders, holding him in place. Taking her pleasure. Her mind filled with all the ways she would please him through the night.

The flick of his tongue, the sweet subtlety of his touch drove her higher. Then she couldn't think about anything but the velvet feel of how he gave and gave to her, taking her so close—

But she didn't want to go alone. He'd already done so much for her. She needed them to be partners in this much as least.

"Hank," she gasped, drawing him upward until he stretched over her again. "Now. I want all of you now."

She arched her hips against him, the thick length of him pressing against her. If she moved, adjusted, angled him, she could have him inside her, flesh to flesh—

Oh, God! Her nails dug into his shoulders. "Condoms… How could I have forgotten?"

She wouldn't trade Max for anything in the world, but the pregnancy had been an accident, the product of a night when she and Kevin had too much to drink and got sloppy about using birth control.

"You didn't forget because you just spoke up—" he cupped her face "—and I have that taken care of."

Rolling to his side, he reached to the bedside table and opened a drawer. The box was still sealed, and she realized he'd bought the condoms for this, for *them*.

She angled up on her elbows, watching as he sheathed himself. Anticipation, and more of those nerves pattering through her. So she looped her arms around his neck and drew him to her, needing the forgetfulness she was

damn certain she could find with him. The thick pressure
between her thighs chased away any doubts.

Hooking her legs around his, she urged him on, welcomed him inside her until he was heart deep. Her eyes
squeezed closed to battle back emotional tears because
finally she had him, after so long wondering and wanting,
and the feel of him moving inside her was even more than
she'd anticipated. And yes, even more than she'd feared
because something this special made her rethink the rest
of her life.

Although the last thing she wanted to do right now
was make plans for the future. She wanted to live in the
moment, just the two of them, the scent of her lavender
soap mixing with his aftershave. The special blend of
them clung to the air. She rolled her hips as Hank thrust,
their bodies syncing into a rhythm unique to the two of
them.

The sound of his voice in her ear stoked her along with
the slick glide of their bare bodies against each other. So
close, he took her to the edge again and again, holding
back at the last second until she clawed at his back, desperate for release until—

Wave after wave crested over her, shattering her with
the intensity of bliss restrained for far too long. A cry
rolled up her throat, and he captured the sound with his
mouth—or maybe he was muffling the hoarse shout of
his own release.

His arms folded, and he blanketed her. Aftershocks
trembled through her, through him, as well, binding them
all over again.

Slowly, awareness returned, bit by bit with the cool
gusts of air from a ceiling fan she hadn't even noticed
before. Her hands roved over Hank's body, a precious
weight anchoring her to the bed. Somehow, the mask had

been crushed between them, but she couldn't bring herself to make him move so she could toss it aside.

For now, the masks were off literally and symbolically. No past or future casting shadows.

Right now, she had Hank in her arms, and she held on tight, scared as hell of how badly it would hurt to lose him if she let herself care too much. Having had her heart shattered once, she wasn't sure she had the strength to risk experiencing that pain a second time.

Hank sprawled naked on his bed, working to catch his breath after round two with Gabrielle. She'd proved to be equally as adept in playing with the mask and tormenting the hell out of him.

Then satisfying the hell out of him.

Being with her had been every bit as world-rocking as he'd expected. Now he just had to work to make sure she didn't run scared. Because already he could see doubts and fears chasing through her eyes.

Curled up beside him, which also kept her face averted, she toyed with the feathered mask. "I hadn't pegged you for the playful type, but I like the surprise."

"Glad to hear it." He stroked his knuckles along the small of her back, just above the sweet curve of her bottom.

"You're different here, away from the squadron, more open."

His father's shadow wasn't lurking around each corner ready to ambush him here. "Everyone wears a facade at some point."

"Being bare is a scary thing, being vulnerable." She shivered and he tugged the satin comforter over her.

He tucked the covers around her and pulled her back to his side. "I'm not going to hurt you."

A choked laugh sputtered from her. "No one can promise that. Life hurts."

He knuckled her chin upward until she had to look in his eyes again. "Are you hurting right now?"

She shook her head. "No, of course not. I'm happy and satiated and a little scared, but not sad. Not hurting."

"Good...very good." He dipped his head and kissed her, lingering until she sighed. "Let's see if we can keep you that way. I have a gift for you."

"Another one?" She crinkled her nose. "You're going to have to get your business partner to invent a new game if you keep this up."

"Trust me." He saw the uneasiness in her eyes, the fear that he would give her something totally inappropriate after they'd had sex. She really didn't know him well at all. But he intended to change that.

He padded across the bedroom floor to the mammoth wardrobe and pulled out a gift bag from a French Quarter *parfumeur*. Her eyebrows pinched together curiously as she tucked the Egyptian cotton sheet under her arms. He dropped the bag into the middle of the bed where it landed with a hefty *thump*.

Tugging out red-and-gold tissue paper and tossing it onto the bed, she peered inside the gold foil bag. A slow smile spread across her face....

"Bubble bath!" she squealed, pulling out one bottle, then the next, digging her way through the bag filled with different scents and bathing accessories with obvious joy.

"You'd mentioned hurried showers before now. There are definite perks to having me and a nanny around. You can stay in the tub as long as you like."

She uncorked a small bottle of scented oil and sniffed, moaning in ecstasy. "Heaven."

Chuckling, he passed her a long skinny box. He had

definite ideas for that oil later. "I know this isn't as nice as diamonds, but I figured you would pitch jewels back in my lap anyway."

"You figured right. Besides, bath pearls are more precious than the real kind because this really was thoughtful."

"So why don't you go try it out now?"

"Right now?"

"Sure. The bathroom's right through there."

She rocked forward on her knees and kissed him fast before gathering up her French milled soaps and gels and whatever else chicks called the rest of the stuff. Nearly tripping over the sheet in her excitement, she raced straight for the master bath.

Hank sat in the middle of the bed, leaning back against the headboard and listening to her hum as she filled the tub. As much as he wanted to have her again, he wasn't going to interrupt her first long bath since her son had been born.

How insane was it that he felt every bit as good about sitting here listening to her sing as he had when making love to her? The sound of her voice stroked him just as completely as her hands.

Damn. Gabrielle might be the one in the tub, but he was the one in serious hot water.

Now that he'd had her, there was no way in hell he could let her go.

Gabrielle toed the hot water on again, reheating the tub for the third time.

There had to be a special place in heaven for whoever invented the tankless water heater. This hour-long bath soaked stress from parts of her body she hadn't even realized were kinked. Tension slipped from her every time she opened the drain.

Although she couldn't give all the credit to the spa bath. Lavender perfume hung in the humid air, Hank's thoughtful gifts soothing her soul and tugging her heart all at once. The man could have bought her jewels, which she wouldn't have accepted. Or chocolates, which she couldn't eat because of nursing Max.

Instead, Hank had paid attention to her needs, to the scent she wore.

She sank deeper into the tub big enough for two and soaked in the mellow tan and butter cream-colored decor around her. Maybe she would finish off with a shower, another pure spa delight with jets lining the corners to spray from all angles.

There was even a flat-screen television mounted high in a corner if she wanted to lean back, hide out and watch a movie.

This place was mama nirvana. She'd never considered herself a materialistic person, but she wouldn't mind having this all to herself at the end of each day.

With Hank waiting for her in the bedroom?

She couldn't ignore that they'd taken a huge step tonight. As much as she wanted to tell herself it was only a fling, she wasn't an affair kind of person. She was still the same person she'd been from the start—the girl who'd lived to be a mother, to have her own happily ever after with the best dressed, most well fed, happiest babies on the block.

Which brought her right back to those fears that had iced her after making love to Hank.

Her last romantic relationship hadn't gone all that great, even before Kevin died. That last fight with him kept whispering through her mind, how he'd wanted her to move near him and she'd resisted.

Was she crazy to be thinking of the future now? If anything, Hank was more tied to the military lifestyle than Kevin had been. As if their shared past with Kevin didn't already make things complicated enough.

She toed the hot water off. There wasn't a heater big enough to chase away the chill settling into her bones.

Listening to Gabrielle take a bath had been pure torture. But as much as he wanted to slide into the water with her and make love to every inch of her body, he was determined to let her have her quiet time alone, soaking.

Pivoting away from temptation, he pulled on sweat pants, left his room and headed for hers. He could check on Max, give Leonie a break if she was awake. Seemed as if the entire household had an upside down sleeping schedule, their lives wrapped up in making sure Max was okay.

As it should be.

He stepped into her room, scanning for where she'd left the nursery monitor. Leonie's voice crooned from the next room as she sang some old nursery rhyme. A memory flashed of his mom singing off-key while she decorated the tree, his dad hooking an arm around her waist and vowing his ears were bleeding from the sound.

Both of them laughing together.

Everyone told him she'd been a great mom and from the videos he'd seen, they were right. His dad hadn't talked about her much over the years, just saying she'd been a real wonder woman, parenting alone most of the time since the military lifestyle kept him away.

Hank trailed a finger along the edge of Gabrielle's makeshift workstation. She'd set up her laptop on the sofa

table behind the love seat and pulled a chair from the hall
to set up a mini-office. For her website work? Or school?
Or both while she took care of her son? She carried the
load of three women. He dropped into the seat and wished
somehow he could absorb some of the burden for her.

His eyes landed on two scrapbooks resting on a stack
of her textbooks. He pulled the album off the top and
thumbed it open.

Kevin's face stared back at him like a sucker punch
from the grave.

Hank studied the photo of Kevin with Gabrielle at the
squadron Christmas ball, a red rosebud pressed to the
corner of the image like a splash of blood. The staged
portrait didn't tell him much other than that it commemo-
rated an event. He flipped the page and found a photo of
the three of them at a Shreveport Captains baseball game.
Gabrielle wore a jersey and cap, her blond ponytail lifted
by the wind. Kevin had his arm hooked around her shoulders. They appeared happy. Really happy.

He looked at himself…and crap.

No wonder Kevin knew how he felt about Gabrielle.
One look at this picture would have told an idiot that
Hank had a thing for her. His eyes were glued to her like
a starving guy on food after a hunger strike.

Yet Gabrielle hadn't picked up on it. She'd seemed
stunned when he'd kissed her a year ago. Or she'd kissed
him, as she kept insisting. Once they started, it had been
mutual.

Would he ever get over feeling guilty? Even now, the
weight of it bored into him like eyes watching him from
the grave.

He glanced up fast. Gabrielle stood in the open doorway wearing a simple satin robe. The fabric clung to
her damp body in places, her face still flushed from the

steamy heat. Her hair was piled up on her head, wisps trailing down and sticking to her neck. Just the sight of her had him wanting her again. His hand fisted on top of the photo.

She walked deeper into the room and sat on the love seat, resting her chin on her arms and staring at him over the sofa back. "I thought you might come join me in the tub."

"I thought the bath was about you having time to yourself. If I joined you, doesn't that negate the whole alone-time point?"

"That's actually a very intuitive thought."

"For a guy, you mean?" He faked a smile. "Hey, call me Joe Sensitive."

"You mean Major Joe Sensitive, right?" She laughed, but something sounded off. "I did enjoy the long soak. I may have even drifted off."

"Good."

Her eyes settled on the scrapbook in front of him.

He closed the album, fast. "I shouldn't have looked without asking you."

She reached to open the book again and turned it toward her. "It's silly to keep one of these and then never let anyone look at it. I'm sorry that seeing pictures of him upset you."

"Actually…" He flipped it to the page in question. "I was more upset with myself."

"I'm not sure I follow."

He tapped the edge of the ballgame photo. "Could I have been any more obvious?"

"I didn't know." Her hand gravitated to his face in the picture, tracing his jaw until he could almost feel her phantom touch. "I mean, I knew that I was attracted to you. But I didn't know you felt the same and especially not on a long-term basis."

"The way I kissed you didn't tip you off?"

"I figured I threw myself at you. You reacted on impulse. Which doubled my guilty feelings because I worried I might have harmed your friendship with Kevin."

"Impulse, like hell." He leaned back, folding his hands over his stomach. "Suppressed frustration's more like it."

She slid from the sofa and walked around to sit on the arm of his chair. Her fingers sketched his jaw for real, her fingertips soft and scented from her bath. "We have about a week and a half left to work those out."

A week and a half and then he returned to base, to work.

And she stayed in New Orleans?

She hadn't been willing to move for Kevin. She sure as hell wasn't going to move because they had one night of crazy hot sex between them. He needed to use his time wisely to persuade her they'd started something here. Guilt be damned, he couldn't let her go.

He pulled her into his lap and nipped her ear. "What do you say I carry you back to my room?"

"I think you should carry me back to that spa tub so I can take another bath—with you."

Nine

Getting used to sharing a bed again was easier said than done. Especially since Hank was a serious covers hog.

Yawning, she struggled to orient herself, having been tugged from a deep sleep by the abrupt rush of air over her body. Gabrielle patted the bed in the dark, searching for a corner of the bedspread to yank.

In the week since they'd started sharing a bed—after amazing sex—she'd fast learned that he was a restless sleeper. Which was only made worse by the fact that she was a light sleeper after so many months keeping her ears tuned in for the smallest sound from her son.

But there were so many good things to offset Hank's cover-snatching habit. Their week together had been packed with more great food and amazing sex. They'd even gone on outings with Max, a long drive, a simple walk along Lake Ponchartrain with Max in the stroller, a concert in the park. People mistook them for a family.

They felt like a family.

She blinked to adjust her eyes, but it was still dark. Moonlight streamed through the dormer window, slashing a pale yellow streak across the bed. She rolled to locate even a sheet and found Hank sitting up.

His eyes were open, but he was clearly still asleep. He'd tossed the covers to the ground. His fists were twisted in the fitted sheet. His mouth moved, mumbling something unintelligible, as if he couldn't force the sound out.

He was in the middle of a nightmare. A really bad one, gauging by the tendons standing out along his neck. Pain, fear and something very dark pulsed from Hank like waves off a toxic cloud.

How could she wake him up without startling him?

She was afraid to touch him. Not that she thought he would ever deliberately hurt her, but he looked ready to snap. A simple touch could make him lash out.

Leaning away slowly, she turned on the lamp, hoping that might ease him out of whatever night terrors gripped him. His head twitched, but still he didn't wake. Words tumbled from his mouth, some taking shape, others not so much.

Look out. God. No. Kevin. Hold on.

Realization seeped through her, that toxic cloud expanding to draw her in, as well. Hank was dreaming of Kevin's death.

Her chest went tight. She wanted to yank on her robe and run far, far away. But she couldn't leave him in that hell alone. He'd already lived through it once, a torture no one should face. Ever.

"Hank," she said softly but firmly. "Wake up. You're in New Orleans with me. Gabrielle. You're all right. It's just a dream. Can you hear me?"

Blinking faster, he hauled in breath after breath until he turned to her. "Gabrielle?"

She rested just her fingertips on his arm. "Are you okay?"

He scrubbed both hands over his head. "Crap. No." His voice came out raw and ragged, as if he was pushing the words over broken glass. "Just give me a second."

"You were dreaming about being in the Middle East, weren't you?"

He nodded without speaking.

"About Kevin?"

He nodded again, pulling away to sit on the edge of the bed. If she let the silence stretch, he would leave. His feet were already on the floor. He would shut her out and deal with the pain on his own.

After all he'd done for her, she couldn't let him shoulder everything. The man put up hefty walls. Time for somebody to be persistent enough to scale them.

She scooted to sit behind him, leaning her cheek on his shoulder blade. "Seeing Max and me must bring it all back. This can't be what the military meant by taking time off to recharge after a deployment." She stroked his arm, up and down, again and again, until the tensed muscles relaxed. "Maybe it would have been better for you if you hadn't come here right away."

"Don't go blaming yourself." He grabbed her hand fiercely. "I could look at a damn penny and somehow it would make me think of Kevin and that day...."

"Can you tell me what happened?" she asked, only half sure she really wanted to know, but she couldn't bail on Hank now.

He glanced back at her, the moonlight casting stark shadows on his face. "Didn't Kevin's parents tell you? They were given the official report."

"I know what happened to him and that you were there." Although they hadn't been overly wordy in sharing the details. To this day, she was foggy on why he'd been attacked on the ground. She'd always expected that if the worst happened, it would come from their plane being shot down. Bile burned as she thought about losing both Kevin and Hank. "I want to hear what happened to *you*."

He stayed silent so long she feared he might not talk, after all.

Then a sigh racked through him. "We were at a checkpoint. Everyone had to get out of the bus and show papers. Should have been quick and easy, wasn't even particularly a hot zone."

His heart hammered faster under her ear as she kept her cheek pressed to his back. She slid her arms around him, holding him, and yes, making sure he didn't bolt away. She just held him and waited.

"A sniper hit Kevin with two shots before I could even move to cover him."

Only a few simple words, and he'd transported her there with the pain in his voice. She could almost smell the acrid air, feel the grit of sand in her mouth because she would have screamed. God, how could anyone not?

"I carried Kevin back to the bus."

She hugged Hank tighter, the ridge of scar tissue on his collarbone suddenly all the more awful. "Is that when you got the scar?"

"Yeah."

She squeezed her eyes closed, swallowed down the push of tears. He had been shot, too. She could have lost them both. But right now was about Hank, being there for him the way he'd been there for her.

Clearing his throat, he continued, "Back in the truck,

I radioed for the medics to backtrack, but the frequency was full of everyone calling in. I tore off his vest, his shirt."

Her mind filled with images of those final moments of Kevin's life spent in a stark military bus in a foreign land. How many others had been on the bus with them? Just his crew or other crews, as well? She could hear the voices, the shouts, imagine the smell of death and desperation.

And Kevin's last thoughts of her had been about how he knew she and Hank had feelings for each other. Guilt blanketed her all over again. Might Kevin have found some comfort in knowing she was expecting his child? She hated that she hadn't shared the news with him. She'd thought it would distract him when he needed to focus and in the end he'd died anyway. She battled back her tears, needing to be strong for Hank.

"I'm sure you did everything you could," she offered, knowing it wasn't enough. Knowing he barely heard her since his eyes were unfocused, and, in his mind, he still knelt over Kevin in a hellish desert.

"I did the only thing I could think to." The words fell faster and faster from him. "I put my fingers in the bullet holes to try to stop the bleeding. He asked me to look after you, and then I watched the life leave his eyes."

Her heart broke at the desperation he must have felt.

Hank stood sharply, her arms falling away. He didn't look back, just grabbed his jeans from the back of a chair, hauled them on and left the room. As the door closed behind him, she realized she'd been so worried about how much being together would hurt her. She'd selfishly overlooked how much being with her must hurt him.

Even if she managed to get past the guilt to take this affair into a relationship, Hank might not.

* * *

Hank charged down the stairs to the kitchen.

He needed a beer but would settle for anything that gave him an excuse to walk out of that room full of memories. The nightmare had been bad enough, but reliving the day Kevin died drained him dry. He'd spent ten months coming to grips with what happened. But coming back to the states, being here with Gabrielle, it was as if he had to learn to deal with Kevin's death all over again.

Biting back a curse, Hank rounded the corner into the renovated kitchen and stopped short.

Leonie sat at the island eating a slice of pecan pie and thumbing through a tabloid magazine while Max snoozed away in his baby carrier. "Hello, Major." She slid from the tall swivel chair, tightening the sash on the robe over her lounging pj's. "Could I get you a plate? There's plenty left."

"No thanks. I'm good." Except actually, he wasn't "good." He was a damn mess inside and would be better off alone. He opened the refrigerator and pulled out a carton of juice. He tipped it back just like he did at *his* condo. To hell with manners. He wasn't in the mood for niceties.

"Glad to see the two of you working things out." Her fork clanked against the plate. "I wasn't too certain there at the outset."

"Why so?" He turned to face her, the carton still in his hand.

"You hired a nanny without consulting her the day her son got home from the hospital." She dabbed the corners of her mouth with her napkin. "Any woman would be upset."

"Then why did you take the job if you knew it was

going to make her mad?" He would never understand women.

"I needed the money. She needed the rest." She smiled, her hand smoothing the light blanket over Max tenderly. "And I love this little fellow."

"You could have clued me in so I didn't piss her off."

"Telling a person what to do never works, not in the long haul." She took her plate to the sink and rinsed off the crumbs. "The real lessons in life are learned from actions, making mistakes and fixing them yourself. That's the way good relationships are built."

"Relationships?" He winced.

"Please, do not be that cliché, relationship-leery man." Sighing, Leonie leaned back against the granite slab countertop. "I pegged you for better than that."

He'd just wanted something to drink, some space to pull himself back together and now he was catching it from all sides from a woman he barely knew. "Why are you giving me such a hard time?"

"Because you don't have a mama, and for some reason you don't have much contact with your family. Who else is going to tell you what you need to hear?"

He cocked an eyebrow, channeling his dad's superior look. But what the hell? He followed in the old man's footsteps just about every other way. "You've been reading too many tabloids."

"I do love my gossip papers." She grinned unrepentantly. "News about your family sells."

He spun the tabloid rag around. A headline blared, Granny Ginger Buys Princess Granddaughter a Pony. The rest of the article detailed some supposedly lavish birthday bash his stepmom had thrown for her newest grandchild—a girl whose mother was an illegitimate princess.

The guest list included everyone from the kids of movie stars to ambassadors.

Since emails from home had included details and photos from that party, he knew ninety-nine percent of the information was bull. His mom had rented a pony, but the very long guest list for the toddler's first birthday was simply all the family members. So what if the family members happened to be Renshaws, Landises and in-law royal Medinas? But apparently stuff like this, touting inside peeks into the lifestyles of the rich and famous, sold magazines.

An ugly suspicion niggled. "How badly do you need money?"

Her smile faded. "Not bad enough to ever do anything to hurt Gabrielle or this little boy, and I'll scratch out the eyes of anyone who does."

He searched her eyes and found nothing but honesty. "Good, we're on the same page, then."

"So you'll think about what I said?"

"Said about what?"

She'd said so freaking much he'd lost track.

"Men," she mumbled, reaching for Max's seat.

Hank grasped the carrier handle. "I'll take him for a while."

"It's okay, Major." Leonie patted his hand. "I've got him."

"Seriously, go nap or read a gossip magazine. It can't be easy switching to the night shift all at once."

"Okay, then." She pulled a baby rattle and empty bottle from her pocket as she spun away. "You're the boss."

He set the juice carton on the island, taking his seat in front of the sleeping baby. Kevin's kid. Gabrielle's son.

Shaking the cow-shaped rattle in front of the boy's face, he tracked the faces of both people he loved in the kid's cheeks and stubborn chin. Max blinked wide blue eyes back at him and all those features merged into one, a unique individual.

Max.

A roaring started in his ears, and he reached to pick up the baby. He cradled Max in the crook of his arm, shaking the rattle again since the boy seemed to like it. Max batted at the air, his little fist bumping Hank's, baby skin softer than anything he could remember. Tiny fingers unfurled and wrapped around his thumb, holding tight.

"Hey, buddy," he said softly, "we're going to have fun together. Do you like baseball? With a grip like that, I'll bet you can throw a mean curve ball. You and me, we're going to be…"

Be…what? He wasn't sure where he stood with the child. What would those scrapbooks show when Gabrielle added photos of him with Max? He didn't want to be a stand-in dad. He wanted to be the real thing. A father to Max and a husband to Gabrielle.

But he also didn't want to forget Kevin, and he wasn't sure how in the hell to cohabitate with a ghost.

Gabrielle woke up alone with the covers all to herself. So why wasn't she happy?

She reached to touch the empty spot beside her, and the sheets weren't even warm. Hank hadn't come back to bed after his nightmare. She'd thought getting him to talk about the dream and what happened ten months ago would make him feel better. But what did she know about war memories? She could have made things worse for him by venturing in full steam when he wasn't ready.

Where did she go from here?

Maybe she needed to stop pushing, to give him some space. Kevin had always talked about how Hank kept his distance from his family, that he was the sort of guy who liked to keep his life private. Today, he had to be especially vulnerable—although she could almost see him bristle if she called him vulnerable to his face. He wasn't one to acknowledge his own emotional needs so she would have to take care of those for him.

She could probably use a little elbow room, too. Things had happened at such a fast and furious pace—moving here, Max's surgery, starting an affair. She pressed a hand to her aching heart and wished life could be simple for a change.

Although some things were straightforward. Like her son's needs. She grabbed her robe from the corner of the bed and shrugged it on. Flicking her hair free and finger combing it, she went in search of her son for his morning feeding. She creaked open the nursery door.

Leonie sat in the window seat reading a gossip magazine. She looked up, bifocals sliding down on her nose. "Max is downstairs with the major. He insisted on watching him and who am I to argue with a hot man taking care of a baby." She fanned her face with the magazine. "*Phew.* Now that's sexy."

"Thanks for the update, Leonie." Gabrielle's heart squeezed at the thought of Hank hurting over the loss of his friend and then having that friend's child right there in front of him. But Hank, being Hank, was so busy thinking about others—letting her rest, giving Leonie a break—he put himself dead last.

Hopefully, she could feed Max quickly then go out for the morning. Take a walk with her son. Proofread a school paper in the park.

Gain some much needed distance and perspective to sort through her life.

She searched each of the bedrooms upstairs, but no Hank or Max. She took the back stairs into the kitchen, also empty other than a dish in the sink and a half-empty juice carton on the island. Her bare feet padded along the kitchen tile to the hardwood of the hall. She pinched the neck of her robe closed, wishing now that she'd taken a second to put on some clothes, or at least to put on a nightgown underneath.

Finally, she found Hank in the library. Curtains closed, the room stayed hazy with only minimal morning light shining through but it was plenty bright enough for her to see Hank. He lay stretched out asleep on the leather sofa.

Max slept on his chest.

Leonie was one smart cookie, because right now, Gabrielle couldn't think of anything more appealing than the sight of her baby napping on Hank's bare chest. His broad hand held the infant, and she didn't doubt for a second that if Max so much as wriggled, Hank would keep him safely in place.

Hiring the sitter had been a thoughtful, generous gesture. But seeing how Hank chose to hold Max, to watch over him as he slept, that nearly brought Gabrielle to her knees.

A low buzzing sound drew her attention to the end table where Hank's wallet and cell phone rested. The buzz sounded again, and she realized his cell was vibrating with an incoming call.

Hank reached over his head, grappled for the phone, and thumbed the ringer silent. He turned his head toward her, his eyes opening, blue and clear as if he'd been awake the whole time. "How long have you been standing there?"

"Only a minute or so. I need to nurse Max."

Her son stirred at the sound of her voice, stretching his tiny arms over his head and yawning. She walked toward Hank as he sat up, adjusting his hold on Max like a seasoned pro.

"Sure, here you go." He passed her boy over to her without touching her or meeting her eyes.

Silence settled between them, full of what he'd told her last night. She would have run upstairs right that second but Max wriggled in her arms, fussy and searching for food.

She sat on the end of the sofa, parting her robe and bringing her son to her breast. He squirmed, rooting frantically for a few seconds before latching on with a hungry sigh. Hank stayed on the far end of the couch, rubbing the back of his neck, looking from her to the hall and back again.

Hank's phone vibrated again, and he snatched it up, turning it off altogether before stuffing it in his back pocket. For a guy who'd been sleeping so peacefully, his mood had certainly done a serious one-eighty now that he was awake.

The minute Max finished, she was definitely going to give herself and Hank some breathing room. She would even take Leonie along with her so Hank could have the house to himself. In fact, she heard Leonie on the stairway now, which gave her the perfect out.

"Hank, I think that—"

The doorbell rang, cutting her off short. She looked up fast just as Leonie rushed the rest of the way down the stairs.

Gabrielle cupped her son's head protectively. Hank shot to his feet. Voices drifted from the hall, Leonie's along with others she didn't recognize.

She cradled her son closer. "Has someone broken into the house?"

Hank dropped back to the sofa, a curse hissing from between his tight teeth. "It's not a break-in. It's my family."

Ten

Gabrielle wanted to run. Anywhere would be fine. Just some place far away from the four adults standing with Leonie in the archway staring at her, their jaws slack with surprise. Not that she could blame them. If only she'd had some advance warning she could have dashed upstairs to dress. But the curtains were closed, and she'd been so wrapped up in Max and Hank and making sure they both were all right, she'd completely missed Hank's family's approach.

She'd read enough articles about the Renshaw and Landis families to recognize the small group. It didn't take gossip magazines to keep up with them. Hank's military general dad stood with his second wife, Ginger. A younger couple hovered behind them. While Ginger's four sons resembled each other, Gabrielle was almost certain this was the youngest, the architect who did renovations on historic homes—and also happened to be married to a woman with royal roots to her family tree. His wife jostled a toddler on her hip, a little girl around a year old.

What must they all think?

She didn't have to ask. She knew exactly what any reasonable person would assume based on the way things looked. Hank stood barefoot, particularly sexy in nothing more than a pair of jeans riding low on his hips. And she really wished that she'd put on something more than just a robe and that she was anywhere other than on the sofa nursing her son.

If she pulled Max away, she risked exposing herself to the already stunned quartet. Plus he would scream himself purple if she cut his meal short.

Were they judging her? Wondering if she was taking advantage of Hank? She wondered the same thing herself. She searched their eyes and only found curiosity.

A lot of it.

She looked to Hank for help just as he stepped toward his family.

"As you can see, we weren't expecting company. How about we step across the hall and give Gabrielle some privacy with her son? Introductions can wait until then."

He ushered them out into the hall, pulling the doors closed behind him.

Voices seeped through, lots of voices, rising with curiosity as they all must be bombarding him with questions. If only she could make out the words. Her son continued to blissfully nurse, unaware of the world turned upside down.

A few minutes later, the door opened again and Gabrielle tensed. Leonie slid through, keeping the room shielded from the rest of the house.

"Cavalry to the rescue, sweetie. I have clothes for you." She held up her hands with—thank God—something to wear. "I'm ready to take the little guy if you're about done." Leonie sat beside her, a clothing stack perched on her knees.

Max seemed to be slowing, and Gabrielle would just live with feeling lopsided rather than taking more time to swap him to the other breast. "You'll just need to burp him."

"Will do." Leonie took the baby and patted him on the back. "Can you believe we're actually under the same roof as a former secretary of state? And royalty?"

"Believe it or not, they're here, all right." Gabrielle just wished they'd called first. Her plans for giving Hank space went out the window.

Shielded by the robe, she stepped into her underwear and jeans, then shrugged on her bra and long white poet's shirt. She shoved her feet into sandals. Dressed, thank goodness.

Maybe she would still be able to make it to her room to freshen up further. She cracked open the double doors to peek out.

No luck.

Across the hall in the dining room, Hank stood with his surprise guests. All eyes homed in on her. Leonie tucked by and took Max up the stairs, which pulled the attention off Gabrielle momentarily.

Holding her head high, Gabrielle rolled back her shoulders. Hank slid into place beside her and palmed her waist. He ducked his head and whispered, "I haven't told them anything. I wanted to wait for you to weigh in, although nobody's going to believe us if we say we're not together."

He kissed her cheek and straightened. She didn't even bother protesting. They *were* sleeping together and denying it would make a bigger deal out of the situation.

"Ginger, Dad," Hank said, "this is Gabrielle."

Hank Renshaw, Sr., nodded silently, a graying, older version of his son, and just as reticent. He didn't need the uniform to look like a general. Even in khakis and a golfing sweater, he carried an air of military authority. She resisted the urge to fidget or salute.

Ginger Landis Renshaw stepped into the silence and extended her hand with a smile that seemed authentic. "Our apologies for showing up unannounced. We really should have called."

Her shoulder-length gray-blond hair was so perfectly styled, Gabrielle resisted the urge to smooth her hand over her own messy mop. She recalled from news reports that the woman was nearing sixty, but she carried the years well. Wearing a pale pink lightweight sweater set with pearls—and blue jeans—Ginger Landis wasn't at all what Gabrielle had expected. Thank goodness, because the woman in front of her appeared a lot less intimidating.

Gabrielle had seen her often enough on the news— always poised and intelligent, sometimes steely and determined. Today, a softer side showed as she looked at her stepson then over to Gabrielle.

"I'm Ginger. Nice to meet you, Gabrielle. Although I don't know exactly who I'm meeting since Hank isn't sharing anything beyond your name."

His eyes met hers. He really had left it to her to say what she wanted. She smiled her thanks.

"A pleasure to meet you, too, ma'am. Obviously, I'm a close friend of your stepson's." Taking the older woman's hand, Gabrielle smiled sheepishly and appreciated the light squeeze of encouragement. "He's been helping me with my son since my fiancé passed away."

There. Now she'd left it up to him to share what *he*

wanted with his family about who her fiancé was and what had happened overseas. She knew how Hank valued his privacy.

The collective sigh of relief that went through the foursome drew her attention back.

Ginger pressed a hand to her pearls. "So the baby isn't Hank's."

Oh, my God, they'd thought…?

Of course they had, and they must have been hurt by the thought that Hank would have had a child without telling them. He had to have known what they were thinking. Yet, he'd let them just hang there wondering while she got dressed? That took needing privacy to a whole new level.

Hank gestured to the younger couple. "This is my youngest stepbrother, Jonah. His wife, Eloisa. And their little girl named Ginger." He shot a look at Jonah. "Suck up."

Jonah pointed to his wife. "Her idea about naming our daughter after Mom. I'm putty in Eloisa's hands. Actually, I'm putty in her *and* our daughter's hands."

Hank rolled his eyes. "You'll remember Jonah since he's the one I spoke to about renting this house."

He shot his stepbrother a quick look, just short of an outright glare.

Jonah pointed to his wife again. "She pried it out of me." He hooked an arm around her waist. "I'm helpless when it comes to her. Remember?"

Ginger placed a hand on her stepson's arm. "We're sorry to burst in on you this way, but *Architectural Digest* is doing a photo shoot of this place to feature Jonah's restoration. It's a great boon for his business."

Hank mumbled to Jonah. "You didn't mention that, either."

"Didn't have time," Jonah said out of the corner of his

mouth. "Mom arranged it yesterday so she would have an excuse to come here. And besides, you weren't picking up your phone. That's what you get for ignoring your family."

The general chuckled softly.

Gabrielle was still stuck on the words *photo shoot.* "They'll be photographing the house?"

"And our family." Ginger smiled proudly. "Beyond being great publicity for Jonah's work, it's a lovely chance for me to show off my relatives without worrying about the paparazzi falling out of trees in the middle of a picnic just to get a picture for some cheap gossip rag."

Leonie better clean out her stash of reading material if she wanted to win Ginger's approval.

The general continued, "We've found if we periodically stage pictures on our own terms, the public gets bored enough to leave us alone for a while."

Ginger hooked an arm through Gabrielle's. "So, you'll join us for the photos? Friends are always welcome."

"I'm not sure what to say." The whole meeting was overwhelming.

"No need to make up your mind yet. I'm just glad to meet you." She squeezed Gabrielle's arm. "You'll have plenty of time to think it over while we unpack. Gentlemen, would you please unload the luggage from the car?"

Panic lit a bonfire in Gabrielle's stomach. She looked fast at Hank. Frustration mixed with resignation in his eyes.

His family was staying here.

"So you're okay with us staying here?" his father asked him.

Hank hefted suitcases from the back of the hybrid Mercedes SUV. "Yeah, General, sure."

"Son..."

His father had been a part of the Joint Chiefs of Staff, handling explosive world dynamics without breaking a sweat. But he still got cranky when his kids called him General. "Yeah, *Dad?*"

"That's better." The general nodded, walking along-side him, loaded down with luggage for such a short stay. Although half of it looked as if it belonged to Jonah and Eloisa's baby. A second car was parked behind Hank and Ginger's, a nondescript black sedan with two men in suits in the front—protective detail. His dad and Ginger kept at least one bodyguard at all times when away from home and undoubtedly extra security came from the royal side of the family.

No more making out on the lanai.

His father's strides matched his own. "Is the boy yours?"

Hank stopped short at the base of the steps. Was his dad calling him a liar? Wind rustled the hanging ferns and oak tree branches while he squelched his rising anger. "You heard Gabrielle say he isn't."

"Was she covering for you?" His father's eyes went into deep search mode, just as he'd done when single par-enting his three teens.

Hank bit back the urge to just leave. It had chapped his hide, being questioned at sixteen, but it really burned now thinking his dad questioned his honor. "No one 'covers' for me, especially not Gabrielle. If Max was mine, you would have heard about it."

"You're not known for being chatty with the rest of the family," his father said dryly.

"Fair enough," he conceded. "But having a child is not something I would hide. Even if I decided to wait to tell you, I sure as hell wouldn't have let Gabrielle stand there alone, stating the kid is someone else's."

The doubt in his dad's eyes faded. "Of course. I should have known. You're an honorable man."

"Thanks for that much." He started up the back porch steps.

"You're also a private man, and that makes this a tough family for you to be a part of."

"Do ya' think?"

A laugh rumbled from his dad's barrel chest and yeah, it felt good to join in. The past week and a half had been beyond stressful. Good in a lot of ways—like hearing from the doctor that Max would be okay, and being with Gabrielle. But there was still enough baggage in their pasts to rival even the piles coming out of the back of that SUV.

His father stayed between him and the door. "So if the baby isn't yours, who's the dead fiancé she mentioned? I assume he'd be the father."

"My buddy Kevin, a pilot on my crew. He died in Afghanistan." Even those few words stoked the barely banked memories of his nightmare.

"Are you sure you know what you're doing here, son?"

He didn't need this kind of probing or interference. Not now. "Dad, I didn't ask for your opinion."

His old man's face creased with a smile. "That's never stopped me before. We don't get anywhere in the world if we sit around waiting to be asked."

"Okay, then. I won't *ask* if you mind if I leave." He turned away, ready to walk all the way around the house to another door, if need be.

"Her guy can't have been dead long." His father's words stopped him on the top step.

"Ten months," Hank answered without turning, the

smell of explosives and blood coming back so damn real
he could have been over there, living that hell again.

Footsteps sounded on the wooden porch as his father
neared. His large shadow stretched over Hank as it had
done his entire life. "Son, are you sure she's through
grieving? I'm not saying she's the wrong woman. I'm
just saying be sure it's the right time."

The shadow shifted as the general backed away, leaving his words hanging out there to cast a shadow all their
own. As much as Hank tried to live his own life, still his
dad's legacy followed him. Was there something in the
genetics that led him to make so many of the same choices
his father had made, even when he worked his tail off to
be different? Hell, his dad had even fallen for his friend's
widow.

Did that mean a guy had to wait more than a decade
to act on it?

Hank stayed standing on the top step long after his
father gathered up the bags and headed inside.

While everyone else unpacked, Gabrielle sat with
Ginger in the sunroom, little Ginger toddling around
while Max napped in his baby swing. The moment felt
so timeless, as if they could have been a family from a
hundred years ago gathering just this way. If she were
snapping photos for a magazine, Gabrielle would want
these over any staged, fancy pictures.

She would want this life.

Well, other than the security detail walking the perim-
eter and talking into radios tucked in the cuff.

Her hands shaking, she gripped the arms of the rattan
rocker. "Do you ever get tired of having bodyguards
follow you everywhere?"

Ginger glanced out the wall of windows at the guards

as if she'd forgotten they were there. "Sure, but I try to remember it's just a part of the jobs I've been lucky enough to have." She swooped her granddaughter up into her arms and spun her around once. "Although being a grandmother is the best job on the planet."

"Better than being Secretary of State?"

"Hands down." Ginger set the giggling toddler on the floor and tugged Max's toe gently. "He's a sweet-natured baby. I hope you don't mind my asking...what are those little incisions on his stomach?"

How strange to have all that worry swept away in a few days. "He had surgery this week for a digestive disorder. He's fine now." She said another prayer of gratitude. "But that's why I'm here. At Hank's house, I mean. He's helping me out since this is his friend's baby. He's acting as a sort of a stand-in dad, I guess you could say."

Ginger sat on the rattan sofa next to her. "Although it's obvious Hank's your friend, too."

Was she asking out of curiosity or as a concerned relative? "We knew each other before..." Gabrielle picked at splinters on the armrest. "So yes, we're friends, too."

Ginger's hand fell on the Burberry diaper bag little Ginger's mother had left before she went upstairs to unpack. "I've known Hank since he was your son's age."

Really? "I thought you married the general more recently than that."

She was just realizing how little she knew about Hank beyond what she'd read in the papers. How much of that was even factual?

"My husband—my first husband—was in the air force with Hank, Sr." Her deep blue eyes, the same color as her son's, lit with nostalgia. "My husband Benjamin wasn't career military, like Hank. He wanted to serve for a few years, to give back to his country. Then he got out and went into politics."

Gabrielle recalled reading that Ginger had served the rest of her first husband's term after he'd died, then she turned out to be an even more savvy and effective politician than her husband. Her career had taken off from there. Even now, she served as an ambassador to a South American country. It was tough not to be intimidated by that much power and success. Gabrielle listened, wondering what the woman's agenda was in sharing her life story. Because no doubt, this savvy stateswoman would be every bit as tenacious in protecting her family as she was in negotiating for her country.

"While we were in the military—and I do mean we because the spouse sacrifices a lot being married to a service member—we were friends with Hank and Jessica. Our children played together, too. When Jessica died, I helped Hank with his children. He helped me with my boys after I lost Benjamin." She paused, staring out the sunroom windows and blinking back a shadowy grief that apparently even time hadn't dimmed. "There was never anything going on between us while either of our spouses were alive, nothing. Believe me, it shocked the hell out of both of us when our friendship turned into something more."

Gabrielle willed herself not to show the shame that dogged her still over that kiss she'd shared with Hank while Kevin was still alive. Kevin may have pardoned them with his dying breath, but she couldn't forgive herself.

She looked out over the lush Garden District lawn, seeking some of the answers or peace that Ginger also seemed to be looking for out the window. Instead, Gabrielle saw Hank. His long strides ate up ground as he made his way toward a bodyguard standing under a shady oak. Hands shoved in his pockets, he stopped alongside the security guy, just talking. Checking out the lay of the land, perhaps? Hank had put on a pin-striped button-down shirt with his jeans, rolled up sleeves and boat shoes. Yet he looked no less in command than he did in his uniform.

Like his father.

Ginger pressed her fingers to the corners of her eyes, drew in a bracing breath, then smiled again. "But we were talking about little Hank."

"*Little* Hank?"

"What can I say?" Ginger shrugged, smiling affectionately at her stepson on the lawn. "To me, he will always be that little boy racing his Big Wheel up and down the sidewalk. He loved to be outside, on the go. He led the pack even then. But he always played fair, too fair."

Gabrielle tore her eyes from Hank and put her focus back onto the conversation. She was reminded of her mother, the whole wonder woman, perfect mom and military wife persona that no human could hope to measure up to. "How can someone be too fair?"

Ginger leaned forward, elbows on her knees, her eyes steely blue with no holding back. She was apparently through taking the scenic route in their conversation. "He puts others before himself, sometimes to his own detriment."

"Are you saying I'm using him?"

"No, heavens no." She waved aside Gabrielle's guilty fears with a manicured hand. "I'm just saying he works so hard to be the good guy, he may not be telling you where he stands. Ask him what he wants. Don't assume. Ask, then ask again until he really talks."

Were there questions she should be asking Hank that she wasn't? Was it possible that Hank was only staying with her for the sake of being the good guy? He'd said it wasn't about a debt to Kevin anymore, but about wanting to be with her. Still. Even before Ginger said anything, Gabrielle had known that Hank was struggling with boundaries.

He'd really poured his heart out to her last night, leaving them both so emotionally raw that he'd needed some distance, seeking out Max rather than returning to bed with her. Obviously, he wasn't in the mood to share more, and quite frankly, she wasn't sure how much more either of them could take.

And Ginger thought she should dig even deeper?

Instead of helping her, Ginger's revelations only made her all the more afraid she wasn't the right person for Hank. She'd been taking, taking, taking from him since he'd stepped back into her life. He deserved someone who could give back, who could break through those high walls of his and care for him, as well. With each second that passed, the possibility of a future with Hank grew more complicated, more improbable.

Ginger shoved to her feet and swept the wrinkles from her jeans. "Enough serious talk for one day. Let's have some fun."

"Doing what?" Gabrielle grasped the subject change with both hands, eager to move on to safer ground.

"A local boutique is bringing clothes by for us to choose from for the photo shoot." Ginger clasped Gabrielle's hands in her own and tugged her to her feet. "Every new mom deserves an afternoon of spa pampering."

Eleven

Hank walked down the hall with a stealth picked up in military survival training. Although damned if he didn't feel about fifteen sneaking around so his dad wouldn't hear him slip into Gabrielle's room. He hadn't been able to steal even a few minutes alone with her since his family arrived. First his mother had abducted her all afternoon to try on dresses then supper had stretched out for hours as they alternated between subtly grilling Gabrielle and discussing the photo shoot for the next day.

Who knew his relatives had become such night owls?

This was his house, for God's sake. Well, his rental house for a short while longer. Not that it stopped anyone from claiming a spare room. Any minor sense of family boundaries had disappeared from his life long ago. He was seriously itching over the scrutiny, more so than usual.

His *father*'s scrutiny dug even deeper than the prying

eye of a camera lens. What if his dad was right that Gabrielle wasn't over Kevin? What if she never got over loving and losing him?

Hank gripped the crystal doorknob outside her room. He'd hung out on the sidelines of her life once before and it had been pure hell. He didn't think he could do it again, not after having been with her. He'd claimed her, and he couldn't see letting her go again. The rest would have to work itself out.

He tapped once softly on Gabrielle's door before sliding inside. Her bed was empty, the covers still undisturbed.

Because she was slumped over her desk, asleep.

How often did she work herself into the ground this way? The afternoon spent trying on dresses with his stepmom must have cut into her schedule. He locked the doors to the hall and the nursery. Anyone wanting to find her would have to knock. His dad and stepmom were good people, but type-A sorts who tended to steamroll over people "for their own good."

Carefully, he slid his arms around her back and under her legs. Her hand slipped from the desk, her short nails sporting the light sheen of a pale pink polish. Ginger's doing, no doubt. His stepmom was a practical woman in many ways, but she did enjoy her manicures.

He scooped up Gabrielle against his chest, her satin robe parting to reveal a nightshirt. His mind zipped back to the uncomfortable interruption this morning in the library. She wasn't going to be caught half naked again.

Damn shame—as long as he was her only audience.

Gabrielle stirred in his arms. "Hank?"

"Shhh… Go back to sleep. I'm just moving you to the bed so you'll be more comfortable."

Her arm draped around his neck, her eyes groggy.

"Wait. Put me down. Almost done with the paper I have to turn in."

"Is it due tomorrow?" If so, he would be right there beside her, proofreading, if she needed him.

"Nuh-uh." Sleepy fog cleared from her eyes and they went smoky with awareness. She rested her other hand on his chest, her fingers tracing the vee of his collar.

"Then you have time to finish it later."

"You're right. I do have time." She slipped a button free, then another. "For this."

She took his earlobe between her teeth and nipped.

A bolt of desire shot straight to his groin. He tightened his grip on her, pressing her closer. She smelled like lavender and Gabrielle, the scent so familiar now he could taste her on his tongue. He fought back the urge to take her right here.

He set her on the bed. More like, he dropped her and took a step back, trying his damnedest to be a gentleman. "You really should sleep."

"I've gotten plenty of sleep this past week, thanks to all the help from you and Leonie." She shrugged off her robe and whipped her nightshirt over her head, wispy blond hairs clinging to the cotton before it fell away. "Trust me to know what I *need*."

Call him a selfish bastard, but as he looked at her lounging on the bed wearing only a sea-green pair of bikini panties, he couldn't bring himself to tell her no.

"What *exactly* do you need?" He took off his watch and placed it on the bedside table with deliberate precision, setting his leather wallet alongside the lamp. He pulled a condom from his billfold, wanting her to know he would always protect her in every way possible. "Because I really want to hear every detail."

"You, here, doing whatever I say."

His eyebrows shot up. "Oh, really. You want—"

"Control. Do you have a problem with that?"

The challenge in her green eyes cranked him higher, his body more than happy to comply.

"None whatsoever." He tugged his shirt off, stepped out of his jeans and slipped into bed next to her. "What are you going to do with me now that you have me?"

Grabbing his shoulders, she shoved him onto his back, straddling him. "You'll have to wait and see."

"And how long will I have to wait?" He throbbed against the warm press of her satin underwear.

"Patience…" She wriggled just enough to tempt him without taking him over the edge. Biting back a groan, he squeezed his eyes shut, cupping her waist and guiding her faster against him.

She shifted to the side and he moved to catch her. Except she wasn't going anywhere. She tugged the sash from her robe and teased it along his chest in a slithering path. A playful smile spread over her face and she leaned forward to—

Holy crap, she was blindfolding him.

Wrapping the tie around and over his eyes twice, she sealed it in place with a kiss, pinning his wrists to the bed. And sure, he could have broken free and pulled it off at any time, but who was he to argue if she wanted control?

Willing his arms to relax, he sank back into the mattress, his head digging into the pillows and anchoring the blindfold. Her purr of approval stroked him with a heated sigh against his chest, soon replaced by her fingers. She used her touch, her lips, the glide of her hair along his skin in a feathery path that mirrored his game with the mask. She teased the silky strands along his shoulders over his chest until his skin tightened at the phantom touch.

Lower, lower still she trailed her hair until…the slide of the strands over his erection threatened to finish him before they'd even started. The lavender scent of her clung to the sash, filling him with each labored breath he dragged in.

Her hands replaced the feathery locks, stroking, caressing, driving him damn near crazy with wanting her. Then her mouth closed over him. His hands twisted in the sheets as he fought back the need to shout, she felt so damn good.

He reached to pull her up, and she shoved his arms away, continuing to take him higher with her lips, her tongue and then to hell with the blindfold. He ripped the sash from his face. "Okay, you win. If I don't get my hands on you soon, I'm going to lose my mind."

She pressed a kiss to his stomach, purring against his skin. "I'm all yours."

Thank God.

Hank hauled her up, flipping her to her back. He grabbed the condom from the bedside table, sheathing himself in record time before he thrust hilt deep inside her.

Holding her hands over her head, he drove into her again and again, watching her face to make sure she was every bit as crazed as he felt. Out of control? Totally. Something about this woman stole reasonable thought, tipping his whole world upside down.

She looked back up at him, her pupils wide and her chest flushing with pleasure, the signs he needed that she was close, too. Still, he held back, waiting, watching until…he saw her fly apart.

Only then did he allow himself to dive in with her, a hot release pumping from him, driving him into her again and again and even as he came, he already wanted more of her.

All of her. Gabrielle would be his wife and to hell with everything else.

And he intended to press hard and press now to make that happen before she slipped away.

Standing in front of the full-length mirror on the armoire door, Gabrielle struggled with the zipper on her new dress, scared of yanking too hard for fear she would damage the gown that cost more than she earned in a month. Who'd have thought a photo shoot of a "family dinner" would include a floor-length formal, complete with a manicure and an up-do? The nails and hair, she could live with and actually enjoyed.

But she'd been vaguely ill when she realized her clothing designer was the same one who'd once decked out Reese Witherspoon for the Oscars. Ginger had told her not to worry. They would be donating their dresses to a charity that raised funds for breast cancer survivors. Her conscience slightly assuaged, she'd accepted the "loaner" for the evening's photo shoot.

The plum-colored satin slid over her skin with reminders of all the ways she and Hank had used her robe's sash the night before. The power play of blindfolds and, later, bound hands had continued until nearly sunrise, leaving them both panting and depleted.

Their lovemaking also left her even more confused as to how they would blend their lives. She couldn't miss the seriousness in Hank's eyes, the intensity in his every move. Things were moving so fast. She wanted more time to figure things out before—if—they went public, but that option had ended the second his family walked into the foyer unannounced.

A tap sounded on the door. "It's me. Hank. Are you about ready?"

Pressing a palm to her chest, she held the dress in place, while hitching up the hem with her other hand and padding barefoot to let him in. She unlocked the door and started to tell him she'd changed her mind about being in the photo shoot, such a public declaration of their relationship no matter what his stepmother said.

She darn near swallowed her tongue. Hank in his formal air force uniform filled the doorway and her eyes. Rows of medals gleamed on his chest, his silver aviator wings pinned above them. She'd seen him dressed this way before, but she'd always been with Kevin, so she'd worked to keep her distance, putting those walls in place between them.

Right now, Hank was one-hundred-percent touchable. Her hand fell to rest right over his heart. "You take my breath away."

"I should be saying that to you," he said, without even looking at her dress. His eyes stayed firmly on her face.

She touched his tie, his chin, his mouth that had brought her so much pleasure the night before. If only they could lock themselves in her room. But they couldn't. There were people waiting downstairs and a photo shoot to complete.

Which reminded her— "I need your help zipping my dress, please."

"As long as I get to unzip it later." He backed her into the bedroom, kicking the door closed behind him. He set something on top of the armoire, then turned her around. He kissed her neck before she could look at what he'd brought in with him. His lips lingered as he inched the zipper up. Her head fell back until he grazed his mouth over hers.

Easing away, she said, "I'm not sure I should be in the pictures. What if people assume…more than they should?"

"They'll assume you're my date, which you are. They may even assume we're lovers, which is true, as well." His hands tracked the dip of her waist, the curve of her hips. "Or they'll assume the photos have been staged with a drop-dead sexy model on my arm."

He palmed her stomach and pulled her flush against his thickening arousal.

"Hank, are you sure we can't just ditch the whole thing? Leonie already has Max for the night. We could lock ourselves in here or walk by Lake Ponchartrain holding hands."

"Either option sounds infinitely more exciting than this dinner. If you're serious about wanting to ditch the gathering, then that's what we'll do."

She was tempted to do just that, but Ginger's words filtered through, reminding her how he always put other people's needs first. "Your family will be upset with you, and I don't want to cause trouble."

"Their opinion has never stopped me before."

Except if he cut out on his stepmother's plans—plans Ginger had concocted just to be a part of his life—there would be deep disappointment. No matter how many boundaries he put in place, Hank clearly loved his relatives, even if he preferred a little less togetherness than the others did.

She rested her arms over his as he hugged her from behind. Smiling at him in the mirror, she willed her nervous doubts away. "Let's go to dinner, and then we can take that walk along the lake."

"If you're sure."

"I am." Sort of.

"Okay, then. We have a date for later. As for now…"
He leaned past her to pull a flat velvet jewelers box off
the top of the armoire.

He creaked open the lid, revealing a wide bracelet band
of diamonds with matching chandelier earrings.

She gasped, in awe of the beauty and in horror at what
the price tag must have been. "Hank, I can't—"

"Wear them for the photos," he interrupted. He clasped
the bracelet around her wrist and passed her the earrings
with enough diamonds to make the down payment on
a house. "If you have any arguments, take it up with
Ginger."

Even as he said it, she knew he was the one behind the
jewels. She put on one earring, then the other. "And if I
lose one of these in the soup?"

He grabbed her shoulders and turned her to face him,
tiered diamonds brushing her neck. "Gabrielle, they're
just earrings."

"Diamond earrings." Lots of diamonds.

"I've never given a damn about money before, but I
find myself wanting to spend it on you, to make your life
easier."

She stroked his rugged face, his intensity tugging at
her far more than any jewels. "Thank you, but I'm not
exactly the kept-woman type."

"It could be more than that." He pulled her hand from
his face and held on. "You could move in with me. Most
of your classes are online now anyway. I can help you
with Max."

Her chest tightened with increasing panic.

"Hank, stop. I've worked hard for this life I've built
here in New Orleans. Let's not rush into anything."

"Rush? I've been halfway in love with you for nearly
two years. Doesn't feel like rushing to me. We were

friends before. We're lovers now." His voice grew tighter and tenser with each angry word. "Damn it, if I had my way, we'd just get married."

Her throat closed up. He'd shocked her silent, *scared* her silent. The roots of her hair tingled, and she struggled for air. She wanted to be with him, was probably halfway in love with him, as well.

His backhanded proposal touched her, without question, tempted her even. But the thought of getting married? No matter what he said about how long they'd known each other, taking such a huge step was definitely too much, too soon for her to handle.

Hank's jaw flexed, his eyes chilling. "Your enthusiasm is overwhelming."

Oh, God, she'd hurt him. She clasped his hand. "Hank, you just surprised me. I don't know what to say."

He let go, shoulders broad and braced in his uniform. "Let me make this easy so you don't have to work on concocting excuses. My dad thinks I should give you more time to get over Kevin. Do you still love him?"

"It's not that simple."

His face closed up. "It is to me."

How had this conversation gotten so out of control? How had her *life* gotten so out of control? She struggled for the right words to defuse the situation. "Kevin and I were having problems. You know he and I argued before the deployment about my leaving New Orleans and moving closer to him. And now you're pushing me to make the same decision."

"Is that what you and Kevin really fought about right before we deployed?" He pinned her with too perceptive eyes.

She looked away. "Of course it is."

"But the two of you had been debating that for months.

I don't know why I didn't see it at the time, but something different must have happened that day, something bigger."

His perception made her itchy. She wanted to leave the past behind her, but that would never be possible with Hank. Their lives were too entwined. "We'd been fighting because the one time I got tipsy, we forgot to use a condom, okay? Are you happy now?" She jammed her feet into the silver heels. "Let's go to dinner."

Hands behind his back, feet planted, he blocked the door. "I'm not happy but I want to hear it all."

What was he hoping to accomplish by pushing this now? Why couldn't he just take his father's advice on this and give her some time?

She did care for Hank, so much, and the thought of losing him scared her almost as much as the thought of moving forward too quickly. She needed to make him understand what had happened between her and Kevin, to share things she'd held back before.

"That day, we fought about it again because he wanted me to go to some party with him and I didn't want to go drinking. I wanted to just be together before he left. Maybe I was looking for some reassurance because things were already rocky between us."

Hank's stoic face didn't give her any indication of whether or not she was getting through to him. She'd been so focused on helping him through his grief over seeing Kevin die, she hadn't considered for an instant that he might be jealous. But she couldn't ignore the possibility now. "Before I could even see it coming we were fighting. I was tired of always having to be the responsible one. Always having to be the grown-up...like with partying and birth control."

The next part was tougher, her words coming back to

haunt her and hurt her. "I told him I wasn't ready for a family. I didn't want to be my mom."

And to think her precious baby boy had already been growing inside her. She'd been working so hard to make it up to Max for not wanting him at the start.

Her voice dipped lower. "I didn't tell Kevin about being pregnant because I was afraid he would throw that fight back in my face."

Hank scrubbed his jaw as if he didn't know what to think. "Why didn't you tell me all of this before?"

"Excuse me for not wanting to talk to you about details from mine and Kevin's sex life."

She'd never shared the truth with anyone. The fight had been private, between her and her fiancé, and no matter what had happened with Hank back then, Kevin had deserved that kind of loyalty.

"I mean, why didn't you tell me the two of you were having problems, deeper than just whether or not to move?" Anguish and anger mixed in his eyes. "Do you know how much I've beaten myself up over kissing you that night?"

"I beat myself up, too. But, back then, I didn't want to betray Kevin's trust by sharing something so personal. And now, I guess I thought it didn't matter."

"There were two of us kissing, and even if we didn't have a relationship then, I thought we were still friends. So yeah, it mattered."

Would things have been different if she'd been more open with Hank that day? She wasn't sure how she could have been so honest with him when she hadn't even been able to be honest with herself. Since nothing else seemed to be working, she tried to shift the tone of the conversation back to lighter ground. "Do you think we could just go back to me tying you to the bedpost?"

His shoulders tensed.

"Not funny. Not now," he snapped, his anger not fooling her for a second.

She saw the depth of his pain, and she didn't have a clue how to make things better. Damn it, she hurt, too. Why was he doing this now? Why was he pushing her for something so soon? "Tell me what you want me to do."

"You don't have to *do* anything. It's not about you being in control in bed or in the relationship I thought we were starting." He shook his head, stuffing his fists in his uniform pockets. "You keep talking about not wanting to be your mother, but you're pulling the same control act that she does. You're driving yourself into the ground trying to prove you don't need anyone."

"That's not fair." She'd come to the house with him. Allowed others to care for her son. To care for her. She was giving up control left and right.

"But it's honest."

His clipped words iced over her. A warning prickled along her skin.

"If you can't accept me as I am, there's no way this will work." She'd fought too long and hard to carve out her independence to throw it away as soon as Hank Renshaw looked her way. She wanted him desperately. That didn't mean she would give up control of her life with both hands.

The silence stretched.

The space between them might as well have been miles. And then she knew: there was no reaching him. His father had even tried—and astutely so. Hank talked about her being a control freak and yet he was trying to call all the shots.

She waited for him to tell her she was wrong, to tell her all the ways this would be fine. But just as Kevin had balked when she didn't live up to his expectations of perfection, Hank was bailing on her, and the failure hurt even more this time.

What a helluva time to realize there was no halfway measure to her feelings. She'd fallen totally and completely in love with Hank Renshaw.

Twelve

Since Hank first saw Gabrielle, he'd wondered what would have happened if he'd met her before Kevin did. What if he'd had the chance to win her over?

Now he'd been given that chance, and he'd blown it in less than two weeks.

Gabrielle's cool hand was tucked in the crook of his arm as he walked down the stairs for the photo shoot. His father waited in the foyer alongside Ginger. His dad wore the same uniform as Hank did, but with stars on his shoulder boards and a chest so full of medals it was a wonder the old man could still stand upright. His wife—Ginger—stood beside him all decked out in red and smiles. She'd maneuvered this whole gathering with such expectations. Had his family's arrival made things worse or simply exposed the inevitable?

Hell if he knew that or anything else right now.

His whole world was exploding out of control and there

wasn't a damn thing he could do about it. Just like when his mother had died, when his sister had been kidnapped, when Kevin had died, nothing he did changed the outcome.

From the foyer, the cameraman clicked, clicked, clicked pictures, snapping shots as fast as rapid gunfire, taking Hank back to that battlefield moment when he'd lost Kevin. Flashes blinded him until he fought the urge to duck. His mouth dried up. He couldn't force Gabrielle to accept what he had to offer. He could only keep putting one foot in front of the other as he had his whole life.

At any other time, Gabrielle would have enjoyed the staged dinner, with all its pageantry of the local history. But right now, it took everything inside her to hold it together through this family event. She couldn't even enjoy the magnificent dress and jewelry. But she refused to embarrass Hank by running crying from the house. She would see this dinner through, then decide where to go next with her son.

Forcing back the urge to flee, she blinked away tears and plastered on a smile as strains of Beethoven piped through the home's sound system. The dining room had been transformed into everything she would have wished for if the house had been hers. Greenery had been scattered throughout to fill in the sparser corners. The sideboard was laden with silver chafing dishes and serving pieces, a server standing discreetly to the side.

A candelabrum spiraled up from the table with a spray of roses and stephanotis trailing down the middle. Crystal, china and silver place settings were set for—she counted—sixteen.

Sixteen?

She glanced over quickly at Ginger and the general,

then at Jonah in his tuxedo with his wife in a glittering gold gown. Who else was slated to arrive and why had Ginger not mentioned it before?

The doorbell rang and the floodgates opened.

Gabrielle took a step back instinctively as all of the Renshaw and Landis offspring poured into the foyer. Ginger's other three sons arrived with their wives, and the general's two daughters trailed behind with their husbands. The whole group filled the space in a mix of more uniforms, designer gowns and a mint's worth of jewels. Introductions passed in a blur of names and photos before they began to take their seats at the monster-size table. Hank held out her chair for her, a silent looming presence behind her. His hand brushed her back briefly before stepping away.

And if this event had been orchestrated for Ginger to meet Gabrielle, then they'd all been called here, as well, to inspect her. No wonder Hank had such rigid boundaries.

She glanced up at him just as his stepbrother leaned toward him while keeping his arm draped around wife.

"Did they forget to tell you the whole family was invited to the photo shoot? They're all staying in another house they rented two streets over."

"*You* neglected to tell me," Hank growled under his breath while his stepmother raved over one of the women's gowns. "Don't bother recycling that excuse about being putty in your wife's hands. If I'd known, I wouldn't be here subjecting myself to this zoo."

"And you wonder why no one tells you anything." Jonah's wife laughed softly beside him. "In this case, however, I can honestly say I thought you already knew. Maybe Ginger thought the general told you and vice versa."

"You don't believe that any more than I do. This was a setup, clean and simple."

Gabrielle gripped his arm tighter. "For what purpose?"

His guarded eyes met hers. "So you could see what you're letting yourself in for, getting involved with this family."

"That seems a little extreme." She eyed the length of the table, her ears burning with the sense that everyone was talking about her.

Jonah shrugged. "Extreme? Maybe. But I've learned to go with the flow."

Easier said than done with their fight hanging over her head. But Gabrielle went through the motions all the same, answering questions from the mass of family by rote. They were wonderful people who at any other time she would have enjoyed. But allowing herself to form an attachment to any of them would only set her up for more heartache.

She hardly tasted the tapas or rich cabernet that was served with them. All through the five-course dinner, she could only think of Hank. His proposal. And how differently that offer could have played out six months from now when they'd both gained more distance from the deployment, her son's health scare and Kevin's death.

By dessert, she was ready to shatter from holding her feelings in check for fear the photographer would capture a shot of her heart in her eyes as she stared at Hank. So she kept right on smiling at stories about all the cute nieces and nephews until the candles burned low.

The doorbell pierced the mingled sounds of classical music, clanking dishes and laughter. One of the three wait staff peeled away from the sideboard and into the hall to answer the door. Ginger's face creased with worry, although no one would have gotten by the security outdoors without decent identification.

Soft voices from the hall carried into the dining room. Familiar voices.

Gabrielle gaped in disbelief at Ginger. "You invited my parents, too?"

Ginger's eyes went wide with surprise. "Your parents?" Then her features smoothed, and she sent a pointed glance toward the photographer as she stood. "What a pleasant surprise."

Jonah brought his napkin to his lips and said out of the corner of his mouth. "We're gonna need a bigger house."

"Gabrielle?" Her mother's voice grew louder, closer, her German accent light after so many years of living around the world. "Where's the baby? Where's my grandson?"

Chairs scraped back. The general pivoted toward the cameraman, his looming frame and military command blocking the photographer. Her parents stood in the archway between the foyer and dining room—her mother looking travel-worn from the transcontinental journey. They weren't dressed with the glitz of Hank's family, but her parents had worked hard to build a life for their kids, even if those hopes sometimes pushed her mother into micro-managing their lives.

Ginger swept up beside them. "Sergeant and Mrs. Ballard—Christine and Edward—" of course Hank's well-briefed, savvy stepmom already knew her parents' names "—welcome!"

Gabrielle skirted around the table and to her parents, ever aware of silent, brooding Hank only a step behind her. Not that she would have expected otherwise. Hank might be angry at her, frustrated with her, even irreconcilably so, but he would always do the honorable thing. He wouldn't embarrass her in front of his family or hers.

She hugged her burly dad, then her mother. The familiarity of her mom's arms and familiar gardenia cologne comforted her in spite of all the tension and heartache threatening to floor her.

She took her mother's hands and whispered. "Mom, what are you and Dad doing here?"

"I'm so sorry to have disrupted your big event." Her mother eyed her gown and jewels with a hint of disapproval. "I didn't know there would be so many people...."

Hank thrust his hand out. "Mrs. Ballard, Sergeant Ballard, I'm Hank Renshaw. It's a pleasure to have you here. Let's go across to the library and talk for a moment while the staff sets a place for you both."

And while Hank's stepmom likely booted out the photographer.

Jonah's wife reached out to Gabrielle, as the other wives clustered in a semicircle, creating a wall of privacy between her and the prying lens. The family moved in seamless sync, having made a science out of handling the media.

Hank ushered her parents across the hall into the library to give them privacy, and Gabrielle couldn't help but think how only yesterday morning she'd come in here to find him asleep with her son on his chest. The world was moving at warp speed.

The doors closed, sealing them in the cavernous room that hadn't been staged for the photo shoot. Empty shelves climbed to the ceiling, as hollow as her heart.

Her mother's face relaxed, and she grabbed her daughter's hands. "We're here to check on you and help. Although it appears you have plenty of helping hands." Her eyes zipped back and forth from her to Hank, curiosity crackling, even as she continued to ramble, "You said you just had Hank's help, and I know it's not P.C. to say so, but a man's help with a baby isn't the same as a woman's help."

An image popped to mind of Hank asleep with Max on his chest, and she almost burst into tears, which would be absolutely *the* worst thing to do around her parents now. Yet, something inside her felt about five years old, and she wanted nothing more than to pour out her heart to her mom while drinking a cup of hot cocoa.

What in the world was Hank saying to her father over in the corner?

Her mother wrapped her arm around her shoulders. "We're staying at a lovely little bed-and-breakfast just down the road. We would have come earlier, but we had to wait for the Mardi Gras travelers to leave town. We're comfortable there with plenty of room. We got a suite, in case you needed somewhere to stay while your apartment's being fixed. We weren't sure exactly what you had set up here with your gentleman friend."

Because Gabrielle hadn't told her. She'd closed herself off from her parents, more intensely than before over these past ten months for fear they would judge her life, her decision to have a child alone.

For fear she would become a child again around them and just let her mother take control.

But she couldn't stay here after the fight with Hank.

These were her parents. Her heart was breaking, and yes, she needed a soft place to land tonight. She wasn't running away from Hank. She just wanted room to clear her head, something she couldn't do with an audience of nearly twenty relatives.

Besides, she owed her parents that much. They'd flown

all this way to see her baby, her dear son that had anchored her in spite of all the hurt clawing at her heart.

"Mom," she blurted out, the last thing she would have expected to ever come out of her mouth. "Max and I would love to spend some time with you and Dad. Give me ten minutes to change and toss some things in a suitcase."

"Don't you think it's a little early in the day for alcohol?"

Parked on the lanai, Hank ignored his father and tipped back the imported beer. His dad did always have the good stuff on hand. As he sat here, looking out at the yard, tormenting the hell out of himself with memories of dancing with Gabrielle under the stars, he couldn't think of a better time to get falling-down drunk.

She'd just up and left with her parents last night, gathered her son and headed out the door, only pausing long enough to hug his mother. Holding Max for all of ten seconds to say goodbye had damn near torn his already bruised heart from his chest. He'd thought he heard Gabrielle murmur a tearful thanks before she booked it out of his life. But what the hell was he supposed to do?

The morning sure hadn't brought any answers so by noon he'd moved his moody self outside away from his hovering family.

He looked up at his father. "Want a beer anyway?"

"Sure." His dad dropped into a chair beside him, and pulled a bottle from the crystal ice bucket Hank had brought outside. "But only so you aren't drinking alone."

"Damn nice of you."

"Count yourself lucky. I'm the only one of the family willing to put up with your bad mood."

Hank set his bottle down with controlled precision,

anger pumping through him. "With all due respect, sir, I didn't ask you to come here. I didn't ask for your help, which sucked by the way."

His father cocked his head to the side. "How so?"

"You're the one who said she needed time to grieve for her dead fiancé. I don't think the Landis-Renshaw clan gave her much time by sweeping in here unannounced. Do you?"

"So you love her?"

Hank reached for the bottle and clammed up again.

The general reclined in the chair, eyes too astute. "That had to have made things tough for you, having feelings for Gabrielle while they were dating."

"What makes you think I had feelings for her back then?" he asked evasively.

"You haven't even been home from your deployment for two weeks and you're not the type to fall for someone fast."

"You would be wrong about that." He'd fallen for Gabrielle the first time her saw her.

His father lifted and eyebrow and his beer. "Oh, really?"

"Wow, I stepped right into that, didn't I?"

"It helps that I know you."

Hell, might as well quit pretending. He sank back into his chair. A strange—and uncomfortable—suspicion drifted through his head. "Did you have feelings for Ginger when Mom was alive?"

"Ginger and I were both married, both in love with our spouses. Then we were both busy as hell bringing up kids." His face creased with…pain? "I can honestly say the feelings came to us later. We wasted a lot of years avoiding it. Tough for a guy like me to admit he was afraid, but I was a big coward. Scared of losing a woman I loved again."

He looked at his big, invincible three-star father through different eyes. "What helped Ginger get over the fear?"

And could that be helpful to Gabrielle?

"You would have to ask Ginger yourself."

"Really?" He shook his head. "Sorry, Dad, but that sounds like a damn awkward conversation."

Ginger had been a part of his life for as long as he could remember, but he didn't exactly excel at the warm, fuzzy parts of family relationships.

"Believe it or not, she's handled tougher cases than you. She's a damn fine diplomat."

"Things just aren't that simple for me. Talk it over and make it all better."

"It can be."

"What about Kevin?" His fingers tightened on the longneck. He met his dad's eyes and let the hurt just roll right over him, regardless of whether or not his father read it in his eyes. "I just say to hell with the fact I made a move on her before he died?"

"That must have been a real bite in those honorable intentions of yours," his father stated simply, not judging, just putting the undeniable fact out there.

"Tough to reconcile." Until he did, he couldn't see a way through to being with Gabrielle although he'd thought more than once that he wanted to be a husband to her and a father to Max. He still wanted those things, but he'd certainly botched his proposal. He understood now that he had to reconcile that guilt first or he would continue to sabotage their relationship again and again.

Kevin could pardon him a hundred times over but until Hank could forgive himself, there was no way to move forward. He could see now that the fight with Gabrielle wasn't about where she would live or which one of them was in control. Because Kevin was steering their relationship, even from the grave.

"Son, it's time to stop punishing yourself for being alive when he isn't."

"Easier said than done." He bit back the urge to shout, anger piling on top of frustration. "You're going to have to excuse me for being slow on the uptake, but this conversation is supposed to help me how? Because the way I see it, I'm sitting here, with my gut on fire and no way out."

"Your gut's on fire? Good." Hank clapped him on the shoulder. "Then you're almost there...."

"You're glad I'm about to put my fist through a wall?"

The general didn't so much as wince, just looked back with wise eyes and a face that was beginning to show the toll of numerous wars. "We spend a lot of time pumping ourselves up for battle. You have to believe you're invincible to hang tough during some of the things we're called to do in the line of duty. That's a difficult switch to turn off once we come home."

Damn straight, he was wired tight. And come to think of it, he had made going after Gabrielle into a personal mission.

He focused on his father's words, looking for something to grab hold of before the grief and rage pulled him under. "Makes sense."

"Screw what makes sense," his dad barked. "Quit thinking logically. Quit running scared. It hurt like hell to lose your best friend, all the worse to be there when it happened. There's only one way to get to the other side of that grief so you can claim the good that's waiting for you."

Each breath seared his throat. "And what would that be?"

"Wade right in."

His dad's words—his dad's wisdom—sliced through the last of his reserves. Hank squeezed his eyes closed as a tear rolled down his cheek. His father's hand fell to rest on his shoulder and finally, Hank let himself grieve.

Thirteen

The quiet was deafening today as opposed to the evening before with Hank's family.

Gabrielle curled up in the quaint little brass daybed in the bed-and-breakfast suite her parents had booked yesterday. Max was asleep. Her parents had gone out for a walk before supper. Surprisingly, her mom hadn't pushed for details.

Leaving Hank's house yesterday had been a crazy whirlwind of throwing things in her bag and gathering her son. Leonie had been confused but busy taking care of Hank's nieces and nephews. Gabrielle had just wanted to get out before she burst into tears, a close call when Hank had held Max to say goodbye.

Once at the bed-and-breakfast, she had slept and slept, and part of her knew she was grieving over losing Hank but she couldn't find a way out from under the confusion and hurt of her argument with him. The longer she was away from him, the more difficult it seemed to find her way through to reconciliation.

The outside door clicked with the opening lock a second before her parents walked through. Her burly daddy, who rarely said much, lumbered into her room with a small white box in his hands. He set the confection store carton on the end table and dropped a quick kiss on top of her head.

"Love you, Gabby girl."

Then he was gone. Much like her growing up years. She'd always been sure of his love but his presence had been in short supply. He passed her mother coming in as he ducked out to his room. The television vibrated lightly through the wall, the sports channel no doubt.

Her mother still hovered across the room. "Do you mind if I sit and join you? Those pralines your dad bought are to die for."

"Sure, Mom, knock yourself out." She nudged the box toward her mother.

Dropping into a fat floral chair by the window, Christine pulled one of the caramel pecan treats from the box, breaking off a bite at a time as she nibbled and stared out the window. Gabrielle kept waiting for the lecture or third degree, but it never came.

Finally, she couldn't stand the pressure of waiting any longer. "Go ahead and ask, Mom."

Her mother looked over quizzically, smoothing back her short blond bob. "Ask what?"

"About Hank and me. You came all this way, so you might as well say your piece."

"I came all this way because my grandson had surgery and this was the soonest I could leave your little sisters. And I came to meet this new man in your life who's obviously very important to you."

"He's not in my life anymore." Gabrielle eyed the box of pralines, but her stomach hurt so badly she couldn't eat.

"Looked to me last night like you're a major part of his life and family." Her mother popped another bite in her mouth.

Gabrielle hugged her knees. "That party was all for show, staged for a magazine shoot."

"I'm not talking about the fancy dinner. I'm talking about the expression in his eyes when he looks at you. That man loves you."

Just hearing those words cut right through her heart. "Mom, he may have had feelings for me, but we never stood a chance. Anything we had would have always been tangled up in his survivor's guilt. He will always see me as his best friend's girl and that's not something I can fight."

"Do you still see yourself as Kevin's fiancée?"

That stopped her short. "Of course not. I understand that Kevin is gone, and I'm helpless to change that."

"*Helpless?* That's a strange word choice. Why would you feel helpless?"

Gabrielle gawked at her mother. "You've got to be kidding. How could I feel anything but helpless?"

Her mother set aside the praline, her attention zeroing in. "There's nothing you could have done for Kevin. You're not Wonder Woman."

A dark snort of laughter burst from her. "That's rich, coming from you. You're the ultimate wonder woman. You make everything look easy."

"Now that's just silly, dear. Life is anything but easy." Her mother moved smoothly from the chair to sit beside Gabrielle on the bed. "Being a military wife and mother is full of tough challenges."

She searched her mom's face for some sense that her mom was joking but found only complete honesty. Her mother truly didn't see herself as the conquer-all woman everyone else perceived her to be. "Why didn't you ask for help?"

"What was complaining going to get me? My family was an ocean away. My husband was getting shot at in another country. And I had five children to take care of." She flattened her hands to her thighs. "Honest to God, I didn't have time to complain."

Gabrielle understood that feeling well enough lately.

"If there had been help available, I would have embraced it with both hands. For more time to read to my kids. Or even to read a book for myself while soaking in a bubble bath." She sighed, rolling her green eyes in imaginary bliss.

Gabrielle's heart ached as she thought of how perceptive Hank had been about her wish for a long soak alone, saturating herself in lavender-scented bubbles. Some might consider that a small thing, but seeing her mother brought a hefty reminder of Ballard family values—thoughtfulness, doing things for others, that's what mattered more than money.

Christine took her daughter's hands in hers. "It's not like I knew how to handle everything in those days. You just don't remember the burned meals or the time I wrecked the car because I forgot to pick your brother up at kindergarten, then I drove too fast scared to death because I was late. Believe me, I cried then. As for the Wonder Woman issue…" Her mother's German accent got stronger when she was fired up, turning her *W*s into *V* sounds. "I am not perfect now, just better at handling things than I was then."

Could her mother be right? That she'd simply forgotten

the more frazzled days? "If you learned over time, don't I deserve the same chance?"

"You have a point." She stroked back Gabrielle's hair as she'd done millions of times, always there, always loving, and that did count for a lot. "I know I interfere quite often. What is it they call that here in the States… Being an airplane mother?"

Gabrielle grinned. "A helicopter mom, always hovering."

"Ah, that makes more sense. I never understood the airplane analogy."

Smiling, Gabrielle leaned into her mom and they laughed together.

Her mother's arm slid around her shoulders. "Do you love this man? Do you love Hank?"

Gabrielle didn't even have to think to know. The truth settled in her heart, the only thing that made sense in her life. Why was it, though, that love had to always bring so much pain? "Yes, Mom, I love Hank more than I've loved anyone in my life, except for my son."

For once, she didn't feel guilty about admitting she did have deeper feelings for Hank than she'd had for Kevin. She had loved Kevin and she'd done her best to be a good fiancée, staying with the relationship longer than she should have. If anything, she'd hurt him most by hanging on too long when there'd been signs the relationship might not be a good fit.

Her mother hugged her tighter. "Then you don't need to have all the perfect answers right now. No one is a wonder woman from day one. Do the best you can, don't give up and the rest will sort itself out with time if you are determined to work at it."

Her mother's advice shuffled around inside her until it settled, making such perfect sense she didn't know why she hadn't seen it before. She didn't have to have everything figured out before moving forward. It was okay to love Hank and be with Hank while they resolved their problems, because yes, she *did* want to find a way to be with the man she loved. Forever. "I am determined, Mom. Very much so."

"Then what are you sitting around here for? Go get your man. Your father and I welcome the chance to babysit our grandson."

Complete love and acceptance radiated from her mother's face. Unconditional love, just like she felt for Max. Gabrielle wrapped her arms around her mom and held on tight.

"Danke, Mama." She adored the nuances of her mother's language. *Danke.* Thank you, but less formal for a family member. A loved one. *"Danke."*

And now she just hoped she wasn't too late to claim Hank's love that she'd so foolishly almost tossed away.

Family dinners two nights in a row?

Hank felt as if he'd set a new record in togetherness. But his relatives had all come to New Orleans for *him.* He couldn't just boot them out of town. So he parked himself at the table while everyone spoke on top of each other. They weren't there to intrude. They simply wanted to be a part of his life, see him after his deployment and show him some love.

And after his conversation with his father earlier, he had to confess that the whole Renshaw-Landis connection was starting to grow on him. He would have to be thickheaded not to recognize the gift of this much support—a room full of people who would drop everything for him.

Tonight's meal was less formal than the photo shoot dinner. Instead of gowns, uniforms and tuxedos, everyone wore jeans or khakis. The children were included, too, the table packed with high chairs and chatter about elementary school plays. The menu ranged from Creole shrimp and grits to hot dogs with macaroni and cheese. Still, even with nearly thirty kids and adults seated, the table seemed lacking to him without Gabrielle and Max.

Since that talk with his father, he'd been wracking his brain on how to win her back in a way that still gave her the time and space she needed. He refused to accept failure. He needed to be smart about this. His whole future was at stake.

As he speared another fat Gulf shrimp that was totally wasted on him tonight, the doorbell rang and Leonie raced to answer it.

Frowning, he set his fork back on the plate. The general raised an eyebrow and two of his stepbrothers shot to their feet.

What the hell? While he knew no one would get by security without the proper identification, it would be helpful if they started announcing some of these unexpected guests. What family members were left?

"Hank?"

His ears had to be fooling him, creating the sound of the voice he wanted to hear more than anything.

Then miraculously, so damn amazingly, Gabrielle stood in the archway to the dining room. His heart got stuck somewhere in his throat. He pushed his chair back and stood, ignoring the weight of his family's eyes all trained on him. He could see only Gabrielle, with her wind-flushed cheeks and her loose, silky blond hair.

Most of all, he saw her beautiful smile.

Relief scoured through him. For whatever reason, she'd come back to him, and he would be damned before he did or said one thing to push her away again. So he smiled back at her, but waited, letting her take the lead for now.

Gabrielle walked deeper into the dining room, her sexy legs striding confidently closer. "I'm sorry to disturb everyone's dinner. Would you mind if I stole Hank from you? I'm not sure I'll bring him back anytime soon. In fact, I may want to keep him for a very, very long time."

Laughter rippled down the table, and he didn't miss how one of his sisters shouted that Gabrielle was welcome to hang on to him permanently.

His stepmother reached for Gabrielle's hand. "I'm so glad you came back."

Gabrielle smiled full out, not a shadow in sight. "Me, too."

Past ready to have her to himself, Hank palmed her waist and followed her out into the foyer before facing her. At first, there were no words. He just took in the beauty of her face that he'd dreamed of so often while he was overseas. The thought of not having her in his life…

He swallowed down a lump in his throat and cupped her shoulders, needing to touch her. "What brought you here tonight?"

Her hands fell to rest on his chest. "I have a surprise for you."

"Your arrival is plenty of a surprise."

"Not by a long shot. Now close your eyes." A mischievous glint lit her emerald eyes. "Trust me."

And he did. He trusted her with his love and his life.

Hank shut his eyes, hopeful as hell that this was going to go well for him. A silky cloth trailed over his fingers, up his arm then over his eyes. Realization slid over him just as Gabrielle tied the blindfold behind his head.

Oh, yeah.

Hank clasped her wrist, his thumb stroking her racing

pulse. "I assume I'll be keeping my clothes on for now since my family's in the next room."

"You're every bit as safe in my hands as I am in yours." Her voice caressed his senses, the words as satiny as the fabric she'd teased over his skin.

Hooking her arm with his, she guided him smoothly toward the back of the house and out the door. The cool evening air wrapped around him while he waited for her next move.

Gabrielle rested her head against his shoulder. "My car's a tighter fit than yours so you'll need to watch your head stepping inside."

So they were leaving. Interesting. But anything Gabrielle did intrigued him, always had. "We can take mine if you prefer. The keys are in my pocket."

"Hmm.... Sounds like you're propositioning me." The tips of her fingers hooked in the front pocket of his jeans.

"I'm hopeful, Gabrielle, but taking nothing for granted."

He could have sworn he felt her lips brush his shoulder, but then his mind focused completely on her hand dipping in to fish out his keys with what had to be deliberate precision. She pulled back out slowly, her fingers rubbing against his increasing arousal.

A low growl rumbled in his throat. "I really hope we're alone out here."

"The security guard has his back to us. He's watching the street."

"I can't wait to get inside the car with you—only you."

"Patience, Hank. I promise this will all be worth it."

With that vow hanging between them, she led him smoothly to his SUV and settled them both inside. Seconds later, they were on the road, with her behind the wheel and him still blindfolded. While he was a navigator, even he started to lose any sense of direction after a few minutes of her speeding around curves and turns.

He resisted the urge to grab for the armrest. "You drive like a maniac."

"I learned on the autobahn." The car veered left hard and fast before jerking to a halt.

"How did I not know this about you before?"

"We have a lot to learn about each other, and I look forward to that." She opened her door and the sound of water lapping echoed.

Lake Ponchartrain.

It made perfect sense.

They'd discussed coming here to talk after the photo shoot, for time alone together, to build on their relationship. Now she was fulfilling that plan that had been cut short.

His door opened and she pulled off his blindfold. Sure enough, Gabrielle stood silhouetted by the lake, the setting sun casting tequila-colored warmth over her face.

He joined her, holding his hand out for hers, clasping in a perfect fit. The blindfold she'd used on him—the satin sash from her bathrobe—trailed from her pocket in a floral splash riding the wind. They walked that way for at least ten minutes, reminding him of times past when they'd enjoyed that rare gift of two people able to coexist even in silence.

As the sky grew darker and the city lights flickered to life, Gabrielle's steps slowed, her attention out there somewhere on the lake.

"Hank, my love for you is like that lake, it's powerful and fluid, and a natural force I can't deny any longer." She stopped, facing him, as serious as he'd ever seen her. "I want to be with you forever, here, Bossier City, wherever that love takes us around the world."

Her declaration was even more than he could have hoped for and almost sent him to his knees. He clasped her shoulders and put his all in what he'd been waiting two years to tell her. He wouldn't botch it this time.

"Gabrielle, I've been in love with you since the first time I saw you. But I'm willing to take it one day at a time if that's what you need, because every day with you is better than a lifetime without you."

"Oh, God, Hank, I want it all with you, so much." She cradled his face in her hands and kissed him, fully, openly and with the promise of more to come. "I love you, more than I ever thought it would be possible to love anyone. I don't want to wait. I just want us to be happy together every day for the rest of our lives."

He hauled her close and let the relief shudder through him until he could trust himself to speak again. He buried his face in her hair. "About my job in the military, if it's a deal breaker for you, I'll get out. I've done a lot of soul searching with my dad since you left. He helped me start coming to grips with what happened over there. He's helping me reevaluate a lot of things. I know what's most important to me now."

"Hank," she gasped, arching back. "Didn't you hear me say that I love you, anywhere that takes us? You don't have to give that up for me. I don't want you to do that."

"Wait. Let me finish. Yes, my job is important to me, but you are more important and I'm not willing to lose you over this. I'm lucky. I have financial choices."

She looked right back at him, her steely resolve glimmering in the hazy sunset. "I love you too much to ask you to give up something that's so much a part of who you are. All I ask is that we're partners, that we keep working at making our relationship stronger. And that we get a permanent home when you retire."

She appeared to mean what she said, but he wasn't risking his future with her by just grasping her offer without careful consideration. "How about we take it a day at a time with the military-life decision? If you change your mind, tell me. I may have followed my dad's career path in some ways, but I have no dreams of being a general."

"But you could be," she insisted with a faith in him that he appreciated.

"I have plans for a business I would like to start, a spin-off with my computer partner. I was thinking New Orleans would make a good home base. In fact—if you agree—I would like to get a head start on that home by buying the Garden District house we've been renting. We'll have roots here, whether I stay in the air force or not."

Happiness and peace spread across her face. "I can live with that plan as long as I'm living with you."

"And about our big, pushy families?" His thumb stroked along her neck, taking note of her speeding pulse and silky skin. "If we decide to invite them into our lives more often?"

"I think we're lucky to have them," she said without hesitation. "Beyond the fact that they're actually pretty amazing people, they're also very eager to babysit."

His imagination sparked with how they could fill their time alone in a deserted stretch of moonlit water. "Are you propositioning me?"

She pulled the blindfold from her jeans pocket. "I have some plans of my own, if you're game."

He spread his arms wide. "I'm all yours."

Epilogue

New Orleans: A Year Later

"Laissez les bons temps rouler!" Let the good times roll!

The cheer bounced around inside Gabrielle Ballard Renshaw's head as she pushed through the Mardi Gras crowd lining the road to watch the informal neighborhood parade pass her house. Her mood was totally partyworthy. But she needed to deliver a message to Hank, a very personal message. Tracking down her boyfriend—her husband of two months—lit her soul.

Excitement powered her forward, one step at a time through the throng of partiers decked out in jester hats, masks and beads. Lampposts blazed through the dark. The parade inched past, a jazz band blasting a Louis Armstrong number while necklaces, doubloons and even candy rained over the mini-mob, that also happened to be all family gathered on her front lawn. It wasn't the official parade, but a smaller one put together in conjunction with a local fundraiser.

She loved this town she now considered her home base, somewhere to come back to no matter where they were stationed.

The past year had been hectic and blissful as she and Hank figured out ways to blend their lives while she completed her degree this past Christmas. She thumbed her diamond solitaire and diamond-studded wedding band, in a simple style they'd chosen together. Her scrapbooking skills were getting a workout recording all the amazing memories.

They'd been married just after the holidays in a simple wedding, only family at the base chapel. Hank had worn his formal uniform and they'd carried Max down the aisle with them. Their one claim to pageantry had been a B-52 fly-over as they'd walked out the chapel doors as man and wife.

Although she did move up to Bossier City with him and he'd stayed in the air force, she'd insisted on keeping some of her business contacts. In a surprise twist during their Christmas gathering of all the relatives at the family compound, Gabrielle had found herself brainstorming with Hank's older brother—the lawyer who oversaw the Landis/Renshaw Foundation. Before the pumpkin pie had been sliced, they'd pulled together ideas for starting a scholarship to benefit children of military veterans who'd died in the line of duty. The funds would be awarded in Kevin's name.

Peace didn't arrive in a single day. But she and Hank were building a future together while still acknowledging a dear man who'd been such an integral part of both their lives. Another gift from Kevin, they no longer iso-

lated themselves. They'd learned to embrace and appreciate their families while building their own life together.

Her eyes tracked to her precious, *healthy* son playing
with his cousins under a sprawling oak with twinkling
lights in Mardi Gras colors of green, purple and gold.
Wearing his pj's, he ran in high-speed circles with his
cousins, all under Leonie's watchful eye. She served as
the caretaker for their Garden District house when they
were away, and helped with nanny duties during visits.

Finally, Gabrielle made her way past their huge extended family to her husband. Hank caught her eye and
peeled away from their male relatives all giving input on
how to tie a piñata from the tree.

His strong and steady arms went around her waist,
pulling her as close as was appropriate around so many
watchful eyes. "Hello, Mrs. Renshaw."

"And hello to you, Major." She toyed with the buttons
on his chambray shirt.

"What did the doctor say? And you'd better talk fast
because it's killing me that I didn't get to go with you."

She'd made an appointment to see her old doctor while
they were in town for Mardi Gras. Hank had wanted to
meet her there, but she'd insisted he stay with the family.
She'd been almost afraid to hope and wanted to keep the
appointment low key.

Wow, had she been in for a pleasant surprise.

Who knew that contentment and excitement could coexist? "This family has more than we expected to celebrate tonight, because, yes, I'm seven weeks pregnant. It
happened on our honeymoon."

"And you're happy?"

"I'm ecstatic! And you?" Although she could already
see the answer in his electric-blue eyes, lighting from
inside.

He cradled her face in large tender hands. "Max is going to love his little sister."

"It could be a boy." She leaned closer, her back foot lifting.

"But it's a girl," he said without hesitation.

"You're a pushy guy, you know that?"

"Thank goodness I found a woman strong enough to stand beside me for life."

And their life together was better than she'd ever dreamed, thanks to her mother's help in realizing she didn't have to be a wonder woman. Doing her best and accepting the best from others bonded them all into a beautiful family.

"Celebrate with me soon?" she whispered against his mouth.

"Celebrate now." He spun her around as the parade marched past. *"Laissez les bons temps rouler,* my love. Let the good times roll."

* * * * *

PASSION

Harlequin® Desire

COMING NEXT MONTH
AVAILABLE MAY 8, 2012

#2155 UNDONE BY HER TENDER TOUCH
Pregnancy & Passion
Maya Banks
When one night with magnate Cam Hollingsworth results in pregnancy, no-strings-attached turns into a tangled web for caterer Pippa Laingley.

#2156 ONE DANCE WITH THE SHEIKH
Dynasties: The Kincaids
Tessa Radley

#2157 THE TIES THAT BIND
Billionaires and Babies
Emilie Rose

#2158 AN INTIMATE BARGAIN
Colorado Cattle Barons
Barbara Dunlop

#2159 RELENTLESS PURSUIT
Lone Star Legacy
Sara Orwig

#2160 READY FOR HER CLOSE-UP
Matchmakers, Inc.
Katherine Garbera

REQUEST YOUR FREE BOOKS!
2 FREE NOVELS PLUS 2 FREE GIFTS!

ALWAYS POWERFUL, PASSIONATE AND PROVOCATIVE

YES! Please send me 2 FREE Harlequin Desire® novels and my 2 FREE gifts (gifts are worth about $10). After receiving them, if I don't wish to receive any more books, I can return the shipping statement marked "cancel." If I don't cancel, I will receive 6 brand-new novels every month and be billed just $4.30 per book in the U.S. or $4.99 per book in Canada. That's a saving of at least 14% off the cover price! It's quite a bargain! Shipping and handling is just 50¢ per book in the U.S. and 75¢ per book in Canada.* I understand that accepting the 2 free books and gifts places me under no obligation to buy anything. I can always return a shipment and cancel at any time. Even if I never buy another book, the two free books and gifts are mine to keep forever.

225/326 HDN FEF3

Name _____ (PLEASE PRINT)

Address _____ Apt. #

City _____ State/Prov. _____ Zip/Postal Code

Signature (if under 18, a parent or guardian must sign)

Mail to the **Reader Service:**

IN U.S.A.: P.O. Box 1867, Buffalo, NY 14240-1867
IN CANADA: P.O. Box 609, Fort Erie, Ontario L2A 5X3

Not valid for current subscribers to Harlequin Desire books.

Want to try two free books from another line?
Call 1-800-873-8635 or visit www.ReaderService.com.

* Terms and prices subject to change without notice. Prices do not include applicable taxes. Sales tax applicable in N.Y. Canadian residents will be charged applicable taxes. Offer not valid in Quebec. This offer is limited to one order per household. All orders subject to credit approval. Credit or debit balances in a customer's account(s) may be offset by any other outstanding balance owed by or to the customer. Please allow 4 to 6 weeks for delivery. Offer available while quantities last.

Your Privacy—The Reader Service is committed to protecting your privacy. Our Privacy Policy is available online at www.ReaderService.com or upon request from the Reader Service.

We make a portion of our mailing list available to reputable third parties that offer products we believe may interest you. If you prefer that we not exchange your name with third parties, or if you wish to clarify or modify your communication preferences, please visit us at www.ReaderService.com/consumerschoice or write to us at Reader Service Preference Service, P.O. Box 9062, Buffalo, NY 14269. Include your complete name and address.

HDES11B

New York Times *and* USA TODAY *bestselling author*
Maya Banks presents book four in her miniseries
PREGNANCY & PASSION

UNDONE BY HER TENDER TOUCH

Available May 2012 from Harlequin® Desire!

"**W**ould you like some help?"

Pippa whirled around, still holding the bottle of champagne, and darn near tossed the contents onto the floor.

"Help?"

Cam nodded slowly. "Assistance? You look as though you could use it. How on earth did you think you'd manage to cater this event on your own?"

Pippa was horrified by his offer and then, as she processed the rest of his statement, she was irritated as hell.

"I'd hate for you to sully those pretty hands," she snapped. "And for your information, I've got this under control. The help didn't show. Not my fault. The food is impeccable, if I do say so myself. I just need to deliver it to the guests."

"I believe I just offered my assistance and you insulted me," Cam said dryly.

Her eyebrows drew together. Oh, why did the man have to be so damn delicious-looking? And why could she never perform the simplest functions around him?

"You're Ashley's guest," Pippa said firmly. "Not to mention you're used to being served, not serving others."

"How do you know what I'm used to?" he asked mildly.

She had absolutely nothing to say to that and watched in bewilderment as he hefted the tray up and walked out of the kitchen.

She sagged against the sink, her pulse racing hard enough

to make her dizzy.

Cameron Hollingsworth was gorgeous, unpolished in a rough and totally sexy way, arrogant and so wrong for her. But there was something about the man that just did it for her.

She sighed. He was a luscious specimen of a male and he couldn't be any less interested in her.

Even so, she was itching to shake his world up a little.

Realizing she was spending far too much time mooning over Cameron, she grabbed another tray, took a deep breath to compose herself and then headed toward the living room.

And Cameron Hollingsworth.

Will Pippa shake up Cameron's world?
Find out in Maya Banks's passionate new novel

UNDONE BY HER TENDER TOUCH

Available May 2012 from Harlequin® Desire!

Harlequin *Presents*®

Royalty has never been so scandalous!

THE
SANTINA
CROWN

When Crown Prince Alessandro of Santina proposes
to paparazzi favorite Allegra Jackson it promises
to be *the* social event of the decade!

Harlequin Presents® invites you to step into the decadent
playground of the world's rich and famous and rub shoulders
with royalty, sheikhs and glamorous socialites.

**Collect all 8 passionate tales written by *USA TODAY*
bestselling authors, beginning May 2012!**

The Price of Royal Duty by **Penny Jordan**(May)

The Sheikh's Heir by **Sharon Kendrick**(June)

Santina's Scandalous Princess by **Kate Hewitt**(July)

The Man Behind the Scars by **Caitlin Crews**(August)

Defying the Prince by **Sarah Morgan**(September)

Princess from the Shadows by **Maisey Yates**(October)

The Girl Nobody Wanted by **Lynn Raye Harris**(November)

Playing the Royal Game by **Carol Marinelli**(December)

HP13066SC